I0699630

ROYALE

KENNEDY PLUMB

First Print
PUBLISHING HOUSE

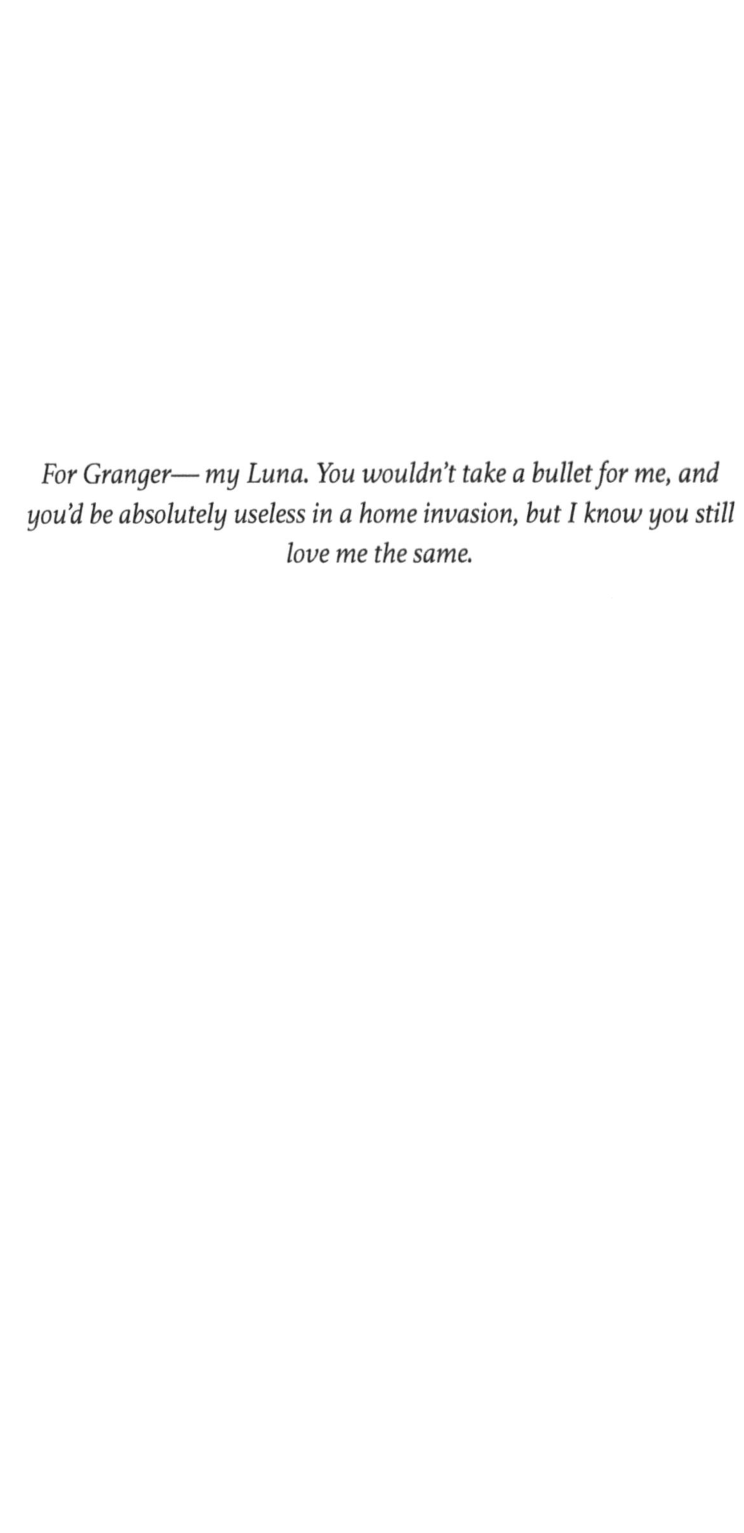

For Granger— my Luna. You wouldn't take a bullet for me, and you'd be absolutely useless in a home invasion, but I know you still love me the same.

AUTHOR NOTE // CONTENT GUIDANCE

This book is recommended for ages 12+ and contains content that may be triggering for certain audiences, including: descriptive violence, death, gun violence, abuse and injury of a child, mention of enslavement of people with disabilities, mention of animal injury, and suicidal thoughts. Contains cliffhanger ending. Proceed with care.

ROYALE

1

HOW RUDE OF THE EARTH TO JUST KEEP SPINNING

SAM

I'm behind the wheel of a truck, my foot anchored down on the gas pedal. It's dark ahead and dark behind. I can't see where I'm going. All I know is I can't stop. The air from the open windows is clouded with dirt and rocks that fly up with each turn of the tires.

Faster, faster.

I feel the engine groan as I push it forward through the dark as fast as it will go.

I squint, finally seeing the pair of lights ahead that I've been looking for, knowing I've found her.

The edges of my vision go red, fury filling my already hazy view.

She will pay.

Faster, faster.

The red of her brake lights flash ahead as her car comes to a stop a short distance ahead.

But I don't stop.

I press the pedal down as far as it will go. I don't even brace myself as I barrel the truck right into the back of her car. My chest lurches against my seatbelt, but I barely register the crunch of metal, the spray of glass, or even the airbags exploding around me. I don't even feel the pain.

All I see is red. I want her to see my face and to know it was me.

Me.

She'll never take anyone away from me again.

I slam my shoulder into my door, pushing it open with a crunch. I stumble out, struggling to limp over to her door, the dust coating the air so thickly it's hard to breathe. My hand feels far away as I fumble with her door handle, but I finally get enough of a grip to yank the door open.

I want her to know it was me.

"Veg—"

I choke on her name as I see her face.

Because it's not her face at all.

A different face stares up from the steering wheel, neck bent at an unnatural angle, eyes glossy. A blank, eternal, lifeless stare. A trail of blood drips from her mouth.

It's not Vegas.

It's Ella.

It's Ella's lifeless eyes staring back at me.

I JOLT up in my bed with a gasp and choke down the sob in my throat as I try to ground myself. I touch my face, my blanket, taking stock of what's real. I breathe in through my nose and out through my mouth.

This is real.

I breathe again, trying to slow my racing heart.

Just a dream. Just a dream.

I try to push that vivid image of Ella's lifeless stare out of my head, trying to settle back into real life. It's then I remember that reality isn't much better. How could I ever forget the fear in her eyes when she looked at me? The way she had hidden behind Vegas to get away from me?

But she's alive. Thank God she's alive.

The room around me is still dark, but I can make out Ponyboy's sleeping figure in the bed next to mine, his breaths fortunately deep and undisturbed. I'm glad one of us is getting rest.

Beardsley kicked us out of the medic tent a couple hours ago, shuffling me out and insisting that Luna and Q were *fine* and to "go get some rest, or else." He wouldn't take no for an answer, so I allowed Ponyboy to show me to one of the sleeping barracks where he, Beardsley, and Red usually sleep. I didn't think I'd be able to sleep at all, but I guess the sheer exhaustion in my body took over my mind, lulling my guilt-drenched thoughts into a well-deserved nightmare.

I don't deserve peace when Steele, Red, and Lala are still there because of me.

My body and brain feel heavy and loaded as I try to slip on my boots as noiselessly as possible, careful not to disturb the quiet of the room, oddly confused by the peaceful sleep that everyone seems to be enjoying around me. Is no one concerned that everything is different now? That everything is completely wrong and backwards?

They always talk about the calm before the storm, the peaceful lull that radiates even as the turbulence is slowly closing in. But something I don't hear talked about nearly enough is the calm *after* the storm. The eerie quiet that comes right after you've just witnessed your whole life come crashing down around you, and now all you have left is the wreckage, the quiet, and the crushing expectation to put yourself back together like nothing ever happened.

My own sister doesn't want to know that she's in the care of a maniac and would rather be with her than me, so what now? The Earth just turns like normal?

I habitually turn my wrist over to check the time on my wristTab, momentarily forgetting that it's still covered with the woven bracelet Red gave me before we went into E2. My heart squeezes as I picture him and Lala and Steele being marched back into Vegas's clutches, and all I could do was watch helplessly from afar, knowing it was all my fault.

I run a finger along the rough texture of the bracelet before sliding it up an inch. The bright LED screen of my Tab blinds me for a second. I have to squint to read the time.

10:41pm.

I sigh. It turns out what I thought was a couple hours was actually only 53 minutes.

Well, Beardsley, I tried.

I push myself off the thinly padded bed and weave through the other beds scattered around the room, some occupied with snoring bodies, some empty. I reach the door and push it open as quietly as I can, careful to let it click behind me softly.

Outside is the hustle and bustle of the settlement here preparing for bedtime seemingly as usual, like it *wasn't* out of the ordinary that a rusty old truck came screeching in with blood and screams and panic just mere hours ago.

I wind through the bustle, unsuccessfully trying to retrace my steps back to the medical building. Well, if you can even *call* it a building. All of the structures here are like huge permanent tents. Big aluminum frames covered with some kind of thick, industrial vinyl material that is sealed around the frame and secured to the ground, keeping the insides comfortable with heat in the cold seasons like now and apparently AC in the hot ones. It makes me wonder how long this "headquarters" has been here, and more specifically *how* this headquarters is here at all.

Whenever I had pictured the *"underground"* organization Q's group works for, Lala's secret connections, I always imagined something more lowkey, more transient for frequent relocation whenever it was discovered or threatened. But this? There's no way the Feds don't know this is here, yet no one seems worried about it.

That kind of scares me.

What kind of powers are we trifling with here if they aren't worried about the FPA at all?

The overhead lights of the upper shell of the Underground are in dim night mode right now, so there are big lights on around the perimeter that brighten the place up like a football stadium.

I pass by people carrying boxes to trucks and groups engaged in casual conversations. People cleaning. There even looks to be a game of soccer going on at one of the edges of the settlement. How many people are involved in this operation? And are all of these people runners like we are?

We.

I snort to myself at the thought, remembering how any prospect of *"we"* exploded atomically right before my eyes earlier tonight. Q will likely and understandably never want to see me again after Vegas revealed my lies about knowing the way out of the Underground, and then I allowed her dog to literally take a bullet for me. Red, Lala, and Steele think I'm some kind of murderer, and probably even more so now that they've been taken into captivity thanks to me. And Beardsley? Well, let's just say if I valued my own life at all, I'd be sneaking away from this entire establishment right now before he finds out the whole truth and guts me like a fish the redneck way. Slowly.

But even still, I couldn't just leave without at least trying to explain to Q why I did what I did, to apologize. And I certainly couldn't leave without making sure Luna was okay.

Even if they do kick me out, which I'm fully prepared for, I will admit part of me does feel a small weight lifted off my shoulders now that the truth is finally out, now that I can stop with the deception and just say, "here I am, take me or fillet me."

That sharp, knife-twisting burden I always felt about using good people, about lying to the group the way I was, is at least a little less sharp. Now I only have one sharp burden left: the one where I have to figure out how to stop the most powerful person in the Underground somehow or lose my sister forever.

But, hey, at least I can be honest about it now.

After a couple laps around camp, I finally find the medical building. I push the door open carefully in case any patients are sleeping inside and pass by rows and rows of hospital beds surrounded by hanging privacy curtains, some closed, some not. Most of the beds are empty, but some are occupied by snoring patients and beeping monitors.

I round the corner past the second row of hospital beds, and things are finally beginning to look familiar. I find Luna still lying on top of the same hospital bed she was on when I left, but now she is sleeping. Her body moves up and down with steady breaths. There is an IV attached to her front leg, saline dripping from a bag propped behind her.

A voice behind me startles me.

"Xanax," the voice says.

I turn to see a young medic standing next to me.

"Huh?"

He nods to Luna's restful body. "We didn't have many animal sedatives to choose from, but luckily we've got our share of Xanax."

"Oh." I huff an understanding laugh. "Elites sure do love their drugs. How is—?"

"She's *fine.*" Q's voice from the curtained bay next door interrupts my question, and it's like I can hear the roll of her eyes just from her voice.

I smile. She's finally up.

I step over to the neighboring bay and find Q lying on the hospital bed, her curls stuffed into a loose bun on the top of her head, no residual makeup left on her face from E2. She's wearing a black sweatshirt for some old rock band, knees crisscrossed under a thin blanket. She looks effortlessly pretty, and so violently annoyed to be here. Great to see her back to her usual self.

"She's *supposed* to be resting," the medic answers pointedly, with a good-natured arch in his eyebrow. He's wearing a surgical mask that covers most of his face, but he looks like he can't be that much older than either of us.

I step closer to Q's bed and sit in the chair next to it. "He's right."

"Like you have any say on the matter, traitor," she says completely deadpan, but there is a tiny playful speck in her eye that you'd never notice unless you had studied every single movement of her eyes and committed each one to memory. I mean *I* haven't... but if *someone* had, they'd notice.

"Okay, okay." I laugh, my palms up in mock surrender. "Traitor's a little harsh, though, considering you guys double crossed me too. I'd say we're about even."

She lifts her chin. "Not even close. Traitor."

"If you insist," I concede with a chuckle. "How are you feeling?"

"Murderous." She flicks her head to the medic.

"Hey, you're the one with the concussion here," he says with a laugh. "I'm just trying to keep any permanent brain damage to a minimum."

She grumbles a string of expletives under her breath.

The medic hangs up a clipboard with Q's chart on a hook outside the curtain. "I'm heading to the Hall for a quick bite to eat. Send someone to get me if Luna wakes up while I'm gone." He begins to step away but stops. "You're lucky she's such a fighter."

Q smiles genuinely, setting aside the jokes and misdirected anger. "Thank you, Matt."

And he's gone.

And we're alone.

She hugs her knees, as if she felt the air get heavier too.

There is a beat of silence before we both start talking at the same time.

"It wasn't all—"

"You know I didn't—"

I laugh humorlessly.

"You first," she says with a flat smile.

I sigh, not even really sure where to start. "I'm so sorry. For Luna. For lying about knowing the way out. Everything."

She looks down at her knees but doesn't respond.

"I never meant for anyone to get hurt. It's killing me that they're all still back there. That Luna" —I nod over at her still snoring body— "got hurt. I just... I honestly *never* wanted—"

Thankfully she cuts me off with a wave of her hand. "I get it."

I must have heard her wrong. "What?" It comes out as a strangled squeak.

She tucks a curl that has come loose behind her ear and messes with the threads of her blanket to avoid looking at me. She takes a moment before answering and the suspense nearly kills me.

"I've never had a real sibling. It's always just been me. I mean I've had foster siblings, but they never—" She shakes her head, cutting herself off. "I don't know, when I saw you with her... the way you held her..." She finally meets my eyes. "I guess I just hope if I ever had an older brother that he would've done the same for me."

I gulp, my throat suddenly tight.

"I'm just saying I get it. You did what you had to do."

I remember thinking the same thing in E2 when I saw that

blank-eyed man who looked like he could have been Foster's dad, remembering what Foster had said about doing what he'd done for his parents. I remember feeling a small shred of forgiveness, an understanding that he did what he had to do.

I hold her eye contact. I need her to know I'm telling the truth, that I'll never let a lie ruin our friendship again. "It wasn't all a lie, Q. I swear. I mean, yeah, the part about my dad and all. But our talks... when I said I'd help you find their names—your parents—I meant that. Truly."

It's her turn to nod. "I'll hold you to that, then."

"When we get outta here, that'll be our first stop."

She huffs. "You really think we can actually get out? After everything that's happened?" She raises a skeptical eyebrow.

"Someone once told me that you just have to keep 'hoping and hustling.'"

She laughs. A real laugh. And it loosens some of the tightness in my chest just to hear it. "It just sounds lame when you say it."

I snort. "Still though."

"Then hope and hustle we shall," she says in a mockingly formal voice.

"Deal." I jut out my hand, and she shakes it like we've just closed a business transaction.

I give her a signature smirk now that the tone has finally shifted and it finally feels like we're back in friendship territory. "Honestly, I thought you'd make me work a little harder for your forgiveness. Make me grovel a bit. Do other unspeakable things to win you back."

She shoots me a look. "I said I *understand* why you did it, I didn't say I *forgive* you for doing it. So yeah, there is a list, and as a matter of a fact, you've just added two more things."

"Well, I look forward to smashing the list to bits." I salute. "In the most respectful earn-your-trust-back kinda way, of course."

Luna interrupts by whimpering in her sleep next door, and I stand to peek around the curtain. I confirm she's still resting.

"You know, she's a pretty good judge of character," Q says, her knees still tightly at her chest. "And she literally took a bullet for you."

I grimace. "Don't remind me."

"I guess that means I have to forgive you eventually."

I blow out an exaggerated sigh of relief. "Well good, because I'm gonna need all the backup I can get when Beardsley finds out the truth."

A gruff voice behind me makes me jump out of my skin. "When Beardsley finds out *what*?"

2

WE ALWAYS KNEW IT'D HAPPEN
EVENTUALLY

MATEO

Zone C9, the night of Sam's expulsion trial

I wait without breathing as the votes of the expulsion trial are calculated. I've threatened just about every Zoner within my line of sight to vote innocent on their wrist-Tabs, or else. I try to make eye contact with Sam, who is lying on his stomach on the platform, a Guard keeping him down with a heavy boot. I just can't seem to catch his eye. I want to tell him it's going to be okay, that we believe him. We're on his side.

Because, come on, treason? They can't be serious.

It'll be okay. It has to be.

I can only really see one side of his face from here, but it's enough to see that although he's trying his best to mask it, he's scared. And I won't lie, that kind of freaks *me* out a little bit.

Sam, the back-talking all-time-record-holder of Penalties in the entire zone... *scared?*

My little brother Eddie knows better than to make a sound, but he brushes my arm, looking up at me with big eyes that say, *"It's going to be fine, right?"*

And even though my confidence in the matter is slipping more and more with every slow second that passes without a decision, I do what you have to do as a big brother and give him a tight smile that hopefully assures him, *"It's going to be fine."*

But then it's not.

It feels like everything around me and inside me bursts when Chief pronounces him guilty of treason with a sentence of expulsion, effective immediately. The crowd of Zoners erupts like a volcano, movement and sound and fury exploding all at once.

"Who voted guilty?" I scream, pushing anyone unfortunate enough to be near me. "Who?"

The crowd gets rougher as the shouts and pushing spreads across the bodies, like we've all been wound so tightly and too closely, and now the bands have all popped at once, releasing a rage that has been forced down for too long. A rage that, for some, isn't even related to what's happening to Sam, but it is for me.

I can't let this happen. He's innocent.

Sam gets pulled to his feet limply. It's like his eyes have glazed over. He can't give up, he can't.

I've finally pushed my way to the front, but the Guards have already dragged him halfway off the platform.

"Stop!" I shout at Chief, who doesn't even try to pretend he's not loving every minute of this. "He didn't do anything wrong!"

I spin around frantically. Where's Foster? He'll tell them. He can tell them their fight was all just a big misunderstanding.

Eddie is appealing to Mayor Ramos on the other side of the stage. "This isn't fair!" his tiny voice cries out. A few other Zoners our age join the protests of injustice, as many of us have been friends with Sam for years.

With a tiny flick of his head, Chief makes a signal and Guards around the perimeter start marching in. Chief turns on his heel and follows after the Guards dragging Sam toward the

Southern Boundaries, the deathtrap of invisible but lethal electric gates that surround the entire Zone and keep us caged in here.

The Guards on all sides of us begin whacking everyone with their batons and throwing people to the ground, and it only seems to make everything worse. The rage intensifies. Zoners start pushing back, fed up with always being thrown around.

This is getting bad. There are still little kids around; someone could get hurt. But I need to follow Sam. I have to stop them somehow.

Panic starts to settle in my ribcage. I'm getting pushed on all sides by waves of Zoners fighting or trying to get away. I grab Eddie's arm. Our best chance is to talk to Ramos, who is speaking in a reassuring way to a huddled group of concerned Elders, no doubt trying to assure them that he has everything under control. I give Eddie a boost up onto the platform and lift my knee to follow, when suddenly I feel myself flying through the air, landing face-first on the ground below the platform.

A Guard presses a heavy boot onto my back. I crane my neck up to see that Ramos is gone.

"*Corre, ¡rápido!*" I yell to Eddie as the Guard smashes my face into the gravel. "Run home. I'll be right behind you!"

He starts to protest, but another Guard jumps to get onto the platform after him. He gives me one last look of concern before bolting in the other direction.

Please be the one time you actually listen, I silently beg.

The Guard yanks me up to my feet. I try to shove him off me, but he punches me straight across the face. My vision goes dark for a second, the pain shooting across my face and down my neck.

But my vision comes back all too clearly when I hear it.

The unmistakable sobering sound of a gunshot.

Four of them.

Bang, bang.

Bang, bang.

My stomach falls to my feet, and I shove the Guard again. "No!" I cry out.

He throws me to the ground again, but I barely even feel it. All that exists to me right now are those gunshots echoing over and over again in my head.

Is Sam really dead?

Can he really be gone?

The edges of my eyes sting with furious tears. How can something like this be allowed to happen?

He was innocent.

The Guard pulls my arms roughly behind my back and cuffs them tightly with a band. I'm pulled back to my feet, but I feel heavy, like I'm packed full of tar. The Guard pushes me forward to walk, and it's all I can do to stumble forward without fully crumbling to the floor.

The Guards have ushered almost everyone back to their Quarters, but there are a few others like me, cuffed and shoved toward City Hall, varying evidence of resistance on their faces. Cut lips, bleeding noses, swollen eyes like mine.

The walk to City Hall and down the stairs to the holding area feels like a sluggish blur.

He can't really be gone.

All this time, we've joked that they would find a way to get rid of him one way or another—he's always been too loud, too stubborn. But it's always been just that. A joke. I can't believe they've actually done it.

The Guard throws me into a tiny cell with six other guys, my arms still cuffed, and I stumble to my knees.

Parker from B-Quarters turns to offer me a cuffed hand from behind his back, and he helps me to my feet.

"Thanks, man," I mumble, and he nods in reply. He has a

busted eyebrow that is already sealed in crusted blood. He catches me looking at it.

"Guards just started throwing punches everywhere," he says. "Figured I'd land a couple while I had the chance."

One more dude gets shoved into the cramped space before the door gets slammed shut with a *clang* and a *click*.

I look around the room in disgust and curse at them, spinning around to make eye contact with each of them. "You selfish bastards. I want to know which of you took the guilty incentive. I want you to look me in my eye and tell me. And then as soon as these cuffs are off, I'm kicking your ass."

I spin again furiously, daring anyone to speak.

Steven from H speaks up from where he sits on the floor, back up against the dirty wall of the cell. "I didn't. My whole Quarters voted innocent. My girlfriend's, too—I-Quarters."

There are mumbles of agreement throughout the tiny room until it's determined that everyone here voted innocent, as well as apparently the majority of the Zone.

I exhale a heavy breath as I process this revelation. They threw the vote. They wanted him gone that badly.

Parker behind me speaks up. "Do they even *count* our votes, or has it all just been bullshit this whole time?"

Steven scoffs. "Really makes you wonder about all the others, if any of their trials were real either."

"I guess I just always assumed everyone else voted guilty every time," someone else says.

Murmurs of agreement.

"I have a feeling things are about to get much worse around here," Steven mutters cryptically.

That lingers in the air for a moment as everyone chews on it. He's right. Something about tonight shifted things monumentally, and now it'll never be the same. We will never be the same. We've taken too much.

"Then we've gotta do something." I lower my voice. "Or each of us in this room is next."

THEY LET us out of the holding cell a couple hours later. I massage my arms, sore and stiff after being cuffed behind my back for so long, as I jog back to my Quarters.

I hesitate before going in, taking a second to fortify myself, knowing Eddie is going to need me to be strong, even though I'm two threads away from falling apart myself.

How do you look into the eyes of your kid brother, who has already been through so much hell in his nine short years, and tell him that everything is going to be okay, even when you know it's a lie?

If there's one thing I know for sure after tonight is that it's *not* going to be okay.

It's only going to get worse.

All my resolve crumbles as I walk into our Quarters and see Eddie nearly hyperventilating, sitting in the middle of the floor, eyes swollen and red.

He runs to me, and I drop to the floor, holding him tightly.

"I didn't know if I'd ever see you again," he splutters in between sobs.

My heart shatters, realizing that he's been here this whole time, all alone, not knowing if they were going to off me the same way they did Sam.

I hold his face in my hands and make him look me in my eyes, which have filled with their own tears.

"Eduardo, I swear on my life and everything I am. *Nothing* will ever separate us. Do you hear me?"

He nods and sobs into my chest.

"Me and you. Always."

I squeeze him tightly, allowing my tears to fall, allowing

myself to mourn with him. Not just for Ella and Sam, but also Mom... our old lives... Everything we've lost feels especially heavy. We grieved losing our mom years ago, when they separated us and sent her back to our old home. Normally that loss feels like a buried numb pain that never quite leaves, but every time a wound like this opens up, it brings the hurt to the surface all over again.

I hold him, and we cry until exhaustion takes over, sending us into a heartbroken sleep right here on the floor of our now empty Quarters.

TYRO B-29

As usual, my body wakes me up at exactly 6:15am, fifteen minutes before the daily alarm rings. I've been told of the concept of sleeping in, but I've never really seen the point. There's just so much to do, so much to learn, and already so little time to do it. Why would I waste good hours of productivity on sleep?

Luckily my roommates agree, so I fortunately don't have to tiptoe around the room all morning waiting for them to wake up. There is an air of quiet contentment as we make our beds and get dressed for the day. There is some quiet chit-chat among some of the others, but I keep to myself, softly humming the tune of a song I don't really know.

I smooth out the creases of the cotton sheet on my bed before folding my blanket and placing it neatly at the foot of the bed. I slip my night clothes off and refold them. Pants, shirt, fold, stack on pillow. I open the wooden chest at the foot of my bed and choose my clothing for the day. I settle on a pair of jeans and a purple long-sleeve t-shirt, my favorite color.

I pause, scanning through my brain to confirm. Yes, right, my favorite color purple.

I slip on the sneakers I was issued, and although they're a little too snug on my toes, I still love them anyway. They have little stripes on the sides that remind me of wings.

The last thing I take from my wooden chest is my toiletry bag before carefully closing the lid and stepping into line for the restrooms.

Lucy, one of my best friends, steps in behind me, giving me a friendly nudge to say good morning.

I smile over my shoulder. "Good morning, Lucy. How did you sleep?"

"Perfect as always, what about you?"

"Perfect," I reply.

It's my turn in the restroom, and I brush my teeth routinely, remembering to sing the birthday song in my head like I was taught. How does it go again? Oh yes, *happy birthday to you, happy birthday to you...* Brush, spit, rinse. Brush, spit, rinse.

I smile at my reflection when I finish, examining my sparkly clean teeth. I spend the next several minutes on finishing touches. Washing my face, using the restroom, brushing the sleep tangles out of my long hair, which I tuck behind my ears. I take an extra second to study my reflection. Wouldn't shorter hair be so much more practical? I shake away the thought quickly, remembering to be grateful for what I have.

Finally, I hold my hand under the dispenser and my daily reds and blues plop into my hand. I swallow them one at a time before showing my open empty mouth to the scanner on the dispenser. It flashes green and unlocks the restroom with a *click*.

I smile at myself one last time in the mirror, crinkling my nose a little bit like it does when I really laugh. Perfect.

Now I get to start another day.

My first class of the day is Etiquette, and I'm really excited for today's lesson. The conference room is a little chilly today, I notice, as we all file in and find our seats, but I remember to feel grateful anyway. The padded red carpet is plush underfoot as I walk to the round table across the room.

Hannah and Josiah are already seated, to my disappointment, as I usually like to be the first to arrive. They already have their notebooks open and ready to go.

"Good morning," they both say as I approach.

Aunty is passing by at that moment, making her way to the front of the room.

"Wonderful manners, you two," she praises. Hannah and Josiah beam at her, soaking up her approval.

I can't help but feel a twinge of—hmm, what is it? A twinge of an emotion I can't quite place the name of, but it feels sour in my chest. I don't like that it seems to fester there, taking on a life of its own. I inhale a discreet breath and take my seat by my tablemates, choosing to smile at them instead of frown like my body would like to do for some reason.

Aunty always says to smile whenever you'd like to frown because a frown doesn't get you anywhere. A smile can unlock doors and stop wars, she says.

I open my notebook and doodle a little bit at the top of the page. I make little stars and whirls around my name. My name. I admire it there on the paper. It was a little stiff at first, while I was getting used to it, but now I love it. I love the way the loops and curves of my letters all blend together like a roller coaster.

Roller coaster?

I'm surprised at myself. I backtrack a little bit, wondering where that came from. I scan my brain, trying to locate something to help me visualize it. After a moment I find a video clip of a train of sorts, with thrilled people in each car, speeding down a sloping track and screaming with joy. The frame pulls back to reveal that the track is made up of bends and loops and curves, and I smile. There it is. Bends and loops and curves just like my name.

My name.

Aunty calls for our attention, and I sit up straighter in my seat.

"Good morning, children," she says with a smile.

We repeat it back to her.

"Today's Etiquette lesson is about table manners. In a social situation that involves eating, it's very important to utilize table manners in order to display your best self to your table companions. And why is it important to display your best self, children?"

"Presentation is manifestation," we all answer in unison.

"Very good."

She uses a clicker in her hand to activate a video on the screen behind her.

"I'd like you to watch this video and tell me what this dinner guest may be doing *wrong*."

I watch the video as intently as I can, hoping to have an answer for Aunty before Hannah or Josiah do.

3

A GINGER AND THE TECH OF MY DREAMS

SAM

"**I** told 'ya I'd skin you alive if you lied to me, boy," Beardsley growls, taking a menacing step forward.

I deserve this.

This definitely has been a conversation I never want to have again.

The puberty talk with Ella? Uncomfy, sure. But we survived.

But telling an unhinged redneck you lied about being able to lead him to freedom, just so you could use him and his resources for your own personal gain?

0/10 do not recommend. Might not live to see another day.

"Chill, Beardsley," Q says, trying to have my back even on the hospital bed I caused her to be in. "You didn't see it there." She takes a hesitant peek at me, knowing it's a touchy subject for me. "This operation they're running is seriously creepy. He needs to get her out of there as soon as possible. I would've done the same thing."

If smoke could actually come out of his ears like in the old cartoons, it would. He points at me sharply. "You're on your own. If you think I'm risking my neck for you again, you have another thing comin'."

I nod. "I know. I just didn't want to leave without telling you how sorry I was first. I really am sorry."

"Leave?" Q scoffs. "Don't be ridiculous. You're not going anywhere by yourself. Right, Beardsley?"

She gives him a pointed look as if she's a scolding mother.

"Get out." His voice is deathly quiet. He points behind him to the exit.

"Beards—" Q begins, but I interrupt her with a smile.

"No, he's right. I should go."

"Go get some sleep," she says with a lethal undertone of *"and nothing else drastic."*

"You too. I'll come back in the morning to say goodbye before I head out."

With a departing nod to Beardsley and a pat to a snoring Luna as I pass, I push out of the doors and into the cold evening air.

Even though, yes, I expected this reaction from Beardsley, it still sucks. A tiny part of me hoped he'd miraculously understand, like Q did. That he'd understand my motives and my desperation, and though frustrated by the deceit, we'd reevaluate and make a new plan together, but now I'm just right back to where I started.

On my own.

I pace outside the hospital building for a while, trying to figure out what to do, a tight pressure building in my chest.

I can't decide if it was better or worse before when I didn't know where Ella was. It was just a blur of the unknowns. I didn't have anything solid in my head to picture or fear. Now every time I close my eyes, I see her face at E2, her real face. Her real eyes wide and scared of *me*, hiding behind that woman.

Vegas.

The very thought of her name makes my blood boil under my skin. The way she smiled so smugly when Ella wanted to stay, just like she knew she would somehow. Whether Ella realizes it or not, I'm positive she's being controlled. Brain-washed, somehow. Who knows what else? I don't know how Vegas has managed to brainwash these kids so quickly, to make them turn on everything they've ever known, their only family, in a matter of a couple weeks, but that's the only explanation. And that's precisely why I can't just respect Ella's choice to stay. If I knew for a fact it was truly her decision, it would be hard, but I'd have to respect her choice. I don't think it's truly her choice like Vegas made it seem, though. I have to figure out what's going on, even if no one else believes me.

A man passes by, and an idea comes to me.

If Beardsley won't help me, maybe there's someone else who will.

"Excuse me?" I ask the passing man. He turns. "Who runs this place?"

He raises a suspicious eyebrow as a once-over makes him realize he doesn't recognize me.

"Like, who's in charge?" I press.

There are footsteps approaching behind me, and the man's eyes widen slightly.

"What's that saying? Speak of the devil, and he shall appear?" a deep voice behind me says.

"Arcadius," the man in front of me says with a nod in greeting before hurrying off.

I turn to find a towering man with copper hair and a matching beard. Like probably the sickest beard I've ever seen. Yeah, Beardsley's is cool and everything, but this is next level and *red*. He's like straight out of a movie.

"I don't believe we've met." His smooth brown eyes look me over.

I don't answer right away because my eyes have narrowed in on what sits at his side.

A robotic figure, made of matte black metal. Four legs, a

stiff tail that wags back and forth mechanically, and a mouth full of lethal teeth.

A robodog?!

A robodog that is now creeping toward me with a growl. There is what appears to be a gun mounted to the top of its back, and I shudder considering the nightmare of being this thing's target.

"Axel doesn't really like strangers," the man says with a warning undertone, prompting me to remember that I accidentally ignored his question.

"Right, sorry." I try to keep it cool, even though I'm feeling like I just had a tech-dream come true right before my eyes in the form of a robotic dog that could kill me brutally but epically. "I'm Sam."

"Pleasure to meet you, Sam." He stretches out his hand. I eye the dog as I carefully, and *slowly*, meet the man's hand to shake it. No quick movements. "I'm Arcadius, but most people around here just call me Cade."

He studies me, like he's looking through my skin to try to figure me out.

Is he part robot too? Maybe he possesses some kind of x-ray vision.

The thought of the man in front of me possibly being a real-life cyborg makes my pulse quicken with excitement. How cool would that be? Obviously probably not, but I won't rule it out just yet, for the sake of being completely thorough. Scientifically.

He gestures around the settlement. "What brings you to the Catacombs, Sam?"

I balk internally at the name. The *Catacombs?* Wasn't that an underground graveyard?

So welcoming.

"I came in last night with Beardsley's crew. They were helping me with a... situation at E2, and things went bad." My throat squeezes in shame, knowing it's my fault that Steele, Lala, and Red are still there. That Luna is unconscious on a hospital bed. That poor Ponyboy is probably permanently traumatized because of it all. "Which is actually what I wanted to ask you about. I need—"

A woman suddenly rounds the corner, looking relieved to see us. "Cade, there you are," she says breathlessly. "The Bransons and Holts are at it again."

Cade barely looks fazed but nods in acknowledgement. "Where?" is all he says.

"The Hall."

Axel seems to understand the woman and without even a command begins to follow her back around the corner.

Cade looks at me again with those analyzing brown eyes, and it's like he can somehow sense that I have nowhere else to go. I'm just a lost stray begging for scraps, and he's left with three choices: he can either shoo me away, call the pound, or take me in.

"Walk with me," he says, without even a question in it. A statement. He's used to making commands that are followed unquestioningly, so he doesn't even wait for my response before turning. He knows I'll follow.

And I do. I feel relieved that he didn't just shrug me off. Maybe he'll actually give me the time of day.

The area seems more deserted than it was earlier as we pass by several lodging structures like the one I slept in with Ponyboy, all the same type of perma-tents. The prior commotion is now replaced with an eerie quiet. *Catacombs*... I shiver a bit.

"Can I just ask how all of this is even allowed to be here?" I ask Cade, still in awe of it all. "Like if I even breathed wrong in my Zone, the Feds would be on me in minutes. How does *this* exist?"

"Ah, a runaway," Cade says simply, as if he has finished putting together the puzzle pieces that make me.

My tongue feels like it slips down my throat.

I really just admitted being a fugitive to a powerful stranger.

He could very well be in cahoots *with* the FPA, and I basically just handcuffed my own wrists together and served myself up on a silver platter.

"No, I—" I try to backtrack. "I just meant *if*—"

He holds up a hand to stop me. "Relax. We have offered sanctuary for many runaways."

I feel relieved at his assurance, but I remind myself to be more careful. I stack a few layers of mental cinderblock around myself, guarding what little secrets I have left. I *know* I can't trust anyone. I've been an untrusting skeptical pessimist my whole life, yet how quickly I forget myself when I'm put in front of a dad-like authority figure and a sick robodog.

I need to be smart here. Be. More. Careful.

I'm struck again by the quiet of everything. We've crossed the majority of the camp and still haven't passed another person. Where is everyone?

"No really," I urge, realizing he never answered my question. "How is an illegal operation of this size not shut down?"

He doesn't answer right away, and for a second which feels way longer than it probably is, all that can be heard are our footsteps crunching against the dirt.

Cade bends to pick up a stray piece of trash on the ground and twirls it slowly like he's about to juggle with it or something.

"Let's just say," he finally answers, "that the FPA knows by now it's in *their* best interest to leave us alone. We've come to… an understanding."

I mull over this information as we approach what must be the Hall, which is just a much larger perma-tent. He tosses the plate into a trashcan before stepping through the door, which the woman is holding open for us.

"Thank you, Meredith."

Well, this answers the question of where everybody is.

They're all here.

Inside the Hall is so chaotic and loud that it takes my brain extra loading time to make sense of the environment. The huge space with lines of cafeteria-style tables is packed with people yelling, arguing, pushing, shoving, like what I imagine a bar fight would look like.

As Cade and Axel walk through the rowdy mass of people, it's like they're parting the Red Sea. As they pass, person after person quiets down until we reach the center of the room, and apart from one final group shouting in the middle, the rest of the room has gone completely quiet just from their presence alone.

There are four furious men standing around a cafeteria table, pointing and spewing curses at each other. I made out a few intelligible bits.

"A dirty thief!"

"—terms you agreed to!"

"Pay me my money!"

The cards strewn around the table, the accusations of cheating and theft. I put two and two together and conclude that someone lost the game and now doesn't want to pay up.

Cade clears his throat, but they don't completely quiet down until Axel makes a digitized bark that seems to bounce off the spaces between the bodies around the room like a zap of electricity.

One of the men addresses Cade defensively. "They *knew* the terms, Cade."

The two men across the table from him explode in protest. "We didn't agree to be cheated. We agreed to a fair game!"

"I don't know how they did it, but they're con artists."

"That's a bold accusation, Holt—"

Cade holds his hands up to silence them. "Gentlemen, please."

He steps toward the table and picks up the cards. He turns them over one by one, analyzing them with that same intensity he looked at me with earlier. Cyborg possibility: still inconclusive.

The two men being accused of cheating shift uncomfortably the longer he examines the cards.

"This deck is marked," Cade finally announces, setting the cards back down on the table.

The watching crowd breaks out into a mixture of surprise and furious confirmation, as it seems the audience was split on whether they supported the accusers or the accused.

"Now this would normally be what I'd consider an offense worth community service for," Cade continues, his tone calm but with undeniable authority. "But in this case, I'd say everyone witnessing your true methods is punishment enough. Debts in this round are absolved, and I'd caution everyone else to remember this before playing another round with the Bransons again."

He looks around the room with a raised brow as if to say, "Any questions?"

The Bransons don't even try to plead their innocence as they collect their cards in silence. They know they've been caught, and there are too many witnesses for them to dispute.

Not to mention lethal teeth of a menacing robodog right next to them, but maybe that's just C9 trauma talking. He's probably lovely.

The Holts watch smugly with arms across their chests. The rest of the audience settles, and everyone carries on with their evenings, the tension oozing out of the room now that the truth has been revealed.

Cade looks back at me and nods toward the door, so casually calming down an entire room without lifting a finger and then getting back to business as usual like it's just another day. I have to shoulder my way through the crowd to avoid being left behind, and he still makes it to the exit before me.

Once I push through the exit, my ears feel suddenly hollow without all the extra noise of the Hall. Cade is talking to a small group, who engage with him easily. He seems less intimidating in a smaller group, his gaze less intense, his smooth expressions more charming than authoritative. Even Axel waiting nearby seems more at ease. It's a relief to see that his people like him.

He sees me coming and gives the closest member of the group a parting pat on the shoulder. "If you'll excuse me."

And then to me, "So sorry for the interruption, Sam."

We meander through the people finishing evening preparations, not really walking anywhere in particular. Axel follows closely behind.

"It's okay," I say, not even really sure how to go about this. I should have been rehearsing some kind of speech in my head. I try to collect the important pieces.

"You were saying something about a situation at E2," he prompts patiently.

"Yes, sir. We attempted an extraction. My sister is being held against her will at the Fresh Air Casino by a woman who calls herself Vegas."

To my surprise, Cade sighs. "Ah, yes. I should have known when you said E2."

It sounds like he's already aware of the situation. Beardsley must have already debriefed him. Great, that should make things easier.

But then the bombshell drops when he says, "I assume things with my wife didn't go over well."

IF AXEL NOT CUDDLY, WHY CUDDLY SHAPED?

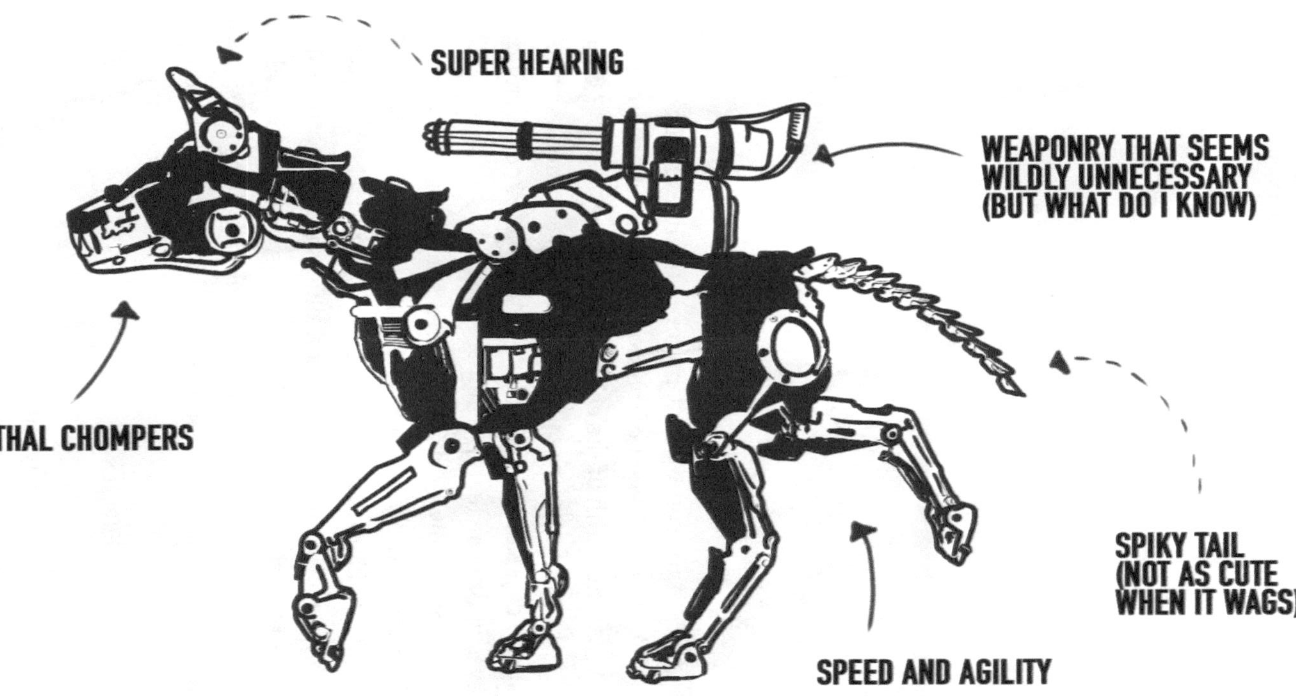

TYRO B-29

6:15am comes, and my eyes open like clockwork to the familiar view of cylindrical air ducts stretching across the width of the ceiling like a maze.

It's comforting to open my eyes and see the same view every single day. Knowing it will always be the same when I open my eyes makes me feel safe and at-ease.

I make my bed with care, smoothing it to perfection, humming softly to a song I long to know the words to.

Night clothes off. Pants, shirt, folded, stacked.

I select denim pants and a blue shirt today, smiling at the cute ruffles that are stacked in layers on the shirt. The ruffles remind me of something—something happy or nostalgic, perhaps—but I can't quite place what it is. I pull it on over my head.

Toiletry bag.

Restroom line.

Nudge on my shoulder.

"Good morning, Lucy," I say. "How did you sleep?"

"Perfect as always. What about you?"

"Perfect."

It's my turn into the restroom.

Happy birthday to you, happy birthday to you. Brush, rinse, spit. Brush, rinse, spit.

I opt for a ponytail today—Lucy and I have been practicing on each other, and I've gotten quite good at it. I'm pleased at the neat masterpiece sprawling down my back. I bring the ponytail length to the front of my shoulder and smile at the mirror, nose crinkled to perfection.

Reds and blues, swallowed.

Green light. Lock clicks.

I hold the door open for Lucy and flash the smile I've just practiced in the mirror.

She smiles back.

"GOOD MORNING, CHILDREN."

"Good morning, Aunty," we parrot back, Hannah and Josiah chiming in next to me at our table. My notebook is open and ready to go. I feel enthusiastic, my body nearly buzzing with the anticipation of what I'll learn today.

The conference room isn't as cold today, and I take note of the gratitude I feel for that.

Aunty says it's good to acknowledge when things are going your way because it is more likely to continue, when gratitude for it is put out into the universe.

"Today's Etiquette lesson is about cultivating efficacious friendships."

I copy that down in my notebook.

F.E.cayshus friendships.

I make a quick mental scan, trying to locate *efficacious* in my vocabulary, but I come up frustratingly short. An unkind thought about my brain's intelligence level threatens to materialize, but I shake it off and refocus instead.

"When making new friendships, it's important to evaluate if their strengths and resources can be of value to your goals." Aunty clicks her remote, and the screen moves to an image of two children playing on a playground. "That way your relationship can not only have social benefits but can also be mutually fruitful as well."

The image sparks a sudden vivid mental image. Another movie scene, perhaps, like the roller-coaster one yesterday. Or maybe a memory? A boy around my age is laughing and playing on a gray playground. A friend? I believe I am watching him from the ground, excitedly waiting my turn, as he flies down the slide. And then, just as quickly as it appeared, it is gone.

I'm surprised at the sadness that engulfs me, like a wave that soaks my body from head to toe. Why am I having an emotional reaction to this image?

Aunty's slideshow clicks to a bulleted list that I immediately start to copy down, trying to blink away the image of that boy from my brain and the strange sadness that accompanied it.

"Let's discuss the strengths and skills that *we*" —Aunty makes a gathering type of gesture around the conference room — "are going to seek out in our friendships."

I've nearly copied the whole list when one of the bullet points makes me pause for a second.

Family members are well-connected.

Family members.

I make a mental scan but come up short. I scan again. Still blank.

I frown.

I take an extra second to reflect, wondering why my brain is unable to provide any insight to this topic. If I'm to seek out friendships with family members who are well-connected, but I have none of my own, who will want to seek *my* friendship?

I glance at Lucy two tables over and feel a strange sharp

feeling in my stomach. I watch her for a moment as she copies down her own notes. Is she considering right now if our friendship is efficacious enough?

I realize I've gotten behind, and my penmanship suffers as I hurry to finish copying down the rest of the list before Aunty switches to the next slide.

"Now, why might we want to avoid cultivating a friendship with an individual who shows signs of fragility?" She points to one of the bullet items and waits for a volunteer to answer. I recite the correct answer in my head, but I'm still trying to catch up after my momentary distractedness, so I don't raise my hand.

Rachel at the table next to ours raises her hand and answers with confidence. "Weakness is profitless."

"Weakness is profitless," we repeat.

"Very good," Aunty praises. "Let me tell you all something my mother taught me when I was young before she died. You are the company you keep."

She pauses for a moment to let us reflect on those words.

"'Company' meaning the people you choose to surround yourself with. If the *company* you keep is weak? You will always be weak. And *we*" —she makes that gesture with her arms again, like she's bringing all of us in close to her— "choose strength instead."

We choose strength instead.

I copy that down.

4

———

BREAKFAST WITH A SIDE OF BLOOD

MATEO

C9, the day after Sam escapes the Zone

Check-in the following morning is tense to say the least. I notice right away that there are much fewer Guards than usual, and the ones that do show up to check-in are still in their riot gear from last night, black helmets covering their faces and matte armor plating them from head to toe. They seem very on edge—irritable and moody, almost like they're looking for a fight today. Chief is nowhere to be seen, which is probably for the best because I don't know how I'll be able to restrain myself when I see him.

Murderer.

And *where* is Foster? He's never late to check-in. I have some words for him too, but at this point I just want to make sure he's okay. He must feel terrible about everything. No matter what went down between him and Sam last night, I know he didn't mean for all of this to happen.

For Sam to be dead.

It's like my very brain is still refusing to believe it because even thinking those words feels like a different language entirely. It can't be true, it just can't.

Eddie and I keep our heads down through formation and as the line moves through BART, the machine that checks us in and assigns our daily functions. Are they seriously carrying on like it's just a normal day after everything that happened last night? I get assigned Kitchen Support, and Eddie's subject today is Math, and as we sit at our regular spots with our breakfast trays, I feel a pang in my chest at the empty seats around us.

No Sam. No Ella. *Still no Foster.*

Where our mornings are usually filled with joking conversation, light-hearted arguments about politics, or quoting the few movies we can remember, today it's just filled with crushing silence. He doesn't say anything, but I know Eddie feels the void too.

I pat his shoulder, knowing there's not really anything I can say.

I chew on my eggs, but I barely taste them as I sit in my worries that are compounded by the silence at our table. The tableTab games don't even sound appealing right now, and the Tic-Tac-Toe one is usually enough to pull me out of any bad mood. But I can't shake off this feeling of deep dread in the pit of my stomach, a sort of Spidey-sense I get when bad things are about to happen. Sam and Ella gone. Foster nowhere to be found. Who knows who's next?

I always knew they were out to get us down here, but I've always tried to stay positive. There was nothing I could do about it, so might as well try to make the best of it, right? Well, look where that's gotten us. We're still just as helpless as everyone else. Our odds are no better because of it. I have no more means of keeping my sibling safe than Sam did. As anyone else does. How will my outcome be any different? How can I still continue to promise my brother I'll keep him safe?

My train of thought is interrupted by a conversation growing in volume at the other side of the Mess Hall. I can't make out what the two dudes are arguing about, but they're getting angrier by the second. I know where this is headed if someone doesn't step in. Soon enough they'll be dragged off to that tiny holding cell or to the Penalty Podium where we all have to witness their electrified beating and listen to Chief give a smug lecture about how "the prosperity of the Zone depends on the choices of the individuals" or some crap like that. Who knows what kind of mood Chief will be in after last night, so it's better not to even risk it. We've got to keep our heads here, even more than usual.

I push myself up off the bench to head over and help mediate, but before I can even take a step in their direction, the punches are thrown. By now everyone else has noticed too, and it feels like the room is on the very edge of chaos. Everyone watches the two circling and punching and pushing like it's fight club or something— some people egging them on, some trying to talk reason from the sidelines.

Someone has to stop this. I know what it's like to have my arms cuffed behind my back for hours, locked in that basement of Town Hall, and I've also felt the sparkling sting of the Penalties. If I can spare these guys either kind of torment, I have to try.

"Stay here," I say to Eddie, having to raise my voice over the new volume in the room.

I try to push through the bystanders, but to my dismay a Guard beats me to it.

Great, now we'll all have to gather for their—

Shots ring out.

Bang, bang.

The screams that erupt throughout the Hall are ear-splitting. Everyone pushes each other to try to get as far away as possible, sending the Hall into a frenzy, but I'm just standing in shock, watching as the blood pools from two bodies.

The life draining out of them as quickly as their fight began.

The Guard raises his gun again and fires a third shot into the ceiling, the bullet firing straight through the wooden beams of the roof.

The screams and movement stop immediately like they've been plucked from thin air.

"Breakfast is over," the Guard yells, his voice muffled from inside his helmet. "Report to your duties immediately."

The only sounds now are scrapes of benches, stacking of trays, and clicking of doors as people exit. I couldn't really taste my eggs, but I can taste this. The fear.

I find Eddie and put my arm around his shoulder, keeping him tightly next to me as we exit the building. The silence extends to outside as everyone silently heads to their assignments.

I raise Eddie's quivering chin and whisper down at him, "Breathe, *Lalito.* Everything will be okay."

He nods. He knows I'm lying, but a little bit of the fear melts away from his face.

Isn't it funny how that works? We can know someone is lying straight to our face but can still take comfort from their lies, from the hope that maybe there is some small sliver of truth to it after all. It's those deluded shreds of hope that keep us going.

After Eddie is safely on his way to his subject, I realize my own hands are shaking.

I knew it, I knew something bad was going to happen. That "Spidey-sense" is never wrong.

But you can know something bad is about to happen, and still never be prepared to witness it coming true.

They didn't even get a chance. No warning, not even the farce of a trial Sam had.

Their deaths are clearly supposed to be a message to everyone that they're still in charge, that the disorder of last night will not be tolerated. But now that I have a second to collect my thoughts, I'm getting a whole different message entirely. Call it that delusion, call it my obsession with a good old-fashioned conspiracy— whatever. But this seems desperate. Like they're grasping at straws trying to keep it together here.

Which seems to *me* like the best time for a little organized mayhem. After all, one loose thread in a sweater can unravel the entire thing. All it takes is the right snag.

AFTER HOURS of the repetitive tedium of washing dish after dish, the bell finally *dings* and signifies that there are ten minutes until check-in for lunch. I take off my gloves, throwing them in an easy spot for me to find later, and wash my hands. Spending hours in the dim lighting of the kitchen makes the outdoor artificial light feel blinding.

I let my eyes adjust and spend a few minutes looking around for Foster, hoping to see him returning from a nearby function, or even from Town Hall. Maybe he spent the night locked up like I did but had to stay longer for some reason.

I wish he would have spoken up last night at the trial.

All that crap Chief was saying about Sam inciting some kind of rebellion, and Foster trying to stop it. Treason this, treason that. I was there. I know that didn't happen.

And so did Foster. If he would've spoken up too, maybe it could have saved Sam. Maybe things could have gone differently. I'm trying really hard not to blame him, but his silence is just making it even harder.

I find my spot in the formation line, and Eddie sidles up next to me. He's quieter than usual, but I don't blame him.

Losing Sam last night was like losing Ella all over again. We both held onto the hope that Sam could find her somehow, that he'd bring her back, and it would all be back to normal. But now that *he's* gone, she's officially gone too.

I lost my best friend last night, and Eddie lost his too.

I wish I was better with words or knew the right thing to say to make it better, but I don't.

We're waiting for formation to begin, everyone scared to even breathe too loudly after what happened this morning. A couple of Guards are standing at the ready with guns in their hands when a group of trucks come squealing in through the Southern Boundaries, past the circular layers of the living Quarters on that side, past the school and hospital. Three trucks whiz by, spraying dust and gravel everywhere. I shield my eyes.

This can't be good.

They squeal to a stop right next to the Podium, and it's like the exact millisecond the wheels stop turning, the doors are already opened and boots of at least a dozen new Guards are stepping out, sporting the same full armor and covered faces ours have.

The doors slam in unison, and they all step with precision into a formation of their own in front of ours.

There is one last slam of a door that follows all the others, with slower footsteps that are separated from the rest of the group.

A woman, unhelmeted and unarmored, steps around the formation, and I have to use every ounce of bodily control I have to keep my jaw from dropping at the sight of her. Eddie doesn't have the same control, and I smack his shoulder as discreetly as I can, shooting a stern look at him. He fixes his face immediately, but his wide eyes look at me like, *"Are you sein' this?"*

The woman steps to the front of the formation, her movements deliberate and slow, a threat that we all receive without words even being spoken. Her dark hair is slicked back into a neat bun, her skin is pale and her eyes are so dark they're nearly black, her green shirt and camo pants are plain and unassuming. Appearance-wise there isn't really anything that special about her... except for the arm made of metal resting at her side. I can't tear my eyes away from it. It looks more like a weapon than a prosthetic, more deadly than functional.

It's actually kind of awesome.

I wish Sam were here. I'd make so many movie references right now.

She brings both arms behind her back into a stance of attention, but we are already so silent you could hear a pin drop.

"Ladies and gentlemen," she says, barely raising her voice. "My name is Sergeant Nova, and I have been appointed as your new Chief of Discipline since it seems Sergeant Hallows went a little too easy on you."

The tension is so thick I can feel it on the hairs of my arms. Easy? He murdered Sam in cold blood.

"I'll say this one time," she continues. "There will be order, or you will pay for it with your life. It's as simple as that."

She makes a motion with her hand, and the Guards around her break formation, moving to different areas around us. Movement begins as they direct us to start checking in through BART for lunch, and we obey silently. I squeeze Eddie's hand.

We've almost reached the end of the food line when I feel the tickle of an incoming alert on my wristTab. I turn my wrist over to read the message, and my throat nearly falls to my ankles.

MATEO AND EDUARDO, PLEASE COME SEE ME IN MY OFFICE IMMEDIATELY.

-Mayor Ramos

MEMORY LANE WITH TEO
EPISODE 1

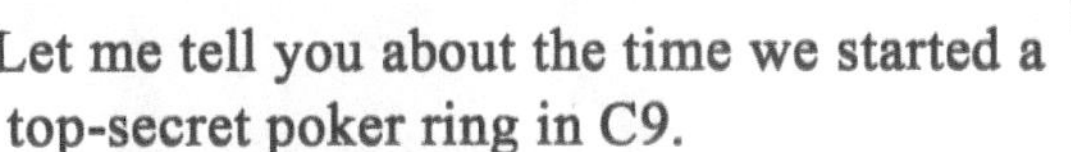

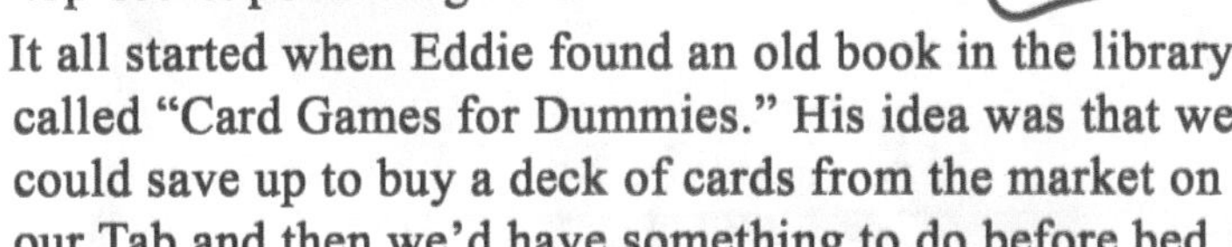

Let me tell you about the time we started a top-secret poker ring in C9.

It all started when Eddie found an old book in the library called "Card Games for Dummies." His idea was that we could save up to buy a deck of cards from the market on our Tab and then we'd have something to do before bed.

We skipped breakfast for two weeks so we could buy the deck, and learning every game in the book became a quick obsession. To the point where Sam began confiscating our deck at 9:00pm each night so HE could get some sleep. Otherwise, we'd easily stay up past midnight.

Once we learned poker it was all over. The concept of gambling was just too enticing to a couple poor orphans. We began whispering around, inviting neighboring Quarters over before curfew to play, but they could only buy in once they had saved up 10 plastic water bottle caps.

It flew through the Zone like wildfire. Everyone began obsessively collecting water bottles, so they could play. The Guards couldn't figure out why Waste Management was suddenly such a popular function.

The caps became a currency in the Zone that was just ours (as worthless as they may have been), a secret only we knew about. We clung to that small taste of freedom AD-DICTIVELY.

It took 3 months for Chief to figure out what we were up to, but until then we lived like kings with our hundreds of useless water bottle caps and tiny shred of normalcy.

5

MAY I SUGGEST MARRIAGE COUNSELING?

SAM

I wake up the next morning in the quiet sleeping quarters with my head buzzing. I barely slept. After dropping that nuclear bomb on me, Cade told me to go to bed, and we'd talk more about it later.

Right. Like I'm going to get any sleep after that.

Vegas and Cade, MARRIED?

My brain has just gone wild all night trying to make sense of that. Are they working together? Am I even safe here? Does this connection give me an advantage or disadvantage? Ponyboy rustles in the bed next to mine as I stretch out the soreness in my neck. The bed on the other side of Ponyboy, which I assume to be Beardsley's, is still empty. I see he couldn't even stand to sleep in the same vicinity as me. Great.

Ponyboy's eyes suddenly flick open, and it's like he immediately powers on to full energy. "Good morning!"

I smile, bringing my finger up to my mouth, reminding him to keep quiet for the other still-sleeping members of our room.

A shadow flickers across his face as he seems to replay the traumatic night before. He begins to ask, but I interrupt before he even opens his mouth.

"They're both fine," I say gently. "Q and Luna are fine. I'll take you to them."

The brightness returns to his eyes, and the bounce returns to his small frame, but his skin looks even paler than it usually does, and his ponytail has come loose.

I gesture for him to come here, and he sits next to me on the bed. I gently pull out the hair tie from his long hair and try to comb through the tangles with my fingers.

"Are Red and Steele and Lala going to be okay?" he whispers, looking down at his hands as I tame his hair.

"I hope so," I answer honestly.

I smooth his hair at the scalp and bring it up into a bun on top of his head like I've done to Ella's hair so many times. When I'm done, I flick his head playfully, and he makes a face at me.

We walk together to the medical building, and I can't help but smile. Ponyboy greets everyone with a sunny "good morning" as we pass and nearly vibrates with contagious energy. It somehow makes me forget for a second that I'm out of resources and prospects and have to save my sister without either one somehow.

By the time we reach the building, Q is already outside, and to my pleasant surprise, so is Luna. You'd never know Luna was even bullet-ridden just mere hours ago as she bounces around Q happily. She has a white bandage wrapped around nearly her entire abdomen, but it doesn't slow her down at all.

Luna sees us coming and bounds over to us, nearly tackling Ponyboy. He squeals with glee as she licks him all over his face. I lower to a knee when it's my turn for her attention, and I bring her face close.

"Hey, you," I say to Luna with a smile, rubbing down her face on both sides and around her ears. Her tongue lolls out of her mouth, almost like she's smiling back. I point my finger at her and speak to her in a stern tone. "No more bullets on my behalf. We're square now, got it?"

She licks my face, and I take that as agreement.

"Q!" Ponyboy squeals, running up to her and hugging her legs. She leans down to hug him back.

"Hi, Pony, nice man bun." She smirks in my direction. "I should've known Prettyboy had some tricks up his sleeve."

"Oh, I have lots of skills in a variety of departments." I make my voice low and sultry, hoping to make her laugh. She just rolls her eyes, but that's good enough for me. I'm just glad she's okay and doesn't entirely hate me.

"I'm starving, let's go eat!" she says, looking down at the two bubbly children bouncing around her, one with fur and one without. Her voice raises to a higher octave whenever she's talking to them, a brightness in her tone that I love hearing.

We make our way to the Hall, and I speak to Q in a quiet voice, so Ponyboy ahead of us doesn't overhear. "I have a crazy development."

She gives me a look like, *"Well? Go on."*

"I met Cade last night. Oh, and Axel. Really, Q, you guys have a robodog here and you didn't tell me?"

She shushes me, her lips pressed into a tight-lipped smile. "Don't say his name too loudly." She nods at Luna. "She haaaates him."

I laugh in shock. "It seems like there's a story there, and I'm going to eventually need every detail, but first." I pause for suspense. "Vegas and Cade. Are *married.*"

Q skids to a stop. "No."

Her disbelief is reassuring. I'm glad I wasn't the only one in the dark on this fact.

"What? *How?*"

"Exactly my same questions." We continue walking, Ponyboy and Luna a few yards ahead, skipping and playing as they go. "He dropped that little tidbit on me and then just told me to go to bed. I know absolutely nothing. Are they working together?"

Her brows pull together in confusion. "That wouldn't make any sense. I don't think so? I mean pretty much all we do here is run deliveries to Elites. I've never seen anything even close to Vegas-level nefarious, and I've been here for *years*."

That sends a little bit of relief through me, although I'm still not sure how a connection like that can exist without there being some level of cooperation. I mean they're obviously a little...untraditional, existing in two separate spaces and all, but that doesn't mean they aren't still friendly.

Q blows out a loud breath. "Dang."

"Right?"

It makes my head hurt.

We enter the Hall and have to weave around people, everyone filling up before getting to work on whatever it is they do here. We step in line, and I'm so deep in my thoughts I don't even consider the fact that I don't have any money until we reach a man standing at a table in front of the food window.

"ID?" he asks me in a bored tone.

"Oh." I shoot a glance to Q over my shoulder. "I don't have—"

She steps around me and recites two strings of numbers to the man; I assume one for her and one for Ponyboy. "He can use mine."

The man looks at Q and then back to me as he types in the numbers into a small device. "We can make an exception today, but tomorrow he'll need his own number."

I gulp, remembering what Red had said to me before we went into E2, when he was telling me that Lala's *"Underground"* removed his wristTab in exchange for a commitment of service. *One cuff to another,* he had said. That makes a nagging dread fill in my gut.

What kind of service will I need to commit to in order to stay here, even temporarily?

We step to the food window and are met with a continental-style breakfast with simple items like fruit, pastries in plastic wrappers, bagels, and small containers of yogurt.

I can't remember the last time I had fresh fruit, so I pile both a banana and an apple on my plate happily, while Q grabs two yogurts and a banana. Luna and Ponyboy wait beside us obediently, Ponyboy chattering away about a topic that, admittedly, I'm not really listening to.

Most of the tables are full, but we find a few seats open near the exit. People pass by and greet Luna, many stopping to pat her on the head familiarly. Luna sits on the ground next to Q's feet and downs the banana Q throws to her in one swallow.

"My question is," I say with a mouth full of apple, but keeping my voice low in case 'the devil' decides to appear again, "if they aren't working together, why are they even married?"

To my surprise another young boy approaches our table and sits by Ponyboy. There are other kids here? In the *Catacombs*? Ponyboy and the boy begin talking right away, a convenient distraction so Q and I can keep theorizing without him overhearing.

"He doesn't wear a ring," she offers through bites of her yogurt. "I know that for a fact. I checked the second I saw him."

The way she says that sends a strange ping to my stomach. I eye her.

"What? He's hot," she says simply with a shrug. Another ping. "I always kinda wanted him and Lala to get together."

"Well, it turns out his type is a little less Beauty and a little more Beast."

Q takes another bite of yogurt. "Nah, Vegas is totally hot, you have to admit. Evil, of course. But yeah. That's a hot couple."

I consider the two of them, like fire and ice. Two powerful people, each commanding their own forces for their own purposes... if they aren't working together, won't there be an inevitable head-to-head when their interests clash?

My thoughts of the Vegas-Cade power struggle are interrupted by a commotion outside. Q and I share a look, both questioning what could be going on. Luna's ears also perk up curiously.

Q instructs Ponyboy to say goodbye to his friend, and we move outside to check it out.

We approach one of the outer perimeters of the Catacombs, which is lined with trucks of every shape and size for easy loading and unloading. There is a buzzing group surrounding a black vehicle that looks like it has just arrived. The driver side opens, and Cade steps out, his long red hair looking ever so slightly wind-tousled, like some warrior on the back of a noble steed.

"Give us some space, everyone," he instructs as he walks to the passenger side of the vehicle, barely even raising his voice over a normal level, knowing that his order will be obeyed. And it is. The group shifts backward, and I stumble a little over Luna as it does. I pat her apologetically.

Cade opens the passenger door and gently helps out a young woman, keeping his arm around her to keep her from falling down. She stumbles a lot, even with the assistance.

I notice right away how pretty she is, but she definitely looks like she's seen better days. She's tattered, disheveled, and unmistakably straight from E1 with her outfit choice—some form of a bikini under what looks like a fishing net with long tassels at the end that fall nearly all the way down to her booted ankles.

What is someone from E1 doing here?

I look over to Q to ask, but she seems to be wondering the exact same thing.

The girl looks to be in her early twenties. Waist-length wavy brown hair with long strands of crystals woven into it. Dark makeup that is smeared nearly all the way down her cheeks, making her look a little bit like someone who has painted their face like a skeleton for Halloween. She looks like she can barely even keep her eyes open. Her head lolls as Cade moves her in the direction of the medical building. A man from the crowd steps to her other side and helps Cade support her.

"I should bring her a change of clothes. We look about the same size." Q nods in their direction. "C'mon, let's go."

Acknowledging that we're in her territory here, I simply follow her lead.

WE PASS off Ponyboy to Beardsley, but I keep my distance. I'm not looking for a fight, and I know he doesn't want anything to do with me. The less he's reminded of my presence the better. I'll get out of his hair eventually, but I'm still lacking any resources or a plan. As soon as I get those? Beardsley, you'll never have to see me again.

When we get to the E1 girl's hospital bay with a pile of Q's clothes and an assortment of toiletries in hand, she is already hooked up to an IV bag on her non-Tabbed wrist and is sleeping deeply.

Cade is sitting next to the bed, Axel lying motionless right by his feet.

Luna makes a low throaty growl as we approach, and Q *tsks* her sharply.

"Do you need to wait outside?" she scolds her through her teeth. Luna lowers her ears in reply and lies down just outside the curtain.

"Hi Cade." Q clears her throat. "I thought she might like a fresh pair of clothes to change into, and we looked about the same size."

Cade smiles. "That's very thoughtful of you. Thank you, Q."

I run the risk of being nosy. "Is she from E1? How did even she get out?"

Cade looks down at her with a faraway expression. "She's the daughter of an old friend. I called in a few favors to make the extraction happen."

"Do you do that a lot?"

I feel a glimmer of hope. If he has those kinds of resources, those kinds of connections, there's no reason he couldn't do the same for Ella.

"We've gotten a couple E1's out over the years," Cade replies. "But unfortunately, it's usually not long before they're begging us to take them back. The withdrawals are just too much for most to handle."

Withdrawals?

As crappy as that sounds, it's hard to really feel bad for them when they just get to party and have a good time every day. No real understanding of what's going on around them, no fear of the day-to-day. Nothing compared to what the rest of us have to go through just to survive down here. Not to mention the people with disabilities they happily enslave to fulfill their every whim.

Q blows air out of her mouth and blurts, "Is it actually true that you and Vegas...?" She makes a gesture with her hand to complete her sentence. I'm thankful she was the one to bring it up because I've been dying to talk to him more about it, but I wasn't sure if a stranger's hospital bedside was the most appropriate place to broach the topic.

He huffs a soft laugh. "Well, I knew her as Veronica, but yes."

Q folds her arms across her chest. "Are you aware of what she's doing over there? It's creepy as hell, Cade."

"My wife and I have been separated for some time." He

seems to be choosing his words carefully, and that makes me suspicious. "We haven't spoken in years, very nearly since coming Under." He leans back into his chair. "She keeps her... business... very private."

I feel a flare of anger beginning to bubble up inside of me. How can he refer to this woman so casually? "If by 'her business' you mean murdering, kidnapping, and brainwashing children, including my eight-year-old sister, then yeah."

His eyes meet mine, the deep brown seeming to swirl inside his irises. "She's always been very... *competitive*, sure—that was part of the reason we didn't work out—but I've had no reason to suspect her scholarship program based on what I've heard. It seems harmless."

I shift my weight, trying really hard to keep my anger from getting the best of me. I can't burn a bridge here.

"Well, it's not," I say curtly. "My sister was kidnapped, and now she's been brainwashed into wanting to stay. I don't know exactly what she's doing or how she's doing it, but there's something off about those kids."

Cade nods slowly as if he's working out the details. "So you attempted to remove your sister from the program— a program that provides her with growth, learning, and opportunity she wouldn't receive elsewhere—and instead of wanting to go back to your Zone with you, she wanted to stay? And this was surprising to you?"

Q glances at me, worried I'm about to flip a lid. I breathe out through my nose. "I know how it sounds. But I know my sister. There's something off."

"Not to mention she tried to kill us, she still has Steele, Red, and Lala, *and* she killed one of her workers. Right in front of us," Q adds, really trying to reason with Cade. She knows how important his help can be, now that he's confirmed his connection to her. "Her employees are all indentured servants basically. Working off some kind of sentence. I really wouldn't be surprised if the kids are too."

Cade nods again, and I can't tell if he's just politely listening or if he's really processing what we're saying. He has to know from personal experience that Vegas is unhinged.

"I was aware of her...methods... with her employees. Like I said she's always been very competitive. We both had different ideas of how we could obtain our goals in the Underground and thus parted ways." He looks between us both. "I'm not saying I don't believe you. I just don't see what use she'd have with 'brainwashed' children, as you say, nor do I think she even has the resources or know-how to accomplish that."

I start to protest, but he holds up a hand to stop me. "But we always protect our own. I will need to negotiate the return of my employees. If you and I can come to some kind of agreement, I'll see what I can do about your sister too."

I breathe a sigh of relief. Is he really going to help me? At this point I don't even care what kind of *agreement* I have to commit to, as long as she's safe.

I look at the girl on the hospital bed, who he just used his resources and connections to rescue. I feel a burning hope that Ella could really be next.

"And the rest of the kids?" Q asks softly, like she already knows the answer.

Cade sighs. "I hate to say it, but the rest of the kids are unfortunately not my concern."

Q WALKS me over to a building near the Hall, insisting we need to blow off some steam. We enter the building, and the smell of sweat nearly gags me. It's a huge room packed with workout equipment. Weights, mats, machines, really anything you'd ever need if you're into that kind of thing.

She leads me over to the back corner where there is a huge red wrestling mat, and two men rolling around all over it. It looks to be a pretty even match, but eventually one of them taps. They both stand, breathing heavily and shoving each other familiarly. They shake hands and separate to take long gulps from their water bottles.

"Hey Q." The one who won waves. He has dark hair and a friendly smile under a cool mustache.

"Hi, Mack." Q nods to me. "Prettyboy here needs a proper ass-kicking."

I gape at her. "No way, I didn't sign up for this."

"Remember my forgiveness list?" she chirps. "This is at the *very* top."

Mack steps closer to us with a grin. He's a little shorter than me, extremely lean, and if I didn't just witness him take down the other guy, I wouldn't be worried at all about going hand-to-hand with him.

I give Q a look, but she sends one back that says, *"You're doing this whether you like it or not."*

"You new here?" he says, holding out his hand for a shake. "I'm Mack."

I shake his hand. "Sam. Do you have a rule for going easy on newcomers? If so, then yes, I'm new."

Guess I'm doing this whether I like it or not. I slip off my boots and leave them at the edge of the mat.

He just laughs, and I gulp, sending Q a glare as he leads me out to the middle. I bear down, determined to give this my best shot. Maybe it won't be too—

He pins me down in seconds.

I tap.

Q cackles from the sidelines. Even Luna yips, bouncing around at the edge of the mat like she's joining in the heckling.

Round after round, no matter how hard I try, he barely lifts a finger and overpowers me every time. After the third or fourth time he begins to give me some guidance. He shows me where to put my hands and how to rock my hips to roll out from underneath him. With some extreme effort on my part, and him going easy on me, I finally escape successfully. Once.

I stand and push my hair off my sweating forehead, breathing heavily. When was the last time I *exercised*? Have I ever?

Mack motions Q over. "Let's show him a basic scissor sweep."

Q stacks her hair into a bun on top of her head, a devious smile on her face. "I'd love nothing more."

"We'll demonstrate, and then I'll show you how to do it," Mack says.

Q lies down on her back and Mack kneels in between her legs. She wraps her legs around his waist.

I press my lips together, trying not to laugh hysterically out of pure discomfort. "Are 'get a room' jokes allowed on the mat?"

Mack gives me a pity chuckle, but Q doesn't acknowledge my comment at all. Instead, she grabs Mack by the collar, shoves her knee into his stomach, and before I can even blink has him rolled over on his back with her elbow on his throat.

"Very good," Mack praises, tapping her shoulder. She stands up and offers her hand to help him up.

"Did you see the scissor motion her legs made when she threw me over?"

"Ah, yes," I lie, unable to admit I was completely distracted by sheer shock. "Very scissor-y."

Q snorts. "Oh, I'm so gonna enjoy this." She lies on her back again. "Your turn, Prettyboy."

I roll back my shoulders with pretend confidence. "Right. Piece of cake."

I kneel the same way Mack did, and I'm suddenly extremely

aware of our proximity as she wraps her legs around my waist. *Don't think, don't think, don't you dare think.*

Her eyes are sparkling with mischief as she pulls me down by the collar, our bodies even closer now. My brain goes foggy. Do my arms usually work? Does my tongue usually feel like this? I really should pay atten—

She flips me over to my back, knocking the breath out of me as her knee thrusts into my breadbasket. Her elbow presses down tightly on my throat in a choke. I try to roll out like Mack taught me, but her hold is firm.

She brings her face closer to mine, so her lips are nearly brushing my ear. "You're right, piece of cake."

I stubbornly refuse to tap, trying to wiggle out from under her. My legs flail as I try to kick, push, anything, but she just presses more weight on my throat. I'm very nearly beginning to see stars when Mack calls it.

She holds it for an extra second, our bodies tightly woven together, our breaths heavy.

My eyes flick to her lips, which are so close to mine.

So close.

It would be so easy to just...

Something flickers in her eyes, a flash of something fiery and fierce, and it makes my skin burn.

Or maybe I'm just starting to go unconscious. Yeah, that's probably it, because as quickly as the flicker appeared, it's gone in an instant, and she lets go of my throat.

"No tap, really?" She scoffs. "You really can't admit you got your pretty little butt handed to you by a girl, can you?"

I stand up woozily, massaging my neck. "Girl? Where?" I pant.

She shoves my shoulder. I laugh breathlessly, trying really hard to lower my heart rate and push the memory of that look in her eyes out of my brain, to push away the thought of her lips so close—*dude.*

I swallow and take a very slow breath out of my nose, committing myself to pay more attention as we switch roles, and Mack shows me what to do.

We practice for the next hour, but I don't manage to pin Q down even once.

TYRO B-29

After our physical fitness class finishes, we are all excused to lunch. My heart is still beating quickly from the exercise as we all shuffle out of the conference room, my shirt slightly damp with sweat. It's crowded in the narrow hallway as the group makes our way to the cafeteria down the hall. As we near the room, the smell of pizza fills my nostrils.

Lucy grabs my arm, and we squeal at each other in excitement. Pizza day is our shared favorite. There's just something about the way the cheese is so melty and gooey, the crust so warm and crunchy. *Mmm.* It's making me drool just thinking about it.

We quickly get our food and find our table. Katie and Amber are already seated, happily nibbling on their slices of pizza. As we make casual chit-chat about friendly topics like we learned the other day in Etiquette, a part of me is tempted to bring up today's lesson regarding friendships. I admit that I'm still a little bothered by it. I would be disappointed if anyone at this table decided a friendship with me wasn't efficacious enough, especially Lucy. But I determine I'm too afraid to know the answer, so I decide not to bring up the topic. No one else seems bothered by it anyway, so perhaps I should just let it go.

I feel a firm hand on my shoulder, followed by a warm voice near my ear. Aunty's voice. My body is comforted by the sound of her voice instantly. It feels like a hug, or a blanket.

"I'm sorry to interrupt your lunch, sweetheart, but can you come with me to the data room for a moment?" she asks. "I need you for a quick download."

I stand, accepting the task eagerly. Katie looks visibly disappointed that she wasn't the one chosen. Something swells in my chest. Pride?

"Wonderful." Aunty gives my shoulder a squeeze. "I'll have you back before your pizza can even get cold."

MY BRAIN FEELS MUDDLED and tight as I walk with my friends to recess. I'm so distracted, I nearly trip on my own shoes walking up the stairs to the courtyard. The brightness of outside is nearly blinding compared to the dim lighting of the basement. There are baskets near the exit with balls, jump ropes, and building blocks. Things are taken out of the baskets quickly as everyone chooses what they'd like to play with today. Lucy untangles a jump rope for us, and I follow her, Katie, and Amber to the grass, still feeling a bit disoriented.

After a few rounds of jump rope, where I uncharacteristically trip over the rope on my turn, Lucy speaks up.

"Are you okay?" she asks, stopping her swinging motion and letting the rope smack to the ground.

"Yes," I assure her with a smile, trying to make it convincing. I don't want to admit to her, especially with Katie and Amber close enough to hear, that I'm feeling a little strange. "I'm fine."

"Guys!"

Another friend of ours, Alyssa, has run over from across the other side of the grass, stopping right in front of our group, panting and out of breath. "Jackson is *touching* the fish in the creek. Come see!"

I perk up, immediately interested and convinced this will be the perfect distraction to get me out of my crowded head for a moment.

Lucy takes the jump rope from Amber's hand and gestures toward the creek. "You guys go ahead. I'll meet you there. I'm going to get a drink of water first."

I run with the girls over to the creek, and I'm surprised to see Jackson and a couple other boys standing in the middle of the creek, their pants soaked from the water. Is this even allowed?

Alyssa is folding her pants up above her knees, and to my surprise, she steps into the water with them, tiny splashes coming off the creek as she makes her way to the middle.

"Come on!" She waves us in with a huge smile. "Come look!"

We giggle excitedly as we fold our pants up like Alyssa did. I set my shoes by the edge and step into the water, pleased by the feeling of the cool water on my bare feet. Just as I hoped, a weight seems to lift off my brain as I relax and play with my friends in the water.

Jackson holds out a tiny oddly shaped fish in his hand and waves it around, laughing with satisfaction as Katie, Amber, and Alyssa squeal. I hold out my hand, curious to know what the tiny creature would feel like on my skin. It wriggles and flops around in my hand, and I laugh, delighted by the tickle.

Then a loud voice nearby freezes my body and sends what feels like an electric shock up my neck and into my brain. It's like all the jumbled pieces my brain has been trying to sort through since the download suddenly settle into place, stacking on top of each other like a tower of building blocks. This voice is familiar. My brain knows this voice.

"Ella!" the voice says.

6

RULE 1 OF ZONE-CODE: DON'T BE A DIRTY RAT

MATEO

As Eddie and I make our way to Town Hall, I try my best to calm the fiery rage that fumes in my chest. I need to tread carefully, now more than ever, even though all I really want to do is make the Mayor pay for all he's allowed to happen. The deaths on his hands. The lives he's responsible for. He killed my best friend, and now he wants a meeting? He expects me to sit across the desk from him and pretend like I don't see the blood on his hands?

"How can he just hide in his office and get away with this?" Eddie whispers, sharing my anger. I shush him, knowing we have to be careful, but I know he has just as much reason as I do to hate the Mayor.

"We have to play it cool," I remind him, and also myself.

The Mayor's office door slides open as we approach, revealing Mayor Ramos sitting at his desk, studying a projected holographic image floating just above the surface of his desk. His office looks a bit weathered. Books are strewn about, furniture looks displaced. The Mayor himself looks tired and disheveled.

"Come in, come in," he says with a wave, swiping away the

projection and turning off the surface of his desk. The deskTab lights go dark and reveal the regular wood surface underneath.

The door slides closed behind us, feeling almost like a jail cell clanging shut. Eddie gives me a look, sharing the feeling. At least if we're locked up in here, this time we'll be together.

Ramos stands, the zipper of his suitcoat nearly bulging at the size of his stomach, which just makes me even more mad. Some nights my brother goes to bed hungry when our ration points just can't stretch through the whole week, and he's up here in this office getting fatter and fatter.

He gestures to the chairs in front of his desk. "Please."

We obey, and as I take in the solemn look on his face, a piece of the anger chips away and is replaced by the inevitable dread that comes before receiving bad news. What else could there possibly be?

There is quiet for an extra second as Ramos lowers back down in his chair and sighs a deeply tired sigh that I actually relate with. His eyes flick back and forth between us, and his expression softens as he seems to remember that Eddie is only nine years old. He's trying to figure out how to soften whatever blow he's about to deliver, which just makes the anger come back fully charged.

Because, dude, you already killed my best friend, and by extension *his* best friend—or at least, stood by and watched it happen, so whatever else you have to say will be nothing in comparison.

He attempts to smile. "Thank you for coming." The smile falters ever so slightly. "I'm afraid what I have to tell you won't be easy for you to hear."

I'm afraid if I open my mouth to even breathe, certain profanities at his expense might slip out, so instead I just nod. I feel the dread oozing and spreading inside me, growing the longer the anticipation of the bad news is drawn out.

"Believe me, if there were any way I could deliver it in a way that—"

"Sir, with all due respect," I interrupt, my skin sizzling with the rage I'm trying really hard to contain. "Considering the fact that we're all still at half rates right now, if we don't earn our points today, we won't be able to afford breakfast tomorrow, so..." I trail off, figuring that what I'm implying will finish my sentence for me.

It does.

He sits up a little straighter. "Right, yes, of course, my apologies." He sighs. "Well, I'll just come right out and say it then, I suppose. This morning, I received word that your friend Foster has passed away."

Eddie gasps.

"What? How?" My chest is so tight, I can barely croak the words out.

Foster too? This can't be happening.

Ramos makes a grim face I can't quite decode, like he's trying to decide what details to keep to himself and what to reveal. "We aren't exactly sure, but there appears to have been some kind of accident."

I can't take it anymore. I shoot to my feet. "Liar!"

Ramos looks startled at my sudden outburst but not necessarily surprised by it. "Mateo—"

"You honestly expect us to believe there was an 'accident' after what you did to Sam? We *heard* the gunshots. We know what you do to them when they're 'expelled.'"

I know I said I'd stay calm, but it's like years of forced restraint come to a breaking point all at once. All the years of being smart, picking my battles, staying quiet to stay safe, saying "yes sir" and "no sir" in the hopes that one day things would get better because of it.

Well, they haven't gotten better. In fact, our lives are up for the chopping block more than ever, but I suddenly can't stay quiet anymore.

Not after Sam, and now Foster, too.

"Mateo, if you'll just listen to me—" Ramos tries to shush me.

But I've listened for too long. "All these years, telling us the trials were fair and democratic, but they've been rigged all along. You just get rid of whoever may be a threat, whoever asks questions a little too loud."

I point my finger at him, like it's a dagger. "You're a liar. I don't know how you can live with yourself."

Eddie's eyes are wide as he looks back and forth between Ramos and me.

"And not only that," I continue, my blood still on fire. "You're a murderer, too. You are a—"

"He's alive, Mateo." Ramos interrupts exasperatedly.

My voice catches in my throat like it has slammed on its brakes. "What?"

"Sam is alive," Ramos repeats, slower this time. "That's what I was trying to tell you."

I look at Eddie, silently asking if we believe him or not.

"How?"

He opens his mouth to respond when suddenly the door to his office slams open, and the new Chief of Discipline, Sergeant Nova, storms in.

"Mayor Ramos, I'm going to need you to come with me," Sergeant Nova says coolly, two Guards standing ready at either side, blocking the entire aluminum doorway.

I scoot Eddie's chair closer to mine in the most discreet way possible, looking nervously between the two authorities each trying to take up more space than the other. How do we get away from this power struggle without getting caught in the crossfire?

Ramos gestures to us with an unnerving calmness. "As you can see, I'm in a meeting right now."

Nova nods toward him, and two of the Guards, their faces unseen under their black helmets, march forward. "Afraid it can't wait," Nova replies with a sneer. "I have been directed to conduct a very *thorough* investigation regarding the deaths of Sergeant Hallows and Doctor Coombs."

Eddie blinks at me, and I know what he's thinking because I'm thinking the exact same thing: *"What the hell?"*

Chief is dead?

And Ramos was responsible?

Did he kill Foster too, and he's just lying about Sam? How do we know who to believe?

The Guards yank Ramos up to his feet, and I'm shocked that he is keeping such a calm composure. Maybe he's innocent after all.

"I'm so sorry our discussion was so rudely interrupted, boys," he says with an easy smile. "We'll finish up whenever this misunderstanding gets resolved."

Misunderstanding? My mind is racing with questions, doubts, and fear. How can he say that with such ease when three people are dead, or possibly more, and he's being taken into custody?

As Ramos is led out of the room, Nova lingers behind for a moment, sizing us up with her cold, calculating gaze. I can feel the weight of her scrutiny, and it feels like she's dissecting every inch of us, trying to determine whether or not we're worth her time.

Finally she speaks. "You two were friends of Foster Jenkins and Samuel Carmichael?"

Why does that feel like an accusation? She can't possibly think we had anything to do with Foster's death? I try to keep my voice steady as I reply. "Yes, ma'am, that's correct."

Nova's eyes remain cold, steely like the metal of her prosthetic arm. "Right. And what were you discussing with Mayor Ramos just now?"

I can sense Eddie's fear from beside me as I try to come up with a plausible response. Even though we didn't do anything wrong, her stare still makes me feel like I'm squirming under the bare lightbulb of a dingy interrogation room with no alibi.

"We just wanted to discuss the half rates, ma'am," I reply as evenly as I can, and I'm not really sure why I'm lying, because I certainly don't trust Ramos, let alone want to keep his secrets, but something inside me tells me to. "We were concerned about making ends meet."

Nova doesn't seem to buy it, but thankfully she doesn't push any further. "Well, you should know I'm taking this matter very seriously. We'll be looking into every angle."

The way she says 'every angle' feels like a verdict, a gavel banging down. Like she has already decided on our guilt, our involvement. There is a beat of silence, her assessing gaze never leaving my face.

"You should head back to your functions now."

We don't need to be told twice. We gather our bearings quickly and exit the room, the weight of the conversation settling heavily on my shoulders as I wrestle with who to believe.

As we make our way back to the Mess Hall, Eddie keeps glancing at me nervously. I shush him every time he tries to speak, not willing to risk being heard. I lead us around back to where the garbage dumpsters are. It reeks back here, so I know there won't be anyone around.

I turn to face Eddie, bringing my hands up to his shoulders. His composure cracks.

"C'mere." I bring him in tightly, too numb myself to cry, but allowing him an unobserved moment to feel whatever he needs to after the news we've received.

It's just one blow after the next. Like a relentless tidal wave that keeps coming in and beating us down every time we try to get our footing in the sand.

First Sam and Ella. Now Foster, too?

"Do you believe Ramos?" he asks quietly, sniffling into my uniform. "Do you think Sam is really alive?"

"I don't know," I admit, my mind still reeling, my heart and body trying to balance what I hope to be true with keeping enough suspicion to hopefully uncover the truth. "But we need to do something."

Eddie nods in agreement, finally stepping away from me, steeling himself with a resolve to help. "What do we do? I mean you heard Nova. What if Ramos really is behind all of this?"

I bring a finger to my lips as I hear the sound of footsteps from around the corner. I flick my head to the left, and he follows me back the way we came.

I look at the time on my wristTab, finding that we still have a few hours left of functions. "We'll talk more at dinner," I whisper. "I think I have a plan."

THE TENSION IS as thick as honey as we wait in line for check-in to dinner. Where the Mess Hall usually has a tone of careful lightheartedness, a place where we can relax in between the strict repetitiveness of our functions, now it's somber. Scared.

The Guards are posted around nearly every square inch of the perimeter, the guns an unmistakeable and unspoken reminder of what happened when we were in here last. It's like the sound of the gunshots still hum deeply in the bones of the room, like the sound of your finger tracing the rim of a glass bottle.

No one makes eye contact as we shuffle in, as if even glancing in a Guard's direction will set off those guns again. Dinner tonight is a gray-looking soup with a crusty piece of bread and dry cob of corn. I murmur my thanks to the kitchen Elder as my tray scrapes along the counter. Eddie is so wrapped up in his thoughts, the overwhelm of the past few days understandably fogging up his brain, that he forgets his manners. I glare at him with a raised brow until he realizes what he forgot. He thanks the Elder over his shoulder.

Wow. It's like I've completely morphed into my mother. I can just see her giving me that exact same eyebrow. *"Mateo Alejandro Francisco Barrajo-Galindo, mientras tú vivas en mi casa..."*

My heart squeezes at the memory of her, the wound threatening to open itself. I shake it away. I have to. I need to stay focused on the family that's *here*, the family that's counting on me. Maybe one day I'll be able to miss her, but it can't be today.

As everyone begins to be seated, the noise-level picks up just enough that individual conversations can't be heard through the general din. Perfect for small talk, social niceties, and maybe some plans for rebellion on the side.

I scan my eyes over the tables, looking for Parker from B-Quarters. When we talked in the holding cell, he seemed just as fed up with everything as me. If I know anything from the movies I watched as a kid, it's that there is strength in numbers. If we want to accomplish anything at all, we'll need all the help we can get.

I take the empty spot on the bench next to Parker, Eddie sliding next to me. His roommate Trevor is sitting across the table. They look to be in the middle of a whispered conversation.

I raise my chin at both of them in greeting, giving them both fist bumps. "What's up."

"Hey, man." Parker's busted eyebrow is scabbed over now but still noticeable. "Crazy day."

"How have you been feeling since the other night?" I ask carefully, hoping he can catch the gist of what I'm trying to imply.

He nods slowly, and fortunately I can see the understanding in his eyes. "Steven," he calls to the table next to ours, to the other guy who was in the cell with us, from H-Quarters. He nods him over, and Steven brings both a tray of food and his girlfriend to our table, sliding in next to Trevor across the table. I can't remember his girlfriend's name, but she's a pretty brunette from I-Quarters. I feel bad when she greets me by name.

"Hey, Teo," she says with a tight smile, touching her hand up against Steven's arm. It's an intimate touch, but one discreet enough for none of the Guards to see it.

The Zoners all know they're together, even though they can't show it out in the open. In fact, there are tons of couples in the Zone, even though it's super against the rules. Tons of people, Sam included—that player— have stolen moments hidden away behind Sanitation Centers or in shadowed corners when the Guards aren't around. What the Guards don't know won't hurt them, which is one of the biggest unspoken rules in Zoner-Code: *Don't be a dirty rat.*

And I'm really hoping everyone at this table takes that rule to heart with what I'm about to say.

They look at me in anticipation, somehow knowing something big is coming. I peek around carefully, making sure none of the Guards are close enough to hear me.

I lower my voice. "Before I start, I need to be sure you want to be involved in this." I look each of them in the eye, hoping to convey just how serious I am. They need to know what they're getting into. "I have no idea what the outcome will be. I have no idea what I'm doing. And we could all face serious consequences, maybe even expulsion. Now is your chance to get up and walk away, no questions asked."

They all look at each other with widened eyes, but no one moves. Well, they can't say I didn't give them a chance to be absolved. I look at Eddie, and he gives me a terse nod for reassurance.

"Sam is alive, but Foster is dead," I say to the group as quietly as I can manage.

Steven's girlfriend covers her mouth with her hand in shock, and I can feel Parker tense up next to me.

"Well, at least that's what Ramos told me."

I fill them in on the rest of the brief discussion with Ramos, and as the time on my Tab ticks closer to the end of dinner, I know I have to make the rest of this quick.

"We need to do something," I finish, and I'm relieved to see nods of agreement from the table. This is it. My numbers.

Trevor leans in closer over the table conspiratorially. "What did you have in mind? I mean we tried to do something last night and look what happened."

"Yeah, and new girl freaks me out," Steven's girlfriend says with a shiver. We all know she's referring to Sergeant Nova.

I see Steven slide ever so slightly closer to her, offering comfort as much as he can out in the open. "Talia's roommate was telling us earlier—"

Okay, yes that's right, *Talia.*

"—that she overheard Nova telling another Zoner the feds are considering shutting this Zone down and separating us all into different Zones if things don't shape up."

He looks at Talia, and I can see the worry there, knowing they very well could be separated if that happened.

"Me and you are close enough to aging out," Parker adds to me with a nudge of his shoulder. "They'd probably just expedite us and send us off for enlistment early instead of re-Zoning us."

Eddie's leg bounces next to me, and I put my hand on his leg, giving him a flat smile to assure him I won't let that happen. Nothing will separate us.

Steven says what we're all thinking. "The only way is to get out. We have to get out of here before things get worse."

The tone seems to settle at our table, the weight of resolve sinking down and coating us in a heavy gloom. We know action is the only way. We can't just wait around anymore, hoping someone—someone like Sam— will do it for us.

"He's right," I say, as Zoners around us begin getting up and cleaning up from dinner, our time nearly up. "We have to get out. Maybe Ramos can help."

"Can we trust him?" Trevor asks doubtfully.

"I don't know." I shrug, my lips tight. "I'll try to figure out how to talk to him again. Maybe he'll tell me more about how Sam did it."

We gather up our trays so we don't arise suspicion. We can't stay all hunched together and so obviously up to no good.

"I think our best shot is to get the Elders on our side," I say quickly before we all have to scatter. "We need them. They can't stay holed up in their cozy little rooms anymore."

The group nods in emphatic agreement.

Parker inserts the final word. "The next time one of us is assigned Elder Assistance, tell the group, so we can make a plan."

We mutter our assent in careful unison, before breaking apart and heading out of the Mess Hall to prepare for curfew.

The overhead lights of the upper shell have dimmed into dusk, casting shadows of the buildings across the gray of the Zone like a black and white sunset.

"Say we do figure out how to get past the gates, then what?" Eddie whispers. "We can't survive out there on our own."

"We—" My heart stops when I feel the rough glove of a Guard on my arm, stopping me in my tracks.

No. Did he hear us?

The Guard's glove moves down my arm and to my hand. To my surprise, he puts something in my hand—paper?—and then turns on his heel and walks off without a word.

Eddie and I look at each other with wide eyes as I finger the sharp edges of the paper. Zoners around us make their ways down the zigzagging trails that lead to the circular layers around the Square that make up the living Quarters. No one seems to pay us much mind, but I pull Eddie into a shadowed corner of the Hall and unfold the piece of paper.

On it is a handwritten scribbled message:

Holding cell. Come through the emergency exit in the basement. Tonight. -Ramos

He wants to meet.

7

WELCOME TO THE CATACOMBS

SAM

Through lunch, I don't see Cade anywhere, and it only fuels my anxiety. I know my sister is not his top priority when he's running this kind of operation, but I'm still anxious to get a plan in motion. Q suggests we go check on the E1 girl to pass the time, and although I grumble about it, I follow her to the medical building anyway.

Ponyboy has chosen to help Beardsley organize supplies today, and I feel a sting at that, even though he's completely oblivious to any kind of conflict between us. It's like we're two parents fighting over custody, and I got set to the side for the one with the fun accent. Even Luna chose him over me when we dropped off Pony, and that stings. I thought we were bullet-bonded.

Q and I arrive at the girl's bay in the hospital building and find her sitting up in bed, looking completely disgusted at whatever liquid she's drinking from a colorful mug. She is tucked into a woven blanket, but she appears to be wearing one of the T-shirts Q dropped off earlier, and her long dark hair has been brushed and pulled up into a bun on top of her head. All the remaining smudges of E1 makeup and glitter have been scrubbed off, leaving her tanned skin clear and fresh, and *wow* how could she possibly have gotten even prettier?

I don't realize I'm staring until Q clears her throat at me, giving me a pointed eyebrow.

I try to play it off with a grin and a shrug, but I scold myself internally. *Why can't you just be normal?*

The girl looks at us over the brim of her mug, big brown eyes flicking back and forth between the two of us. She lowers the mug and nearly gags as she swallows the liquid. From here it looks like it's straight egg yolks, and I can't blame her. I want to gag just looking at it.

"Hey," Q says with a smile as if they're already friends. "We just came to see how you were feeling. I'm Q. This is Sam, but he actually prefers to be called Prettyboy."

I scowl at her. "I thought we left that behind in E2," I say through gritted teeth

Q smiles at me, replying with a sickly-sweet tone like she's talking to Luna. "We did, until I found out there that you're a dirty liar. I have to exact my revenge somehow."

I look back at the girl with a flat smile. "Sam is fine."

She sets her mug aside, and I'm nearly blinded by the bright smile she gives us in return. "I'm Zara, and um *hello* aren't you two just absolutely adorable? How long have you been together?"

Q busts out a laugh that is way too loud. Like insultingly loud.

I tell Zara in a stage whisper, my hand cupped over my mouth for emphasis, "She's been after me for a while, but I'm just really hard to get."

"You wish, Prettyboy."

"Maybe I do."

Q ignores me completely after that, but I saw it, I saw the smile. A small win, but a win, nonetheless. Progress toward restoring friendship.

Zara kicks her legs on the bed, her voice coming out nearly a squeal. "Eeee the *tension*, oh this makes everything worth it. I'll take another hangover any day to watch this all play out." She grins conspiratorially. "I don't mind a slow burn."

"There is absolutely nothing to burn, believe me." Q laughs, pointedly changing the subject. "*Anyway*. How are you feeling? Cade said E1's can sometimes have a hard transition."

"Oh, I feel like absolute dumpster grime," she says nasally as she pinches her nose to take another sip of the egg yolk concoction. "And everything is, like, slow and weird. How are you not completely bored out of your minds out here? It's like everything here is in slow motion."

Q side-eyes me, seemingly able to tell I've forced myself to take a big calming breath. Listening to an Elite complain about boredom, or actually anything really, would normally be enough to send me straight over the edge, but look at me. Breathing it out like an evolved human.

I open my mouth to respond, but Q cuts me off quickly, not trusting my mouth, which is completely fair. "We stay pretty busy," she replies with a stiff laugh. "It seems awesome in E1, though. Everyone always seems to be having so much fun when we drop off deliveries."

I blink at Q, impressed with how diplomatic she's being, when I know she hates the Elites just as much as I do.

Zara's brightness dims for a second, her smile faltering ever so slightly at the edges. But before I can even blink, she has already shaken it away.

"Yeah," she says, her smile stretched back to its regular fullness, though it doesn't quite meet her eyes. "It's so fun."

Her hands move under her blanket, and I'd recognize that fidget anywhere. She's messing with her wristTab. Just like I do when I'm anxious or nervous.

And it's then that I realize I'm not seeing a spoiled, rich, carefree, faceless Elite. I see a girl. A girl from a Zone—yeah maybe not a common Zone, but she's scared and alone, just like me. Maybe we're not so different after all.

"Are you sure you're okay?" I ask, stepping closer to the bed. I take off the woven bracelet that Red gave me and flash my wrist at her, showing her that I have a Tab too. Q looks back and forth between us, trying to catch up, not seeing the signs of distress I was able to recognize more quickly.

Zara's hands freeze under the blanket. "Were you in E1 too?"

"I was in a Common Zone. C9. We were always told how great it was in the E-Zones..." I try to put my words together carefully. "But you guys were trapped just like we were, weren't you?"

I hand her Red's bracelet, knowing I don't deserve it anyway. She puts the bracelet on and twists it around on her wrist, her eyes welling up with tears. She doesn't answer.

Q lowers herself onto the edge of the bed. "You're safe here," she assures her, resting a comforting hand on Zara's blanketed calf. "It might help to talk about it, if you want to."

Zara sniffles. "It's all such a blur." She presses her fingers into her temples like she's trying to press out a headache. She is quiet for a second, her eyes closed.

"Do you want us to give you some space?" Q asks gently. "If we're making things worse, please tell us to leave."

She frowns. "No, please don't go. I hate being alone, and my brain is especially annoying right now."

Her face looks busy as she seems to be working on some kind of mental puzzle. We give her a moment of quiet to process whatever it is.

"Maybe you guys can help me fill in some gaps," she decides, a distant look on her face. Then she sucks in a big breath like she's about to dive off the edge of a cliff into the ocean and doesn't know when she'll get to take her next breath. "I lived with my parents in E2 for a few years when we first came under, but then I got dumped, and they hated seeing me all mopey and sad. They thought I could use some time to have fun and make friends, so they moved me to E1. They had no idea what it was really like." Her voice cracks, and she closes her eyes.

Q and I share a glance, seeming to share the same thought. We both saw it there, and nothing seemed so bad. All the Elites seemed to be having the times of their lives. Constant fun, any luxury you'd ever dream of. Sure, they couldn't leave—electric gates and wristTabs make sure of that—but if it were so bad, why did they seem so happy? The weightless feeling there was so palpable. In C9 you could feel the misery in the air, just walking through the Square. It seemed so different at E1. But was I just distracted by all the shiny glamour?

"I tried to keep it lowkey when I first got there. I didn't know anyone, I was heartbroken, and I was never really into the party scene anyway," Zara goes on, looking so distracted, as if she's processing this all for the first time herself as she speaks it aloud. "At first the messages seemed normal enough. I'd get a popup on my Tab every morning checking in to see how I was adjusting, but the longer I kept to myself in my apartment, the more... frequent the messages became."

I cross the room to the other side of the bed, to the chair that Cade had been sitting in earlier. I lower myself onto it quietly, trying not to interrupt her story. I listen intently, feeling unsettled by the way she's telling it, feeling like I'm about to learn that yet another thing I've believed about this place for the past eight years has been a lie.

"They showed up to my door after about a week. I remember they were so...plasticky, like their whole faces were manufactured. Their smiles were so fake. They pretended to be concerned about me, but they left me with an ultimatum basically. Engage in the Zone 'culture,' or I'd have to go to a Common Zone instead."

"Culture?" Q repeats slowly. "Like the clubs and stuff?"

"Everything, the whole lifestyle." She looks down at her blanket. "I found the cameras in my apartment that night. They were everywhere. My room, my shower."

The hair on the back of my neck burns with a slow growing fury.

"Are you serious? Your *shower?*" Q's voice is thick with a disgust that matches my own.

"I made a friend in my early days there," she continues determinedly, like she's trying really hard to get this out before she crumbles. "She was like me. New, but she had another week on me, not 'engaged' in the culture either. She'd been visited once more than me. They told her it was her last warning. We went to our first party together, but she left early, said she wasn't feeling well. The next morning at brunch she told me she was having some doubts about the whole place. She seemed scared." Zara wrings her hands in her lap. "I never saw her again."

"Did they actually send her to a C-Zone, or do you think they—?" I whisper it, even though there's no reason to keep my voice low. It's not like I have to worry about Guards or higher-ups from the Zone listening in here, but it's just habit.

"I don't know." Zara shakes her head. "I went fully in after that, though. Too scared of them showing up again. That was... four years ago I think?" She takes another sip of her egg yolk mixture, tapping the outside of the mug for effect. "Haven't been off Vibe or whatever variation of it since, hence the super fun side-effects."

I think of unknowingly intaking Vibe through my blood just by simply walking through one of those clubs. The way I had forgotten everything I came there for. I remember feeling so at peace, so at home, never wanting to leave. That's a dangerous feeling when you're in a shiny, glamorous, neon-coated prison cell. They barely even have to lock the doors.

Q and I are on the same wavelength. "Does every club and

restaurant shower the drugs, or can you just go to the ones that do if you want to?" she asks hesitantly, like she doesn't quite want the answer.

Zara blinks at us, her voice lowering to a feeble whisper again. "I don't know. It's all a blur. I can't even remember the last time I spoke to my parents."

Q stands furiously as she works through all the information we've learned. "So let me get this straight." She paces back and forth next to the hospital bed. "They entice people in, promising fun and friends and community. Then they force you to get the wrist whatever things." Her voice rises the longer she talks, her anger rising with it. "Then they force you to go to places that shower a mind-altering drug, and you have no way to protect yourself against it?"

"When you put it that way, that's even worse than C-Zones," I admit. "At least we were allowed to stay conscious. We were consciously *miserable*, but at least we were in our right minds."

Zara brings her knees up to her chest and puts her face in her hands. Her voice is muffled by her palms. She sobs, "What's worse is I literally don't even remember the last 24 hours *like at all.*"

Q is quick to put a hand on her shoulder to offer comfort. "What do you mean?"

Zara looks up, a shadow crossing her tear-streaked face. She whispers, "Everything from the last few years is a blur, yeah, but I've never like *blacked out.* Except for 24-hours ago. Everything since then is gone. Everything."

She keeps her voice low. "I have no idea what happened before I came here, how I got here, nothing. When I woke up he told me something about my parents wanting me out, but I just feel weird, like I'm forgetting something important. Or someone." She shakes her head. "I don't know."

"I'm so glad Cade got you out when he did then. You're safe now," Q assures her with a smile.

Zara gives her a small smile in return, wiping her tears with the back of her hand. "I just wish everyone I left behind could be here, too. You guys are so nice."

That makes a tiny pinprick of an idea begin to sizzle in my mind. I lean forward, resting my elbows on my knees as I try to coax the idea into full form. "What if they could?"

Q gives me a look like, *"You better not be suggesting what I think you're suggesting."*

"No," she says simply. "No."

I stand up, feeling goosebumps as the idea begins to take shape and energize my blood. "Hear me out." I put my hands up in a *"now wait a minute"* gesture. "Zara, what do you know about the 'live free or die' thing?"

She looks back and forth between us, her brows pulled together. "I don't know, some of my friends were into it, but it always seemed a little culty to me."

Now it's my turn to pace by the bed. "Your friends. Was it just a saying to them, or did they really want to get involved in something?"

Q repeats herself. "No. *No.*"

"Like some kind of..." Zara lowers her voice to a whisper. "Revolution?"

I feel electrified. "'Support life, support freedom' right?"

Q turns on the bed to face me. "What good would Vegas's followers do us anyway?"

I quit my pacing and face them both. "We hijack her followers before she can use them herself."

They both look at me like I've grown a second head. Zara is allowed to be confused, but there's no way Q can't see how genius this is.

I lower myself onto the other side of the bed. "Think about it, Q. She's already done all the work. She's been laying bread-crumbs for some kind of rebellion already, right? We just have to swoop in and steer them our way instead. They'd never know the difference, and they could be the bodies we need to stop her." A laugh bursts out of me and comes out a little too mad-scientisty, but I can't help it. "We use her own followers against her."

Q blinks at me, and I can see the wheels turning in her head. "I'm not saying I support this, *because I don't and you're insane,* but how do you plan to get them past the gates?"

Okay so I haven't thought that far ahead yet, but my heart is in the right place.

"Strength in numbers, right?" I say, seeing the tiny glimmer of support in her eyes and feeling deludedly encouraged by it. "And we have Zara. If anyone can take down E1 from the inside out, it's her."

We both turn our heads to Zara, who so far has been playing ping-pong back and forth between us with her eyes, trying to keep up. They widen now that we're looking at her. "I feel like I'm missing a key detail or two here."

I smile. "Don't worry, we'll fill you in."

TYRO B-29

I look up to locate the source of the voice calling my name from across the creek. When I see his face, even more pieces fall into place, and images that are so vivid fill my memory. I'm nearly knocked breathless by the weight of these new images and scenes filled with this person, heavy new emotions attached to each one. Everything clicks into place exactly where it should, and everything is suddenly clear. My heart swells with a new feeling. Love.

"Sam!" I say, my tongue taking over and saying the name that came attached to the images. My body takes over, acting on pure instinct, muscle memory perhaps. My body wants to be near him, wants to hug him. I close the distance between us, splashing through the creek to meet him as he runs toward me.

He picks me up, and it feels so natural, so pleasant. I feel so much love in my heart that it nearly chokes me as he spins me around. "Ella, you're okay, I've been so worried about you."

His hug is so tight that it squeezes a laugh out of me. I love the closeness. I want to stay wrapped up in this feeling forever.

"Sam, you're crushing me!" I giggle as he squeezes tighter, but I really don't mind. It just feels so right.

He brings me over into the grass, holding my face in his hands. "I can't believe it's really you." His brown eyes are so deep, so sincere. They're filled with tears. He cares about me. Another feeling swells inside me, and I can't help the instinct to hug him again.

"I've missed you," my tongue says, taking over again. And it feels true.

I can't wait to get to know this person more, to understand these strong emotions and images stacked in my brain. I want to keep feeling like this. I take his hand, pulling him up off his knees. "I'm so glad you're here too now! Let me show you around."

I can't wait to introduce him to Aunty and Lucy. Two people that mean the most to me. To my luck, Aunty steps in behind, already close enough for an easy introduction. Perfect. I turn to look for Lucy, but Sam stops me. The look on his face sends a chill up my neck. Gone are the eyes that were just filled with love and care. They are now replaced with a shadow.

"Ella, we're not staying here," he says, with an edge to his voice that makes me feel unsettled. "We have to go."

My heart drops. Go? I was so excited to know him, to understand him. To introduce him to my friends. And he wants to go? Go where?

"What, why? I like it here."

The thought of leaving makes me want to cry. Leave my friends? My bed and the same view of the air ducts I see when I wake up every morning? Leave Aunty?

He kneels in front of me. "This place is dangerous. *She* is dangerous."

Confusion washes over me. "Aunty? No, she takes care of us. She loves us."

He cuts me off. "Ella." He squeezes my hand. And while my body, my instincts, want to draw into his warmth, *I* can't shake off this fear that tickles the edges of my skin, a fear that makes me want to run far away. It's like I'm at war with my own nature.

"You have to trust me. We need to leave. Now."

I step away, overwhelmed with the conflicting feelings whirling around inside me. All I know for sure is I don't want to leave. I won't leave.

He reaches out for me again, but I don't want to feel that tickle of fear again. I want this feeling in my body to go away. I take another step back.

"I don't want to leave," I manage to say, my throat tight.

To my relief, Aunty steps around the boy and to my side.

"Are you alright, sweetie?"

I nod. That warm feeling from her voice washes over me, and some of the tension in my body melts away. Her arm around my shoulder feels comforting, like an answer, washing away the conflict I felt. This is where I'm supposed to be.

I breathe a sigh of relief, feeling safe again, until the boy grabs my arm and pulls me toward him. I'm terrified as he drags me through the grass, my attempts at freeing myself from his grasp useless. This is my home. He can't take me away.

"Sam, stop!" I shriek, desperate to make him listen. "I don't want to go with you. I'm happier here."

He loosens his grip arm at my words, and the look on his face makes my body and heart react in a surprising way.

He looks sad.

I made him sad.

Why is he so sad?

I scan my brain, trying to reconcile these questions with an image, a memory, anything to make sense of this reaction. I'm feeling nearly out-of-body as Aunty approaches again. I step closer to her in a haze, still watching him from a distance.

"If you don't want to leave, I'll stay with you," he says, shaking off the tug of his pretty friend next to him.

A happy spark in my heart flares. He wants to stay. Perfect. I'll find Lucy.

But Aunty puts her hand on my head, running her fingers through my ponytail. "Well, it looks like she wants to stay, and it's time for you to go."

I look at her, confused. Why does he have to go? I care about this person, and I want to know why.

I feel sadness as I watch the guards take him away. Why can't he stay?

"No! Ella! Please!" he begs, but they force him across the grass and away from me.

My heart feels like it is being squeezed tightly. A wetness falls down my cheek, and I touch it in surprise. A tear.

Aunty squeezes my hand and lowers down to wipe the teardrop off my cheek. "Are you alright, darling? I know that must have been overwhelming for you."

I nod, not sure how to verbalize how I'm feeling.

She smiles at me, her hand still on my cheek. "You were so brave, my dear."

"Thank you, Aunty." I sniff, trying to feel that warmth from her voice again, to take away these other feelings I don't understand.

She stands and raises her voice so the rest of the group can hear. "Children, recess is over." She smooths down the fabric of her dress. "I'd like you all to go sync up before the remainder of our lessons."

We shuffle back in through the stairs that lead to the double doors of the basement, setting the play equipment back in the baskets as we go. I don't know where Lucy or any of my other friends are, but at the moment I don't really care. All I can think about is that look on Sam's face. His sadness, my own sadness. I can't shake away the feeling of love that I felt so strongly when he held me. I wish I could feel like that again. In comparison to that, all I feel now is... empty. Alone.

I follow the group through the dim hallway on autopilot, not really in control of my movements. We squeeze into the data room, spaces filling between us as we separate to our own areas. The machines beep in a familiar rhythm. The otherwise quiet atmosphere, even as we all shuffle in, makes me feel a little better. This is routine. I'm used to this. I'm not used to all those new feelings and conflicts I felt outside. This is familiar.

I pass by bed after bed, nearly knocking over Zachary as I go, not paying enough attention to where I'm going.

"Sorry," I whisper to him.

I reach the area of the room where I belong.

She lies on the bed, eyes closed, the monitors she's attached to beeping rhythmically. Her cheekbones are a little more sunken than they were before, as if she was extra drained by the download earlier. I take her wrist to complete the sync, everyone around me doing the same next to the other beds, but I can't shake his face. These feelings. So I don't sync, not yet.

I look around, making sure Aunty isn't close by, or any of the surgeons. They don't like it when we talk in here. It disturbs their recoveries.

I squeeze her hand gently.

"Ella," I whisper, shaking her hand a little bit. "Ella, wake up."

Her eyelashes flutter at my voice.

"I met Sam," I say. "He was here."

Her eyes open wide at the sound of his name, the sapphire blue of her irises a little duller than normal, but still alert.

"Tell me more about him," I beg quietly. "Please. I need to know."

8

THE DEVIL AND A DAYDREAM

SAM

The medic who operated on Luna has requested a follow-up visit to make sure her stitches are healing up okay, so while Q is occupied with that, I decide to track down Cade once and for all. Q gave me rushed directions to where his office is, but my brain turned off after the second "turn left at...," so I've pretty much just been walking around in circles hoping I run into it. The walkways are busy, people walking with intention like they're on their way somewhere important. It seems like everyone has something to do here. He really runs a tight ship. I'm acutely aware of the contentment here. No fear, no impending danger. Just purpose.

I finally decide to swallow my pride and ask a passerby for help. They are friendly and point me in the right direction. I pass the Hall and walk up to a dark brown perma-tent that is smaller than the others but has the same vinyl-type material stretched over a rooted structure.

I stand in front of the door, waiting for just a moment, and I know it's just a door, but it feels more than that. Daunting. Bigger than just a door because I know as soon as I pass through it, I'm giving up the freedom Ramos sacrificed everything at C9 for. I dread what kind of commitment I'll have to agree to, but I know there's no other way.

I knock on the door softly, part of me hoping he doesn't hear it, or maybe he's not even here, and I can have more time to—

"Come in," a voice from inside says, and I push the door open before I can change my mind.

The air inside the tent is even chillier than the winter temps outside, and I almost feel like I'd be able to see my breath if I tested it. Once my eyes adjust to the dim lighting inside, I see the tent has been sectioned off inside. I've stepped into a small room with office furniture, cabinets and shelves lining the sides, and a huge computer at the back wall. There is a door in the back that leads into a separate section. Living quarters, maybe.

I pass by Axel as I enter the room, who is lying flat on his metal stomach very still, his legs bent to either side, and at first I think he's off, but then he blinks as I walk by. That will never not be terrifying.

Cade is sitting at the desk in the middle of the room, looking over papers that are scattered all over the surface. He looks up as I walk in, gathering the papers and arranging them into a neat pile as I approach. "Hello, Sam," he says, his brown eyes analyzing my every move in that way they do, just like Axel's.

"Hey." I shift uncomfortably under Cade's piercing gaze but try to appear confident and composed. "I know you're busy. I'm sorry for interrupting."

"No need. Just organizing some research, but it can wait." He gestures for me to take a seat across from him at one of the four chairs lined in front of his desk. He leans back in his own chair. "I assume you're here to discuss your sister."

Okay, so we're getting straight to business. I plop down into the chair.

"Yep, I guess I'm ready to sell my soul, or whatever it is people do here." I hold out my wrists mockingly like he's about to put handcuffs on them.

He chuckles. "I'm sure we can work something out where your soul can stay intact."

I shrug, dropping my hands back to my lap. "Eh. It's not worth much these days, anyway. Just ask Beardsley."

"Yes, I'm sure he's not happy about the capture of his friends."

I rub the back of my neck. "Yeah, I feel horrible. Do you think you'll be able to get them back?”

He clasps his hands together and rests them on his desk. "Like I told you before, I haven't spoken to my wife in some time, so I'm not sure if she even knows they are my employees. I'm sure we can come to a diplomatic agreement. I'll send a messenger to E2 tonight and ask her what her terms for release are."

I hesitate before responding. *Diplomatic.* That wasn't exactly what I had in mind. I feel a little silly for wanting to storm back in guns blazing. Do I just let the adults talk it out? Is that even possible with someone like Vegas? She seemed pretty unwilling to negotiate, but maybe I just interpreted "*I won't stop until every man in power has to answer to me*" wrong.

He sees my hesitation. "What is it?"

I drum my fingers on the desk. I decide to keep my E1 idea to myself for now. Maybe he's right, and they can settle this like adults. We can leave sparking a revolution in E1 for another day, I suppose.

"I'm just worried about my sister, sir. What do you need from me to include her in your negotiations?"

"Well, what do you have to offer?"

I hold out my wrists again, and he smiles, waving a hand at me to lower them.

I consider his question. Realistically speaking, I don't have anything to offer this man, a man so powerful the FPA doesn't even bother him. I'm just a tiny flea in comparison.

I decide to just be honest. "Truthfully, I really don't have anything to offer except my life. And you can have it if that's what you need. I'd trade my life for my sister's every single time."

He smooths his beard. "Let me ask you this, Sam. How do you see yourself as an adult? You're what, sixteen? Seventeen?"

"Almost seventeen." It sounds so puny when I say it, so pathetic.

"So in a year you'll be an adult," he continues. "What kind of adult do you see yourself being?"

I find myself floored by his question. Every time I considered adulthood, I imagined it still in chains, trapped in the FPA's clutches. Except instead of trapped in a Zone, I'd be drafted and off doing their dirty work. I've never considered a future that was my own.

"I've never really had the chance to imagine that, sir," I reply honestly. "I always thought I'd be enlisted, like the others in the Zone are when they age out. But now that I'm not in a Zone anymore, I don't know. But I'd like to think I'll be someone my sister would be proud of. And my—" I choke on the word and have to clear my throat humiliatingly. "Parents."

He looks me over intensely, but he's impossible to read. I can't tell if this is a positive or negative reaction to what I said. Was he hoping I'd say something else? Is he disappointed? Surprised? Impressed. I have no idea.

After what feels like several decades, he nods slowly. "Well, in that case, why don't we just agree on an IOU? I'll include— Ella, was it?—in my negotiation, and you'll owe me a favor."

"A favor?" I question with an uneasy chuckle. "Did you forget the part where I said I have absolutely nothing to offer? What kind of favor could I possibly do for you?"

He smiles. "I'm sure something will come up."

I feel a tug of dread in my gut. I hate the prospect of owing someone, especially something like this. If he saves my sister, how could I ever repay him? It'll just be a debt that hangs over my head. But do I have any other choice?

No. I really don't.

If this man is offering a way—and someone with his resources, it's a way that could actually work— I'd be stupid to not do anything he asks. He wants me on my knees for who knows how long? Fine. My knees it is.

I jut out my hand. "You have a deal."

He shakes my hand, sealing the deal. I'm one step closer to getting Ella back. I should be happy, hopeful. But instead, that dread is still clawing at me.

Did I just make a deal with the devil? What kind of favor did I just commit to?

AT DINNER LATER THAT NIGHT, the energy in the Hall buzzes with excitement.

"Calix is back," Q explains with a contagious bouncing enthusiasm. I find myself matching her excitement even though I have no idea who that is or what that means. "And it's a Saturday night." She pauses and leans forward, ending her non-explanation with a single summarizing word. "Paintball."

The hair on my arms stand straight up under my long sleeves like I've just been electrocuted. She's just said every teen boy's biggest daydream. Well, one of them, at least. "You're kidding."

My lips stretch into a giddy grin at the thought, and she repeats herself with a conspiratorial smile. "Paint. Ball."

"You've really been holding out on me here. The Catacombs was this cool, and you guys really had me sleeping in the back of a dusty truck for days on end making deliveries? Tell me everything."

She drops a chunk of stew from her fork down to Luna at her feet, who swallows it in a grateful gulp.

"Calix is Cade's right-hand-man, but he's the fun one," she explains, taking a bite of her roll. "Whenever it lines up where it's a Saturday night and he's not off on business or delivery, he organizes paintball matches. He calls it team-building, but it can get pretty cutthroat. Last time" —she laughs in memory— "I got Beardsley right on the buttcheek, and he couldn't walk straight for a week."

"Well for my buttcheek's sake, I better stay as far away from you as I can," I tease.

She smiles sweetly. "Like you could, even if you tried."

I open my mouth to argue, but Ponyboy runs up and nearly strangles me from behind.

"Did you hear!" He cheers. "Paintballllll!"

I laugh and massage my neck. "I heard, man, save it for the arena."

His smile dims for a moment. "Oh, I'm not allowed to play."

I hate myself. Of course he's not allowed to play. He's a kid, idiot.

But then he perks right back up. "I get Luna duty!"

At the sound of her name, Luna leaps up excitedly, nearly knocking Ponyboy down, her tail wagging uncontrollably.

The pair's enthusiasm is contagious, and I can't help but smile. "Well, someone has to keep this wild animal in control," I say, scratching behind Luna's ears. She nuzzles against my hand, her tongue out like she's smiling at me, her dark eyes creepy but in a different way than Axel's. Hers are just so human-like.

As dinner comes to an end, Q and I make our way outside, Ponyboy heading a different direction with a couple other children and Luna who bounces along next to them. We follow the growing crowd past the tents and trucks, past the medical building and living tents, and outside the Catacombs perimeter. There is a huge sectioned off area of dirt, and inside it are makeshift structures of every shape and size. This must be the arena. It's shadowed since the overhead lights are beginning to dim with post-dinner dusk.

The air around is charged with energy and excitement as people begin to gather. The sound of laughter and chatter fills the night, a stark contrast to the stiff tension I grew used to at C9. Even the rare "fun" we were allowed to have there still had undertones of fear.

A tall broad-shouldered man meanders through the crowd, talking and laughing familiarly with people as he makes his way to the center. His black hair is buzzed short, sleeves rolled up on muscled forearms. Why is every man here superhuman? It's just unfair at this point. He has a big uninhibited smile and a silly energy that makes no attempt to play it cool or assert dominance. He simply exudes an easy lovable energy that people seem to like.

I assume this is Calix. The fun one.

"Come on," Q says, and a surprised jolt shoots down my back as she takes my hand and pulls me through the crowd behind her. I follow numbly. It's like all the nerves in my body zero in on the surface area where her skin meets mine. Warm, soft, and before I can even begin to spiral about what this could possibly mean, it's over anyway, and she has dropped it.

"Alright, folks!" Calix yells to the crowd. There are people of all ages gathered, but most are adults. I can't wait to make some old people cry.

"We're shaking things up a bit," he continues, pivoting as he talks to acknowledge the people in all directions. "No teams this time!"

There is a surround sound of chatter, not angry or upset

chatter, just intrigued and excited. Q looks over her shoulder at me and pumps her fist excitedly.

"It's Battle Royale, people. Every man for himself."

More chatter.

"Objective — be the last one standing. Everyone else is an enemy. If you survive, you win. Let's gooo!"

The crowd responds in volume. There are yells and whoops all around which charge through me, revving me up. I feel buzzed and excited, energy coursing through me. I haven't felt this excited since I took that first cruise on my magboard just after escaping C9. I feel that same weightless exhilaration, like for once I don't have to worry about everything else. I can just have fun.

There are a couple tents off to the side that people move toward. I just follow Q, staying close, part of me hoping she'll hold my hand again. She doesn't. It's fine. What friends hold hands anyway? She leads us to a tent with boxes of gray clothing. I freeze in place when I realize what they are, feeling like that weightless energy is plucked right out of me and replaced with cement instead.

They're uniforms. Common Zone uniforms.

They are mismatched with washed out paint splatters from previous matches, but they are unmistakable. Light gray canvas shirts and matching pants with huge cargo pockets.

Q digs through the closest box for her size, but I'm still stuck to the ground.

I spent eight years in that uniform.

I thought I'd never have to put it back on again.

I feel a little nauseous. Maybe I'll just sit this one out.

But as I watch Q's excited expression and feel the buzz of anticipation in the air, something stirs inside me. A longing to feel that weightlessness again, to feel alive again. C9 doesn't have to haunt me. This can be one thing C9 doesn't have to take away from me. I can take it for myself. With a deep breath, I reach into the box and grab a uniform, feeling the familiar worn fabric between my fingertips.

Q looks up and notices my hesitation. "You okay?"

I force a smile. "Yeah, just a little weird to be putting this back on after everything, you know?"

She looks back and forth between the uniform in my hands and my face before realizing what I mean. She steps over to me, putting a hand on my shoulder. "You could always let me ruin it for you. We can really make the uniform pay. I'll make it nice and colorful for you."

I chuckle, relieved she lightened the mood instead of letting me dwell in it. "And let you beat me? Never."

Q grins. "Oh, it's not about *just* beating you. It's about making sure you never forget who handed you the most humiliating defeat of your life."

"Well even more embarrassing for you when you get annihilated by the new guy," I joke back, following her to the next tent where the equipment lies in neat rows on tables. Some serious hijacking of an Elite supply truck must have taken place to get all this stuff. I support it wholeheartedly.

There are so many different shapes and sizes of paint guns, and I look over them, trying to strategize possible strengths and weaknesses of each one, a little overwhelmed by all the pieces and possibilities. I admit that I'm at a little bit of a disadvantage here since I've only been paintballing once, and I was only six years old, so it's kind of a blur.

Rather than be mature and ask for help, I watch Q assemble hers discreetly while pretending to strategize and pick my pieces.

She has picked up a paint gun so big it almost looks like a rocket launcher. She clicks the CO_2 tank in and loads up her hopper with pink paint balls like it's second nature. She slings it over her shoulder so casually, you'd think she was simply putting a backpack on and heading to school. I feel a chill down my arms as I watch her effortlessly prepare for battle, which, I have to admit, is pretty attractive.

"You ready to get wrecked Prettyboy?" She waves her gun at me tauntingly. "How pretty you'll look covered in pink."

"Very funny." I try to assemble my pieces like she did, but I'm struggling to not be distracted by how good she looks right now. I've seen Q in so many different looks over the last few days. Her overalls and goggles getup, her golden goddess E1 outfit, the sleek pantsuit of E2. But looking at her now, the ease and confidence she has in this place, mixed with her huge curls messily tied up on top of her head, head to toe in C9 gray plus a combat vest, paintball gun in her hands. Man, she's never looked so good. I guess tactical is what does it for me.

I shake the distracting thoughts away, recommitting to focusing on my equipment before she notices I don't know what I'm doing. It takes me a second, and I may have done it a little clunkier than she did, but I figured it out on my own and didn't have to do the unspeakable and ask for help. Like a real man.

She tosses me a pair of black goggles and a vest that I pull over my chest as we return back to the geared-up group. We all spill into the dirt arena that is peppered with structures to hide behind. I catalogue them and try to strategize the best route. The largest structure is in the middle. It's like a small house. There are two levels, hollowed out windows, and a roof that would be a great vantage point. If I can make it over there in one piece, that is. There are probably twenty-five or so other competitors armed and waiting. I size them up. 3/4 of them I should be able to obliterate no problem. The remaining 1/4 will be a fun challenge.

Mack from the gym awaits nearby, goggles sitting on top of his dark hair, mustache as cool as ever. He'll certainly be a worthy opponent.

But I don't really care about winning or losing. The only

one I'm worried about beating is the one right next to me—Q. Smug, cocky, arrogant, gorgeous Q. All that matters is that I slaughter her with all the blue paint I have in my hopper with absolutely no mercy. Like the gentleman I am.

Calix, who is decked out in all-black battle gear, has been shouting instructions from the front of the group, and I really should have been paying more attention. I catch the last of his speech. "Three strikes, and you're OUT. There are extra paint balls, canisters, and other upgrades in the center trove. Laser sights, enhanced VR, silencers, you name it. At the first sound of the horn you can move. At the second horn" —he pumps his gun in the air— "we fight to the death!"

Everyone cheers, including me. I pump my gun in the air with him. Q whoops next to me, and pulls her goggles over her eyes, which make her look like she's about to go snowboarding down a snowy mountainside. Only her lips are visible, and it reminds me a bit of the first time I saw her. She clicks a button on the side and the entire rim of the eyepiece lights up with a dim blue light.

She gestures to the goggles in my hand. "You're gonna want those."

"You plan to go straight for my eyeballs, or what?"

Her lips quirk, and I hate that I can't see her eyes. "Good luck, Prettyboy. You're seriously going to need it."

To my horror the first horn blows while I'm still fumbling with the goggles. She takes off at lightning speed toward a structure behind us, while nearly everyone else runs toward the middle. That must be the trove.

I run as I'm pulling the goggles on, cursing myself for not paying more attention to the instructions. I speed to the nearest structure and crouch behind it, snapping the goggles on over my face and clicking the button on the side like Q did.

I fall back onto my butt in surprise at what materializes in front of me. The goggles are VR. The dirt arena has completely transformed into a vibrant landscape so realistic I could easily forget this isn't real life. The center trove is now a towering half-demolished medieval castle, complete with tall turrets and sprawling flags that flap in the virtual wind. The landscape around is lush and green, rolling hills pocked with crumbling brick structures, and a star-speckled navy-blue night sky above. I take a moment to admire it all, allowing myself to pretend I'm really up there in the fresh air.

The second horn blares, and I spin around, trying to locate Q in the transformed arena. Half of the competitors are disqualified in seconds, eliminating each other easily while they all greedily fight over the upgrades in the trove. Like a flash of lightning, I spot Q racing atop one of the castle towers, her figure silhouetted against the light of the virtual moon. I'd recognize the shape of her hair anywhere. She shoots at someone on a lower level before disappearing from sight.

Game on.

I spring into action. It takes a second to find my footing, to get used to navigating an actual physical landscape while looking at it through a colorful fictional lens. But I find confidence quickly and begin darting from bricked cover to bricked cover, speeding through the virtual landscape with ease and shooting at anyone who comes into view. I don't know if Beardsley is playing, but I secretly hope I catch a sight of him among the structures, so I can also shoot him in the buttcheek too.

The adrenaline fuels my determination as I strategize. Now that most people have dispersed from the trove, I inch closer to it, determined to claim that roof-top vantage point. I scan across my view, carefully looking for any sign of movement.

As I near the central trove, paintballs whiz through the air. I'm dodging them left and right, hearing paintballs buzz right by my ear on several occasions and splattering right next to me.

I approach the trove and catch a glimpse of movement out of the corner of my eye. Q, like a shadow in the night, slides down from one of the castle towers and lands on the ground with a soft thud.

She spots me, and her lips curl into a sly smile before slinking into a nearby structure. My heart races, fueled by the thrill of the chase. I can't let her outmaneuver me. I follow her trail, my footsteps quick and light.

A paintball pelts me on the front, and I dive into the structure Q went in. From my new shelter, I look down at my uniform, annoyed by the splatter of red that bleeds down the shirt, as well as the throbbing pain in my chest from the hit.

Three strikes, and you're out.

I have to be more careful. I peek out the window and see Calix squatted behind the trove, shooting paintballs the other direction. I take the opportunity and pull my trigger, aiming right for his back. He howls at the force of my hit, my blue paint splattering all over the back of his black vest. He buckles forward and rolls inside the trove before I can hit him again.

"Prettyboy." Q's sings the nickname like a siren from somewhere above me, and I realize I've fallen right into her trap. She lured me here, hoping I'm nothing but a stupid sailor who will hurl himself into the dark depths of the sea.

"Q," I sing back, crouching low behind the ancient looking stone of the wall before me. There are lit medieval sconces on the walls that cast a fiery glow across the ground as I creep down the hallway, keeping my gun aimed and scoping out each corner like I'm an FBI agent looking for my suspect.

I hear a clatter ahead of me, and I rush toward the sound, my gun aimed and ready. I speed around the corner, my finger eager on the trigger. But the room is empty in all directions. I move to find a wall to hide behind and wait for Q to come out of hiding, but a noise from above makes me fall back into the stone wall behind me.

It's her. She leaps down from a hidden alcove and lands like a cat right in front of me.

She steps closer, so closely I can feel the warmth radiating from her. She has a strange smile on her lips I can't decode. Her eyes are hidden, but her lips are *right there*. So full and soft. I can't take my eyes off them. My brain completely goes blank as she steps even closer. I want to close the distance, I want to feel her breath on my lips, but I can't get my limbs to move.

She leans in, her face so close to mine that I stop breathing. I can smell the flowery fragrance of her hair, the mint of her breath. I lean in, everything blurring out of my view except her lips. I'm going to do it, I'm really going to —

Bang, bang.

I moan in pain, her paintballs hitting my gut like a hammer. Two of them.

Her lips spread into a grin, but she's still so close I can feel her whisper on my lips. "I win," she says, before blowing me a kiss and skipping out of the building.

Wow.

I guess I am nothing more than a stupid sailor, after all. Except I didn't just hurl myself into the depths of the sea. I freaking cannonballed in.

RULES OF PAINTBALL
(FOLLOW AT ALL COSTS OR GIVE UP YOUR DIGNITY AND MANHOOD FOREVER)

5. Safety first! Always keep your protective gear on to avoid any not-life-threatening-but-still-painful injuries!

4. No pushing or shoving! Aggression and pent-up accepted as long as the gun is used as a vessel!

3. No kids allowed! Or dogs! And certainly no robodogs!

2. Three strikes and you're out! And it's impossible to cheat because everyone can see your failure splattered all over you!

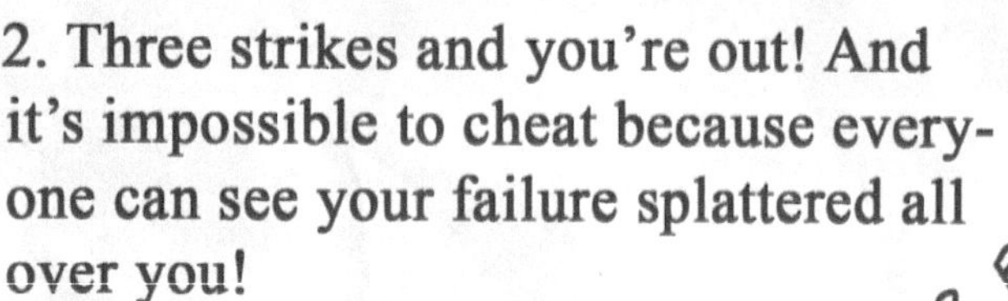

1. And most importantly, if a beautiful girl lures you into a dark corner, she can't be trusted! All is far in love and war!

TYRO B-29

I await anxiously by Ella's bedside, waiting for her to tell me something, anything that will help me make sense of these feelings I have. To make sense of this Sam person. Some people are already finishing up their syncs, and the surgeon is lingering nearby.

"Ella, please," I beg.

She struggles to keep her eyes open, but I see a flash of determination that livens up the cold blue of her eyes for just a second. I squeeze her hand to offer some encouragement.

"He's—" Her voice is hoarse, barely audible over the beeps of the monitors. "He's my brother. He raised me. I was so ungrateful. Can't believe" —her eyes begin to flutter closed again— "he actually found me."

Something inside me, something deep inside that I've never even realized was there, sends a thought to my brain. A bone-chilling thought: *Don't sync.*

I've never skipped a sync before. It's against the rules. The very thought has never even crossed my mind before. But I can't ignore the feeling, the warning. I've always felt better after a sync—lighter, my brain less muddled. But what will happen to these feelings, these memories? Will I still remember the way it felt when Sam held me? That warmth, that love. Will I still remember it? Do I even want to? I remember the aching sadness that came with it, the crushing loss I felt when he was gone. The loneliness I feel now, knowing I'm alone here.

All of that could possibly be gone within minutes.

I stare at the cuffs on our wrists. All I have to do is attach them, touch mine to hers, and I can be free again. Free and happy, like I have been my whole existence thus far.

It's like my brain snaps into place, making the decision for me. My brain and body feel united for once, and they seem to take control. I can't give up what I know now.

I squeeze Ella's hand and place it gently back on her bed. I slowly stand and walk toward the door, trying my best to pretend like everything is normal.

Everyone has begun to gather toward the cafeteria for dinner, and I follow, even though I know I'm way too anxious to eat anything. I'm convinced everyone can see the lie all over me, like I'm doused in red ink. *I broke a rule, I skipped a sync.*

I see Aunty talking to a few Tyros near the stairs, and I know I have to avoid her at all costs if I can. I fear that one look in my direction, and I'll confess everything immediately.

I feel a ping of... is it guilt? Is that how I feel? It's a twisting feeling in my chest—for breaking a rule, for deceiving Aunty when she's the one person who cares for me most.

I collect my dinner on my tray and join my friends at our table. I don't make conversation with them, I just sit with the guilt I feel, trying to make sense of all these new feelings whirling around inside of me. Trying to decide if it was a mistake to keep them.

∿

THE NEXT MORNING, I wake up with a clearer mind, but I'm surprised to find how much my body aches. I stretch my limbs before pulling myself out of bed, but it does little to help the soreness that seems to go all the way down to my bones.

I do a quick mental scan, hoping it's all still there. *Please tell me he's still there.*

Sam. Brother. Protector.

A memory comes up in my mind, and it's so vivid it's like it has been freshly painted. He's reaching for my hands. I feel energetic and excited in the memory. My hands take his, and within seconds it's like I'm flying. He's spinning me in circles, the world around me blurring as I spin around and around and around. I scream in delight, giggling as the spinning gets faster. When he puts me down, I stumble, unable to stay upright, feeling like the earth is being shaken like a snow globe.

He laughs. I laugh. I feel happy, unexplainably happy in such an ordinary moment.

I return to the present, and feel a wet tear fall down my cheek.

Lucy nudges me from behind to say good morning, and I swipe it away quickly before she can notice. I clear my throat.

"Good morning, Lucy, how did you sleep?"

She smiles, as she always does, and I can't help but feel sorry for her that she likely hasn't felt the kind of happiness I just witnessed in this memory. The kind I felt yesterday when I met Sam. "Perfect as always," she says. "You?"

I try to muster a smile. "Yes, great, fine, thanks."

Her smile falters a little. "Are you okay?"

"Yes, I'm great." And although she may be noticing the lingering guilt or confusion on my face, the stiffness of my movements, it's actually the truth.

The truth is I've never been better.

When it's my turn for the restroom, I feel that same deep

instinct speak to me again as the red and blue capsules drop into my hand from the dispenser. The same feeling I had when I was sitting next to Ella. It had told me not to sync up.

I look at the pills in my hand. What's wrong with vitamins? Why is my body urging me not to take something it needs? What if these instincts are my body working against me, betraying me, getting me to destroy myself from the inside out for some reason?

I pop the pills in my mouth, with every intention to swallow them, as I have every day and night for my entire existence. But I just can't shake that feeling telling me, begging me, not to take them. It's like my throat is tightening itself, refusing to swallow them.

So I break a rule for the second time in my life.

I hide the pills under my tongue before opening my mouth for the sensor, which, to my relief, unclicks the lock on the door like it always does.

I give a tight-lipped smile to Lucy as I hold open the door for her and then walk straight to my bed. When I'm sure no one is watching, I spit the pills into my hand and set them under my pillow.

My whole body buzzes as I walk to breakfast. Who is this person I'm becoming? A rule-breaking, crying liar? It goes against every ethics lesson Aunty has taught us. So why does it somehow feel so right?

BY LUNCH, my body has taken a turn for the worse. I feel feverish, randomly breaking out into a sweat at odd times. I scold myself for skipping my reds and blues this morning, certain it's the lack of vitamins doing this to my body. I feel foolish for thinking I knew better than the people who take care of me.

But somehow, mentally, I feel better than ever. Where my mind usually feels blocked, like a section of it is taped off from access, now it feels open and clear, filled with Ella's knowledge and memories. It seems like every second, something new is brought to the forefront. Like a core memory, or a lesson she'd learned throughout the years.

As I stumble clumsily through the lunch line to collect my sandwich, my muscles nearly throbbing with the soreness, a memory comes to mind of Ella waiting in a very similar line. I feel her excitement. She giggles almost hysterically with a boy next to her—that same boy I thought of yesterday, the one on the playground—as they wait their turn in a line just like this one.

I don't get to see what happens next in the memory before I stumble to my knees, dropping my tray onto the ground with a *clang*. A blackness creeps into my vision, clouding over me like a storm that I have no choice but to succumb to. The storm takes over.

I AWAKE TO A RHYTHMIC NOISE.

Beep. Beep. Beep.

I stay an extra moment in the comforting darkness before opening my eyes. I'm in a dim room by myself. I'm hooked up to an IV at my bedside that drips every so often, at different intervals than a different monitor, which is hooked up to my heart. The room is small. There is a tiny perimeter of floor space around the bed I'm lying on. The door is closed, but the crack underneath the door reveals a brightness just beyond the room that I'm curious about.

How long have I been out? What time of day is it?

The door cracks open, and a heavily-browed eye peeks through the crack before shutting it again.

I take stock of my physical state, wiggling my fingers and toes, stretching my neck. I appear to be fine. Why am I here?

My last memories are fuzzy. I think I remember waiting for lunch. How could such an ordinary event cause me to end up here?

The door fully opens, and I feel instantly lighter as Aunty walks into the room, followed by the bushy-eyebrowed man I saw earlier, who appears to be a doctor. I try to sit up, but Aunty holds up a hand.

"Ah-uh," she says. "You need to rest."

The doctor stands next to the monitors and interprets whatever signals they're putting out.

"Do you know why you're here?" Aunty asks carefully. They are both staring at me, and it makes my hands prickle with sweat, like I'm in trouble.

"Have I done something wrong?" My voice is cracked and dry. I strain to try to remember. Why does my brain feel so clogged? It's like every mental direction I try to go, every pathway I try to go down, a brick wall builds itself right in front of me.

"Ella," Aunty says softly, taking my hand. "Do you remember skipping a sync?"

My brows furrow in confusion. "Skip a sync? Why would I do that?"

Aunty and the doctor glance at each other. "We were hoping you'd tell us, sweetheart."

"I—" Suddenly everything feels overwhelming, like there is a building being constructed on my chest. My eyes fill with tears. "I don't know. I can't remember."

This time the doctor speaks up, his tone stern. "Do you know the risks of skipping a sync? Do you realize what could have happened if we didn't catch it so soon?"

A sob threatens to burst out of my throat. Why can't I make sense of my brain? Everything feels so mixed up.

Aunty holds up a gentle palm to the doctor. "We aren't trying to scare you. Luckily, you're fine, my dear. We just want to understand why you'd risk it. Did she tell you not to sync?"

A tear falls down my cheek. "I don't know."

9

THE ILLUMINATI IS AT IT AGAIN
MATEO

I wait until the upper-shell lights have darkened to their post-curfew level, feeling jittery with nerves at the anticipation of sneaking across the Zone after curfew. Even before Nova showing up, that would have been a consequence-worthy offense, probably in the form of forced exercise or even a Penalty. But now, who knows what kind of unhinged punishment Nova would come up with if she caught me. Her "order or death" policy seems pretty straightforward. And we thought *Chief* was the psychopath.

"Okay." I let out a breath and push myself off the lower bunk that used to belong to Ella. It's easier sometimes than going all the way up and down off my top bunk. "It's time."

Eddie steps up from his own lower bunk on the other side of the room. "Let's go."

"Uh, what do you think you're doing? You're not coming."

Eddie huffs a laugh. "Yes I am." And he just looks at me, his jaw firmly set, as if the matter is completely settled just because he says so.

I gawk at him. Did he completely forget who's in charge

here? I let him attend *one* rebellion-themed discussion, and suddenly he thinks he's Keanu Reeves or something?

"I admire the confidence, but no, you're still not coming." I have to hold back a smile at the stubborn little look on his face.

He folds his arms across his chest, challenging me. "I want to help."

"Too dangerous." I fold my arms back.

"You said we'd never be separated."

We stare at each other for a beat, and a part of me is almost proud of the way he isn't backing down at my glare. When did he get so grown up?

Man, I really do sound like my mom.

He takes advantage of my lack of response. It's like he knows my resolve is softening the longer I go without replying. "I deserve the choice, Teo. Can't there be one thing that's *my choice?*"

He's got me there, and he knows it. I let out a relenting sigh. "You better not slow me down."

He pumps his fist in victory. "I won't, I swear."

I use the wallTab by the door to turn off the lights, so anyone walking by our steel cabin would assume we're asleep like we're supposed to be. Luckily our uniforms are already a drab gray, so we don't have to worry about sticking out too much.

The door swishes open when I wave at it. Eddie and I share a look before crossing the threshold to outside. Somehow, we both can sense that leaving this room, deliberately breaking curfew, is a decision. A commitment we can't return from. We're committing to change, to getting things in motion no matter the risks. Once we leave this room, there's no going back. He nods, assuring me that he's sure he wants to be involved.

And just like that we're on our way. My heart is pounding in my chest as we move stealthily through the shadows, the only sound our footsteps and heavy breaths, avoiding possible patrol routes of the Guards.

We approach Town Hall from the side, avoiding the main pathway that leads up to the entrance, which is lit along the edges by street lamps that cast a warm glow onto the neat landscaping. Our footsteps crunch on the gravel as we cross to the southern side of the building, the side Eddie had shown Sam and me just mere days ago when we were searching for Ella. This was his special hideout area with Ella. I'm sure he has so many feelings, having to come back here without her.

I let him take the lead. He guides us over to the shadowed corner next to the wall of Town Hall. The wooden basement door is covered with leaves that camouflage it from view, and I help him kick them off. I look around, making sure no one is around before hoisting up the wooden door, revealing the basement stairs underneath that lead further underground. I try to not think about the spiderwebs that tickle my arms as we take the first steps down.

Once we're fully inside, and I've used the strap to close the door above us, we switch on the lights of our wristTabs. The lights bounce off the concrete walls as we descend, which freaks me out. I keep seeing the movement of the lights and think it's Nova or another Guard waiting here in the darkness for us.

It's colder the deeper we descend into the basement, and with each step I can feel my breath turning to ice. The stench of rot and mildew makes me feel like I'm trapped in a coffin, and that makes me wonder if we're walking right into an elaborate trap. I don't know what Ramos would have to gain by leading us here under false pretenses, but I don't know who to trust anymore.

We pass by the pile of miscellaneous supplies that Eddie and Ella had stored down here for their shenanigans, and I take the opportunity to rub his shoulder. I know he misses her. Hell,

I do too. There's nothing I want more than to believe that Ramos is telling the truth and that Sam really got out, and maybe, just maybe, he actually found Ella. What if they're even on their way back as we speak? As much as I wish I could see them again, though, I hope they never come back here. I hope they find a better life out there.

We make our way further into the basement and detect a faint light at the end of the narrow hallway. We switch off the lights of our Tabs just in case and stay close to the cold walls. The hallway curves around, and I peek around the corner, instructing Eddie to stay behind me. The curve of the hallway opens into a line of dim holding cells, one of which I spent the night in just last night, though it feels like a lifetime ago. Through the bars of empty cells, I see him. Ramos is pacing around his cell, his suit jacket lying crumpled on the wooden shelf of a bed and his sleeves are folded up over his elbows.

There is a Guard standing stiffly just outside his cell, alert and waiting.

Man, this was really just all a trap after all? He lured us all the way here just to get us in trouble?

I turn to Eddie, gesturing back the way we came. We need to get out of here and make a new plan. This was a really bad idea. Eddie's eyes widen, and he takes a few slow inhales.

Oh no, I know that look. *Seriously?* Allergies in a time like this?

He covers his mouth with both hands as if he can squeeze the sneeze away if he presses hard enough.

"No, no," I whisper, adding my hands over his own. He squeezes his eyes shut.

Eddie's sneeze comes out a garbled snort through both pairs of hands, and we freeze, praying by some miracle the Guard didn't hear us.

"Mateo, is that you?"

Ramos's voice seems to echo and rattle through the metal of

the cells between us. To my horror, heavy footsteps round the corner before we can even run. The Guard.

"It's alright," Ramos calls. "He's with me. You're safe."

The Guard gestures for us to follow him. "Come with me." His voice is muffled under the metal of his helmet, his face covered from view.

We hesitate, knowing the likelihood of this being a trap is still quite high. Especially since Ramos could still very likely be a murderer, responsible for the deaths of both of my closest friends.

Ramos sighs, sensing our mistrust from the other side of the room. "Do you want to know what happened to Sam or not?"

I look back to Eddie to see what he wants to do. This choice affects him just as much as it does me, and I agreed we would do this together. He nods, confirming he wants to know no matter the risks. I agree. Even if it is a trap, I have to know. If there's any possibility that it could be true, I want to hear it, if nothing else but to feed a naive hope that there's a chance for us too.

I take the first step into the exposing light of the holding cells, following the Guard to Ramos's cell. The Mayor looks exhausted—the wrinkles around his eyes seeming deeper than usual, his usually bright eyes dim.

"Nice place," I joke to try to ease some of the heavy tension.

Ramos's lips quirk upward in a near-smile. "Thanks," he replies. Then his face falls. "Listen, we'll need to make this quick. Sergeant Nova will likely be back any minute to continue my interrogation."

"Is Sam really alive?" Eddie speaks up from my left side.

"Well, he was as of last night. If he's managed to get himself killed already... well that would be a disappointing waste of energy."

Eddie and I share a look. This so far hasn't been very reassuring.

Ramos exhales slowly and closes his eyes, lowering himself onto the wooden shelf behind him. "Sorry. No time for not-funny jokes. It's been a long night. What I meant to say is, yes. He was not actually expelled last night. I helped him escape, and he's on his way to find Ella."

Eddie hoots in triumph, but I'm not so easily convinced. He's saying he turned off the electric gates and allowed Sam to just step right through? And let him walk into the dark unknowns outside the Zone, just like that? I want to believe him. I want more than anything to believe Sam is alive, that he got out. If he got out, maybe there's hope for us too. But how am I supposed to know for sure? How can I know if Ramos can be trusted, especially when I loathed him with a fiery passion just a few hours ago when I thought he murdered my best friend?

Ramos must see the doubt on my face because he continues without waiting for a verbal response. "He said you'd be suspicious. He told me to tell you, and I quote, 'Looks like the Illuminati will have to try again another day' whatever that means."

Eddie grabs my arm with glee, and my eyes widen. We always used to talk conspiracies after our siblings fell asleep, and I had always insisted the Underground is too Illuminati coded to ignore. Which is true, don't even get me started, but that's a story for another time.

I can't believe that crafty son of a gun really talked himself out of an expulsion *and got himself out.* What a legend.

I have so many questions, but I know we don't have much time, so I try to formulate the most essential ones. "Where is Ella? Do you know what happened to her?"

Ramos sighs. "Dr. Coombs told us about some experiment he was paid to perform on select gifted Minors by some mercenary that calls himself Vegas... We think Ella's alive, but"—he shakes his head with a heavy sadness— "unfortunately the five other kids didn't make it."

"No," Eddie gasps.

"Why?" I can barely speak, feeling the weight of what he's just said. Did he say *five* Zoners? Minors, like Eddie? Just experimented on and discarded like they were nothing? I feel sick.

Ramos leans forward in a way that makes us both lean forward too. "We have reason to believe that this mercenary, Vegas, is collecting children in E2 for some reason. That's all we were able to find out. Sam is heading there to look for her. I hope he gets there in one piece."

"So Ella's going to be okay?" Eddie's voice is so full of hope, it nearly makes me choke. I don't have the heart to tell him that if this weirdo mercenary kidnapped her, it might not be the best outcome, so I decide to just let him hope for the best. I don't have to talk reason with him. Not this time. He can believe his best friend is alive and well, just like I am.

Ramos seems to decide that too because he just smiles at Eddie. "Yeah, I think Sam will make sure she's okay."

But then his smile falters, and his voice gets quicker, more urgent. "We're running out of time. Long story short, I need your help. I don't know how much longer the FPA will keep me around after everything that has happened, but my guess is not long, so we have to get things moving quickly."

I don't like the sound of that. What things? We?

"Can't we just help you out?" Eddie suggests. "Tell us where the keys are. We'll unlock it, so you can get away."

He stands up from the sleeping shelf and steps up to the bars, holding onto them from his side. He's close enough now that I feel his warm breath on my nose. We're nearly the same height, but I still have to look up ever so slightly to look into his eyes. "That's very sweet of you. There may be a time later where I'll take you up on that, but for right now I don't want to risk Nova's retaliation on all of you until I have more of a plan. I want to help set things in motion first, in whatever time I have left."

"Things" again. *What things?*

"Listen to me closely," he continues. His eyes darken with an urgency that sets the anxiety I feel on fire. "I've received intel from a source that a dangerous person is going to be moving into this Zone, who sees an opportunity with me down and Chief gone. An opportunity for power."

"The Feds? That mercenary?"

He shakes his head. "My source didn't specify. Whoever it is, they plan to use the kids here for leverage, to negotiate more control and resources in the Underground."

My eyes widen. "Like a hostage situation?"

"Exactly like that."

"So what does that mean?" I try to keep my voice steady. I don't want to scare Eddie with a strong reaction, even though a panicked scream is threatening to bust out of me. *Stay calm, stay calm.*

"It means you have to get out before they get here." He clarifies through gritted teeth, repeating himself slower, "You have to get *everyone* out. War is coming to the Zone, Mateo. And it's coming soon."

10

AND NOW A MESSAGE FROM OUR SPONSORS

SAM

The morning after paintball, I wake up with a sore body and a bruised ego. I hardly slept at all. The events of the paintball game replayed in my dreams over and over, my subconscious mocking me like I imagine an older sibling would. I grab a fresh outfit and the shower caddy they gave me at the supply tent when I provided the ID number I got from Cade, grumbling to myself as I walk sleepily past Ponyboy's cot and the others who are sleeping in on this lazy Sunday.

I should've known better than to be so fooled by Q's tactics. Of course it was all to win. It was a fight to the death. I *knew that*. I don't know why I let myself forget so easily. It's actually laughable the fact that I really thought she was going to kiss me, ME, but... also the baffling reality that I wanted her to... The disappointment I felt after was undeniable, and that's just confusing. As much as I have tried to brush it off as just being swept up in the moment... no, I wanted her to kiss me. I can't deny that. I can't deny the sizzling energy I felt when she was close.

Time moves so differently down here, making days feel like

years, but I have to confront the reality that I've only known her for a few days. I just need to stop overthinking everything before I ruin our fragile friendship. I'm finally making progress toward earning her trust back, and that's what I want more than anything else. I can't mess things up.

I was so mesmerized by the ruse, I completely forgot that there is absolutely not a single reality in this dimension, or any other where Q—pro-wrestling, paintball-gun wielding, thrill-seeking, fearless, gorgeous Q — would ever see me as anything other than an annoying pain in her side. A "pretty" pity project.

Deep in thought and deeper in wallowing, I step up into the shower truck someone pointed me to, which is basically a reconstructed horse trailer hooked up to a potable water tank. I select an empty stall. There is a mirror on the wall that separates my stall from the one next to it, and in it I examine myself. So skeletal you can see my ribs and collarbones. Purple bruises across my chest from the paintballs. My brown hair shaggy and nearly to my shoulders. Dark circles under my eyes from stress and haunted dreams. No wonder Q couldn't get away from me fast enough. I look like the Grim Reaper.

As I'm showering, I think back to the Sanitation Centers in C9, the dark chambers with a timer projected on the wall, constantly reminding you that nothing there was free, not even your own hygiene. You had to earn that. But there are no timers here. And I didn't even have to pay for this soap.

For the first time, under the relaxing heat of the water, I allow myself to imagine staying here long-term. I visualize seeing Ella hop around with Ponyboy and Luna, hearing her uninhibited laugh. Seeing her brightness finally not restrained by the gray of C9 and whatever illusion Vegas has convinced her to believe.

Could we be happy here?

I'm sure Beardsley will come around once Cade gets

everyone back, and maybe the favor I've committed to with Cade won't be so bad with Ella here, safe and happy.

And Q.

But I try not to think about her right now. I'm bruised enough.

By the time I get back to my bed, squeezing wetness out of my hair with the towel, mostly everyone else in the room has left for breakfast, Ponyboy included, but I'm not really hungry.

Am I *avoiding* Q? No, of course not. Am I intentionally going a different place than she is, so I don't have to see her and potentially humiliate myself further before I've had time to lick my current wounds? Maybe.

I just don't think I can handle her smirk right now.

Her beautiful, perfectly sculpted smirk—

Shut up, Sam.

I wander around outside for a few minutes before I decide to go check on Zara. Maybe ask her a little more about E1 and distract myself from my pathetic reality.

The medical building is quiet and sterile, except for the occasional beeps of machines and monitors. The curtain of her bay is only halfway closed, so I can see her sitting up on the bed, working on something very determinedly on her lap. I knock on the nearest wall and clear my throat.

She brightens when she looks up and sees me. "Hi! Come in."

I sit down in the chair next to her bed, offering a warm smile. "How are you feeling?"

She flaps the IV in her arm with a roll of her eyes. "This thing is getting old. They're trying to make sure I don't get dehydrated, yes, I get it. Still annoying though."

I look at the object in her lap, a sketching pad. She has filled almost the whole page with angry black scribbles. "What are you up to?"

She sighs, tapping the paper with her marker. "One of the

medics suggested art to help me untangle the memories of my blackout." She clicks her tongue. "The problem is that I'm not an artist."

I gesture to her scribbles. "You're going to sit there and lie to my face? With that masterpiece?"

She laughs, straightening her posture like she's an art critic. "It does have an aesthetic of chaos, undertones of madness, very intriguing."

"Exactly, I mean just look at the linework," I add with a grin.

"Hey—" she says sharply all of a sudden, waving her marker to the curtain, her abrupt change of tone making me jump. "Where's your NOT girlfriend, Q?"

I shift in my seat. "I'm sure she's around. We just haven't bumped into each other yet."

Zara raises an eyebrow, sensing my avoidance. "Okay, spill it. What happened?"

I play dumb. "What do you mean?"

"The second I said her name you looked like a heartsick puppy."

"That's not true," I insist. "We're just friends. Really. I haven't even known her that long."

To which she gives me another look. "Something obviously happened between you two, and I'm extremely nosy, extremely bored, and extremely invested in your NON-relationship."

I sigh. As reluctant as I am to relive the humiliation, I give her a rundown of the paintball game, finishing my story with an adamant reminder that we are *just friends*. Or at least, making our way there again.

"I just have one question," Zara chokes through a suppressed laugh. "Did you pucker up and everything?"

I glare at her, and the laugh she was holding back explodes.

"You did, didn't you!" She is laughing so hard that she's nearly wheezing.

"Maybe a little," I grumble, but I have to make a notable

effort not to laugh along with her. It really is all so silly and juvenile. How am I this hung up on something so frivolous as a kiss, when my sister is being ensnared in Vegas's webs as we speak?

Zara exhales a sing-songy sigh, wiping a tear from laughter off her cheek. "I'd say I could help you make her jealous, but I'm too much of a feminist."

I chuckle. "It's okay. I'm happy being friends, if she even considers me that. I may have started off our friendship on a foundation of lies, so now I just want a fresh start."

She smiles, reaching over to squeeze my hand comfortingly. "You seem like a sweet guy. Just be patient. Trust takes time to build, but it takes even longer to *re*-build."

"Hey Zara, have you seen—? Oh, there you are." Q's sudden voice from the curtain startles me, making me jump. Her eyes are like lasers flicking from me, to Zara, to Zara's hand—which is still on my hand. I stand up a little too quickly, guiltily, throwing my hands in my pockets as if they're on fire. Even though I haven't done anything wrong, it still feels like I was somehow caught in the act.

"Is everything okay?" she asks, a strange look crossing her face I can't figure out.

Zara mutters something to herself about feminism, but I'm not really paying attention.

"Yeah totally, what's up?" I say too loudly. Nice, why don't you yell at her some more?

"I've been looking for you. Cade said his messenger from E2 should be back soon."

"Wow, already?" My spirits brighten immediately. If he was able to reach some kind of agreement with Vegas, does that mean I'll have Ella back tonight? Tomorrow? The thought fills me up so tightly with hope and excitement that I might need to scream or risk exploding.

I look back over my shoulder, nearly out the door already.

"Bye Zara, thanks for the help!" and she mouths back to me "good luck."

Q follows me outside the medical building, and I can't ignore the thick awkwardness between us, like honey oozing from a honeycomb. Luna nearly knocks me over outside which is a welcome distraction from the weird tension, and I return her affection by kneeling down and taking her face in my hands. I can't wait for Ella to meet her.

That thought makes me realize she's never even *seen* a real dog before. She's never seen any animal, actually.

It infuriates me how little of life she's gotten to experience down here. How many tiny moments have been taken from her.

I can't wait to experience all those firsts with her when we get out of here someday, and I actually allow myself to envision that as a possibility.

"Where have you been?" Q asks with a casual tone that seems too forced, giving a hand command to Luna to follow as we amble toward Cade's office. "I didn't see you after the game last night, and you missed breakfast."

I force my voice to stay casual too. "Oh, last night, yeah, I was just tired, so I headed right into bed. And then this morn-ing, I just wanted to clear my head."

"With Zara?"

Before I can respond, the air around us cracks with a deaf-ening blast.

I throw myself to the ground, pulling Q and Luna down next to me. Q grips Luna's collar as she barks wildly into the chaos. We cover our heads as explosions roar one after another, seeming to be surrounding us on all sides.

Screams from around camp are barely heard as the cracks ring in my eardrums. I keep my head covered, relieved to feel Q's hand in mine, knowing she's right next to me.

After several minutes, the blasts seem to let up. I put a hand on Q's back, scanning her for injury, grateful she's close.

"Are you okay?" I ask her, brushing dust off her jacket and her hair.

She looks at me through her curls and nods, though her eyes are dilated. She's scared, but she'll never admit it. Some kind of realization crosses her face suddenly, and she leaps to her feet, keeping hold of Luna's collar in one hand and my hand in the other.

I don't even bother asking where we're going because I suddenly realize I'd follow her anywhere regardless.

She pulls Luna and me behind her, nearly jogging toward the Hall. The camp itself appears mostly untouched by the blasts, but that doesn't lessen the chaos or the thick fear radiating off everyone. People are running toward the boundaries from all directions, mismatched weapons in hand. From the direction of the wreckage, they seem to only have affected the outer perimeter, like whoever was responsible for this only wanted to send a message, rather than hurt anyone. Was it the FPA? Did they finally decide this operation here was worth going up against?

Q drops my hand and bursts through the entrance of the Hall, the doors bouncing off the inner walls with a *clank*. She runs past the tables to where a group of children have huddled in the corner.

Ponyboy among them.

He comes running toward us when he sees us, tears in his eyes. The sight of him so scared and alone rips a hole right through me. He probably hasn't even recovered from everything that happened at E2 only days ago, and now this?

Q falls to her knees and holds him. "Are you okay?" she says into his hair, and he sniffs. He says he's fine, even though he's visibly shaking as he clings to Q. Luna licks his face relentlessly.

I check on the rest of the kids, who are scared but not hurt. Are these kids like Ponyboy? Kids that someone smuggled out of a Zone and brought here for refuge, or were they born here? The fact that children could be born in the Underground is really not too far-fetched, but it's something I've never even considered before. Who would *want* to bring children into this hell?

The doors to the Hall slam open and to my surprise and horror alike Beardsley storms in, a pickaxe in one hand and a gun in the other, face red with fury. I shrink a little, wondering if he's finally come to serve me the redneck reckoning he always promised. He scans the whole room, and when he sees Q and Ponyboy safe and together, visible relief softens his wrinkled face for a moment.

But then his face hardens again as he marches straight toward me, and I'm certain this is it for me, but he tosses me the pickaxe instead of slicing me open with it. I fumble with it for a second before getting a good hold. He doesn't give me an explanation or even a second glance before turning on a heel and marching back out the door. Could this be Beardsley's idea of a peace-offering? I accept, as confused as I may be. Touching how explosions can really bring people together.

I share a look with Q before she gives me the silent go-ahead, still sitting cross legged on the Hall floor, stroking Ponyboy's long hair in her arms, Luna's head resting on his leg. I know she'd normally be holding a pickaxe right next to me, but with Lala, Red, and Steele gone, she has had to take up more of the slack with Ponyboy. I respect her ability to do both, to be both nurturing and fierce. To know when each side of her is needed and to switch into that side of herself so effortlessly.

I run out of the Hall to catch up with Beardsley, who has already nearly reached the border of boxes and trucks, where basically every other able-bodied person of the Catacombs is armed and waiting too.

Sweat gathers in my hands against the cool metal of the pickaxe as I take in the wreckage from the blasts. Remnants of the explosives show that they were placed closely together, surrounding the entire camp in a tight intentional circle. Several trucks are damaged, one is completely overturned. Hundreds of boxes of materials and supplies are destroyed. Message only maybe, but the message is loud and clear: *we could have done much worse.*

From the tangible fury of the people all around me, it appears the Catacombs is not receiving that message well.

Cade, Calix, and Axel are at the front of the rowdy crowd, examining the remnants of the closest bomb. Axel sniffs each bomb and barks when he clears it of the possibility of detonating further. People shout at them, asking permission to retaliate, demanding action. Cade ignores them, but Calix holds his hands out trying to reassure them and calm them down. I stretch my neck to watch Cade over people's shoulders. He squats down in front of the bomb, black smoke still billowing out of it in swirling tendrils. He picks up a few items that are scattered around it.

The crowd quiets as he stands slowly. He turns around, scanning the area and looking for someone in the crowd. I blink in surprise as he meets my eyes. Me? My brows furrow in confusion to be the one he was searching for, but it all makes sense when he holds up the items in his hand.

Playing cards.

TYRO B-29

Aunty assigns a guard to supervise me today. She said it is to monitor my symptoms, to make sure I've fully recovered from the missed sync, but I suspect it's also to make sure I don't try to do anything else life-threatening and against the rules.

I didn't sleep at all last night after they let me out of the hospital room. Since then I've been trying desperately to figure out what was going through my head when I skipped that sync, but I come up short every time. It's like there is a blip in my brain, an entire chunk of time just completely carved out from existence and now nothing makes sense without it.

Lucy, Katie, and Amber have been treating me differently since word got around of what I did. They speak to me very gently and softly, like their regular volume might break me in half. I think everyone just assumes I had some kind of mental break, and I suppose I did. That's the only explanation I can think of, too.

I wish I could ask Ella if she knows anything, that maybe she could make sense of my actions. Like did we perhaps talk about something that would make me forget to sync? But unfortunately, she wasn't awake for our sync this morning, and the "supervisor" hanging right over my shoulder made it impossible to even breathe in her direction, let alone to try to wake her.

I'm hoping I'll have better luck with this sync. I walk with Lucy toward the data room. It's later in the evening than our syncs usually are, but Aunty wanted us to sync right before bed today. We walk quietly into the room, and Lucy gives me a side look that silently asks me if I'm okay before we part to our different sides of the room. I give her a grateful nod. My supervisor is just a few feet behind me as I make my way to Ella's bedside. She stirs a little when I approach, but her eyes stay closed.

"Hey, Gordon, come help me out here for a minute, will you?"

A surgeon by the exit is struggling to fit through the door with the stack of boxes he's holding, a stack he can barely see over.

My supervisor looks at me hesitantly, but speed-walks toward the surgeon, keeping me in his sight the whole time. A clear message that says, *I'm still watching you.*

I take Ella's hand and prepare to sync, holding my wrist cuff up to hers. To my surprise she squeezes my hand. Her eyes remain closed, but I see her eyelashes flutter for a second.

I can barely make out her whisper, as she talks through her teeth without moving her lips, so as to avoid alerting any of the surgeons. "Is. Sam. Okay?"

"Sam?" I whisper back. "Who is Sam?"

Ella lets out a breath through her barely parted lips, and I sense some frustration tensing in her hand. She whispers again, slightly more urgently, "You have to remember Sam. *Sam.* He. Can get us. Out of here."

My body reacts to that name for some reason. Why does it feel so familiar, yet my brain is telling me I've never heard it before in my life?

"What do you—?"

The presence of my supervisor back in my proximity cuts off the rest of my sentence. She squeezes my hand again, and I wish so deeply I could talk with her more. Get some clarity. She seems to know something, and I desperately want to make sense of the gaps in my brain. I squeeze back before touching our cuffs together, clipping the cable in place, and letting the sync take place.

I feel the familiar rush of cold shoot up my arm and across my shoulder as the sync begins, cringing at the chill that cuts down my vertebrae. The cold pulses in my wrist for one minute that always feels like ten, and the wrinkles in my brain seem to smooth themselves out slowly and gently. Then my cuff blinks green, and it's over. I disconnect the cable.

"Good night, Ella," I whisper, and my supervisor clears his throat in warning.

Before I walk away, I hear her so softly behind me say, "Remember. Sam."

EVEN LONG AFTER I have slipped into my night clothes and cuddled under my blanket for the night, I can't stop thinking about Ella's hoarse whispers.

Sam.

He can get us out of here.

Here, as in our home? Why would we want to "get out of here?" And what, leave Aunty? Leave safety, and family, and the future we're trying to build?

I squeeze my forehead and close my eyes, as if that will help me draw out some recollection of this Sam. When I think the name, my body remembers somehow. It feels warm and familiar. I just can't get my brain and my body to connect. I can't seem to visualize a person. There are only clouds of feelings and vague associations.

I stretch my arms, trying to release some of the frustration that is settling in my muscles. I stop when I feel something under my pillow. I try to make sense of it in the dark.

Two small round... capsules?

I realize with horror it's my red and blue, that I've for some reason hidden away. On the day I skipped my sync, did I also skip my vitamins? Why would I do that?

The more I try to think, the more frazzled I get, so I eventually concede into a strange restless sleep where I dream of red and blue capsules, pizza day with Lucy, and even weirder: the warm embrace of a stranger whose face I can't quite unblur.

WAITING in line the next morning for the restroom, I can't help but feel like I'm slowly spiraling. I'm frustrated I can't trust my own mind, otherwise I'd already know what led me to make the decision to skip a sync, as well as my reds and blues on the same day. What would have made me take such a risk? I'm never reckless, always careful and sensible. I always follow the rules, so it must have been something. What could have happened, or what could I have heard, that would have made the risks seem worth it to me?

It's my turn in the restroom now, and I can barely look at myself in the mirror. I'm still pale from the last few days of recovery, and my eyes lack their usual sparkle. I pull my hair into a braid and hold my hand out to the dispenser for my capsules. They drop into my hand, and static seems to shoot up my arm at their touch, remembering the forbidden pair under my pillow.

I toss them in my mouth and swallow, but to my horror they come right back up with a gag.

I try again, using water this time, but it's like they keep getting caught in my throat. I decide to try doing them one at a time, going slow. I breathe a sigh of relief when they finally go down. I show the dispenser my mouth, and the door unlocks. I'm about to exit, but I have to sprint back to the toilet instead, where I vomit mostly stomach acid. Acid, a red capsule, and a blue capsule.

I just stare at them floating in the toilet water. Horrified. Confused.

A sinking feeling settles over me, a confirmation that my body must know something my mind has forgotten. That's the only explanation. And that terrifies me.

I'VE BEEN DOING my best to pay attention during Aunty's Daily Life lesson today, but I'm so distracted that my notes look like a tornado. She is teaching us about the basics of money, which normally I would be very interested in, but my mind keeps wandering back to this morning. Am I going to end up back in a hospital room again because my body wouldn't let me take my capsules?

Will they believe me when I try to tell them I really tried, that it wasn't my fault?

The door to the conference room opens and all eyes turn to the guard who weaves his way through the tables and up to the front. He whispers something to Aunty, who has paused mid-sentence. Is it just my imagination, or do I see her eyes flick to me for just a second?

My heart pounds. Do they know I didn't take the capsules? How could they know? It's not my fault. I tried to take them.

"Children, will you excuse me for a moment?" Aunty places her clicker down on the table next to her with a stilted smile. "Ella, can I have a word with you outside, please?"

It's like the blood drains from my entire body. Everyone's heads whip back in my direction. My knees shake as I stand and follow them out the door.

The door closes behind me with a *click*.

"Ella." Aunty's voice is gentle, but her face is stern, which makes my eyes immediately well up with tears. Is she disappointed in me? Am I in trouble?

"My friend here tells me they found your vitamins hidden under your pillow this morning. Have you been skipping your reds and blues?"

I lower my chin in shame. "I don't remember."

Aunty sighs, and a tear rolls down my cheek. She *is* disappointed in me.

"My friend is going to bring you to a quiet place to think for a little bit until we can figure this out. You know we don't tolerate rule-breaking here, Ella, and this is your second offense this week."

I sniffle. "I'm so sorry. I don't know why I did it. I can't remember why."

She puts a hand on my arm. "You were given such a rare opportunity for this life here, my darling. Are you really willing to give that up?"

I shake my head, trying to swallow down the sobs.

"Very well," she says. "I'll be by later to talk more."

She goes back into the building, and the guard walks me down the hallway, taking a turn to a door I've never seen before, that he uses a key to unlock. A blast of cold air from inside the room hits me as we walk inside. The lighting is dim, and it has a distinct smell of sweat. In the room there are several smaller rooms lined up next to each other, the insides exposed through metal bars.

A flash of a memory appears in my mind, but it's gone before I can make sense of it. My body reacts strongly to it though, almost like it remembers something significant happening in a room just like this. I start to feel scared.

The guard unlocks one of the barred rooms and gestures me inside. There is a small bed and a toilet in the corner. The door closes behind me with a *crash*, which seems to knock the sobs right out of my chest. I drop to my knees and cry into my hands.

I hear the guard's footsteps leaving and the click of the main door being locked back up.

A voice close by startles me. "Are you alright, *mija*?"

I look up from my hands to see a woman in the room next to mine, looking at me through the bars. She has long dark hair and kind eyes. There is another woman in the room with her. She is lying on the bed on the other side of their room. She sits up to look at me. Her hair is cut short, mostly gray. Her eyes are sharper but show concern as she watches me.

I sniffle and nod, wiping away a tear with the back of my hand.

"Did they hurt you?" It's a man's voice this time. I look up to see a man behind them standing, looking through bars from his room on the other side of the women's. He looks through their room into mine. His voice is deep but gentle. I look at him curiously, interested that he doesn't have any hair. His head is just the same bare, smooth black as the rest of his skin.

I shake my head. "No," I croak. "I'm not hurt. I—I made a mistake."

"And they put you in here?" The gray-haired woman sounds angry about it. Didn't she hear me say it's my fault? "You're just a kid."

The kind-eyed woman reaches through the bars for my

hand. I hesitate, not sure if I should trust someone who is obviously being held in here for a mistake of their own. But her eyes are so genuine. How could she not be trusted? I take her hand and instantly feel warmth.

"What's your name?" she asks gently.

I sniff. "Ella."

And something about me saying that makes the three of them look at each other in surprise.

11

TRUST ISN'T MY STRONG SUIT. I PREFER NATURAL SUSPICION.

MATEO

The next morning following our meeting with Ramos, I feel fidgety and anxious as I wait at attention during formation. It feels like a thick sludge has replaced all the blood in my veins, making me feel heavy and weighed down as I stand here. I didn't sleep at all after we got back from visiting Ramos in jail last night. His words just kept repeating over and over in my brain.

You have to get everyone out. War is coming to the Zone, Mateo.

You, you, you. Everyone, everyone, everyone.

When I was talking with Parker and the others—brainstorming the *beginnings* of a plan together— it was a shared load, a shared responsibility. And it was just us. We'd look out for each other, and we would figure out how to get each other out.

But everyone? That's a responsibility I never asked for.

I flick my eyes across the rows and rows of Zoners around me, the people I've stood beside for the last seven years, and it really dawns on me that even though we're treated like adults-in-training, future soldiers to do the FPA's bidding, we're all still just kids. *I'm* just a kid. And all of this is really up to me? I'm really responsible for saving everyone? Ramos has to know that he's asking too much. It's all too much.

I try to keep my breaths calm, but I feel a panic starting to rise up my bones. How can he expect this of me? I've only ever just been in the background. I never wanted to be a hero. All I've ever wanted was to keep my brother safe. How did I get mixed up in something this big, this dangerous?

Nova marches in, flanked by two Guards on either side like she was yesterday when she collected Ramos from his office. I straighten my posture and sharpen my focus. I can't get in trouble today because I'm already fragile from the weight of these new expectations, and even under the slightest scrutiny I can't trust myself not to blurt out everything Ramos has trusted me with.

Nova stops at the Podium and evaluates us all for a moment, looking across at our formation, no doubt looking for less-than-perfect Zoners she can make an example out of.

To my horror she locks eyes with me, and I swear I can see her eyes grow even colder, misting over with some kind of frozen hell-fire.

"Barrajo," she barks, her voice echoing across the courtyard.

My heart stops. Does she know Eddie and I went to Ramos last night? Does she know we broke curfew?

Does she know what he asked me to do?

Several pulse-stopping seconds pass. This is it, this is where it ends. And all because I decided to act for once. A tremor begins to move up my legs, causing my knees to shake against my will.

"What are you staring at?" she finally says, and it's like my airways let down actual physical barriers and finally allow air to pass through. She doesn't know anything. This is just a show of power.

"Nothing, Sergeant," I shout in a monotone voice the way I'm supposed to, careful not to move, not even my eyes, keeping my posture rigid even as my insides are fusing themselves back together after nearly melting away to nothing.

Nova's lips twist into a sneer. "Right. Keep it that way." Her attention widens to the rest of the formation, and my whole body seems to sigh with relief. She addresses the group as a whole this time. "I would like to address some of the rumors that have been circulating."

She pauses to let her words carry across the rows of Zoners. No one dares to move, but I can feel the tension and anticipation radiating off everyone's bodies, like it buzzes in the air around us.

"It is true that Sergeant Hallows is dead."

She says it like a dare, a threat to break formation. No one falls for it, but that buzzing feeling in the air intensifies.

"It is also true that Foster Jenkins is dead. I plan to find the person responsible for these deaths. We already have a suspect in custody."

Ramos.

"Especially while this investigation is ongoing, I will have no patience for second chances. My earlier warning still stands, and I won't sugar coat it. Step a toe out of line, and everyone who loves you will have to watch you meet the same end as those two trouble-makers yesterday."

A chill runs down my back, just considering her words and what would have happened to Eddie if we had been caught last night. I wish he didn't have to be involved in this. I wish he would have listened to me when I asked him to stay behind, to not get himself involved. But he's too stubborn, too strong-willed.

Just like Mom.

Nova dismisses us, and I have to blink away the memories that try to surface when I even think the word 'Mom.' I can't be distracted. There's too much at stake now.

Eddie hurries over to me when the formation breaks, and

we step in line behind BART for check-in. He looks me over, concern creasing his forehead. "Are you okay? You thinking about last—"

I shake my head to cut him off. I can't let him worry. He can't know I have doubts about my capabilities, that I have no idea what I'm doing. He can't know I might not be able to keep my promise to keep us together, to keep him safe. I plaster on a reassuring smile. "Everything's fine."

He doesn't seem convinced, but he doesn't press me on it. I try to shift my focus from worrying about the unknowns and instead to getting through one task at a time. That's all I can control right now. Task one: I need to tell the group.

Before we know it, Eddie and I each have our breakfast trays loaded up with a meager helping of bland oatmeal and a banana, and we're nearly speed-walking to Parker's table.

I slide next to him on the bench so quickly that my tray nearly slams down onto the table. He looks startled at first, but then his eyes flash with understanding. He locks eyes with Steven and Talia who are still waiting in line and makes a discreet gesture in my direction, signaling to sit with us when they're done. Trevor next, who sets his tray across from Parker just where he was yesterday.

Rachel and Amanda, Talia's roommates, slide in next to Trevor. I send a look to Parker, but he gives me a reassuring smile that says, "*We can trust them.*"

I'm nearly vibrating with anxiety at the wait, but soon enough Steven and Talia finally make it through the line and join us. I take note of where the Guards are located. There is one at each exit, and another who is passing through the Hall row by row. He's on the other side of the Hall now but will be close enough soon.

"I spoke to Ramos," I whisper, and everyone leans close while trying to look as natural as possible. I'm grateful for the noisy cafeteria that muffles the sound of my voice. "Things are even worse than we thought."

Trevor and Parker share a look, and so do Talia's roommates.

"I mean we suspected things were getting bad, but what did he say?" Parker says, keeping his voice low.

As much as I can't wait to relieve some of this burden—to finally share the weight of it with others—as soon as I tell them what he told me, it becomes real. I can no longer just pass off the conversation as a figment of my imagination or a dream. It becomes a reality that I have to do something about. The pressure to act becomes real because then there will be accountability. I take a deep breath. "He said war is coming to the Zone, and it's coming soon. He said we need to get everyone out."

A crushing silence descends over the group as my words sink in. War. It's a word we've obviously all heard before, but it's never been a direct reality. Always just something that was happening somewhere else. Easy to forget it was happening at all, even though we're living underground because of it.

Rachel vocalizes what we're all thinking, her whisper cutting into the group's silence like a knife. "How are we supposed to do that? That's impossible, we'd never even make it past the gates."

"Sam got out," I say as if this solves everything. "He's on his way to look for Ella."

Their jaws drop in shock.

"No way," Parker barks a disbelieving laugh.

"Ramos helped him out."

"And you believe him?" Trevor asks with mirth, and it's a fair question.

"I do. He got out, we can too."

"We can't just stay here until things mellow out again?" Amanda squeaks, a tremble in her voice. "If we just keep quiet and keep our heads down, we can wait it out. The FPA can't hurt us."

"Oh, they can't?" Trevor shoots back sharply across the table. He holds up his fingers and counts them off one by one. "Tell that to Walter West. Foster. Josh and Markus yesterday. And whichever one of us is next."

"They won't keep us here forever." Amanda's voice rises to near hysterics. "My grandpa is an Elder in C3. He's going to come for me when this is over. We just have to keep waiting."

Talia takes her hand and squeezes it. "No one is coming, Amanda," she says gently.

"She's right." I push my tray of uneaten oatmeal aside, her doubt suddenly giving me the fuel I needed for the decision, locking my resolve into place. This is what needs to be done because like she said, *no one is coming*

"The point of waiting it out has passed," I continue quietly but firmly. "The Zone is going up in flames, and if we don't do something, we're going to burn right here with it."

Amanda rips her hand away from Talia's and jumps to her feet, her face twisted with anger. "If you guys want to get yourselves killed, that's fine. But leave me out of it."

She snatches her breakfast try off the table and storms off.

Rachel looks at me apologetically. "We'll talk to her. She'll come around."

I wave off the apology. I don't have the time or energy to worry about her. If she wants to help, great. If not, just stay out of the way.

"Check your functions," I say to the group that remains, waving my wrist at them in explanation. The sooner we can talk with the Elders, the sooner we can develop a real plan. Ramos agreed they are our best shot at an escape, but he warned that they may not agree to help.

"They've grown accustomed to their safe, comfortable routine here," he had said before we left last night, which enraged me. "Don't be surprised if they don't want to give that up for a dangerous unknown."

How can they just tuck themselves away in their cozy cabins and pretend not to hear us while we're getting beaten, and even killed, just outside their doors? I think of Ella's screams while she was getting that Penalty just mere days ago and shudder. I'll never forget the way it sounded when the batons cracked over her skin. And they just ignored it.

There are a few quiet moments as everyone checks their wristTabs for their job assignments for the day. I touch the function option on the LED screen of my Tab, hoping it'll say Elder Assistance. To my dismay, an animation of a little dancing swing set pops up instead. Park Maintenance.

"Kitchen Support," Steven says with a sigh, and while there are typically a few Elders there that oversee the kitchen, it's not enough. We need all of them on board for this to work.

Talia and Parker both have Waste Management, Eddie is a Minor, so he doesn't have anything useful—just Reading Skills — and Trevor has Park Maintenance with me.

I blow out a sigh of disappointment. "We need to figure out a way to meet with as many of them as possible, and we have to be quiet about it. We can't risk Nova hearing anything."

Eddie fidgets in his seat next to me, and I know that means he wants to say something. I look at him and raise a brow, giving him the ok to speak up.

"Doesn't Amanda have a baby sister?" Eddie says slowly, as if still formulating the sentence while he's saying it. "She could get us into the Nursery. That's where most of the Elders are, right?"

He's right. She made it pretty clear just now she didn't want to be involved, though.

Nova calls us to attention for the pledge, the FPA's message of the week, which has been the same for the last two weeks in a row for some reason, and then the morning announcements.

"I'll talk to her," Talia promises through the scraping and bustle of everyone in the Hall standing up to recite the pledge. "Give me until dinner."

During announcements, the reality and risk of involving the group is starting to settle in on top of my shoulders, and all I can think about is how much of this plan is riding on trust. Trusting that Ramos is telling the truth. Trusting that I can count on these people I've confided in. And trusting that no one will turn us in before we even get a chance to try.

THE GUARDS OVERSEEING Park Maintenance sent Trevor and me to opposite ends of the Zone, so we couldn't even see each other through functions, let alone formulate more of a solid plan than just hoping Amanda will come around. So by lunchtime, I'm no closer to figuring out what to do now than I was a few hours ago.

At least it's finally time for lunch. I begin the walk toward the Square from my assigned park—the one by the Northern Boundaries, closest to our Quarters. I massage my hands, which are sore from hours of scrubbing and shining the play equipment. My mind is so busy, trying to think of every possible angle of an escape and what failure could mean for every kid here, that I don't notice the buzz right away. The buzz of something happening.

Everyone with functions on the outskirts, like me, move into the Square quickly as we all notice it at the same time. I try to stretch my neck to see what's going on, but I can't see anything yet. This is why I kept Sam around for so long—it pays to have tall friends. People are gathering around the Podium, which is not out of the ordinary considering we always gather for formation before checking in for lunch, but what is out of the ordinary is the *buzz*. People moving just a little bit quicker, the tension just a little bit stiffer, the whispers like hisses as everyone tries to figure out what's happening.

I shoulder my way through the crowd, and my heart sinks when I can finally see what—or *who*— has joined Nova and her Guards on top of the platform.

Talia, Rachel, and *Amanda.*

No.

The Guards push Talia and Rachel to their knees. A Guard holds Amanda's hands firmly behind her back a few steps away from her kneeling roommates. She begins to cry.

Amanda, what did you do?

I can barely breathe as Nova steps up to the front of the platform, her one metal arm reflecting the warm afternoon overhead lights. She looks over all of us, and apart from Amanda's sobs, it's so quiet you could surely hear a pin drop. Without moving my head too much to avoid drawing attention to myself, I try to find Eddie in the crowd and strategize. If this gets to that point, do we run? Where would we go? Would we even get far before they just shoot us in the backs?

Nova regards the girls behind her with a look so sinister, it would have given even Chief a run for his money.

"Amanda here has made the brave choice to come forward with some very interesting information about her roommates. Information that, unfortunately, has warranted a punishment."

I can't breathe.

Talia and Rachel's heads are forced down by the Guards, their hair covering their faces, so I can't even look at them, to try to glean any idea of what happened from the looks in their eyes. Talia was so confident she could get Amanda to come around. *What happened?*

"Amanda tells us they were talking about an attempted escape."

A collective gasp comes out of the crowd around the Podium like a wave rolling toward shore.

Nova makes a gesture to the Guards, and they remove their weapons from their belts. A chill moves down my back. The last time we were all here witnessing a Penalty, it was Ella's. Her punishment for just a silly prank on the Guards. I can still *feel* Eddie's screams as I held my hands over his mouth to muffle them when her body went limp from the continued blows. Sam's screams that echoed off the beams seem to still be lodged there like ghosts.

The Guards press a button on their club-batons, and the electricity powers up, sparking and sizzling off each spike.

I feel like I'm going to be sick. This is all my fault.

The Guards rip the backs off Rachel and Talia's uniform tops as Nova continues. "After being blessed with the privilege of safety and care in this Zone, you dare even speak of leaving? Inciting some kind of rebellion? From what I was told, the last person who did that was expelled."

What do I do? I'm the reason they're here. I can't just stand here and watch this happen. But if I act, won't they punish Eddie too? I know they will, just like they did to Ella. I can't risk that. If it were just me at stake, I'd jump up there without question and take the fall for everything. I feel paralyzed by the weight of the impossible decision before me.

The Guards stand behind the girls, waiting for the final order to begin.

"Let this be the last reminder to everyone here. I said it before, and I'll say it one final time. There will be order, or there will be—"

"No!" someone yells from the crowd. There is a commotion as someone pushes their way forward.

It's Steven.

Talia's head jerks up at the sound of his voice, surprise and fear flashing across her face. She shakes her head, a frantic pleading look in her eyes.

Steven pushes his way forward and is about to jump onto the Podium when—

Bang!

My ears ring, and the screams around me are muffled. Everyone in the crowd ducks, covering their heads instinctively. My own heartbeat begins to slow as Steven's body jerks back against the force of the gunshot, as if I were the one hit by the bullet.

Nova stands at the Podium, her metal arm aimed toward Steven's limp body.

Her arm. It shot him.

Talia's screams slice through the muffled ringing in my ear. "Steven!"

Nova lowers her arm, a mechanical clanking sound coming out of it as the end of it moves back into the shape of a hand like a damn Transformer. She steps to Talia and shoves her head back down with the hand made of skin and bones, ignoring her sobs. She gives a final gesture to the Guards, and they raise their clubs to deliver the blows.

I squeeze my eyes shut, but nothing can block the sound of their screams.

WHAT REMAINS of our group is deathly quiet at the lunch table. The space of missing bodies feels like a blackhole that is consuming everything around it.

Steven, gone.

Talia and Rachel, gone. Alive, fortunately. But their absence is still loud.

The girls were allowed to visit the medElders at the hospital for their Penalty wounds instead of spending the rest of the day in a holding cell, but I suspect Nova wasn't being charitable, she just doesn't want anyone seeing Ramos down there.

I haven't touched my food and have less than no appetite to eat after what I just saw, so I slide it over to Eddie next to me who is picking at the remaining crumbs from his sandwich. I know the servings they give us aren't enough. I know he's still hungry. He tries to slide it back, but I refuse it until he gives up and nibbles on it quietly.

With a sigh, I break the silence. I know it's time to acknowledge the blackhole, especially since it's my fault this even happened. My voice is barely a croak. "I'm so sorry I involved you guys in this." I look Parker and Trevor in the eyes, so they can hopefully see I mean it.

Parker waves a slow hand, his voice heavy with the loss of his friend. "This isn't your fault, man. We all knew the risks."

Trevor's eyes are nearly on fire. He leans in and hisses, "They can't get away with this. I'm in now more than ever."

"Same," Parker whispers with an emphatic nod. "I want this place to burn."

My eyes flick up when I sense someone approaching our table. My senses automatically jump to high alert. If it's a Guard, I need to be ready. But it's... Amanda.

She rushes to our table, hands flailing, eyes red from crying. "Parker." It's only one word, but it makes what's left of her crumble. She breaks into a sob again.

Parker goes rigid. "Get away from me, Amanda. I can't even look at you."

"It didn't happen like she said," she begs through her sobs. "I was just talking to Jess, venting, I guess. I didn't know what to do. But I didn't know the Guards could hear me, I swear. I swear on my life."

"Tell that to Steven."

Amanda's mouth snaps shut, like he's slapped her. She looks back and forth between us, as if trying to make a decision. A resolve crosses her face. "Talia said you needed to get into the

Nursery. I'll do it. I'll take you there. Please. Let me try to make it up to you."

"Steven is *dead*, Amanda," Trevor whispers through his teeth. "Make it up to us? Nothing you do can change what you've already done."

Amanda sniffs and uses the back of her hand to wipe off her tear-streaked face. "You're right. But I can try to make sure his death wasn't for nothing." She turns to leave. "I can get you in tonight, take it or leave it."

THINGS THAT CAN (AND PROBABLY WILL) BE OUR DOOM

THIS ANGSTY DIAGRAM FEELS LIKE SOMETHING SAM WOULD DO

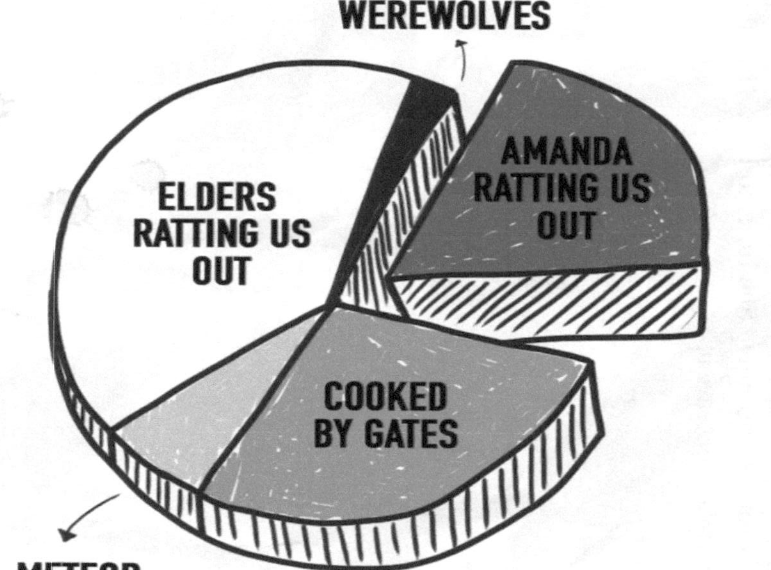

TYRO B-29

The three adults gawk at me through the bars.

"Ella, as in *Sam's sister*, Ella?" The gray-haired woman asks in shock.

That name.

Sam.

That's the same name Ella mentioned at our sync last night. What had she said?

Remember Sam. He can get us out of here.

"Do you know him?" I ask, remaining careful in case this is some kind of test. I have to figure out how to learn more about him without revealing that I was talking to Ella at our sync. That would just make me look even more guilty.

The dark-haired woman holding my hand seems to hesitate before answering, a flash of uncertainty crossing her face. "Sam was travelling with us to find you. He told me that you knew my sons—Mateo and Eduardo. He said you and my Eduardo were best friends. Is that true?"

She holds my eyes, as if my answer is very important to her. It makes me nervous, overwhelmed. I don't like feeling this kind of pressure when everything is already so confusing.

I pull my hand away and put a few more inches between us. "I don't know. I can't remember." My voice is no louder than a whisper.

The gray-haired woman hisses something under her breath before dropping back down onto the bed. "I guess the casino lady was right. He really lied about everything."

I bury my head in my knees, wishing everything could just make sense.

"What do you mean you can't remember, sweetie?" the woman presses gently.

"I just can't remember," I cry into my hands. "She told me to remember Sam, that he could help us, but I can't. I can't do it."

"Who told you to remember? Remember what?"

I look at her through tears. "Ella." I sniff. "Well Ella-A."

The gray-haired woman stands again. They both look at me in confusion. "Ella-A?" she says it slowly, like as if she's trying not to scare me off or make me cry again. I don't understand what they're not getting. Isn't it obvious what I'm saying?

"Like the real Ella," I explain, trying not to get flustered. "I'm Ella-B. I'm just—well, I don't know what I am."

All three of them stare at me in silence, the man's stare just as heavy as the women's even though his is further away. The silence is weighted, and it makes me feel frustrated that this is just more to figure out and untangle.

"Did I say something wrong?" I ask carefully. Maybe this was a test after all, and I've just failed, and Aunty is on her way here right now to let me know I have to leave and never come back.

The long-haired woman stands and exhales slowly, putting her hands on her hips and beginning to pace back and forth around the room. Both women move closer to the man, and the three of them talk too quietly for me to hear, but with their hand motions they look agitated.

I suddenly feel exhausted, the poor sleep I got last night

finally catching up to me. I pull myself off the floor and lie on the bed. It's uncomfortable, but not unbearable.

I drift to sleep quickly.

I'M AWAKENED by the sound of clanging keys. My eyes flutter open and see my door being opened, a different guard stepping through and setting a dinner tray on the floor just inside the room. He does the same for the two women and the man on the other side of them. I didn't think I was hungry, but the sight of the food on the tray makes my stomach growl on its own. I sit cross-legged in front of it, admiring the perfectly round roll, the mashed potatoes and gravy, and the slice of meatloaf.

Someone clears their throat, interrupting my evaluation of the meal before me. It's the long-haired woman. "Can we talk more? I'm sorry if we upset you earlier. Your... situation was just surprising to hear."

I push my tray over closer to the bars that separate our rooms, unable to stay away from her kind energy and warmth.

"I'm *La Reina*, by the way. Lala for short." She gestures behind her. "And these are my friends, Steele and Red."

I remember the basics of an Etiquette lesson Aunty taught a while ago. I think it's one of my first memories. I'm proud I remember what I'm supposed to say when someone introduces themselves. "Nice to meet you," I tell them.

Lala and Steele both join me on the floor, facing the bars and enjoying their own dinner trays. The man, Red, is also eating, but he's pacing around his own room as he does. He looks like the kind of person who doesn't like getting comfortable, especially in a place like this.

"We have a few questions, if that's okay. If you feel overwhelmed at any time, just let me know, and we'll stop," Steele says, setting her cutlery on the tray while she speaks.

I confirm with a nod, taking an ungraceful slurp of gravy before remembering my manners.

"You say there is a 'real Ella.' Is that right? She's a different person than you?"

I suddenly feel shy. She's being polite, but the tone of disbelief underneath the niceness, makes me feel abnormal. Why are they acting like this is abnormal? Is it?

"How..." Steele hesitates, carefully wording what she's trying to ask. "What does that mean exactly? You just have the same name, so they call you A and B?"

I furrow my brows. "No... we're the same. I'm her double. I was made from her."

The women look at each other, and I don't have much experience reading people other than my friends, but it looks like this information has confirmed something they feared. Which means my... "situation"... as they called it isn't normal after all. They must think I'm some kind of freak.

I start to cry again at the very thought. Just when I thought everything was already confusing enough in my head.

"Oh, *mija*, don't cry," Lala says. "It's okay, we're just trying to understand."

Red sighs from the other room. "Steele, you're terrible at this. Let Lala do the talking."

"I'm sorry," Steele says to me, her voice gentler than it has been this whole time. "He's right. I'm not very good with kids."

"Do you want us to stop asking you questions?" Red asks. "We just thought we may be able to help each other if we knew more about you."

I sniff and look up at them. What kind of help do they think I need?

I shake my head. I just want to organize the mess in my brain. They seem to know this Sam I'm supposed to remember, so maybe they can tell me more about him, and I can start to make sense of everything.

"What do you know about... *how* you were made?" Lala continues the questioning with a kind smile.

Her question makes me pause mid-chew, mouth full of meatloaf. I realize I've never given that much thought. I scan my brain. Huh. I swallow the food before answering, like Aunty taught us.

"I don't know. I just remember existing one day. They gave me enough access to her memory, so I'd have the skills I need for someone of my age. I've always known how to read, count, basic math. I even got some of her abilities too, like she's a really good singer."

Lala nods, but I can tell by her eyes that this only adds to the amount of questions she has. "When you get hurt... do you bleed?"

I remember the paper cut I got once during Etiquette, and the tiny drop of red that dripped onto my paper. I remember studying it curiously for the rest of the lesson. I nod.

Steele looks at me in wonder. "How is that possible?" she whispers.

"You don't know?" I just assumed adults knew everything.

Lala looks at Steele again, and it's interesting to me how they keep communicating with each other without talking. I wonder if one day Lucy and I will be able to do that.

"I don't want to upset you," Lala says softly. "But your...situation, you 'being made' from someone else...It's—well, it's never been done before. I didn't even know it was possible."

I blink at them. Does that mean the other Tyros and I were some kind of... experiment? The thought of that makes an awful feeling grow in deep in my chest, but I try really hard to keep from crying again. I swallow it down and force myself to breathe evenly through my nose.

"The other Ella... Ella-A, I mean," Steele asks hesitantly, carefully, like she's worried she'll make me cry again. "Is she okay?"

I think of Ella lying on her recovery bed, face pale and sunken. Voice hoarse. Aunty has always assured us they were just recovering, that eventually they'd get to be our partner. A teammate we would get to have for life. But now that I think about it, she doesn't look any more recovered now than she did in my earliest memories. If anything, she looks worse.

I gulp, considering not telling the truth. Will they think I'm hurting her? Will they think I'm more of a freak?

"I'm not sure," I answer as honestly as I can. "We have to sync every night, but she's not usually awake. Except the other night—" I stop myself.

"What happened the other night?"

"That's when she told me to remember Sam, that he could help us. But I'm not sure what she meant by that."

"Have you met Sam before?" Red asks, pausing his pacing to join the questioning.

I consider his question. I think of how my body reacted to hearing his name, how my body has been acting strangely, the feeling I've been having that there could possibly be some kind of disconnect between my mind and body.

"Maybe," I admit. "But I can't remember it, as much as I try."

"Did he see you here the day we got here?"

"He was here?" I ask, but my body already knows the answer to that somehow.

"We all came together. We were trying to rescue Ella," Steele answers, a bitter undertone in her voice for some reason. "He got away, we got caught. That's why we're in here."

"*Rescue*, Ella?" I whisper. I'm scared to know the answer. I'm scared to know the truth. It brings to mind the question I had earlier. What do they think I need help from?

Lala sighs and reaches for my hand through the bars. I take her hand and bite my lip to keep my eyes from welling up again. "Yes, my dear. Sam told us she had been kidnapped. Taken from him and brought here."

Kidnapped?

Aunty always made it seem like our doubles wanted to be here. That they came here because they wanted to for a better future. But I think of her just lying there on her recovery bed... who would want that?

Lala looks at me gravely. "We made a mistake to believe Vegas—your 'Aunty.' Don't trust her. If you help us, we can help you."

I'm startled by the sound of the outer door being pushed open and a pair of footsteps approaching. My heart starts pounding like I've just been caught doing something wrong. Was I doing something wrong to speak to these people? I feel more confused than ever.

The two women leap to their feet and lie on the bed in their room. I follow their lead and bring my dinner tray to the bed, hoping to make it before—

"Hello, darling."

It's the first time Aunty's voice has ever sent a chill down my spine.

12

———

NOT EXACTLY FORGIVENESS, BUT HEY I'LL TAKE IT

SAM

Cade directs Calix, Axel, and a few other men in the front row to survey the surrounding outskirts, assuring everyone else that everything is fine and to resume regular activities. Cade points sharply at Beardsley and me, demanding we follow him to his office.

"You know somethin' about this, Prettyboy?" Beardsley mutters gruffly as we shoulder through the crowd.

"The playing cards..." I keep my voice quiet from listening ears. "It's Vegas's calling card, remember?"

Beardsley's face is busy as he works it out in his mind, tucking the black gun into his waistband. Are they just handing those out like candy to every unhinged hillbilly here? "Well, I guess we pissed her off a little bit then, huh?"

"Guess so." I come to a stop. "Beardsley, listen, I—"

He puts up his hand to interrupt me, stopping a little way ahead, his face unreadable. "If it were up to me, I'd knock you cross-eyed and throw you to the roaches."

It's the kind of sentence that usually has a 'but' at the end of it, but he just stops there. I can't help but laugh. "Understood."

"Good."

"Good," I repeat. I try really hard to match his seriousness, but I'm unable to keep the laugh out of my voice, and I worry I'm going to ruin whatever progress he's made toward forgiving me. But I spy a tiny twitch of a smile at the corner of his lips, so I take it as a win and run with it, feeling a weight lift off my shoulders.

"Q and Ponyboy both insist I'm just being a stubborn jackass," he adds, folding his arms over his flannel jacket. "Seems they're both quite taken with ya."

"I mean I *am* the ultimate master of deceit, so how could they resist, right?"

He gives me a look as if he's considering ripping the pickaxe out of my hand and slicing me open with it after all. "Don't push it, boy."

I salute with mock formality. "Yes, sir."

Beardsley mutters expletives under his breath, and I know I'm testing every ounce of his patience, but I can't help it. He's given me a tiny inch, so I have to take the whole mile, I just have to.

"Despite my *very* adamant protests," he grumbles, "the boss has spoken. Says you're on my team now, and that I need to play nice."

"I really am sorry," I say genuinely, setting aside the goofiness. I hope he can see I mean it. "I never wanted to lie to anyone, but I had to, Beardsley. She's only 8-years-old. I'm all she has. Wouldn't you do the same for Ponyboy? Q?"

He doesn't answer the question, but he doesn't have to. I know he would. I see it every time he looks at them.

"Let's get this mess straightened out." He nods his head toward the direction of Cade's office, and I take that as a welcome end to the discussion.

All I can do now is prove it. I've said all I can say, and it's about actions now. Hopefully eventually he'll see I meant well all along. Helping to get Steele, Red, and Lala back to safety will be a good first step in the right direction. Maybe I can make a home here for Ella, after all. I feel a glimmer of hope at the thought, even as the smoking leftovers of Vegas's threat still billow around me.

Q, Luna, and Ponyboy are outside the Hall when we pass by. Other adults have joined them now and are helping to attend to the other children. I give Q a look, and she straightens, seeming to understand that I know something. She whispers something to Ponyboy, stroking his face and leaving him and Luna with the other children and adults. She mutters a command to Luna and she straightens with responsibility, going into protective mode over the children she's being left with.

Q jogs over and falls into step with me, raising an arched brow. "What happened?"

Beardsley steps into Cade's office-building, a rush of cool air replacing him. I whisper over my shoulder to Q from the doorway, "Playing cards around the bomb sites."

Her eyes widen. "Like as in…?"

I nod. "Guess that confirms they aren't friendly anymore, after all."

She's stunned. "But an act of *war*? That's another level."

I shrug and hold the door open for her so she can step into the building, the dizzyingly strong floral scent of her hair basically punching me in the face as she passes.

The atmosphere of the office is tense, and it makes me want to shrink into the corner. It feels exactly like how I imagine stepping into a principal's office would feel. Cade's ever cool demeanor melts off as he unfolds without everyone's eyes watching. He throws the playing cards at the wall, cursing loudly.

"Explain," he yells at the three of us, his face almost as red as his hair and beard. "What the hell is this all about?"

Q doesn't shrink under his anger. "We told you she was

deranged, Cade. Honestly, I'm surprised this is the first time she's ever tried anything."

"Plus, her Elites…" I add. "She's getting bolder as her numbers increase."

I shift uncomfortably at Cade's impaling gaze. "What?" His voice is lower in volume, but no less intimidating. It's like power is effortlessly laced into every timbre of his voice.

Q folds her arms across her chest when she meets my eye. She turns her head to Beardsley and Cade. "I would just like to state for the record that I already told him his plan was insane."

Suddenly Cade's office door is thrown open with a loud *clank,* causing me to nearly jump out of my skin. Calix storms in, his lips set in a grim line. He's breathing heavily. Axel pads in behind him, the glowing white of his LED eyes looking especially lethal as he stalks through the room in this defensive mode he's in. He sniffs around the entire room for potential threats.

"We can't find Liam anywhere," Calix says in between breaths. "As far as I can tell, he never came back."

Cade curses and overturns his desk chair. It rattles across the floor.

"Well dadgum, Cade," Beardsley bellows, and the three adults begin yelling unintelligible exclamations back and forth.

"Who is Liam," I whisper to Q as the adults argue, trying not to move my lips like a ventriloquist for fear of setting Cade off more. Seeing him unravel further and further when he seems to be usually so composed makes me feel off-center.

Q chews the side of her cheek the way she does when something is on her mind. "He was the messenger."

The messenger Cade sent to negotiate with Vegas.

Q was right.

This means war.

WHEN THE ADULTS finally take a breather from arguing, Calix moves across the room to straighten Cade's chair and gives me a second glance when he realizes for the first time that he doesn't know who I am. I think back proudly to when I nailed him with a paintball just last night, and he didn't even know I existed. But then it deflates as I remember what else happened at paintball.

I wave at him awkwardly with a flat smile. "I'm Sam. I'm new here."

He assesses me, with a serious but still kind face. The fun, carefree goofball from last night has morphed now into this definitely-not-free-from-cares man, but he still somehow remains patient and approachable. He and Cade really are opposites.

It makes me think about something Vegas said when she was holding a gun to my head.

You don't get to where I'm at by playing fair or playing nice.

Would Cade agree? What has *he* done to get to where he is? And Calix?

"Well, I sure missed a lot," Calix says, blowing out a breath. He sits on the edge of the desk.

Cade lowers himself into the righted chair and seems to be making a noticeable effort to stay calm.

"Forgive me. I have an unfortunate temper sometimes. Please—" he waves to the chairs in front of his desk. We all sit, though Beardsley plops down stiffly with arms folded like a tantruming toddler, apparently offended by something that was said. "—tell me anything that may be helpful. I'm struggling to understand what game my wife is playing at."

Q and I give him a broken and disorganized rundown of what we saw at E1—the following Vegas has recruited there, our predictions about her using them for some kind of rebellion, how she already seems to have 'eyes and ears everywhere.' Beardsley stays unhelpfully quiet.

"If she really pulls off an EI exodus…" I pause for emphasis. "All that extra manpower? She'd be unstoppable."

The two men look at each other. Calix looks skeptical, but I see the gears working on Cade. He's hearing me. He knows I'm right.

"If we intercept her, that manpower could be ours instead," I add, gaining enthusiasm, emboldened by the tiny seed of support I see growing on Cade's face. "Think of what we could do with the extra hands, how many people we could help, how many other Zones we could save people from. We could take back the entire Underground."

Cade meets my eyes, and I see it flicker there—he sees the potential.

Beardsley finally speaks up, giving me a side-eye. "Look, I ain't gettin' in the middle of no rebellion. I just want my team back."

Q calls him out across me with a teasing smirk. "*Now* you're suddenly backing down from a fight? What kind of Southerner are you?"

Beardsley narrows his eyes at Q, his drawl thickening with irritation. "One who ain't lookin' to get himself killed over some power struggle that ain't mine."

"Sounds to me like you're losing your edge in your old age, but what do I know?"

I can't help but chuckle being in the middle of them, knowing full well only Q can talk to Beardsley this way. If it were me, or anyone else for that matter, we'd be crying for mercy in seconds.

"While I did intend to keep things… civil… with my wife, it seems she's left me with no choice. I can't sit back after she put my people in blatant danger with this stupid light show, and this stunt she's pulling with Liam. And Sam's right," Cade says with his eyes closed, rubbing his temples, and I sit a little straighter at his approval. "If she actually manages to rally the Elites in E1, who knows what she'll do next."

Q fidgets with the threads from a rip in her jeans, her knee bouncing anxiously. It matches the anxiety I feel inside. I've been at war with Vegas all along, that's nothing new for me. She fired the first shot when she blackmailed Foster to abduct my sister, and since then I've been in the trenches of the battlefield. But let's be honest, I've never been a real player in the game. How could I be, up against someone like her? She knew she could do whatever she wanted, and an insignificant boy from C9 could never really stop her. I was only ever a "loose end" as she called it. She knows I have always been completely at her mercy, even if I have been too stubborn to admit it.

But now I have a powerful ally. Somehow who can actually equip me with the resources I need to oppose her, to save Ella, to maybe even save all those kids from whatever operation she's running.

But the fact that I can see that reality materializing in front of me like pixels taking shape, I feel a humbling anxiety about it, like maybe I've just been all talk all along. Do I really understand what this plan will mean? Am I prepared to set those consequences in motion?

This could tear the Underground apart limb from limb.

But I know I'll do it if it means getting Ella back.

Despite Cade's declaration, Calix still doesn't look convinced. "So, what, we're just supposed to slide into E1 and somehow get them lucid enough to organize a mass escape?"

"Not an escape," Cade replies slowly, as if he's still making the decision even as he says it aloud. "Not yet. As much as I'd like to retaliate after what she pulled this morning, we have to be smart. Start small. Begin by planting seeds and shifting their alliances, and we'll go from there in time."

I deflate a little at that. I don't have time for planting seeds. *Ella,* doesn't have time. I need gunpowder, not gardening soil.

Calix opens his mouth to ask more questions but is interrupted by the office door banging open again. Axel jumps to life at Cade's feet, crouching on his front legs and growling as the threat enters. But it's just Zara standing in the doorway, breathless, the outer lights illuminating her from behind like a halo.

"Your small friend told me I could find you here," she says, her face pinched with worried determination. "I just wanted to tell you I'll do it. I'll help you at E1."

13

SEDITION IS MY MIDDLE NAME. JUST DON'T TELL ANYBODY.

MATEO

"Are we sure about this?" I whisper to Rachel as we follow Amanda to the Nursery after dinner in the downtime we're allotted tonight before curfew.

Rachel walks a little stiffer but fortunately seems mostly okay after the Penalty. Talia stayed behind. She'll understandably need some time. But from what I've seen of Talia so far, I know this will be the ignition for her once she can see past her grief. She will not let Steven's death be for nothing, as Amanda put it. I gave Eddie the task of staying back with her and made him feel like he had the important task of taking care of her, but really, I just didn't want him to come. The less things he has to directly participate in, the less likely he'll be punished if we get caught. Plausible deniability, right?

"I talked to Jess," Rachel whispers back. "That's her best friend, from N-Quarters. She said the Guards were hiding out, trying to listen for any trouble, and they stumbled right into the trap. I believe her."

That makes my stomach clench a little bit with guilt, with how hard everyone was on her at lunch today. She has to feel terrible—I know I would—but we *did* trust her with that information... And whether it was directly her fault or not, you have to be so careful around here, everyone knows that. Steven's death could have been completely avoided.

The closer we get to the Nursery, the more frenzied my nerves get, like they're all hopped up on caffeine or something. This is the biggest risk we've taken so far. So much of this depends on the Elders not just turning around and reporting us to Nova right away, and *that* is all riding on what I say and how I say it. The problem is *I'm not good with words.* If Sam were here, he'd know just what to say. He was somehow so good with people without even trying.

But I'm all we've got, and for some reason Mayor Ramos thinks I can do this.

Amanda looks over her shoulder for confirmation as she approaches the entrance. Her face asks, *"Are you sure you want to do this?"* and I wish there were another way, so we could just call it off and go back to our rooms to prepare for curfew. But I know this is it.

So I nod. Parker nods. Trevor nods. Rachel nods. We all know this is our best shot.

Amanda steps up to the scanner at the entrance and waves her wristTab at it, pressing a few buttons to indicate that she has brought guests. It beeps, and the entrance swishes open, allowing us into the vestibule. The door closes behind us, and the vestibule swishes in a circle around us, scanning us for weapons and diseases before the main entrance opens and allows entry into the Nursery.

As we enter, I feel a wave of nostalgia wash over me, even though Eddie was already old enough to attend toddler lessons in the schoolhouse when we arrived to C9. The sweet smell of baby powder, the sounds of cooing babies, and even the cries... It all reminds me of when Eddie was a baby, of his room back at home. I suddenly feel a deep sadness that these babies don't have that. The love and comfort Eddie and I had as babies from a real home, a real mother. That's something you can't replicate, especially in a sterile room underground with a bunch of strangers.

The lights are relatively dim, but the huge room is brightly decorated. There are clear sections of the room. The vestibule spits us out nearest the play section that is sectioned off from the rest of the room by a circular gate. In it are a few babies crawling around on a colorful rug and cooing and laughing at each other, a young Zoner sitting cross-legged in the middle. There are toys scattered about the rug, and their happy playful noises brings a smile to my lips. How long has it been since I've heard a baby laugh?

We follow Amanda past the play area and toward the section with baby swings and cribs. It is darker in this corner of the room, and there is soft music playing as some babies are already asleep in their cribs.

Elders are everywhere, and most of them give us questioning looks as we pass, but others are too busy with the babies to even notice us. Some are overseeing the babies playing, some sit in rocking chairs in the far corner holding bottles to tiny mouths, and some gather in small groups, talking to one another softly. There are a few Zoners around, caring for their baby siblings in various ways. I picture Sam being one of these Zoners all those years ago when he and Ella arrived, and I smile at the thought.

Amanda brings us to the center of the room and stops. She gives us a tight-lipped smile. "Good luck. I'm so sorry again for everything." She waves and then heads over to a crib to pick up her baby sister who reaches for her with the cutest little chubby arms.

Everyone looks at me for guidance, and I feel a cold fear taking icy roots inside me. I look at the men and women around the room. These are the people we're entrusting everything with. They have the power to help us or to betray us.

"Maybe this was a bad idea," I whisper to the group, my already fragile confidence wavering completely now. There is too much at risk, too much that can go wrong.

"We're here," Parker says resolutely. "We need to at least try."

Rachel places a reassuring hand on my shoulder. "We're in this together."

Trevor nods to add his own reassurance in the mix. "How should we do this? Split up? Make an announcement?"

I look around the group, opening it up for their input, but before anyone can speak, we're interrupted by someone clearing their throat.

An Elder.

"Is there something you need?" he asks, his wrinkles stacked on top of each other in what looks to be a permanent grimace. He has a long Santa Claus-like beard, but his eyes lack the twinkle. I wish they twinkled. That would make this so much easier.

It's now or never.

"Yes, actually." I say, as confidently as I can. "I need an audience with the Elders. It's an emergency."

He cocks an eyebrow at me. "We don't get mixed up in Zone squabbles, son."

My jaw goes slack. "I'm sorry, *squabbles*...?" I look to Parker on my left to make sure that wasn't just some conjuring of my imagination. "Hold on." I shake my head in absolute disbelief. "By *squabbles* do you mean when innocent children get killed?"

I feel my temperature start to rise. Rachel puts her hand on my shoulder, but I don't stop. I can't. "Or no, surely you just mean when they're beaten to the point of unconsciousness? Mutilated by Zone surgeons and sold off to the highest bidder?"

By now I've gotten the attention of the rest of the room, including the group I came with. I hadn't gotten to that part of the story with them yet, so that's news to them too. The bearded man in front of me crosses his arms across his chest. "That's enough, boy, I think you need to leave."

More Elders have come in from the conjoined living quarters at the commotion. Well, looks like I got my audience. They're here for a show? Guess they'll get a show.

Just seeing them all gathered here in one place makes me even more mad. There has to be at least 20 Elders in this room alone, not counting any others who may be in their living quarters or out on various duties in the hospital, school, or kitchen. *Twenty* adults who choose to hide back here behind brick walls where they can pretend they can't hear the screams instead of doing something about it. Just think if even half of them had ever stood up to Chief? To Nova? All of the terrible things they could have stopped just by speaking up.

The thought boils my blood. "You all remember Sam and Ella, I assume, considering the years they spent here. I'm sure you heard about *their* little squabble. Oh, but did you know that Minors have been going missing here for weeks? Ella included." My arms get more animated the louder in volume I get, and they're nearly flailing at this point. "Well, turns out they've been undergoing an experimental surgery—*against their will*, I might add— because Doctor Coombs took a payout. Guess what happened to them?"

Even the babies seem to understand the gravity of what I'm saying, because the room is as silent as a graveyard.

I turn to the rest of the room. "Anyone have a guess? No? I'll tell you what happened. *They died.* Some as young as six years old."

Rachel gasps quietly, covering her mouth with her hands. "No, Zoe…"

I feel bad I didn't have the chance to tell them about this beforehand. I'd forgotten that they could have known those other children, the others that just disappeared without a trace, just like Ella.

The Elder in front of me moves to make me leave, but Parker and Trevor both step in his way, arms crossed. His face flashes with anger, but he doesn't say another word.

A woman holding a sleeping bundled baby speaks in a loud whisper from the crib area. "If this were true, why are we only now hearing about it and from a kid, no less?"

There are murmurs of agreement from around the room.

"And if you had heard about it elsewhere?" Rachel answers, her tone admirably level but reproachfully nonetheless. "You would've done something about it?"

The woman seems astonished she'd even suggest otherwise. "Of course we would have."

"Right, and when a fifteen-year-old boy was shot and killed right outside those doors, just a few hours ago?" I ask.

The silence is so thick I can nearly see it.

I scoff. "That's what I thought. Once we're less" —I wave around the room at the infants they're holding— "cute, and more... complicated... that's when our lives aren't worth saving anymore. That's when our deaths don't matter anymore, right? Because we're just annoying little teenagers with squabbles."

The bearded Elder fumes. They've all gotten too used to not being challenged like this in here. "It's not that simple. There are rules for a reason. There has to be order, there has to—"

I shake my head in disbelief. "You know what I see when I look at all of you here? So safe and comfortable, tucked away in your little rooms night after night? Sleeping so soundly after washing the blood off your hands and pretending it was never even there? You know what I see?" My voice is low, but it still carries. "I see a bunch of cowards. You can keep turning a blind eye to the suffering going on right under your noses, but they're coming for you too. Maybe then you'll care."

I gesture at my group, hands shaking with anger. "Come on guys, let's go. This was obviously a waste of time."

I walk back the way we came, shouldering through groups

of Elders that are scattered across the pathway out. I'm nearly to the exit when I stop. "We're getting the kids out before this place burns to the ground," I say over my shoulder before I step through the door. "If any of you have a *sliver* of dignity left, you'll at least not get in the way."

THE NEXT FOUR days are relentless. I've visited the Nursery building every night before curfew, hoping to talk to the Elders again, to attempt to soften my tone a little bit and follow up on our conversation... but they don't even let me in the building, which is really not a good sign.

I am so mad at myself for getting so heated. I feel like I messed everything up.

Now because of it, not only do I feel a pressing anxiety that one of the Elders will turn us in at any moment, Nova is also picking a new victim daily and punishing them mercilessly for the tiniest indiscretions, and we're still at half-pay for our functions—one of Chief's final parting gifts to the Zone. So in conclusion: I'm anxious, watching my back more than usual, starving most of the time, and guilt-ridden that I'm watching Eddie feel all of the same exact things. I know everything is really weighing on him hard, and I hate myself every time I hear his stomach growl.

For example, my function today has been Greenhouse Maintenance, and I've been assigned the task of weeding the vegetable planters. The greenhouses are right next to the school, so at lunch time, I finished up a little early so Eddie and I could walk together to formation. I snuck up behind him when his Subject released, to surprise him, but instead of the laugh I expected, he immediately burst into tears.

I hate what this place has done to him.

If there's anything better out there, and I still believe there *has to be*, I hope it's enough. I hope it's enough to put his bruised pieces back together the way they should be, and that one day I get the true Eddie back. The Eddie he'll hopefully have the freedom to be someday.

I glance at the time on my wristTab, and I'm relieved that functions are almost over. All this thinking isn't good for my general outlook on life, and the greenhouse is especially muggy today since there is an Irrigation Rain ongoing this afternoon. I finish spreading the compost in the freshly weeded planter I've been working on and pat the soil off my gloves. The other Zoners begin wrapping up their assignments too, and the air is already lightening up with every minute that ticks closer to quitting time.

I add my gloves to the stack by the door and prepare myself for the moisture that awaits as soon as I open the door, Zoners behind me doing the same. Irrigation Rain days are usually among my favorite days... in the summer. During the cold months, though, the cold rain-like water that falls from the upper shell at scheduled times in order to water their feeble attempts at greenery and experimental crops, just makes it even more miserable down here.

It's time, and it's like everyone does a group exhale to be off the clock.

I throw the greenhouse door open and power-walk over to the school. Small puddles from the rain splash under my boots as I march across the gravelly trail.

I look for Eddie among the children racing out of the school's exit. They laugh and play as they make their way out of the building and toward the Hall for dinner formation. I have to smile as I watch them, somehow mostly immune to the darkness all around them. Innocent, despite what they've had to witness in their short lives.

Watching their infectious happiness, for just this one small moment where nothing is going wrong, and they are allowed to just be children, it gives me a new motivation for what Ramos has tasked me with.

My childhood may be over— I don't have their innocence or child-like optimism. I've been too hardened by this gray suffocating underground hell, but they haven't yet. Like Eddie, there's still a chance for them, for all of them, to still have what remains of a real childhood if I can get them out. Assuming we don't all get lost underground and die horrible deaths of dehydration and/or starvation, of course.

No, if I can actually do this, figure out a way to get us out and then find the exit?

Many of them would be seeing sunshine for the very first time.

I want to give that to them.

My eyes burn at the thought. It may be impossible. But I have to at least try, or we're all going to die down here anyway. Might as well die trying.

I'm still looking for Eddie among the children, when a young boy I don't recognize comes up to me. His gray eyes match the gray of his uniform, his skin as pale as you'd expect for probably never seeing the sun. He steps way closer to me than I'd prefer, and I resist the natural urge to push him away.

"You're Teo, right? Eddie's brother? Is it true?" he whispers, gray eyes filled with awe.

I blink. "Is what true?"

"You're really going to get us out?"

My heart stops. How did word get out? How many people know? *Does Nova know?*

He seems to see the questions cross my face. He rushes to reassure me. "I'm Jess's brother," he adds, as if that's supposed to help.

Who?

Right. *Amanda's best friend.*

Amanda the *rat.*

My eyes widen with realization. My name is connected to Talia and Rachel now... it's only a matter of time before this gets back to Nova.

"Don't worry," he says, seeing the panic in my eyes. "I promise I won't say anything. I was just excited to meet you, that's all."

I move slowly, nearly paralyzed by the worry of what will happen to Eddie if Nova gets word of this. "Um, yeah. Well, I'm at least going to try."

"Cool." He smiles. "I want to help."

Eddie finds us. I sidestep the boy and steer Eddie away by the shoulder, nodding goodbye to the boy. "Sure, I'll keep you in mind if I need anything."

We walk to formation and Eddie gives me a look. "What was that about?"

"Just a sign it's time to expedite things," I whisper as we pass a group of Guards on the trail to the Hall. "We need to talk to Ramos again."

DINNER IS quiet among our group. Things have been tense after what happened to Steven and the Elders refusing to help. None of us are really sure what to do next, considering our sheer lack of resources and connections. Every plan we come up with still lands the same outcome — getting baked by the electric gates the second we try to leave. Without a way to get those off, we have no chance. And as far as I know, the only one who can turn those off is Nova and Ramos, and one of which is the actual spawn of Satan, and the other is inconveniently incarcerated. I have to talk to him again. We can't do anything without his help.

The bell signals our dismissal, and I say goodbye to the group. Eddie and I make our way over to Town Hall. I know we can't just go down to the holding cell in broad daylight and spill the whole can of beans in front of whichever Guard is on duty, but maybe we can at least get a message to Ramos.

We step into Town Hall, and I sigh as the warm air inside hugs me tightly like a heavy blanket. It's silent in here, apart from our own footsteps and maybe some Guards in different hallways on various assignments from Nova. We make our way down the hallway to Ramos's office and come to a stop.

There is a Guard posted in front of his office door.

His covered face turns in our direction as we approach. "What do you need?" he asks gruffly through the helmet.

"We need a word with the Mayor," I respond, hoping to look completely casual.

"He's not in," the Guard says simply.

"We'd like to set an appointment." I decide to take a risk. "We can manage if it's at an... alternate... location."

The Guard doesn't respond, and he's so still for a moment you'd think he's just a robot that ran out of charge. If I could see his face, I feel like I could get a much better feel of where his loyalties lie.

"Names?" he eventually replies, and I exhale in relief.

"Mateo and Eduardo Barrajo. Our schedule is pretty open. *Any time* works." Another risk. Did I really just imply right to a Guard's face that I'm willing to break curfew to meet with Ramos?

The Guard gives a curt nod. "I'll relay the message. Depart to your Quarters to prepare for curfew."

"Yes, sir," I say, and we scurry away, praying we won't regret this later.

⌁

It's not until the next afternoon during lunch when a Guard, I have no idea if it's the same one as before or not, discreetly drops a paper in my lap as he passes by my table. The group all leans in with curiosity, begging me to read it aloud.

I unfold the paper to reveal a ripped, handwritten note just like before. All it says is: *second function, same way*

My whole body relaxes. My conversation with the Guard. It worked.

"During the *day?*" Talia asks in bewilderment. Her and Rachel's wounds from the Penalty have already begun to scab over, but I know the biggest wound—Steven—will take much longer to heal. But she seems to be doing okay, all things considered.

I shrug. "I guess so."

"I can ask to go the bathroom, and then meet you—"

I interrupt Eddie before he can even complete the sentence about coming with me. "Nope. Solo mission this time, dude, sorry."

He slouches and grumbles under his breath something about *missing everything good.*

Luckily, I have Kitchen Support today. It's one of the functions with the most Zoners and the least supervision. It should be easy enough to sneak away for a few minutes.

I wave to the group in farewell as we split up for our various assignments, tell Eddie not to do anything stupid during his subject, and then I head through the doors into the kitchen area. Zoners are there already putting on aprons and rubber gloves to begin the huge task of washing all the dishes and trays from the very lunch we just ate. I say hello to a few Zoners, and even wash a couple dishes, so anyone monitoring security camera footage would see me doing exactly what I'm supposed to be doing. After a few minutes of being deliberately seen at my assigned function, I put my gloves down and dry my hands. I look around to make sure no one is watching before stepping out of the back door and past the dumpsters.

I walk across the Square to Town Hall briskly, but as casually as possible. My strategy is that hopefully if I walk with purpose and confidence, no one will question it. It was dark last time I came over here, but I think I remember a shed tucked away in the corner back near the hidden basement door. If any Guard questions why I'm lurking in the shadows over here, I can just say I'm grabbing extra lawn supplies from the shed.

So far no one is paying me much mind as I pass. The Zoners in front of Town Hall are too distracted with raking up leaves from the small trees that line the pathway up to the Hall. I avoid the main pathway, and instead approach from the side. From my quick look around, the closest Guards are across the Square near the Podium, and they are grouped together talking to each other.

With a breath of relief, I make it to the basement door, which is still covered with the leaves Eddie and I covered it with after leaving Ramos the other night. I kick them off with my boot and take one last look around before heaving up the wooden door. I cringe as its hinges groan and squeal, alerting anyone and everyone nearby that someone is opening it. It might as well have a neon arrow that lights up and a siren that goes off every time it's opened.

I step into the stuffy stairwell as quickly as I can and pull the door shut as I descend. Even in broad daylight, it's still completely dark down here. I light my way with the flashlight on my wristTab. I feel a tickle on my neck and smack it off so aggressively I will probably have a massive bruise in the morning. *It wasn't a spider. It wasn't a spider. It was not a spider.*

I walk carefully down the curved hallway, keeping my footsteps slow and quiet in case there is anyone untrustworthy down here. Luckily Mr. Allergies didn't join me this time, and I can just move as quietly as I want. There are footsteps from the level above my head, along with the normal aches and groans of the wooden building, but other than that it's completely quiet. I peek around the corner at the holding cell area. There is no Guard this time, but—

I freeze.

Ramos is sitting on the ground at the front of his cell, his head leaning against the bars, his head drooping at an unnatural angle. Is he...?

I rush over to him, dropping to my knees in front of him. His arm is limp as I grab it through the bars. His eyes are swollen shut, his entire face nearly completely purple and red with a collage of bruises and cuts. I can't tell if he's even breathing.

I tap his cheek. "Mayor Ramos?" *Tap, tap.* Please be alive, please be alive. "Mayor Ramos, are you okay? It's me, Teo."

I shake his shoulder, but he doesn't react, his head still drooping against the bars.

I leap to my feet and pace back and forth in front of the cell. *What do I do, what do I do?* I can't just leave him here, but is there even anyone I can tell? Are there any other adults here I can trust? My heartbeats feel like thunder in my ears as my pacing turns into full panic mode.

"Mateo?"

I stop, my head whipping around at the sound. It's him, he's moving. *Oh, thank God.* I kneel in front of him again, grabbing his hand and squeezing it.

"Mayor Ramos, what happened? Are you alright?"

His left eye doesn't open at all, it's so swollen, but he looks at me through the tiny slit of his right eye, his blinks slow. "Why? Is there something on my face?"

I bark out a single disbelieving laugh.

"Right," Ramos says with a groan as he tries to stretch out. "Everyone keeps reminding me I'm not funny, but I have yet to get the message."

"Did Nova do this to you?"

He doesn't answer. Instead, he grabs the bars of the cell

with both hands and moves like he's going to pull himself up from the floor. I crouch to help, pulling up under his elbows. He winces as he heaves himself up to his feet. He stumbles backward to sit on the wooden shelf of a bed.

"I spoke to the Elders," I say. "They didn't want to get involved. You were right."

Ramos hisses through his teeth, massaging the back of his neck. "I didn't want to be right. Selfish bastards."

"So what do we do?"

Ramos leans his head back against the wall with a wince and takes a deep breath. "I was able to get Sam out by turning off the electric gates just long enough for him to pass through."

I nod, encouragingly. So this means he has a plan, right?

"The gates require a unique code and authorized fingerprint to disarm. Chief and two other Guards had their own codes, but they were... *taken care of,* shall we say, while I was investigating Ella's disappearance. My guess is the FPA remotely created a short gap in the gates to get Nova in as soon as possible, but I doubt they've had time to get her fingerprints programmed in yet. It'll take time before they can send someone out to do that. So that means the only person who can disarm the gates in this Zone is me."

"And you're here," I say slowly, my brain whirring as if this is a riddle or puzzle, trying to figure out the solution or the pattern, but I'm not seeing one.

"And I'm here," Ramos repeats. He shuts his eyes and begins to mutter to himself, thinking aloud. "Maybe we can time an escape just right with a delivery gap. Should be one any day now. No... there's no way all of you could get out in time before it closes itself... Too risk—"

"Did your contact say how long we have before the other guys get here?" I interrupt his train of thought.

He doesn't answer for a while, and that terrifies me. "You're not going to like it," he finally replies, turning his head on the wall to look at me through his one slitted eye.

I steady myself by grabbing onto the bars of the cell. "Just lay it on me."

"My source says no more than two days."

I press my forehead into the cool metal bars of Ramos's cell, trying to stay calm.

Two days.

That's it.

Two days to solve an equation that actually has no solution.

"So what do we do?" I ask, trying to take controlled breaths in and out.

Ramos scratches his head, and I can tell he's formulating. That gives me at least a little hope. "How do you feel about breaking and entering?"

"I mean, can't be worse than sedition and treason," I joke, but saying the words out loud sends a shiver down my spine. Two crimes punishable by death.

He nods, and a slight smile quirks at the corner of his busted lip. "Right." He pushes himself off the wooden bed with extreme effort to stand in front of me through the bars. "In my office, I have a spare key to this cell that I doubt Nova has found yet."

I feel a glimmer of hope. "Okay. Yes, right. If I can get you out of here, you can disarm the gates."

"In theory," he says, biting his cheek in a way that's really not very reassuring. "They could have terminated my authorization code already since I'm under investigation."

The realization of what this means feels like a vise closing in on my lungs. "So we could get supplies gathered, get everyone all ready to go, we could take care of Nova and the Guards, we could bust you out... and we still might not even be able to get through the gates."

Ramos presses his lips together. "Yes. That's a possibility."

Well, at least he's honest. There is a beat of silence as I process this. Is it even worth it to try, considering the risks? Putting so many people in danger on a *maybe?* I hate these odds. I hate that I have to make this decision. I hate that there is so much depending on *me.*

He must see the overwhelm taking over. He steps closer, putting a hand on my shoulder. "You don't have to do this, you know. I know this is a lot."

I look at him, staring into his one open eye, seeing a genuine concern there. I already made my decision; it just still feels heavy sometimes. "The alternative is waiting around for my turn to die. For Eddie's. I'm no longer okay with that."

Ramos smiles sadly. "I'm sorry, son. Tonight, the Guards on night patrol will change shifts at 11:00pm. There is usually a gap of about four to five minutes. If you time it right, you can slip across the Zone and get into my office while they're switching out."

"I'll try."

"Don't come back here until I send word. We will have to time it just right, so Nova doesn't have time to retaliate. Make a plan for how you'll get everyone in one place, maybe start setting supplies aside if you can, and then wait for my word."

All I can manage to do is nod.

"You should get going," he says with a wave toward the secret exit. "Nova will be back soon to continue my...'investigation.'"

"What is she trying to get out of you?"

He sighs. "Information. She knows I killed Doctor Coombs and Sergeant Hallows and wants to know who I'm working for. Her patience is wearing thin, though. I don't think I have much time left on her watch."

"Do you have two days?"

"I think so," he replies.

"Well, I'll do my best to hurry."

He grabs his suit jacket that is crumpled on the ground in the corner. He digs through the pockets and pulls out a pen and a small scrap of paper that looks like it used to be a full page, but pieces of it have been ripped off little by little. He scribbles something down on the paper.

"The code to my office." He hands it to me. "Be careful, Mateo. Keep your head. Don't trust anyone."

I thank him, say my goodbyes, and head back the way I came, looking over the scrap of paper and committing it to memory in case I lose it. I cringe at the time on my wristTab. I spent far too long here. Hopefully no one has noticed I'm gone.

I push open the basement door just a crack, peeking out and making sure it's clear before climbing out, squinting from the change in brightness, though the overhead lights have started to cool and dim as the afternoon gets later. I leave Town Hall and jog back to the dumpsters and through the back door I came from. I turn the corner into the kitchen and freeze at what awaits me there.

It's Nova and a group of Guards.

"There he is. Grab him!"

TYRO B-29

The guard standing next to Aunty unlocks my barred door with a key from his hip and gestures me out. I follow wordlessly, glancing back to the three adults behind me. Steele gives me a nod so imperceptible I almost don't notice it myself.

The pressure building on top of my chest is almost unbearable.

"Don't trust her," they had said.

This is my home. Aunty takes care of us. She loves us. I'm supposed to risk everything I've ever known blindly? Trust the word of a stranger? Help them somehow when I can't even guarantee I'll remember this conversation tomorrow?

I follow Aunty and the guard out of the cell room. The hallway is brighter, and it hurts my eyes. They lead me to a different room next door that simply contains a plain bare table, with two chairs on each side. The guard gestures for me to sit, and he and Aunty both do so, lowering down into the chairs on the other side of the table across from me.

Aunty smiles at me, but it doesn't send its usual warmth through my body. I'm confused by that.

"I'm sorry for the dramatics, my dear. I'm sure you are so overwhelmed."

I wring my hands in my lap. I'm scared to even open my mouth, for fear of what might come out. Vomit, secrets. My body has been acting strange lately, so who knows what it could say against my will?

"Do you have anything to tell me, sweetheart?" Aunty's eyes evaluate me, their brown so deep I feel I might fall in and drown.

There are so many things I should tell her. That Ella spoke to me. She told me we needed help. The three new friends in the barred rooms next to mine, and what they told me.

Kidnapped.

My hands feel nearly raw from how hard I am wringing them.

I know exactly what I need to tell her, so why won't my mouth open and tell her? I have to say *something*. Maybe I don't have to tell her everything, just enough of the truth to get those imploring brown eyes off of me. I decide on something she might already know.

I drop my eyes, trying to convey regret, although I'm not really sure yet if I even regret it. "I flushed my reds and blues down the toilet this morning. The ones you found under my pillow were from yesterday. I'm sorry. I don't know why I did it."

Aunty's eyes never leave my face. "Thank you for your honesty, Ella. I'd like to have the doctor check your vitals before you sync up tonight."

I keep my eyes down.

"Feeling curious about boundaries and rules is completely normal at your age." She reaches out for my hand across the table. I take it, hoping to feel that familiar safety and comfort I always feel at her touch, which would confirm what I believe in my heart, that she loves us. She loves me. That would finally resolve these confusing feelings, and I'd know that the people in the other room were lying.

She squeezes my hand.

And all I feel is cold. I try not to cry, but it feels like I've lost the only person who loves me. Or at least I thought she did.

"Rules are meant to be followed, Ella. I've decided to give you another chance, because I believe you want to be here. I believe deep down you're grateful for this life I've given you."

The coldness spreads. Why is it so cold?

"The life I've given you, that I can just as easily take away. Is that what you want?"

I meet her eyes, and where I've always seen warmth before, there is now only that same coldness. Have I just been seeing her through some kind of lens? Has this been her all along? Or am I allowing the other three to alter my perception of her, to plant these seeds of doubt?

I shake my head, knowing she's expecting a response. "No, Aunty. I'm so sorry. It won't happen again."

She squeezes my hand again and stands. "Oh, I'm so glad to hear it. Let's go make sure you aren't experiencing any adverse side-effects from skipping your capsules again."

The walk to the doctor feels like a blur, like everything is speeding around me, but I'm stuck in slow motion.

How do I know what to believe? My body, my inherited instincts, seem to not trust Aunty. Lala, Steele, and Red also told me not to trust her. But *my* mind, my own made memories and recollection, my *heart*, is telling me this is my home and I'm safe. Nothing from my own experiences has ever indicated otherwise. How do I know what to do? Will I ever know for sure?

The doctor sits me down on the same bed I was just lying in yesterday and puts a cuff around my forearm that squeezes it uncomfortably. He asks me questions about my general state, which I do my best to answer the way I think he wants, to which Aunty nods approvingly. He snaps a pair of gloves onto his hands, and it's like I'm snapped into a different reality. A memory.

I'm lying in a hospital bed, much like this one. My left wrist and both of my ankles are held down by leather straps, keeping me from being able to move. I feel scared. A doctor with deep wrinkles stands above me, and I feel a strange sense of betrayal when I look at him. He is holding my right wrist, examining my cuff and taking measurements on my arm and palm. When he turns around to gather his instruments, I desperately try to use my free hand to undo the strap at my left wrist. It's too tight.

The doctor returns with a tray of instruments, and he pulls on a pair of latex gloves with a snap. He picks up a syringe with a needle and gives it a flick.

I begin to cry as he takes my hand again.

"Please, Dr. Coombs," I find myself saying, begging. "Let me go. I want to see my brother. Please."

The doctor doesn't respond, only inserts the needle into a vein on my arm.

Everything goes black within seconds, but the memory continues holding me hostage.

When I come to in the memory, I'm in the back of some kind of vehicle. It's dark. There is something over my mouth that keeps my lips from being able to open. Tape, maybe. My hands are bound together. My wrist is sore, a throbbing pain that aches all the way up my arm.

The vehicle comes to a stop next to a building. The driver steps out and talks to a group waiting by the building. There are dim lights illuminating the alleyway, but the figures remain mostly shadowed. Except for the unmistakable image of a woman standing in the center, doling out instructions with the wave of a hand.

Aunty.

Her voice pulls me out of the memory, and I'm back on the hospital bed.

"Well, looks like we're all good to go," she says sweetly. "I don't suspect we'll have any more issues. Will we, dear?"

I shake my head. I rub my wrist above my own cuff, convinced I can still feel the phantom throbbing from the memory.

They were right.

I was kidnapped. I mean, *she*. She was kidnapped. Ella didn't choose to be here at all. She didn't choose me.

Her image, pale and sunken, lying on the bed in the data room.

I've just been sucking the life out of her this whole time. I feel sick.

"I have to use the restroom," I manage to choke out.

"Of course, dear," Aunty says with a smile, gesturing to the door. "Your friends are still at dinner. I'll send an escort to bring you to this evening's sync. You may go."

I run down the hallway to the nearest restroom, throwing open the stall door with a *crash*. I barely make it to the toilet in time before vomiting.

"I'M SO SORRY," Lucy says, eyes wide, when I join her, Amber, and Katie at the table. "I had to tell them. I was just so worried about you."

"Huh?" I blink at her. I have absolutely no appetite for the tray of food in front of me, but I don't want them to worry, so I try to nibble on it.

Lucy cocks her head, as if confused that I'm confused. She answers slowly. "I saw you put your reds and blues under your pillow, and then when you passed out, I got so scared. I had to tell someone."

"Oh," I say, numbly, not sure how to process the betrayal. My mind is too distracted with other things to think through the proper reaction to Lucy's revelation. I have too many other things to worry about.

Like the sync tonight.

I still can't figure out why I would have risked everything to skip it. I know the dangers of skipping a sync. I know my body will slowly shut down if I don't sync with Ella, so why would I have risked that?

Maybe she told me not to do it for some reason, or maybe it was an instinct buried deep down, a warning of some kind. Maybe the syncs do more than just recharge me physically. I know I always feel much more clear-headed after a sync. Maybe it wipes away any mental excess, too, like those random memories and emotions that slip through sometimes.

Which of these memories and emotions will the sync deem as excess? Will it make me forget all of them? Truth be told, I don't like feeling this way. I hate these questions, I hate these doubts and fears. I miss my old normal. Waking up under the same view every morning, going through the same routine every day, the same... feelings... every... day...

But can I even consider that reality if there are memories and experiences I *could* have access to, but they are being held from my brain for some reason? Shaved off like waste with every sync? Why only give us select memories? Why only give us a fraction of what it means to be human?

Like the memory of Ella and that doctor... her pain and fear and worry as she waited in the car. I hate feeling those emotions, I hate feeling her fear, but am I really living if I don't?

Do I want to go back to my fabricated, but comfortable, existence?

I watch Lucy and Katie talking to each other. They laugh at a joke I didn't hear the punchline to. They are completely carefree. No heavy fear, or responsibility, or confusion to have to shoulder. They're just happy.

I clear my throat. They look at me.

"If you knew you weren't really free," I begin quietly, not sure if they can even hear me. "I mean, if you knew you could be *more* free, but it would mean your whole life would change. Would you do it?"

They look at each other. Amber laughs uncomfortably. None of them answer me for a long while.

"Why would I want my life to change? I have everything I need and want here," Lucy finally answers with a certain nod. "Ella, are you sure you're ok? Do you want me to call the—"

"No," I say quickly. "I'm okay. I'll see you guys later."

I stand, taking my still-full dinner tray over to the trash can to dump it.

I decide I can't live like them anymore. Not after what I've seen. Not after knowing what I know.

They want us to believe we have everything we need. But it's not real. None of this is real. And our doubles are paying for our fake existences against their will. *Kidnapped.*

I need to do something. If I don't, who will?

I can't sync up tonight. I can't risk forgetting what I know.

So I have to do something about it, and it has to be now.

14

HOW AM I THE ONE GIVING LIFE ADVICE, WHEN MY OWN LIFE IS A DUMPSTER FIRE?

SAM

I shift uncomfortably in the stiff hospital bed, my empty stomach churning but not from hunger.

Luna senses my nerves and rests her head on my lap, her tongue lolling out of her mouth and drool dripping onto the paper-thin blanket. I pet her head gratefully, glad Q let her be here while we wait.

Q sits in the chair next to the bed and gives me a squeamish look that is really not very reassuring. "You gonna be okay?"

I finger the metal of my wristTab, goosebumps popping up across my arms as I remember the jagged scar Red showed me. "It is what it is, I guess."

It was me who had made the realization in Cade's office. The realization that I couldn't go back to E1 with my wristTab, knowing I could be taken from my consciousness at any time. I'd be a danger to the whole team. A liability. Zara too.

And sure, the plan could go on without us, but I'd have to stay behind like a helpless child while my friends go into the battlefield without me? No way.

So, it was me who asked if it could be removed. Like Red's. After a walkie-talkie call to one of the surgeons in the medical building, the plan was set in motion: I'd get it removed. And to my surprise, Zara asked for hers off too. I felt a camaraderie with her in the decision, the nervous resolve almost like an unspoken pact between the two of us. We are shedding off our Zones once and for all.

But now that I'm actually sitting here, waiting for the surgeon to arrive, even with Zara sitting in the bay next door waiting for the exact same thing, I feel the nerves big time. I remember the dull throb I felt for days after Dr. Coombs' procedure to insert the scrambler—and I guess it worked because the FPA hasn't found me yet— but it still sucked. And that was just an insertion. I can only imagine what's in store from a full removal.

I plaster on a devious smile for Q, hoping I can at least lighten the mood to distract me from the nerves. "Admit it, you'd miss me so much if I bled out."

She sighs over-dramatically. "What will I ever do without you? Who will I demolish in paintball when you're gone?"

I feel a pang in my gut, the humiliation of that almost-kiss still too fresh to joke about. My smile falters, and I laugh half-heartedly, any sarcastic comebacks I may have had completely drying up on my tongue.

Q blinks at me with a strange look and opens her mouth like she's going to say something but clamps it shut when the surgeon walks in. Q takes Luna by the collar and steps out of his way, trading places with him, so she's at the exit.

"Well, I'm gonna go check on Zara, make sure she's ok. Good luck." She still has that look like she wants to say more, but she just turns and leaves, taking Luna with her next door.

I barely notice as the surgeon takes my vitals and hooks me up to various machines. All I can think about is that almost-kiss and how nothing this surgeon can do to me will cut me apart like that did.

~

THE SOUND of Zara's screams is the first thing I register when I come to consciousness.

The second thing is the teeth-clenching agony throbbing in my wrist.

Fogged up by a haze of anesthesia and the near darkness of the hospital room, I fumble with the cords and monitors that are hooked up to me, trying to rip them off with shaking hands, Zara's screams piercing through the darkness.

I try to call out to her, but my tongue feels thick in my mouth, her name coming out more like a gurgle. I finally get the last cord off me, causing the closest monitor to yell at me with shrill beeps. I slide off the bed but nearly fall straight to my knees, like the bones in my legs have been replaced with play-doh.

She's still screaming.

I reach for things around me for support as I stumble across the floor causing several stands to knock over with a crash. My bare feet are cold on the floor, that chilly shock causing some of the fog to lessen. Like a baby deer I finally make it over to Zara's bay next door. Her eyes are closed, but she's screaming and thrashing in the hospital bed. It's hard to tell if she's conscious or not. Am I? This could definitely be a dream, and I wouldn't question it.

I stumble to her bedside, nearly getting hit by her thrashing arms. I take one of her hands, trying to gently wake her up, let her know she's not alone, but her screams are so loud and shrill it makes my eardrums ache.

My knees shake as her screams take me back to a memory I wish I could forget, to the last time I was this useless against screams like this. In an instant I'm that helpless little boy again, holding my mom's hand as I let her die right in front of me.

I try to shake the image away, but it holds, only getting

stronger as Zara's screams continue. Footsteps rush in all around me, and the doctors begin talking at once, looking over her, trying to get her to calm down. It's all starting to blur together, the memory of my mom morphing into the reality in front of me.

It sounds like Zara suddenly chokes on her scream. She gasps, and her eyes fly open. She grabs my hand tightly, her eyes bloodshot and wild.

"Sam," she gasps. Then her voice grows more hysterical. "I remember Sam, I remember!" She thrashes in the bed, repeating it over and over until it's a scream. "We have to tell Q, we have to—"

She is cut off as the doctor stabs a syringe into her arm, her head slumping forward as she loses consciousness. Her words repeat in my brain like an echo, the fog returning, my eyelids falling. I look down at my own arm, seeing the doctor's syringe sticking out just before everything fades to black.

I RETURN to consciousness back in my own hospital bed, all the sounds around me back to a quiet normal. The hum of the generators outside, the steady rhythmic beeping of the monitors. It's so normal it's making me doubt if last night even happened. My eyelids feel like mud as I force them open, trying to sort through what was real and what was an anesthesia-fueled dream. There is a medic looking over my chart, but otherwise the room is empty. I feel a small stab to the chest that Q isn't here. I know if it were reversed, I never would have left her side. Although I don't blame her, considering we're still basically strangers, it stings every time she reminds me that the depth of our friendship is unbalanced, like a seesaw. I've fallen into the friendship way deeper than she has, which is okay, but it still sucks sometimes.

I turn my wrist over to look at the time, expecting by habit to see the LED screen of my wristTab shining up at me, but I blink at the thick white bandages encircling my whole wrist there instead. I hold up my wrist in awe. Could it really be gone? After all these years, it's really just off? It almost feels like I should have sent it off with a better goodbye. It was basically a part of my body after all.

Well, good riddance.

I clench and unclench my hand, noticing that the excruciating pain from last night has lessened to a dull ache.

Last night.

Zara.

I clear my throat, and the medic finally notices I'm awake. She sets down my chart and comes over to check my vitals.

"How are you feeling?" she asks, pressing a stethoscope to my chest.

"Surprisingly fine," I answer, taking a breath as she listens to my lungs.

"Good, so the vicocet has kicked in." She reads my blood pressure as her cuff tightens on my non-bandaged forearm.

"Is Zara okay?"

She is counting to herself and doesn't answer right away. "Hm?"

"Zara," I repeat. "She was screaming last night. Is she okay?"

Maybe now I can try to sort through what was real and what wasn't. I remember the screaming. So much screaming. I remember her grabbing my hand and telling me something. What did she say?

"Oh, she's been fine since we brought out the big guns," she explains, picking up a syringe next to me and flicking it for effect. "Everyone tolerates pain differently, and some people just need a little extra. Especially with her body going through withdrawal right now, I think her whole system just went into shock."

I think of her thrashing on the bed, like she was possessed or something. Her eyes bloodshot. Her screams so shrill.

Didn't seem like shock to me, but I guess I'm no medical professional.

I remember. I remember, she had said. Didn't she? Remember what?

"Can I see her?"

She sets a tray of food on my lap. "Unfortunately, I was given strict orders to fill you up, so you can head out for a field assignment. I'm of the opinion that you both need to rest the remainder of the day, but, hey, boss's orders."

That sends a shiver down my spine. It's happening. And it's happening now.

She holds up a small plastic bottle of white pills and gives it a shake. "Extra vicocet. Stay on top of it over the next few days to manage your pain. No more than one pill every twelve hours. Any more than that will knock you out within minutes."

I thank her. She sets it on the small table next to me and leaves me to my thoughts. I attempt to eat, but I can barely taste any of it, anxiety itching at the back of my throat and making everything taste like mush. The reality of how messy this is going to get is settling in on me, making my heartbeat quicken.

Before Zara, the thought of using the Elites in E1 for my own purposes would have never bothered me. I never would've even thought twice about it. But the more I learn about E1, the more I see it for the gilded cage it really is. Pretty on the outside but still a cage, nonetheless.

And here I am, willing to just thrust them into the crosshairs of a fight they know nothing about, for a conflict that really doesn't even affect them. Regardless of how "slow" Cade wants to take it, we're still using them like pawns.

How many Elites am I willing to sacrifice to stop Vegas?

How many Zara's will I throw into the fire to get Ella back?

I know my answer. I know I'd throw every single one of them in the fire if it were between them or her.

I shudder. I know war is ugly. I just never thought it would feel so personal.

When did I suddenly grow this conscience? Caring about Elites? Who am I?

I force a few more bites of food into my mouth, chugging the water bottle the medic left in a few gulps before sliding off the hospital bed and padding over quietly to Zara's bay, careful to avoid any medics who may insist I return to my bed and rest while I can.

I peek around the corner into her room and see her doodling on the bandages around her wrist, covering nearly every inch with colorful flowers and swirls, her tray of food basically untouched too.

"Hey," I say, and she startles at the sound of my voice, the marker in her hand clattering to the floor. "Sorry."

"No, it's fine." She blows out a breath with a laugh, her hand on her heart in relief that I'm not a serial killer or one-eyed monster. "I'm just a little jumpy from the painkillers. They said an increase in anxiety is a possible side-effect. Love that for me."

I guess that explains my own anxiousness. I bend down to pick up her marker and hand it to her.

"You feeling better after last night? Got kinda rough there for a minute."

Her eyebrows knit together in confusion. "What do you mean?"

I stare at her. "You... were screaming. Like a lot."

This really isn't helping me sort through what's real and what's not real. I remember the screams, though. Don't I?

Her eyes widen. "I was?"

"Yeah... and you said you remembered. You just kept repeating it. You don't remember any of that?"

She looks away, a busy expression clouding her face, no doubt also trying to untangle things in her mind like I am. "What did I say I remembered? Was it from day I came here?"

"That's what I was hoping you knew. You passed out before you could say. I think. I don't know, it's all cloudy for me too."

She lets out a groan and runs a hand through her long hair, the colorful markers slipping from her grasp as she leans back against the pillows. "I wish I could remember. It's all still so patchy. Every time I think I've almost filled in the blanks, like it's on the very edge of my brain, it just blinks away."

"Are you sure you want to go back there?" I ask hesitantly, knowing that asking is the right thing to do but still scared to hear her answer. I'm relying on her so much to say yes.

She sighs. "I'm hoping going back will help jog my memory. Like retracing my steps almost. It's just so unsettling having such a big gap. It just makes me feel...unwhole."

I hold up my bandaged wrist. "Hey, at least we're officially not prisoners anymore. That's a plus."

She chuckles. "And yet here we are, handing them the key and stepping right back in."

A quiet second passes, but it's an easy quiet, it's a quiet without pressure to fill it. She hands me one of the markers, and I help her fill up the white space on her bandage. The scent of the marker sends a strange wave of nostalgia over me. I notice she's still wearing Red's bracelet I gave her on her other wrist.

"You must be so worried about her," she murmurs, breaking the silence as I doodle a lightning bolt on her wrist. "Your sister."

I lower my eyes, remembering what I admitted to myself just a few minutes ago, about sacrificing her and the other Elites for Ella.

"I always wanted a sibling." She draws a swirling pattern with the blue marker. "But I guess I'm kind of lucky I'm only responsible for myself down here. You must feel so much pressure."

I've never allowed myself to feel like caring for Ella was a burden. Because it's not, even still. Even as I risk everything to save her when she doesn't want saving. The responsibility *is* a constant pressure, though. It's a weight I'd carry even if it crushed me, but yeah, it's heavy. Zara's acknowledgement of that makes it feel a little lighter somehow.

"I promised my parents I'd take care of her," I reply simply, not bothering to relay the whole train of thought my mind just went down.

"I know desperate times call for desperate measures, or whatever, but you're just a kid, too. They shouldn't have put that on you. She's their child to take care of."

"I mean they kind of had no choice," I protest, not sure why I'm feeling defensive over people who are long gone. "They didn't know this is how everything was going to end up."

"Every adult had a part to play in what was done to us," she says, out of characteristically bitter. "Whether they contributed actively or not. They made the world this way and then threw us into it to fend for ourselves."

I feel a surge of anger at the truth in her words.

She's right. We're just kids, forced to navigate a nightmare of a world created by the adults who failed us. The world crumbled around us, and we were left to pick up the shattered pieces of our existence, forced into roles we never asked for.

Zara's eyes soften, seeming to see the war going on in my thoughts. "You're a good guy, Sam. Not everyone would go to these lengths for someone else."

I give her a tight smile. "Thanks. Hey, maybe one day we'll be able to have a conversation outside of this hospital room."

As if on cue, the medics return and don't bother making me go back to my own room. They give us the discharge information together, explaining the process for our recovery, handing

Zara her own bottle of pills, and a reminder to take it easy and stay hydrated.

Right, that's totally my priority right now, taking it easy.

My head still feels a little cloudy from the painkillers as we amble out of the medical building to the bustle of morning errands. People are loading boxes into trucks, sweeping out perma-tents, hanging up laundry, cleaning windows. I spot Q and Luna by the familiar white truck with mismatched camper shell, and I feel that annoying sting at the back of my neck again at the sight of her. But Luna perks up when she sees us approach, and it makes every negative feeling fade away quickly.

She bounds toward me, ears flopping as she runs. I drop to my knees, and she nearly knocks me over, unknowingly whacking my sore wrist with her vigorous tail. She puts her front legs up on my shoulders and licks my face.

"There's my good girl." I laugh but then promptly lock my jaw before she can lick straight in my mouth.

"Oh, she's adorable," Zara coos admiringly but from a noticeably tongue-free distance.

Luna bounces next to me as I follow Zara to the back of the truck where Q is stocking it with supplies.

"Hey," Q says breathlessly as we approach. Her hair is pulled up out of her face in a twist, and she's wearing a plain gray sweatshirt. Her goggles are hanging out of her back pocket, and it sends a nostalgic wave over me, even though it was only a few days ago when we were sitting by the campfire talking about her goggles after that night with the bounty hunters.

She sets a box in the bed of the truck and slides it under the camper shell. "How are you guys feeling?"

Zara shakes her orange bottle with a grin. "I feel better than I have for days."

I snort. "Same. It's weird not having the FPA spying on me at all times, though. Kinda lonely actually."

Q smirks and slides in another box. "Welcome to off-the-grid life." She dusts off her hands and meets my eye. "I'm really sorry I didn't get in there sooner to check on you guys. Ponyboy is... having a moment, so Beardsley has been trying to talk him down, and I've had to load the truck myself. Cade wants us to head out as soon as possible."

"Is Ponyboy okay?" I ask as I step in to help loading the boxes, which are heavier than I expected, but I try not to let that show on my face.

Q sighs. "He's taking it really hard that he won't be coming on this one." She looks at me. "He really wants to help save your sister. Well, and Lala, Red, and Steele. We've told him it's too dangerous."

That sends a tender jab to the heart. His precious innocence, totally unaware of the dangers at hand, and yet completely willing to sacrifice his own safety to help Ella anyway. I can't wait for them to meet each other. "Would it help if I talk to him?"

"Maybe." She chews on the side of her cheek. "I hate seeing him so upset. He wouldn't listen to me."

I'm sure there won't be anything I can say that hasn't already been said, but maybe I can help somehow. I can at least try. She sends me to the living quarters I've shared with Ponyboy the last few days, apart from my hospital getaway last night. Zara and Q stay to finish loading up the truck.

I step into the building, surprised to see the lights on. I've never been in here midday, so I had no idea there were even lights here. Beardsley and Ponyboy are tucked away near the back where my cot is nestled by Ponyboy's, the rest of the cots uncharacteristically empty.

Ponyboy is wailing and thrashing his arms around furiously. I smile as I see Beardsley sitting patiently on the cot next to his, whispering reassurances as he cries. He puts up a hard front, but he's really a softie on the inside.

Then again, Ponyboy can bring that side out of anyone. He won me over in a matter of minutes after all, even despite my hands and ankles being zip-tied together, with me watching helplessly from afar as he messed up all the controls of my magboard. He's just adorable and usually so contagiously happy, how could you not love him immediately?

He sees me coming, and his wails increase in volume. Beardsley actually looks relieved to see me, and I wonder how long he's been here trying to talk him down.

"Hey, bud," I say gently, sitting next to Ponyboy on his cot. He looks up at me with huge crocodile tears sliding down his cheeks.

Beardsley stands and pats him on the back. "I gotta go help Q with the truck Pony, I'll see ya back in a couple days. You listen good for Miss Jennifer while we're gone, y'hear?"

That warrants another guttural wail, so loudly you'd think he was being impaled. "I want to come!" He punctuates the yell by hitting the cot with tiny fists. Beardsley gives me a flat-lipped *"good luck"* smile and that old man leaves the building quicker than I've ever seen him move before.

I put a hand on Ponyboy's shoulder, and his fury simmers down into the saddest whimper. "Why can't I help, Sam? I want to help."

I sigh deeply, letting him know I sympathize with him. "I know it's hard to understand. It sucks. I don't blame you for being mad."

He sniffles, wiping his nose with the back of his hand. "You don't?"

"Not at all. I would feel the same way. And I have before, actually. Can I tell you a story about me when I was your age?"

He nods, and I try to push past the tightness in my throat I feel as this memory bubbles to the surface. I usually try to swallow them down, to avoid thinking about the past as much as possible. It does nothing but bring up unnecessary hurt. But for Ponyboy I can make an exception.

"My" —I clear my throat when my voice catches on the word as it usually does— "*dad* used to be a police officer. Do you know what that is?"

He nods enthusiastically, a glimmer of brightness beginning to return to his eyes behind the tears. "Yeah, like they used to take people to jail."

"Mhm. He would sometimes have to leave in the middle of the night if he got a call, and most of the time it was when I was already sleeping, but one time I heard the call come in from my room. It said there was someone on the run who had robbed a nearby gas station. I jumped out of bed, threw on my jacket and Spider-Man shoes, and ran down the stairs, ready to help him save the day." I chuckle at the memory, but the pain of remembering is still there, underneath it all like a molten lava that is always bubbling under the surface.

Ponyboy's eyes are wide. He hangs on to every detail of my story. It squeezes my heart a little bit that these are normal everyday childhood experiences that *he should be having* right now. Not all this. Will he ever get to experience some semblance of a normal childhood?

"Did you?" he breathes.

I shake my head. "Nope. My dad sent me back to bed. I cried and yelled, just like you. But he told me even though I felt strong and capable and wanted to help, the reality of life means you have to sit it out on the bench sometimes."

"Bench?"

Right. No normal childhood. Does he even know what sports are? I might have picked the wrong metaphor... Well, too late now, I've already committed. Hopefully I can explain this in a way that makes sense to him.

"Yeah, like in sports. You don't always get to play the game every time, even when you really, really want to. Sometimes the coach has a bigger plan for the game and knows best, which means sometimes you gotta wait it out on the bench until it's your turn."

"But that's not fair," he whines, his lower lip trembling.

"I know. It's not." I give him a sympathetic smile. "But every player on the team has different skills and is needed at different times. Q, Beardsley, and me are the players they need in the game this time."

He sniffs, looking down at his lap. I tousle his hair until I finally get a tiny smile out of him. I put my arm around his shoulder. "I know it sucks to wait it out. You'll have your turn, I promise. But for now, you have to sit this one out, bud."

He nods slowly, giving in. He looks up at me with sad determination. "You're going to get them all back, right?"

"We will. I promise."

TYRO B-29

Standing in front of the trash can in the cafeteria, this new resolve fuels me, giving me this thrilling burst of energy I've never experienced before. It somehow makes the fear fade to the background.

I decide to trust the deep instincts ingrained in my body rather than my misleading mind. I can't trust my own mind. I need to trust my body instead. *Ella's body. Ella's instincts.*

As discreetly as I can, I pull the lanyard that has my identification card on it off my neck, peeking around my shoulder to make sure no one is looking before dropping it in the trash in front of me.

I take a deep breath. I will trust Ella's instincts.

I walk over to the guard who is posted by the exit, keeping my face smooth and innocent. Something inside me knows he will be more likely to trust me this way.

"Excuse me?" I say with a sweet voice.

He looks down at me. "Yes?"

"I got in trouble today." I lower my chin, trying to seem regretful and shy. "Aunty put me in one of those rooms with the bars so I could reflect on my choices. Do you know what room I'm talking about?"

He furrows a brow in confusion. "The holding cells? Okay, why?"

I gesture to my bare neck. "I realized when I got to dinner that I didn't have my ID lanyard. I must have dropped it in there by mistake. Can you take me there to get it? I'm really hungry, and they won't let me eat without it."

He considers it for a moment. Did he see straight through my lie? He waves to the guard posted at the other side of the room. He nods to me and then in the direction of the exit. The other guard seems to know what he's saying, even though no words were spoken, and makes his own nod in confirmation.

He has me follow him out of the cafeteria, and I do, making sure to stand on the side of his body where his keys dangle off his hip. I study his keychain, trying to figure out how it detaches as we walk down the hallway.

A doctor passes us, and the two men nod to each other in passing. We turn the corner to the hallway I recognize from earlier.

I stay back as we approach the door to the room, the 'holding cells' as he had called it, watching and hopeful. I learn, to my frustration, that his key ring doesn't detach each time, but rather he stretches it on some kind of cord. He stretches the key to the lock, unlocks the door, and then when he lets it go, it zips itself back into place on his hip. There is also some kind of speaker clipped there too, and a muffled voice comes through it periodically.

I feel lightheaded as a wave of nervous nausea begins to douse me from the top down. This already isn't going to plan. I dig around in Ella's instincts, trying desperately to figure out a backup plan in the seconds I have. I linger behind him and lean in for a closer look at the speaker and key ring, trying to figure out how they detach from his hip. The key ring appears to be a clip attached onto his belt loop.

He pushes the now unlocked door open, and we enter the dim room, which feels even darker than it did earlier. I notice that the overhead lights in the room are off, but some of the individual cells have their own lights on, so it is enough to light our pathway.

"Which one?" the guard asks.

A voice crackles on his speaker, echoing through the silence of the holding cells, which are still mostly empty.

My voice cracks as I answer, betraying the nerves I'm trying so hard to keep hidden. "This one over here." I wave to the empty cell next to Lala and Steele, whose heads turn as we approach.

A flash of recognition lights in their eyes, but they thankfully make no other indication that they know me. Their cell is lit up by a single bare bulb, and I notice my cell has one too, but it is off. A shadow of an idea materializes, and I acknowledge that it might not work, but I hope so badly it does.

Please work. Please.

The guard stretches out his keys to unlock the barred door and waves me in.

"Thank you, I really hope it's in here."

My knees shake as I move to stand under the dark light bulb. I make a show of reaching for the chain that hangs down from it. I even jump for it feebly, but my fingers don't even come close, just like I knew they wouldn't.

"I can't—" I jump again, my shaking knees nearly buckling as I land this time. "Can you—?"

The guard steps through the door to help me with an annoyed sigh.

I jump one last time and this time when I land, I throw myself to the floor, pretending I've come down on my ankle the wrong way. I let out a feigned shriek of agony.

"Ow, ow, ow," I whine, lying on my side and reaching for my ankle.

The guard looks alarmed and unsure of how to help me. "Are you okay?"

I pretend to cry. "I think I hurt my ankle. I can't move it."

He tries to help me up, but I stumble and fall, trying to make as much commotion as I can, so hopefully he won't notice as I...

Please work, please work.

I reach for the clip on his belt loop slowly, crying loudly and stumbling as he keeps trying to help me stand up. *Reachhh...*

My fingers fumble clumsily with the clip. It catches on his belt loop. It's stuck.

He has helped me to my feet now.

I'm running out of time.

"It hurts, it hurts," I cry in pain, doubled over.

"You gotta try to walk it off," he says, trying to help me stand straight. From this angle I have one last chance.

I reach for the belt loop and push in the clip...

It comes free. I snatch the speaker off his hip too.

I don't have a second to lose. With the key ring and speaker finally in hand, I dart for the door, letting it slam behind me with a *clang.*

The adults whoop in the cell next to me, Red's booming cheer nearly vibrating the metal bars of the cells, and I'm exhilarated by their encouragement, happy to make them proud of me even though I barely know them.

"Hey!" The guard rushes to the door, slamming into it, but it's too late. It locked itself right when it closed.

I back up as he paws through the air, reaching through the bars to try to grab me, spitting curses and threats at me.

"I'm sorry," I tell him instinctively. But I'm not sorry, and a thrill of energy pulses through me at the thought of that. It's a buzz unlike anything I've felt before.

I did it.

I step to Lala and Steele's door.

"Great job, *mija,*" Lala praises proudly, a genuine smile stretched on her lips that meets her eyes in a way Aunty's never seems to do.

She's pleased with me. That makes me smile.

I fumble with the keys, trying out different ones on the lock until one works.

The guard bangs on the bars, but I try to ignore him as their door swings open. I open Red's next. My hands are shaking as I unlock his door.

Within seconds that feel like a lifetime, we're all standing outside the bars, hugging and cheering. The speaker in my hand crackles to life again. I clip it to the waistband of my own pants.

"So what do we do now?" I ask, really hoping they can take the plan-making from here.

Steele straightens, taking the lead. "If we can just get out of this godforsaken casino, I have a place we can lie low at until we can get in contact with Beardsley."

They look at me, and I try not to shrink under their stares. I've risen to the challenge so far. I tell myself I'm capable.

"Do you know how to get to the main lobby from here?" Red asks.

I stare at them, my fragile confidence waning as I decide whether or not I should tell them I didn't even know there was a main lobby. I can barely hear them over the guard's yelling and cursing.

"We stay pretty contained to one area," I answer slowly. "But I've seen people eating lunch on the patio sometimes when we're at recess. They watch us play. Could that be where?"

"Yes, probably." Red nods encouragingly. "Can you get us there?"

I take a big breath. I am capable, not weak. "Yeah, I think so.

It's near the data room, so after we get Ella, we can get there pretty quickly."

They look at each other, and it sends an uneasy chill up my arms.

"We are getting Ella, right?"

"Maybe we can come back soon and—" Steele begins, but I cut her off.

In an out-of-character moment of boldness, I hold up the guard's keys. "You're not going to get very far without these, and I'm not leaving without her. You were right about everything. She didn't choose to be here. None of them did."

Red puts his hand on my shoulder. "You know we can't save all of them," he says gently.

"I know. But we can save *her*. I owe her my life. I'm not just leaving without her."

"Well, in that case—" Steele smacks her hand on her thighs before approaching the furious guard. He reaches out for her, snarling and scratching like a rabid dog. Steele grabs the collar of his uniform and in a quick motion, jerks him forward. His forehead bangs off the bars of the door. She does it again, and this time he crumples to the floor.

She dusts her hands off. "That should buy us some time. Now, where's Ella?"

15

IN THEORY, A BIONIC ARM SHOULD HAVE BEEN COOLER

MATEO

The sound of Nova's voice makes all of my insides melt, including my brain, so luckily my instincts take over and put my hands up for me. I stay very still, remembering all too well the way Steven's body flew back through the air at the force of Nova's prosthetic, like he'd run straight into a brick wall. The way he crumpled to the ground, lifeless in seconds.

I'm surrounded by the Guards within two blinks. They grab my arms and throw me to the concrete kitchen ground, a sickening crunch from my shoulder on impact, followed by a red-hot blast of pain shooting down my arm. I cry out in agony when they shove my arms behind my back, straining my shoulder further. They cuff my wrists together tightly and shove my cheek down into the floor.

Nova crouches down beside me, her voice low and deadly. "Want to tell us where you've been?"

"I was going to the bathroom," I reply breathlessly, a heavy tug in my chest that any answer I give will be wrong if she already knows where I was.

"I don't like liars," she says simply.

A Guard yanks me to my feet, and another surge of pain shoots through my shoulder as well as a cold fear when I remember Nova's warning. "Order, or death." Something about the finality of her tone, the roughness of the Guards, the thick tension all around, tells me I'm not just headed to an everyday Penalty. She's going to make an example of me just like she did to Steven, in front of everyone, in front of Eddie. They drag me out of the back door and toward the Podium.

Maybe if I can provoke her, she'll finish me off over here where Eddie can't see. I just don't want him to have to live with that image for the rest of his life. I mentally take the pain in my shoulder and shove it down deep into a box in my mind where it can't hold me back. I throw my head back as hard as I can into the Guard escorting me from behind, and it collides with the chest-piece of his armored uniform.

I see stars in my eyes and a throbbing pain in my head, but I take advantage of his startled stumble to jerk my cuffed hands out of his grip. I know I won't get far, but I run as fast as I can anyway, pushing my legs as fast as they'll go. Will she shoot me from behind? Will she draw it out? She doesn't even call after me. She knows I won't get away.

It's like a twisted game of tag. *You're ' it,' Nova.*

The Guards catch up to me, and are even rougher this time, now one on each side of me, holding both of my arms even tighter than before. They're still dragging me to the Podium.

"Hey Cyborg Lady," I call to Nova, who is marching a few paces ahead of us. She stops in her tracks, turning to me slowly, lethally. Her face is expressionless, but a sharpness in her eyes reveals the anger flickering there. "Did you—"

She doesn't even give me a chance to insult her like I planned before she delivers a blow to my face with her metal arm so forcefully that I nearly lose consciousness. I feel dizzy on my feet, but I don't let myself fall.

"I know what you're doing," she hisses, her face only

inches from mine. "You're trying to stall to give baby brother and your little friends time to get away." Her eyes turn venomous. "Don't worry, they'll all get their turn right after you."

No. My soul leaves my body.

"I worked alone," I force through my throat that is getting tighter by the second. "My brother had nothing to do with this. I'll do anything. *Please.*"

"Ah, quite the change of tune." She continues walking toward the Podium, and they drag me along after her. My brain is whirring at full speed, trying desperately to think of a way out of this. I can't let them die like this. It's my fault for bringing them into this.

As we approach the Podium, I notice with horror that they're already there. Lined up. Cuffed. All of them—Eddie, Talia, Rachel, Trevor, Parker, and even Amanda. It must have been the Elders who turned us in, and that make my blood boil. So not only are they cowards, but they're murderers as well. They are just as complicit in our deaths, their souls just as guilty, as Nova is.

There are Guards everywhere, armed and ready. No matter what I do, they'll end me one way or another. There's nowhere to run, there's absolutely nothing I can do. I've never felt so helpless. A Guard throws me into the lineup, and I stumble to Eddie. His hands are cuffed like mine. I expect to see fear when he looks at me, but he smiles, like this time he's the one telling *me* that it's all going to be okay.

"I'm so sorry, *Lalito.*" My voice cracks, and my eyes fill with tears at the sight of his brave little face, the rebellious fire still flaring across his expression while my own fire has given up. "I don't think I can get us out of this one."

Eddie nudges me with a shoulder as Nova makes her way to the front of the Podium, calling all Zoners to attention, Guards pulling them out of their functions to witness this. "We're together," he whispers, and it feels like a knife to my chest. "Like you always said we would be."

I look the rest of the group in the lineup. Parker and Trevor wear a similar fire on their faces as Eddie. Rachel and Amanda are crying. Talia just looks exhausted. "I'm so sorry I got you guys into this," I say to them. "I really thought we had a shot."

The last of the Zoners gather, the smallest kids right in front. My heart aches for them. The awful things they've had to witness in their short lives so far will be enough to give them nightmares for life.

Nova doesn't get flowery with it like Chief did at Sam's trial. She just gets straight to business. "These Zoners have been caught making plans for escape and are therefore guilty of treason. They will be punished accordingly."

So not even the appearance of a trial? Just a verdict without even pretending it was a democratic decision? We all figured out that the trials were rigged anyway, but at least Chief had the decency to keep up the appearance. And we never had to watch it happen. They were always far enough away where we could still somewhat tell ourselves it wasn't happening. Far enough away that we could sometimes convince ourselves that "expulsion" didn't mean a life was ending.

I look around, hoping to see something *anything* that can help, that maybe someone has a plan, or maybe some miraculous idea will spring to my mind, but all I see is no way out.

Nova announces my name, and a Guard pushes me forward. Nova leans down, her face so close to mine that I can feel her breath on my face as she whispers, "I'm going to let you in on a little secret, since I have a feeling you'll be really good at keeping them here shortly."

I keep my eyes locked on hers, but I don't react at all to what she's saying. I refuse to show her any of the fear that has been bubbling up for the past week, the past seven years, really.

"I may have an official position with the FPA, but I'm less

patriotic and more what you'd call... financially motivated. So when a dear friend in the gambling industry found out I was being sent here to C9, she asked me to clean up some loose ends, and I agreed. For a price, of course. Your friend Sam really did make quite a mess of things, didn't he? "

I don't even blink, keeping my face completely neutral, even as my mind speeds a hundred miles an hour processing what she's saying. Is she talking about the person who took Ella and those other kids? The mercenary? How else could she know about Sam?

"It was just a really convenient coincidence that my Guards overheard your friends talking about your little escape plan. Gave me the perfect excuse."

She takes a step back, seemingly pleased after conferring this little 'secret' to me, and she presses a combination of buttons on her bionic arm, and it begins to whir and warp, the metal pieces rearranging. Within seconds, the end of it has shifted into its gun form. The one she killed Steven with.

A Guard pushes me down to my knees, and hearing Eddie's quiet sobs behind me is enough to shatter me to pieces. He doesn't deserve this. I don't deserve him. I try to look back at him, but the Guard shoves my face forward.

"I love you, *Lalito*," I choke, wishing I could hold him, or at least see him. Can he even hear me? "I'm so sorry."

As Nova raises her arm, I think of my mom. The last time we were together. She swore she'd come find us, swore she'd get us out. I believed her. Just like Eddie believed me when I said I'd keep him safe.

Amazing how easy it is to lie to the people we love most.

I close my eyes, letting the crushing weight of the people I've let down take over my body, awaiting the inevitable pain of Nova's gun.

But seconds pass, and nothing happens.

It seems everything has frozen for a moment. I open my

eyes in confusion. Nova's arm has lowered. Everyone seems to be looking behind me...

By the time I turn my head to see what everyone is looking at, there is an explosion of sound and motion at the Southern Boundaries. Nova and the Guards step off the Podium to get a better look at the commotion. An FPA delivery truck, one of the armored ones that comes regularly to drop off deliveries of food and necessities for the Zone, is speeding toward us, throwing up dust and gravel along its way, ripping through the landscaping of the Square.

The formation in front of the Podium scatters, everyone screaming as the truck races right toward us. We all huddle in together on the platform, still cuffed, but hoping to be far enough from the truck's path if it crashes into the Podium.

"Hey! I order you to stop immediately!" Nova yells at the truck, waving both of her arms in warning. It's getting closer. She fires off a blast from her arm at its front tire, and it swerves sideways from the force of the blasted tire, coming to a screeching stop just before the platform of the Podium.

The truck doors are thrown open, and the deafening pops of spraying gunfire explode in my ears, echoing off the steel shell above us. Zoners scream, covering their heads and running in every direction. Nearly a dozen men have jumped out of the delivery truck. Within seconds they're shooting at each other.

It's here. Just like Ramos said. War.

16

CURSE YOU, ALADDIN

SAM

I feel a little woozy from the vicocet as we load up the trucks for E1, and I'm starting to agree with the medic that this might have been too soon after a major arterial operation. But no time for rest until Ella is safely by my side, and luckily, I've got these pain meds in my pocket to get me through until then. We press on! Medicated!

Cade is too busy preparing trucks for a delivery, but he sends Calix in his place to send us off. Calix gives Beardsley the location of which service entrance at E1 has the gap in the electric gates today, and some parting words of advice.

"Do what you can in 48 hours to sway her followers, and then we'll meet you outside to launch the rescue mission. Remember, just a little extra leverage is all we need right now, not a full-scale exodus," he says, mostly to me as if *I'm* the biggest wildcard in the group. Although he may be right, considering the last thing I want to do is play the long game when my sister is enduring God knows what right now.

So I just nod in confirmation. 48 hours until Ella. I can do that.

We say goodbye, gather last minute supplies, and before I

know it, I'm sitting in the shotgun seat on the way back to E1, the truck lumbering over mounds and deep trenches. Beardsley is in the driver seat, Q and Zara in the backseat, and Luna in the bed sticking her nose out the back window. The girls in the back chat together enthusiastically, but the blur of the outside through the window puts me in a sort of zombiefied state, and now I can't stop thinking about my conversation with Ponyboy. About that memory with my dad I told him about. They're sticky, these memories. Once I let them in, open the crack of my inner fortress even a little, it's like they glue themselves onto my every thought.

I can't shake away the feeling of his heavy hand on my shoulder, talking to me exactly like I was talking to Ponyboy, the deepness of his voice seeming to reverberate off the shadowed walls of our front room. It's like I simply blink, and I'm transported back there. To that room. The room the soldiers surrounded my dad in the day they took him away. That very room where Mom... Her screams, the blood, her limp shoulders in my lap.

The room where I lost both of them.

The room where I lost myself. In a matter of minutes becoming a person no longer living for me, but for *her*. For Ella.

And she doesn't even want me.

"I'm happier here," she had said, stepping away from me in disgust, clinging to that woman instead. A woman who wouldn't bat a single eyelash over her but convinced her somehow that she didn't need the only person who has ever truly cared about her. My eyes burn at the edges with angry tears.

What more can I sacrifice? What more can I do to prove to her that she is the only thing I live for? How can I show her that I love her more than Vegas ever could?

Why am I not enough?

The truck hits a gnarly bump, and I whack my head on the

window. The pain forces my eyes closed. I squeeze them shut, trying to squeeze away the pain in my head, the pain in my wrist, and the pain in my heart, too. Before I even realize it, I've drifted off to sleep.

THE TRUCK COMES to an abrupt stop, and my eyes fly open. My hands jerk out on instinct. Everyone in the truck laughs.

"Enjoy your beauty rest, Prettyboy?" Beardsley chuckles.

I let my head fall back onto the headrest. "Very funny," I croak, my throat dry and rough. Everyone steps out of the truck, the doors clanking shut around me, but I take an extra moment inside alone to wake up. I wince, finally coming to. There is an aching pain near my right temple where my head hit the window, and an even worse aching pain throbbing under the bandages on my wrist. Guess the pills wore off.

I grab my water bottle from the center console and chug the whole thing, strongly considering popping one of the pills, or the whole container of them. I decide not to, though. I really need to have my full cognitive ability, however limited that may be, if we're going to pull this off. I breathe and center myself, remembering my purpose here. I set aside the sadness and focus on my deep-rooted fury instead.

Remember: Vegas deserves this after all she's done.

I nod in agreement with myself. She does. I only wish I could see the look on her face when she finds out we stole her own Elites from right under her nose.

And the thought of that alone is enough to get me to step out of the truck and toward an objective that feels like a snail-paced detour. Whether it feels like it or not, I tell myself this is one step closer to Ella. 48 hours to Ella.

48 hours to getting her back, even if right now she can't see that it's best for her.

Because that's what being an older brother means—you protect even when they think they don't need to be protected. You love even when they don't love back.

So that's what I'm going to do.

I step out of the truck, sling my backpack around my shoulders, and meet the others, recharged, recommitted, appropriately re-furious, and ready to do what it takes.

We're parked behind a very familiar and still very smelly dumpster that brings me back to just the other day when we were in this exact spot. The others are already changing into their EI getups, and I groan internally, remembering the torture of this step from before. Luna greets me happily, and I give her a pat on the head.

Q tosses me a bag, pulling out some kind of black fabric from her own bag that resembles something you'd toss into the ocean to catch fish with.

Zara squeals excitedly as she takes a glittering rhinestoned outfit out of her bag. "Oh, you guys do your *research!*" She brings the shiny fabric to her face and inhales it. "I needed this today."

Beardsley has already put on his blue beard wig, grumbling to himself about what a waste of time this mission is, and to my relief he begins pulling the orange and purple ruffled monstrosity they made me wear the other night over his own head. He works next on Luna, combing her fur out and then coating it with a colorful sticky glitter.

Q and Zara step around the dumpster to change into their outfits, and I peek into my own bag, terrified of what I might find. However, I'm pleasantly surprised to see a welcome lack of ruffles and the color purple. I set my backpack down, the cube of my magboard *clanking* inside as I set it on the ground. I reach into the bag Q handed me and begin struggling with whatever is in it right away, unable to untangle all the *many* pieces. Why are there *so many pieces?*

I look at it in confusion, turning it around a couple times to figure out which way is up, and which way is down. Is it supposed to be a shirt? To me it just looks like a random mass of gold tassels arbitrarily stitched together.

I give up on the top momentarily to look in the bag again and see pants, yes, I'm sure those are pants. Odd pants, for sure, but at least they're an identifiable shape. I take the opportunity of the girls being behind the dumpster to quickly trade my canvas work pants for these. They're a flowy black material with stripes of black sequins down the sides, cuffed at my ankles. They're unexpectedly breezy, but it's kind of... nice?

I pull my shirt off over my head and give the tassels a second go. They're hanging off me strangely, barely covering any of my torso. This can't be right. Goosebumps pop up on the exposed skin of my chest and back.

Q and Zara come stumbling and giggling around the dumpster and completely against my will, my jaw drops to my ankles at the sight of her.

Q.

Zara covers her mouth at my reaction, muffling the sound of her signature excited squeal, but my eyes are just locked on her.

She is dressed in a black one-piece that I would think was a swimsuit if not for the glittering black jewels covering its entire surface. Black fishnet fabric covers her legs, apart from the diamonds of brown skin that peek through the tights. Her hair is pulled back tightly, the curls slicked back so her face is fully visible.

Her face.

Her eyelashes are long and curl up nearly to her eyebrows. Her cheekbones are gleaming with the same shimmery gold of her last E1 outfit, but her lips are different. Apart from the new black lipstick coating them, lips which are usually curled into a variety of smirks, are smushed together now. Almost shy.

She looks like a shadow of night, one that could stalk after me into an alleyway. A shadow so sharp it would slice me right in the back with only a look. But I'd let her.

It's like my brain glitches, my tongue not sure how to put words together. "Q— your outfit... you look—"

Zara jumps in to complete my sentence with a grin. "Hot. She looks *hot,* Sam, it's okay, you can admit it."

I would, if my mouth and brain could communicate properly, but I'm unfortunately just completely dumb stricken.

Q chuckles shyly and clips a small black bag around her hips, shaking her head as if trying to make us believe what we're seeing right in front of us is simply a figment of our imagination.

She gives me a once-over and then an exasperated sigh. "How did you manage to—?" She closes the distance between us to examine my failure closer. I'm nearly knocked unconscious by her closeness, her scent. "Honestly, Prettyboy, it's like you've never even worn yarn before."

I flick some of the tassels at her to disguise how her proximity is affecting me, trying really hard to not think about the fact that the last time she was this close to me I almost kissed her. My cheeks threaten to warm at the very thought, so I force my tongue back into cooperation before I really lose it for good.

"Now don't take this as a complaint, because I know the torture you're capable of..." I nod my head toward Beardsley's ruffles, covering my bare chest in mock bashfulness. "But it feels like it may be missing a few pieces."

Zara chimes in happily. "She told me herself she wanted to see if you had a six-pack."

To my surprise, Q's face darkens to a deep mahogany. Is she... blushing?? I suddenly feel ashamed by my scrawny and near-skeletal upper body, hating myself for not doing more pushups over the last sixteen years of my life to prepare for this exact moment in time.

"No I did not," Q hisses at Zara sharply, who makes a deliberate show of dancing away from us and leaving us alone.

"I didn't," she repeats fervently to me, but she avoids my eye, still busying herself with the tassels.

I could just let her off easy, change the subject like any sane person would do. But I take the blush on her cheeks as encouragement to be myself.

"Sorry for the unfortunate lack of six-pack," I whisper. "There might be two in there though, do you need a closer look?"

She gives me an icy glare that I just take as further encouragement and laugh. She moves behind me to try and fix the tassels, her fingers brushing against my skin lightly in the process. My heart skips a beat at the contact, but I play it cool, hoping she can't see the little hairs on the back of my neck sticking straight up.

"Mack made this look a lot easier," Q grumbles.

I feel a twinge in my gut at the thought of her seeing Mack like this. He probably looked way better in it, his more muscular arms and chest filling the gaps where mine fall flat.

"We might need to just start over," she says with a conceding huff.

"Starting over might be a good idea," I agree, determined to not let my jealousy of Mack slip through the false confidence. "But if you wanted me shirtless, all you had to do was ask, Q." I make a show of pulling the material over my head and handing it to her with a grin.

"Maybe if you had more than just a two-pack to offer I would've." And her smirk is back. Despite the low-blow, it feels almost like a relief, like we're back in familiar territory, instead of stepping into the unsureness of blushing and shy smiles and uncooperative hairs sticking up on the back of necks. I can deal with smirks and jokes.

"Touché," I chuckle. "In my defense I've been pretty much malnourished the past eight years."

She takes a moment to untangle the top and then lifts her arms to put it over my head. I have to duck a little to compensate for the height difference, which makes my face end up right in front of hers. I hold my breath.

Her face is so close. Her lips.

She doesn't look at me, but I study her, hoping maybe up this close I can finally find answers in her eyes or in the pores of her skin somehow. My eyes never leave her face as she straightens the shirt into place, her fingers grazing my skin and leaving burning trails of fire behind.

I don't move, I don't even breathe, even after her fiery hands have left my torso, my face still close to hers. There is a stretch in my neck, but I don't care.

"Thanks," I murmur softly.

She finally looks at me, her eyes flicking up to mine. "You're welcome."

I see a new depth in her dark eyes, which are somehow an even more dimensional brown. It's like there is usually a blockage there, some kind of dam that is usually so meticulously in place, but now it's wide open. I study her face, every inch, looking for those answers but still finding none. Her lips are so close. Would they leave a burning fire behind like her hands did?

Her eyes blink to my lips, and it almost looks like she's wondering the same thing, but it could be completely my imagination. An illusion maybe.

Her brow creases to a determined line, and her eyes move back to mine. She opens her mouth to say something. "What if—?"

Beardsley's purposefully louder-than-necessary voice makes my heart leap into my throat. "Hey, you lovebirds, we gotta go if we're doin' this thing."

My hand thinks for itself and grabs hers before she steps away. I'm desperate to know what she was going to say.

"What if what, Q?" It comes out as a croak.

She yells back at Beardsley over her shoulder, her sudden volume making me jump. "Shut up old man, before we all team up and throw you in the dumpster." She looks back to me, the determined spark in her eye still bright, but it dims when Beardsley interrupts again.

"I'm leavin' with or without y'all." Followed by the sound of doors slamming. My eyes don't leave Q's.

She takes her hand back with a sigh, and it's like that passageway in her eyes seals back up again, pushing me out into the cold on the other side. "I was just going say Zara has some ideas to get a message to the Elites."

I throw both of my hands in my pockets, feeling a sting that I try to smile off. "Right. Guess we better get going."

She gestures to my top. "At least you won't embarrass me in there anymore." And I look down to assess her handiwork.

It seems to be a vest instead of a shirt, which makes a lot more sense now that I'm seeing it in its intended form. The tassels are arranged now into horizontal lines that fall down from shoulder pads and cuff at the waist, gathered to frame the middle of my still-bare-but-now-more-intentionally-bare chest. The combination of gold tassels and breezy pants makes me feel kind of like some party-going version of Aladdin.

He probably would have a six-pack though. Bastard.

"Great. Thanks." Although I don't intend them to, my words come out short and flat as I pick up my backpack off the dirty ground and step around her. I don't look back as I follow Beardsley, Zara, and Luna past the dumpster and toward E1, repeating a phrase in my head for the second time today: Why am I never enough?

EVERY PERSON THAT CAN PULL OFF THIS TASSEL ATROCITY BETTER THAN ME

-Mack, unfortunately

-The obvious ones such as Keanu Reeves (obviously), Indiana Jones and Han Solo

-Teo because he makes everything cool some-how

-Ponyboy because he makes everything adorable

-Arcadius, the Ginger Thor of the Catacombs because he's probably secretly shredded

-Luna and/or Axel would bring a certain canine charm to the ensemble

-Shrek. He's green and ripped, need I say more?

-A gutter rat straight from the sewers

-An extra-terrestrial with three heads

-Your left sock you lost in the laundry three years ago

-A wadded up receipt at the bottom of your grandmother's purse

-Your grandmother's purse

-Your grandmother

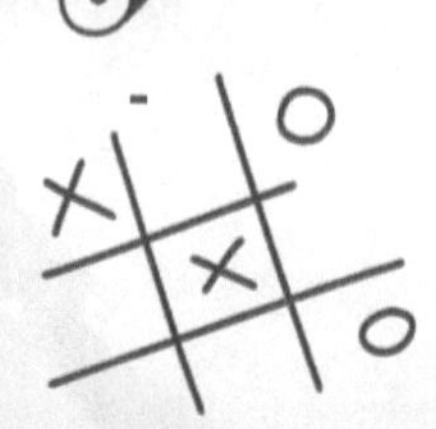

Maybe if I were any of the above, Q wouldn't be so disgusted of me.

17

JUST A CASUAL STROLL THROUGH HELL

SAM

As if I wasn't already grumpy enough, we enter through the coordinated service entrance and find Q's unfortunately attractive tattooed friend there to greet us again. She smiles at him brightly, and I bristle at the once-over he gives her in return, his eyes lingering on her outfit an extra second too long for my liking. Beardsley shakes his hand, clapping him on the back in greeting as if they didn't just see each other a couple days ago. Luna hops around him excitedly, which is just an added level of betrayal.

"Prettyboy, Zara, this is Jones," Q introduces with a smile, and I'm still bristling, but I give him a polite handshake anyway.

Zara holds out her hand to shake his, but he kisses her hand instead. She gives him a dazzling smile. "Oh, we have a gentleman on our hands."

To my annoyance, he so very graciously offers to let us stay in his suite for as long as we need. Zara accepts a little too quickly and explains it's probably for the best she doesn't return to her own apartment.

Jones holds out his hands widely. "What do you need? How can I help?"

Beardsley looks at me with crossed arms and a raised brow like, "*Well, you're the one who got us into this mess, so what now?*"

I pull my shoulders back. I'm determined to do the most damage possible while we're here, make the "wasted" time count. "Is there anywhere we can obtain a ton of playing cards?"

Jones thinks about it for a moment. "I know a guy who runs poker out of his suite. I can take you there, but—" he drawls the last word, pulling at his collar "—he doesn't really like strangers... He might not let you in. And it's probably best if only one of you comes."

I look over my shoulder to Beardsley. "I votef whoever's oldest in the room has to go."

Zara and Q agree quickly, which makes Beardsley's face curl into a scowl.

He shoots a glare straight at me. "If I end up left behind like Steele, Red, and Lala, I'm tannin' your hide and givin' it to Luna as a chew-toy."

I open my mouth to defend myself, to insist I didn't leave them on purpose, but Q jumps in, sensing that the amends Beardsley and I made back at the Catacombs are still fragile. "Beardsley will go." And to him a little more pointedly, "*No one will be left behind. Thanks Jones.*"

He nods and flashes her a frustratingly perfect smile. He opens his mouth like he's going to say something back, so I jump in to deliberately change the subject.

"In the meantime, we should probably start laying some groundwork," I say, looking to Zara, the resident expert.

She grins. "I know just the place. Follow me."

～

Jones gives nonsensical directions to Zara on where his apartment can be located, which luckily, she seems to understand, and we promise to meet back up there tonight for dinner. We part ways and follow Zara out the service hallway, passing by other workers, none of whom even meet our eye as we pass.

The hallway door spits us out into a huge lobby so gaudy and thick with cigarette smoke it makes my head spin. Giant crystal chandeliers hang from a mirrored ceiling, reflecting the gold walls and a marble floor that *clacks* as we walk across. Eclectic people of every variety are scattered about, relaxing on lavish velvet couches, enjoying catered brunch, smoking, or chatting. Sometimes Luna trotting along next to us will get us a double-take, a look of confusion crossing their face briefly before returning to their carefree afternoon unbothered.

Zara walks out of the double doors of the lobby with Luna, and I follow behind Q, a noticeable tension still tightly wound between her and I, even now. I won't push her on it, but I can't stop thinking about what she would have said if Beardsley wasn't such an ass.

"*What if—*" she had said.

What if what? The possibilities are killing me. It could have been, "What if I'd never met you, wow my life would have been so much easier." But it also could have been, "What if there is more here than either of us admit?"

That question lingers in my head like an echo, and I barely register the daytime opulence of E1 as we make our way down the cobblestone sidewalk.

No. Because of course it's not more. We've just barely met. We're basically strangers. Not only that, but we're both stuck in an underground wasteland with no possibility of a normal future. Wanting anything more than a friendship with another person here is just a waste of time. Isn't it?

I mean, sure, there's attraction —she's gorgeous, that's

undeniable. She's also funny, smart, witty, brave, kind-hearted. Who wouldn't fall for her?

I'm so shocked that my mind even brought that to consciousness that I trip on my own feet, stumbling forward right into Q herself. She has to throw out a hand to the building we're walking by to keep from breaking her ankle in her booted heels.

I apologize profusely, expecting a glare or, at the very least, a teasing smirk, but her eyes only hold concern. She holds onto my arm, like she's trying to keep me upright. "Are you feeling drugged again? Did something get through your bandages?"

I should lie. Being drugged again would certainly be less embarrassing than, "Oh I was just thinking about how any sane person would fall for you without question, and then I literally fell. Not like that's a metaphor or anything."

I shake my head, probably more vigorously than necessary, worried any of those thoughts could spew out against my will. "No. No, I'm good, sorry I just tripped."

She narrows her eyes at me, assessing me for any signs of losing myself again, her hand never leaving my arm. When she's satisfied with my level of cognizance, she nods and pulls me into step with her. We catch up to Zara and Luna, who weave easily through the busy sidewalk. Q doesn't take her hand back, and its soft warmth on my bare bicep feels like it could burn straight through my skin.

I try not to make it obvious that I'm flexing a little, making the pathetic muscle on my arm a little tighter as she holds onto it. It kind of feels like I'm escorting her into a ball.

Damn you, Ei for not having a ball I can take her to.

I try to shove away the thought that keeps replaying in my head, nagging and nagging relentlessly.

Who wouldn't fall for her?

I peek at her out of the corner of my eye, and something inside me tightens just by looking at her. A completely involuntary motion that has been happening for days, but I try to ignore it every time, never allowing myself to acknowledge it.

I curse to myself as I allow the acknowledgment to take full form for the first time, to fully register it.

Sam, you idiot. You absolute moron. How could you let this happen?

Meandering down the sidewalk of E1, her hand on my arm, walking without speaking but the awareness of her so close to me it's almost painful, it finally articulates in my brain.

I could be falling for her.

Who wouldn't?

Now this makes two people I'd burn the entire Underground down for.

And neither of them want me.

THE DAYTIME E1 scene is no less extreme than the night version I witnessed last time. People are still ridiculously and impractically clothed, drinking and smoking and stumbling in and out of bars and clubs already like it's not barely lunchtime. Zara leads us into a building with a huge gold sign above the doors that says THE GENOAN.

Zara steps in with Luna first, then Q, then me, my body feeling heavier now that I've allowed myself to admit that yes, Sam, you *do* have feelings like a normal person. I thought "love" was supposed to make you weightless, not like your veins have been injected with cement. So far being an emotionless robot seems the far superior option. Maybe Axel can give me some pointers.

The lobby is sickeningly massive inside, with huge golden chandeliers hanging from delicately painted vaulted ceilings, draped above a sprawling staircase. We pass by opulent suites and elegant lounges where Elites laugh and drink with every imaginable extravagance, and I try really hard to keep my temper under control, long forgetting about once feeling bad for them for using them as pawns in our conflict. Especially when back in C9 — my heart squeezes at the thought of Teo and Eddie still back there so helplessly — we'd often go to bed cold and hungry. I bet these Elites have never felt hungry in their entire lives.

Zara steers us under a marble archway and down a more secluded hallway. I struggle to keep up as the mental distractions stack up like heavy bricks. Luna hangs back with me and licks my fingertips, somehow sensing I'm not quite myself right now. I pet her head reassuringly.

"You good?" Q cocks a brow at me over her shoulder as I fall behind a few feet.

I straighten my shoulders quickly, pulling at the straps of my backpack. I jog a little to catch up, Luna quickening next to me. "Yeah, sorry I was just... taking it all in."

That will be my strategy with Q. Keep all discourse necessary and professional. Short and sweet. Otherwise, I could risk spilling my guts, and how humiliating would that be, considering there's no way she feels the same. I mean, just *look at her*. There's no way in this universe or any neighboring universes, that *she* would be interested in *me*.

It stings a bit because it's so fresh. I just need some time to come to terms with that fact, to push the feelings deep, deep down inside like I always do, and it'll all be okay.

And until then: necessary and professional.

Zara leads us to a discreet door tucked away at the end of the hallway. It has the same white moulding as rest of the wall, and the tiniest golden doorknob you'd never even notice unless you were right in front of it. She looks back at us and smiles so big her mouth nearly stretches off her face. I give her a thumbs up while Q attaches Luna's leash to her pink floral collar. Luna looks annoyed by this formality.

Q assures her in a soothing tone. "It's a crowded area, Loon. I know *you* can handle it. It's everyone else I don't trust."

Zara knocks on the door three times, and we wait in bated silence. Just when it seems there's no one there, the door finally cracks open just the smallest sliver to allow Zara to whisper in some kind of passcode to the unseen person behind the door.

What is this, some kind of illegal speakeasy or gambling ring?

Honestly either would be kind of awesome.

The door creaks open all the way and Zara claps excitedly, motioning for us to follow her into the dark passageway beyond the door. It makes me a little uneasy to not be able to see where we're going as we step inside — my parents always said 'don't follow strangers into poorly lit illegal speakeasies or gambling rings' after all — but I follow anyway. What's the worst that could happen? As we stumble down a dim passage-way, I hear faint music that grows in volume the further down the hallway we get.

Q looks at me over her shoulder with an excited smile that just about kills me, her face shadowed by the darkness but still so achingly beautiful.

Oh, I am *so* far gone.

How have I been able to deny it this long? How have I not physically combusted, living with that much denial?

Zara is practically skipping ahead, her delighted laughter echoing off the walls, and the thrill of it all, mixed with the heavy bass of the music vibrating through my bones is kind of exhilarating. I can't help but feel tingles of that contagious excitement, though it's tinged with the guilt I can never quite shake off that I'm here and Ella's *there*. And here I am sneaking into a hidden club like a teenager in the old movies sneaking out of their house to go to some late-night party. But then we approach a red velvet curtain, which Zara shoves to the side, and Q's face lights up with such excitement that I can't bring myself to regret anything that makes her look that way, even if it's only for a moment.

Luna's whole body seems to twist side to side with how vigorously her tail is wagging. Q has her leash wound around her hand several times to keep it short, and Luna is tugging on it impatiently, wanting to dart after Zara through the curtain.

The room revealed behind the curtain is just as dimly lit as the hallway, but there is red LED uplighting that lines the edges of the entire ceiling and casts a red glow on every inch of the space. I do a double take. Giant statues of ram skulls sitting on top of tall columns in every corner of the room. What appears to be real fire blazing out of gothic sconces on the walls. Scantily-clad women dancing in cages hanging from the ceiling. I put the pieces together just as Zara squeals, "Welcome to Hell everybody!"

I snort. Ah, yes. I always assumed I'd end up here one day.

The pulsating music envelops us as we step further into the room, and it's so loud it seems to squeeze out any of the heavy thoughts, guilt, inadequacies that have been weighing me down, to make room to intake the sheer volume.

I can feel my heart rate increasing with every beat of the music, and I take a second to evaluate my sobriety. Maybe, like Q suggested earlier, the showered drugs have managed to wiggle their way in somehow and this excited adrenaline is just a drug-fueled haze.

But I feel normal enough, despite the ache in my wrist that is becoming as much a part of me as the wristTab itself was.

Zara grabs our hands and leads us through the crowd toward the middle of the room. Luckily, Luna parts a crowd well, so it's not too hard to get through. People on all sides admire her and pet her as we try to move through. She soaks up the attention happily. Zara takes us to a raised platform with a figure in a dark hooded cloak working a turntable. As we weave through the throng of people, I catch glimpses of masked faces, horrifying body modifications, garish outfits.

Zara leans in, having to nearly scream at us to be heard above the music. She does a lot of pantomiming to fill in the gaps. "Microphone. Spread the word. Who? I have to stay low-key."

A look of horror crosses over Q's face, and she shakes her head vehemently. "Nope, definitely not me, absolutely not."

They both look at me, and I groan. I can barely manage to form coherent sentences to individuals, let alone to an entire room of Elites, whose support could turn the whole tide of this war with Vegas. But I guess I have no choice, considering I know from experience how unbudgingly stubborn Q can be.

I shrug off my backpack, which lets a welcome rush of air to my sweaty back. I hand it to Q, which she slings over her own shoulder. With her free hand, she straightens my tassels, giving me a toothy, squinty-eyed grin like, *I'm a completely innocent bystander who didn't just force you into this* and says in an overly sweet voice, "Good luck!"

Zara tugs on the DJ's cloak and yells something at him when he bends down to her level. I don't know what kind of bargain she's running here, but the DJ passes me a microphone almost immediately and offers his hand to help me up onto the platform. I take his hand begrudgingly and feel my mouth go completely dry as I take in all the people around.

The DJ turns the volume down slightly and gestures at me that this is my chance.

The people around look up at me, still dancing to the music, but watching and waiting. For me. To say something.

"Uh," I say into the mic, and it screeches. People cover their ears.

Q gives me a smirk and a thumbs up. "You're doing great," she mouths.

"I have something to say." I'm stalling. Maybe inspiration will just come to me.

How can I possibly say something even remotely relatable to these people, when our lives are on completely different playing fields? Entirely different planets? I take a big breath and dig deep, trying to pull out any single thread of common ground I can find.

I decide to pretend I'm just talking to Zara, remembering the camaraderie I have felt with her in our conversations.

I'm just talking to a room full of Zara's. I can do this.

I swallow. "Do you ever—" My voice is not nearly loud enough. What is wrong with me? I try again, louder. "Do you ever feel trapped?"

This elicits a few whoops of agreement from the crowd, and I feel a little more encouraged, until I realize it was probably just Zara and Q. The majority of the audience still just bounces to the music I'm trying to speak over.

"They're not going to like me saying this," I yell into the mic, deciding just to completely send it. "I'm just going to say what everyone's too scared to. This Zone is a cage!"

That gets their attention.

"You—*we*— are kept distracted by the music and the fun, so we don't think too much about the fact that we are prisoners here!" My volume increases as more and more people from the crowd engage with what I'm saying. "Taken from our homes, trapped underground for a war that wasn't even ours, carefully watched and controlled. Where is the freedom we deserve?!"

This time more than just Q and Zara cheer, and I feel emboldened by their participation. There is something so thrilling—*freeing*— about screaming forbidden things into a microphone, when I've always had to keep them locked away in my head for fear of being accused of rebellion or treason. For fear of the very end I wound up with anyway, however rigged it may have been. The irony that now here I am "expelled" from my own Zone for treason, inciting the very rebellion they were always so scared of me inciting, yelling the forbidden things they were always so afraid of me yelling.

"They forced *us* underground, so the Underground should belong to *us*. We can take it back for ourselves!"

I lock eyes with Q just below the platform I'm up on. There is a strange expression on her face that I can't figure out. As our eyes meet, she smiles at me. A smile so genuine, so encouraging. She may not feel the same way about me as I do for her, but she has always believed in me. It's because of her I've even gotten this far with Ella in the first place, that I haven't given up.

And it's because of her, that smile, the belief in her eyes, that I have the confidence to finish this speech strong. I have to take some liberties here, and I run the risk of making enemies with several people, but I have to do it. "We're meeting tomorrow night at L'Deaux to plan. The only power we have is *together*. Support life, support freedom. LIVE FREE OR DIE."

The crowd roars it back. "LIFE FREE OR DIE!"

I hand the mic back to the DJ, and he cranks the music up right on a bass drop. The new energy in the room lights my already-adrenaline-spiked veins on fire. We might be able to pull this off, after all.

I step off the platform, and Zara jumps up and down. "*Eeeee* that was amazing!" She hits me repeatedly on the shoulder.

Q laughs. "L'Deaux, eh? Willie is going to kill you." Her eyes sparkle with pride though, and it's intoxicating, her being proud of me. Maybe it's just the dim lighting, or the adrenaline, but the way she's looking at me makes me desperately want to close every inch of space between us and kiss her. But I shake it away. I know better. *Professional and necessary*, I remind myself.

"Yeah, probably." I make myself laugh, while keeping my words guarded like I decided earlier. I have to protect myself here, otherwise she'll lure me into vulnerability and shoot me at close range with paintballs. Metaphorically, of course. "Well, too late now, I'll send him a thank you card or something."

"No time to waste," says Zara cheerfully, linking her arms with each of ours and steering us back toward the exit, Luna being dragged behind on the short leash, looking like she is considering just chewing through it. "We have three more clubs to hit up before we meet back up with Beard...Man. Whatever his name is."

I laugh and beg her to call him BeardMan to his face.

We pass through the exit, and something about exiting Hell arm-in-arm with two unexpected friends feels kind of metaphorical and reassuring. Like maybe I'll actually be able to crawl out of my own personal hell— being without Ella—as long as I have them by my side.

TYRO B-29

I lead Red, Steele, and Lala through the hallway silently, squeezing into shadowed corners whenever a doctor or worker passes by. I feel a mixture of exhilaration and fear as I consider the risks, being caught and ending up right back in that cage of a room, or worse.

I feel a certain loss as I betray Aunty, giving up the only home I've ever known. Leaving her and everything behind. Lucy, everyone else. I've only ever felt an assured comfort here, never scared or uneasy, never once suspicious of what Aunty could be hiding. Now that I know everything—and can confirm with my very own mind that Ella didn't choose to be here—the very thought of Aunty's presence sends a shiver down my back.

We reach the data room, and with a sigh of relief I see that tonight's sync hasn't started yet, so the room is empty aside from the children lying on their beds, hooked up to their machines as usual.

I push the door open carefully. "I need someone to help me carry her, and then maybe someone should watch the door," I whisper.

Red nods and follows me inside.

I've never thought twice about the data room. It has never even crossed my mind that it could be out of the ordinary, or even nefarious. But as I watch Red's face contort into disgust as we move through the room toward Ella's bed, passing the others sleeping quietly, I feel a squirm in my stomach, realizing for the first time that this is anything but normal.

I feel a deep guilt as I see this room with new eyes. The real reality washes over me about the true cost of my life, and who is paying it. I feel like crying as we reach Ella's bed, her face pale and sunken. I've been doing this to her. This is my fault. Once I get her out of here, I'll never sync again. I don't care what it does to my own life. She didn't choose this.

Red whispers something under his breath that I can't make out, but from the disgusted shake of his head, I can pretty much get the gist of it. I'm disgusted with myself too.

I glance at the clock above the exit. Only a few more minutes until the evening sync. We have to move fast. Not to mention, a doctor could enter at any—

I freeze as the door opens and a white-coated woman enters, with a clipboard in her hands. Her eyes widen as she sees us, and she moves her hand to grab the speaker clipped to her own pocket. She doesn't see Lala creeping behind her from the shadows, and she certainly doesn't expect Lala to hit her over the head with a keyboard from the machine in the corner. The doctor crumples to the floor in a heap.

With shaking hands, I stroke Ella's forehead, brushing a piece of her hair out of her eyes. Red begins disconnecting her from the monitors, and I try to gather what we might need from around her bed, picking up whatever wires and cables and materials look important and portable. She rustles in her sleep a little as Red scoops her up into his arms, but she doesn't wake up.

We hurry back to the exit where Lala is waiting, arms full of medical supplies she appears to have taken from cabinets and drawers around the room. She dumps wires out of a plastic bag from a nearby counter and puts all the supplies inside, throwing it over her shoulder as we peek outside the room, waiting for a cue from Steele to signify it's clear.

I step out first at the signal and gesture where to go, leading them to the hallway near the patio where I've seen patrons eating lunch.

My heart has never beaten this fast before, and I'm concerned it may completely bust its way out of my chest cavity. I guess I get to test the limits of this body, seeing what it's really capable of. We hurry down the hallway, and the noise level rises. We must be getting closer to this main lobby they were talking about.

Just when I thought my heart was going to beat out of my chest, it stops completely when I hear the thundering sound of running footsteps approaching behind us.

"There they are!" a booming voice behind yells. "Hey! Stop right there!"

A quick glance over my shoulder reveals a group of guards that have rounded the corner at the opposite end of the hallway, the direction we just came from.

"Stop them before they get to the—!"

We turn the corner, a corner I've never been around before, and I'm nearly breathless at the sight. There are more people than I've ever seen squeezed into this room, a room more mesmerizing than anything I could've imagined in my head. Some people's heads turn when we come running around the corner, but for the most part people are distracted. Laughing, talking, playing some sort of game around boisterous tables.

A tug on my arm from Lala pulls me out of a hypnosis created by a huge water tank with colorful floating sea creatures. I do a quick mental scan, and I realize that Ella's knowledge of the vast oceans that once existed, is also only secondhand. I feel a little comforted to have that in common with her.

I struggle with the bundle of wires and cables that are still cradled in my arms as we push our way through the crowded room. To my relief, Lala takes them and adds them to the plastic bag of supplies slung over her shoulder. I shrink a little as I realize we're getting a lot more looks. People around us have begun to realize Red is holding a young unconscious girl.

The guards have taken up a more casual pace in this public area but are following us closely. We'll need a miracle to get out of here.

Steele looks past me over her shoulder, and it's like I can somehow see her mind working something over.

"We need some commotion," Steele says, and Lala nods, taking my free hand and squeezing it. We're nearly halfway across the huge lobby, but the guards are gaining on us, and it seems to be even thicker with people the deeper in we get.

Steele shares a knowing look with Red before pointing to a random person in our proximity. "He has a gun!" she shouts at the top of her lungs. "This man right here, he has a gun!"

The chaos that erupts around the room is immediate. The people near us panic right away, and their panic is enough to get even the people further away who couldn't have heard Steele to panic as well. Within seconds people are running and screaming in all directions, many not even sure what they're running from.

We take advantage of the chaos and bolt for the doors too. There is a bottleneck at the exit, but there is now enough distance in between us and the guards that we manage to push our way out the doors, spilling out onto the street with the rest of the panicked guests.

It's nighttime and dim out here, the only light coming from small black streetlights scattered down the sidewalk. Lala is pulling me behind her, but I'm struggling not to trip over my own feet as we run down the shadowed street.

"I have a contact on the east side," Steele yells over her shoulder.

I'm already out of breath from the running, and I also feel slightly dizzy that I just left everything I know behind. Left Lucy, Amber, Katie... Aunty...

A loud pop explodes behind us. I scream and duck my head. Lala keeps me going me forward, as much as I want to crawl into a ball and hide.

"Stop!"

It's the guards. The one in front is pointing a gun at us. Ella's memories relay the danger of this to my own consciousness, and I feel a pang of fear. We swerve around other pedestrians, keeping our heads low.

Ella jolts awake at the next gunshot, nearly jerking out of Red's arms like a fish out of water. She looks disoriented at first, but then a spark of fear comes to her eyes when she realizes she's being carried by a stranger, with no idea where she is or what's going on.

"It's okay, Ella," I shout breathlessly a few paces behind Red, Lala still holding my hand tightly. "We're going somewhere safe."

She begins to cry when the next gunshot sounds.

"Steele, how much farther?" Lala asks, an urgency to her voice that makes me feel nervous, adding an additional layer to the fear I already feel.

"22 East Main Street," Steele says, and repeats it a couple more times. "3 blocks and a right, then two blocks and a left."

Red slows, sensing something in Steele's voice. "Don't even think about it." His voice holds a lethal tone that makes me shiver.

"My bounty here is still significant," Steele yells back. "I bet these guards can be bought. I'll hold them off. Take the next left sharply and hide there until the coast is clear. Then get to 22 East Main Street, ask for Penny."

Lala and Red argue with her back and forth, visibly angry with her, but I'm not really sure what's happening. I'm just trying to keep my legs moving and my lungs pumping.

Steele gives them a salute before slowing to a stop. I look over my shoulder, but Lala yanks me forward, not wanting me to see whatever is going to happen next.

Red yells in fury, like a battle cry, but doesn't stop running. He punches a shop sign as we pass by, but then I hear him gently apologize to Ella as her cries amplify in volume at his anger.

We make a sharp turn like Steele instructed and find ourselves in a crowded alley. Red leads us down the alleyway to the open back door of some kind of salon. We squeeze inside, breathless and sweaty, and Lala closes the door quickly. She has tears in her eyes but still tries to smile at me reassuringly. She brings me in to her side.

"You were so brave, *mija*. Are you okay?"

Red sets Ella down next to me quickly and straightens to run right back out, but before he can even push the door open, there is the unmistakable pop of gunshots. Three of them.

Bang, bang, bang.

Lala covers her whole face with her hands, and Red punches the door with a furious wail.

I somehow know in my bones what has happened, and even though she was basically a stranger to me, I start to cry.

18

WHAT DOESN'T KILL YOU MAKES YOU WISH YOU WERE DEAD

MATEO

Eddie's screams of fear jolt me into action. More trucks have flown in from the Southern Boundaries, more armed men jumping out of truck beds and joining the gunfire. We have to act, now, or we will be collateral damage in their crossfire.

"Zoners, follow me!" I scream into the gunfire, hoping enough of them can hear me as they run for cover. I'm not even sure what I'm doing, but my instincts seem to be taking over. I really have no plan, but I can't just sit back and watch these kids get hurt or die.

Talia and Trevor catch on the quickest and try to help me get the attention of as many Zoners as we can before we jump off the Podium. We keep our bodies crouched low, unable to cover our heads because our hands are still cuffed behind our backs. I make sure my shoulder or arm, hip, anything, is touching Eddie at all times. I don't want to be even an inch apart.

We take cover on the far side of the Podium, and Zoners begin to gather around us. Their fear feels so heavy. I know the pressure is really on me now. It's a reality now, not just a future concept I had time to worry over. The time is now.

One of the armed men from the trucks throws a gun to Zach from B-Quarters next to us, another one of Parker and Trevor's roommates, and I'm shocked when Zach doesn't even hesitate before shooting the closest Guard straight in the chest. The Guard flies backward from the impact on his body armor, hitting his helmeted head on the Podium. He is dazed for only a second, but it gives Parker the opportunity to kick his gun out of his hand. Parker bends to pick up the gun, tosses it to Trevor, and then yanks the keychain off the Guard's belt. Zach gives us a small salute, before hurrying off with his gun in hand to go after more Guards.

What, they're trying to recruit us now? I can't think about that right now.

We stay crouched behind the platform for an extra second to give any other Zoners a chance to join us, our crowd growing so big most of us aren't even covered at all anymore. We need to move fast.

One of Steven's roommates, Jed, helps Parker use the Guards keys to take off his cuffs and then they help us one by one. My wrists nearly cry from relief as mine fall to the ground. I peek up around the stage. I don't see Nova, but Guards and these rebel men alike are fighting, with weapons and without. It's so eardrum-shatteringly loud—screams, gunshots, crying, my pulse. We have to get out of here, or someone's going to get hurt.

"What's the plan?" Talia asks. She's holding a small crying boy in her arms. The sight of him reminds me of reality. There are small kids here. We need to get them to safety. The weight of that responsibility is nearly debilitating. But I can't freeze up now, not when Eddie is one of those kids who needs saving.

Parker, Trevor, and Rachel lean in, all close by and ready to help however is needed. I look toward the Mess Hall. It would be big enough for us to take cover in. The route there is wide open, though, and it's right near the thickest action. I peek the other direction, toward Town Hall.

The basement.

It's slightly further, but the route is spotted with potential covers: the trucks these men came in.

I look behind me and shrink a little when I see that nearly a hundred Zoners have gathered. The older Zoners have taken in the little ones, covering their ears and comforting them, many holding them in their arms. I look down at Eddie. I try to ask him, "Are you okay?" but my voice can barely be heard over the gunshots. He seems to have read my lips and gives me a reassuring nod.

I almost lost him...

He almost lost me.

I shake my head. No. I can't think about that right now. I have to stay strong and get us out of here, alive. We just need to make it to Town Hall, and then we can figure out what to do next. I am relying on the fact that the Guards and other men don't seem to care about us as much as trying to get the upper hand with each other. They seem to know we can't get very far anyway, with the gates intact. They've surely already closed themselves after the delivery gap, like Ramos was saying.

I lean in closer to Parker and the others. I have to scream to be heard. "Town Hall, south side. Use the trucks as cover to get there."

They all nod, and I feel kind of like a quarterback, getting ready for the next play. Except the objective isn't to score a point. It's to stay alive. It's to keep all of these children who are counting on me *alive.*

Parker, Talia, Rachel, and Trevor spread the word around the group to the older Zoners and prepare the younger kids to run. Trevor and Parker each pick up a kid in each arm, Rachel grabs the hands of two girls, even Eddie takes a young girl's hand. I touch the shoulder of the boy by me. He looks up at me with wide brown eyes. I hold my palms out to him, a universal question. He holds up his arms, accepting. I bundle him into my arms, grateful for his weight to help ground me. To remind me of the literal lives in my metaphorical and literal hands.

I look down at Eddie, and my throat feels so tight I can barely breathe. He's doing that face he does when he's trying really hard to be big. He's trying so hard to be brave. I hate that he has to do that. I wish I could just let him be a kid like he deserves. But he gives me a nod, anchoring me like he always does.

"Together?" I say, well aware I could be leading us right out into a bloodbath.

He nods. "Together."

"Stay right by me, Eduardo, do you understand me?"

"I understand." He looks down at the girl whose hand he holds, and she nods too, her blue eyes wide and scared.

I put my hand on the little boy's head to keep him close to my chest. I tell him to hold on tight, and his whole body clenches with effort. I blow out a big breath, and before I lose my entire nerve, I run for the closest truck as fast as I can. There are small fires everywhere as well as fallen bodies of Guards, rebel men, and to my horror, Zoners, too—some that chose to join the rebels, and some that didn't. This wasn't even their fight, and yet here they lie anyway.

I take a millisecond to scoop the gun off one of the dead Guards as I run by him. In a sobering moment I realize I'm holding a real gun. I've never held one before, much less learned how to use one. With my one free shaking hands, I tuck it into my waistband like I've always seen them do in movies. I'll have to worry about that later. Eddie grabs one from a body too, and at my stern look he tosses it to Trevor, who has to balance the kids he's carrying on his hip and his knee in order to catch it. I stop behind the closest truck. The gunfire is all around us. It seems like the whole world is exploding into dust and smoke.

"You okay?" I ask the little boy in my arms, and he sniffles in reply.

Eddie is breathless, but he gives me a thumbs up.

Not everyone has made it yet, but I know there isn't enough cover behind this truck for even a quarter of us. We have to keep moving. "Let's go."

I peek out from behind the truck. The adults are still busy killing each other. Still no Nova that I can see. I mentally scoff. What a coward. Hiding the second there's actual danger? Abandons the very children she's paid to protect? Not to mention her own men that are out here dropping like flies.

I give a nod to Eddie and take off for the next truck, kid in hand. A pop of a gunshot cracks behind me, too closely. My head jerks around, searching for anyone hurt. Eddie is right next to me, and safe, thank God.

Parker, safe. Trevor, safe. Talia, safe. Rachel, safe.

Eddie and I make it to the truck and take a second to catch our breath. Everyone is breathing heavily when they stumble in around us. I look around at the people who have gathered.

"Is everyone okay?" I ask between breaths, and everyone confirms.

Almost half of us haven't even made it to the first truck yet, and I watch with bated breath as they make a break for it after us. Watching such young kids running through literal gunfire makes me want to simultaneously cry and punish every adult responsible for this. Amanda, Jess and her brother, and a line of other older Zoners, run behind them, shepherding them through the warzone like sheepdogs.

Another gunshot *cracks* and to my horror, Amanda drops,

her whole body tumbling forward like she's been kicked in the knees.

Rachel screams. "Amanda!"

No. No, no, no.

Jess looks back, and I see the battle in her eyes. She knows she can't stop. She has to get her brother and the other children to safety. She arrives at the truck in hysterics. "Someone help her, we can't just leave her there!" she begs through sobs.

I try to set the boy in my arms down, but he wails and won't let go. Talia steps next to me, and I half expect her to tell me to leave Amanda. She was responsible for getting Steven killed, after all. But she takes the boy from my arms and comforts him as he sobs. Eddie is at my side in seconds, looking up at me with those big eyes. He sees the battle on my face too, I know he does. He knows I don't want to leave his side.

"Go," he tells me.

I hesitate, but he pushes me away. "Go!" he yells.

It kills me, but I have to let him be that big brave boy he tries to be. I can't just leave Amanda to die. "Take everyone to the basement. Ramos will know what to do."

And then my baby brother takes off running with the young girl to the next truck without even hesitating, groups of Zoners following him unquestioningly.

Parker gives the two children in his arms to another Senior, understanding what I'm about to do.

"Follow Eddie, Ramos is in the basement of Town Hall," I yell to Talia, Trevor, and Rachel, who watch with expressions of worry, waiting to hear how they can help. "Go!"

They prepare the children to run again while Parker and I nod at each other, knowing what we have to do. I blow out a few breaths in sharp succession, like we're at the starting line of a 100-meter sprint. I race out from behind the truck, Parker following closely. We run toward Amanda, who lies about fifty yards away. It's hard to tell if she's breathing or not.

I skid to a stop next to her, dropping to my knees. To my relief she groans as I jostle her, I pull her arm over my shoulders and support her at the waist. Parker does the same, and we work together to pull her to a stand. She's in and out of consciousness, her canvas uniform shirt wet with blood.

"Teo," she croaks, her head lolling forward as we move for cover as quickly as we can. "Teo, please get Lilly out. Please, promise me."

My chest squeezes, remembering the way she held her baby sister closely in the nursery. "You'll get her yourself," I assure her, my voice strained under the exertion of dragging her weight toward the truck. "You're gonna be okay. Let's get you out of here."

We make it to the truck, panting heavily.

My legs feel like jelly, and it takes everything I have to not allow myself to fall under Amanda's weight. My muscles burn and protest with every step. But we're close. We're finally close. The gunshots have slowed, but the smoke seems to be spreading. It billows around us like a dark fog, stinging my eyes.

We approach the trapdoor of the basement, and I stomp on it a few times to let them know we're here. The door groans as it opens a few inches, and Trevor's brown eyes peek out.

"Teo?" he calls out from the crack.

"It's me, we got her."

He pushes the door all the way up and helps us get Amanda down the stairs. I nearly collapse as we descend, but with Trevor's help we get her down safely and shut the door above us. Every time I've come through here before, it's always been dark and dank and empty, but now it's so packed we have to squeeze our way through. There are Zoners everywhere, filling every inch of available space. Some are crying, some are lying down on the floor, some are arguing. It's tense and cramped.

"Move. Back up," Trevor orders as we push through the

small path toward the cells. We just need get Amanda to Ramos. Then he can figure all of this out.

We turn the corner to the holding cell area, and my heart stops. Eddie is waiting there, just like I told him to. But the cell that Ramos has been in every time we've come to visit, is empty.

Ramos is gone.

THE BIGGEST PLOT TWISTS OF ALL TIME

(THE ONES I CAN REMEMBER, AT LEAST.
IT'S BEEN A WHILE OK?)

6. He sees dead people.

5. The dog dies at the end :(

4. He's his father.

3. She was actually alive the whole time.

2. The house was haunted.

1. The mayor wasn't in the cell.

19

WWTD: WHAT WOULD TEO DO?

SAM

My voice is basically gone by the time we stumble into Jones's apartment, and the pain level in my wrist has really turned a new corner. The ache has begun to radiate up my arm, but I don't have time to worry about that now.

After three more passionate speeches to Elites who probably won't even remember them in the morning, I'm somehow both droopy-eyed exhausted and also buzzing with adrenaline. It feels good to be doing something that matters. Well, matters to me. Whether we can help the Elites or not will all depend on if they want to help themselves, but either way it will all lead to Ella. And she's all I care about.

Well.

As if on cue, Q's arm brushes mine as we plop onto Jones's stiff but functional sofa, and a shiver shoots up my arm, which is still humiliatingly bare thanks to this ridiculous outfit. She throws herself back into one of the throw pillows, absolutely unaware of the affect she has on me. She could completely wreck me with a single touch, and she'd have no idea. Her world would just keep turning. I shake the thoughts away and dote on Luna at my feet instead, who soaks in my attention like I'm her whole world. Crazy how dogs can love so unconditionally and expect so little in return.

Zara unbuckles her heels while Jones fills up cups of water for us. His suite is small and quiet, despite the racket from partiers outside. It's pretty standard issue. It looks like it came fully furnished, and since then no one has bothered to do anything else to it. There is no uniqueness or personality to it at all. No homely touch. It almost looks like a hotel room.

Beardsley, who met us here shortly after we arrived, steps out of Jones's restroom almost drunkenly with a big stretch and yawn combo, having traded his E1 outfit for a cotton pair of pajamas he brought in his backpack. "The bathrooms here are the best part about comin' to this freak-fest, I tell you what."

"My turn!" Zara says, claiming the restroom quickly before anyone else can, pulling her rolled up change of clothes out of the bag clipped around her waist.

I slurp the water from the cup Jones hands me gratefully, the cold liquid soothing my aching throat. Safe to say public speaking is not my forte.

Beardsley dumps a plastic bag over on Jones's square dinner table, and hundreds of cards spill out. "Have at it," he says, tossing the empty bag on top of the pile. "'Night y'all."

And with that he lies down onto the second couch that makes an L shape with the one Q and I are sitting on and drapes his arm across his face.

Q snorts. "It's only 7 o'clock, old man," she jokes, but he's already snoring.

I want to contribute a witty reply, to keep the banter up with Q we always have, to just talk with her like normal, but my throat feels tight. It's like my body knows things are far from normal and is taking matters into its own hands. Self-preservation instinct maybe?

So instead of talking easily with Q like I want to, I run from my feelings and join Jones in the kitchen instead. I scoop myself some fried rice and beef from the takeout containers he has set out on the counter, my stomach rumbling at the smell. Jones has traded his black and white server attire for jeans and a rock band t-shirt that looks frustratingly cool with his tattoos, and just makes me feel even more ridiculous in my tassel getup. I look forward to the moment I can pull my own t-shirt out of my backpack and finally adequately cover myself again. I mutter my thanks, and he tries to make polite conversation, but I really want to just shrink away. Luckily, Zara joins us in the kitchen and takes over the conversation with Jones, which takes the pressure off me for social niceties, and I can happily ignore him completely.

I sit away from them at the table, taking a handful of cards in my hand, then letting them fall one by one through my fingers back onto the pile as I shovel rice into my mouth. There are hundreds of playing cards here, an assortment of suits and numbers, half red and half black, and I don't even want to think about what Beardsley had to do to get all these.

My skin bristles against my will as Q comes back in the room from the bathroom and joins in talking to Jones, both of the girls laughing loudly at everything he says. I eat my takeout in brooding silence, yearning for a hot shower and a solid nap.

A sudden shrill beeping noise comes from the other side of the room, and it makes my heart leap.

"What is that *awful* noise?" Zara clamps her hands over her ears and squeezes her eyes shut.

Luna hops back and forth on the carpet, barking at nothing as if she can snatch the beeps right out of the air herself. Beardsley still snores on the couch, completely undisturbed by the noise, and I kind of envy the sleep he's managing to get right now.

Jones sets down his plate of takeout with a laugh, seemingly used to the noise, and walks over to a small table in the corner with some kind of square device on top of it. The shrill noise beeps in a repeating pattern, and a small piece of paper juts out of it slowly with every beep.

Q brings her plate over to the machine and watches over Jones's shoulder curiously. "Is that a... telegraph? What are you, two hundred years old?"

Zara gasps. "Jones are you secretly a two-hundred-year-old vampire who lures beautiful women into your apartment on the premise of takeout and a quiet night in?" She claps her hands with a concerning amount of enthusiasm at that prospect. "Please say yes."

"That sounds like something that would be pretty confidential if it were true." Jones sends her a wink over his shoulder. "But I mean, now that you're already here in my apartment completely coincidentally, you might as well grab some takeout and make yourself comfortable."

When he turns back around, she grabs the spoon from the takeout container, raises it to her forehead and makes a show of pretending to faint in a dramatic swoony way. I laugh, shaking my head at her in feigned disappointment.

"What, can you blame me?" she mouths at me with an unapologetic grin. "He's *unreal*."

My laugh catches when Q whips around, holding the piece of paper from the device with wide eyes. Luna is at her side immediately, sensing her unease.

I stand right away, my heart hammering. "What happened?"

Jones nods toward the device to provide some context. "The radiograph is how the Catacombs contacts me without the Feds knowing."

Q reads the message on the paper, and it sends a jolt of electricity through my veins.

"For Beardsley's team: Full speed ahead. Battle Royale. Sam —cashing IOU. Will send aid tomorrow."

"Does this mean...?" Q breathes.

Zara has leaped across the room to look at the paper herself, as if it will yield different answers to different eyes. She finishes Q's sentence, "He wants a full-fledged EI revolution."

They look at me. *Cashing IOU...* the favor I owe him to get Ella back.

A chill runs down my back. I understand his threat loud and clear: Pull this off, or no Ella.

Luna barks once anxiously, reminding everyone that she doesn't know what's going on, but she can sense the shift in mood. Q kneels and squeezes her cheek to Luna's, whispering reassuring things to her that I can't hear, even as her brows are knitted together in concern herself.

Jones blows a breath through his teeth. "Well, that's a little more than I signed up for."

Same. I had kind of gotten really comfortable with the "plant seeds, do what you can, and then we'll go pick up Ella in 48 hours" idea. Now this?

I think back to paintball, when Calix was explaining the rules of the game to the awaiting group. If I remember correctly, didn't Battle Royale mean... only one survivor? No teams, no ranks. Everyone for themselves. That doesn't give me much reassurance here. Surely, he means we'll triumph as a united front against Vegas *together*?

Q seems to be thinking the same thing. I can see the anxiety etched all over her face.

"What happened to make Cade change his mind so suddenly?" I wonder aloud.

"I hope everyone's okay," Q says softly, chewing on the inside of her cheek.

The air feels thicker as the reality of it becomes clearer and clearer in everyone's minds. Everyone's thinking it.

Forget planting seeds, the actual war is gaining traction, and people are going to get hurt.

No one wants to be the first to speak, but I feel a bit of responsibility here, since this was my idea after all. I wanted this. *Want* this.

Don't I?

Am I willing to start an actual war just to show Vegas I'll do whatever it takes to get my sister back? To carry out my idea of justice for taking her in the first place?

I blow out a breath, steadying myself to do what needs to be done.

Because the answer is yes. It's always been yes. I'll burn down every inch of the Underground to get Ella back.

Now I have to prove it and light the first match.

"Well," I say, breaking the silence, apart from Beardsley's uninterrupted snoring. "We better get to work."

We spend the next few hours writing a tiny, barely visible message on each playing card: *All of it can be ours. L'Deaux tonight 7:00pm. LIVE FREE OR DIE.*

We loop each message around the curves of spades and clubs, in and out of crowns of kings and queens, inside numbers, anywhere discreet, so any Guard who might pick it up off the street wouldn't think twice about it. He'd just think it was a regular card someone had dropped. Only someone looking for a message would find one.

By the time we're done, I feel nearly cross-eyed. Q stacks all the cards together like she's going to shuffle them and deal them out. She doesn't. She yawns instead, and I can't help doing the same. Jones sets out a pile of blankets and pillows and asks if there is anything else we need.

"I think we're good. Thanks, man," I say, and I mean it.

I'm feeling a little less insecure ever since allowing myself to change into the spare clothes from my backpack, finally grateful to get to stop baring all my weaknesses on full display to someone who appears to have none of his own. So now beyond the haze of vulnerability, I can acknowledge that he's shown us a lot of generosity tonight, which I'm sure goes far beyond his pay grade. And I guess I can admit that he's pretty cool.

He gives me a friendly slap on the back before saying good night to the girls with a one-armed hug for each of them and excuses himself to his room. Zara and Q side-eye each other for a second before racing to the last remaining couch, laughingly pushing and shoving each other out of the way trying to get there first. They reach the couch at the same time and breathlessly declare the matter can only be settled through rock-paper-scissors.

I laugh at them as I spread out a couple blankets and a pillow on the carpet for myself next to where Luna is already curled up and snoring. Q falls to her knees with a dramatic sigh to do the same after Zara's rock smashed her scissors to bits. Zara giggles almost maniacally as she makes herself comfortable on the couch.

Settling down on the floor, I stretch out the soreness throughout my body and pull a blanket over me. I stare up at the texture in the ceiling as the exhaustion of the day quickly catches up now that I'm horizontal. The world suddenly goes black, and Q snickers wickedly next to me. She has not only thrown her pillow at me but has done so with what feels like a year's worth of pent-up rage. Luna startles awake at the motion, and I hear her paws shuffling to the other side of the couch and plopping down with a passive-aggressive huff.

"I guess I deserved that," I say through the pillow, my voice muffled. I don't move the pillow off my face right away, and for a moment I weigh the pros and cons of suffocation and slipping off into quiet oblivion.

Pros: I don't have to think about Ella's face full of mistrust and fear the last time I saw her ever again. No need to worry about these pesky confusing feelings for Q. I wouldn't have to wear the tassel vest again.

Cons: I guess it would be an uncomfortable death. Luna might miss me. Ponyboy might too.

When my lungs finally tell me it's time, I move the pillow to find Q already tucked into her blankets a few feet away. I toss the pillow back at her, although I spare her my own pent-up rage.

She laughs, and I don't understand how just the very sound of it can have so much of an effect on me, but suddenly quiet oblivion doesn't seem so appealing if it means I could never hear her laugh again. Even if being apart from Ella is slowly killing me, at least it feels manageable as long as I can keep hearing that laugh.

Huh???

Who am I?

How and when did I become this mopey, jealous, "I jUsT wAnT tO hEaR hEr LaUgH" person basically overnight? As if I didn't hate myself enough.

Zara switches off the lamp at the side-table next to us, sending the whole room into near darkness. She bids us both good night from the couch and turns over on her side away from us, pulling the blanket nearly over her entire head. There is an abrupt strangeness in the room as all the noise dissolves so quickly into an awkward quiet. It's like the darkness just sucked it all up, absorbed it into its shadows. The only sounds now are Beardsley and Luna's soft snores, the repetitive swish of the internal heating system turning on and off, and the faint din of the night festivities carrying on outside.

There is just enough light from the oven light in the kitchen to illuminate the shapes of the furniture and any obstacles I'd need to avoid if I have to make a late-night run to the bathroom. I don't dare peek at Q. It's still way too hard not to spill my guts every time I talk to her, but it takes everything in me not to acknowledge the silence, or at the very least to make some kind of joke to ease the awkwardness. I just keep my gaze fixed on the ceiling above.

Just when I'm sure she must have fallen asleep, I hear the rustling of her blankets and a small sniff.

Don't do it, Sam. Professional and necessary, that's what we agreed. Don't you dare —

I turn onto my side, having only three seconds worth of restraint in me. If anything, it's just to get one final look at her before I fall asleep.

I'm not prepared to see her lying on her back, tears streaming down her face and hands covering her mouth to stifle sobs.

I move until I'm on my side, propped up on an elbow right in front of her. I put a hand on her shoulder. "Q? What's wrong?"

She covers her whole face with her hands and shakes her head, answering me through her hands. "I'm fine, it's nothing— I'm good."

Her body convulses with sobs, even as she tells me she's ok.

"How can I help?" I feel so helpless. I especially don't want to make it worse by doing the wrong thing, which seems to be default for me.

She doesn't answer. She wipes her eyes with her hands and blows out a breath through her mouth. And then another one. And another.

Oh no. I think she's hyperventilating. Her whole body begins to shake.

"Q—" I start to panic. "Luna," I whisper with a low whistle, and I hear her collar clink from the other side of the couch. She sleepily steps around the couch and lies on her belly next to Q. She crawls forward until she can rest her face on Q's stomach. Q is sucking in short breaths but puts a shaky hand on Luna's head. Still trying to reassure her that everything is fine, even as her body is not allowing the denial any longer.

Luna blinks at me with accusation like she's saying, *"Well? Aren't you going to do something?"*

I replay the night, mentally searching for clues for what could be wrong. I quickly realize she has tried to hide it all night. Laughing a little too loudly at times in the clubs, trying really hard to seem at ease, but I saw all the eyebrows creased with worry, the chewing on her cheek, the general fidgeting. And did she even actually eat any of the takeout?

A sudden memory from C9 comes to my mind, remembering Teo's quiet whispers in the darkness of our quarters as Eddie hyperventilated just like this. Panic attacks, Teo had called them. Ok, Sam, think. *What would Teo do?* I pull myself off the floor and rush to the kitchen to fill her a glass of water.

I kneel to help her sit up. Luna drops her chin to the floor, and I know she feels just as helpless as I do. Q protests through sobs. "I'm ok, really, I just need a second—" She is barely even able to croak out the words.

I bring her knees up to her chest and stay close so she can lean against me if she needs to. I hand her the glass of water.

"Just take a couple sips," I tell her, and thankfully she actually does. The glass trembles in her hand as she brings it to her mouth. I take it from her when she's done and set it aside.

"Try to breathe," I whisper, rubbing her back as she sets her forehead on her knees and takes a few shaky breaths. "I'm right here."

To my surprise she crumples into me. I steady myself, forcing my body to be sturdy for her. She cries into my chest, and it shatters me to see her like this. Resilient Q. The forever optimist. Always reassuring everyone else. Always so strong so everyone else can lean on her. I know I have. What is she carrying that she doesn't even show?

I breathe in the fragrance of her hair as she cries, the coils nearly engulfing my whole face. Her hair's soft texture feels just like how I imagined it would. "It's okay. Everything is okay. Breathe."

She blows out a few more breaths, and I offer her the glass of water again. I wish there was more I could do. I'd take every single worry away if I could, absorb hers into mine like I've tried to do for Ella.

"Something just feels off, I don't know why," she finally says into my chest. "I just have such a bad feeling about this."

I don't interrupt, knowing how hard it is for her to be vulnerable like this. I mean, isn't that the exact reason I've been so scared to talk to her all night myself? Because this very well could have been me? I've been one fake laugh away from being cradled in her arms just like this myself.

"I know I gave Beardsley a hard time about it, but I've never wanted to get into something like this either," she whispers. "I've only ever wanted to bide my time until this was all over. Until I could find them."

"Your parents," I whisper back, understanding what she's trying to say.

I feel her nod against my chest.

"And you will. *We* will. This is just a pitstop along the way."

She sniffs. "I know the odds. I know I'll probably never find them anyway."

I pull her chin up to make her look me in the eyes. "Don't give up," I tell her with every ounce of conviction I can muster. "We'll find a way, I swear."

"Why?" she whispers, searching my eyes for answers, her own eyes more bare than I've ever seen them. "Why do you care?"

A chill shoots down my spine. I know why. I know exactly why. If I'm not careful here, I—

It spills out on its own before I can stop it.

"Because I want to find them myself. Your parents," I nearly blurt. Part of me wants to look away, to run, to hide, but the intensity in her gaze is too mesmerizing. Her eyes won't let me stop. "I want to find them, so I can ask them myself how they could ever give you up? How could they not fight for you with every last breath they had? Because I can't comprehend how anyone could ever let you go."

I blink in pure shock as she suddenly leans forward and presses her lips to mine. For a second I'm frozen, scared that this could be a dream, and if I even breathe, I might wake up.

But then I realize: I can feel her lips on my lips. They're soft. They're real.

Holy crap. *This is real.*

So, I kiss her back, pouring into it every fragment of emotion I've kept carefully boxed away for as long as I can remember. Every fiber of my being zeroes in on her lips, to her heart beating so close to mine. It doesn't feel the same as those occasional hidden make-outs with C9 girls, where we would use each other for mutual distraction.

Because she seems to be pouring emotion right back — I feel so many unspoken words on her lips, but I can't piece them all together. Is there a chance she feels the same way? Or is this just from heightened emotions after a vulnerable moment?

She turns her body to close the space between us, and I pull her even closer, suddenly feeling like the very air between us is too much distance. I never want to feel air between us again.

We kiss in the quiet darkness of the apartment, and whether or not this kiss means the same to her as it does to me, I allow myself for just these few moments to feel chosen.

20

WWSD: WHAT WOULD SAM DO?

MATEO

Ramos is really gone. There are a million questions being thrown at me from every direction right now from Eddie and the others, but I have so many of my own that it's like I'm trapped in my own dimension. Did he get out? Or did Nova finally finish the job? I think of the state he was in when I left. The black eye, the cuts, the bruises. He said so himself he didn't think he had much time left, but it's only been less than an hour. The reality of it dawns on me slowly, like a replay shown in slow-motion.

If Ramos is dead... *we* are dead. We can't get past the gates without his code.

"Shut up, *shut up*," I bark, everyone's questioning and arguing stressing me out so much my skin is nearly crawling. "I need a second to think."

I give my half of Amanda's weight to Trevor and turn to walk the other direction, out of the holding cell area to the stairs that go up into the inside upper levels of Town Hall. With an exhausted sigh, I plop down onto one of the stairs and hang my head in my hands.

What am I supposed to do now?

I feel like Sam would know exactly what to do, and I wish for a moment he didn't leave me here to do this all on my own. I know he did what he needed to do, but his absence feels heavy right now.

Amanda needs professional medical attention. There are *kids* in here who need protecting. Everyone is looking to me for a plan. So what would Sam do?

I feel a panic attack coming on, my breaths getting shorter and less controlled the more I think on how much everyone is relying on me. Tears well up in my eyes against my will as I try to control my breathing. The reality is that I have no idea what I'm doing.

I feel a buzz of an incoming message come through my wristTab, the vibration tickling my entire forearm. Huh?

"ZONERS OF ANY AGE WHO WOULD LIKE TO BE PROMOTED TO A SPECIAL ASSIGNMENT OUTSIDE THE ZONE WILL REPORT TO THE SOUTHERN BOUNDARIES AT 6:00PM. -SERGEANT NOVA"

Special assignment? It's obviously a trap, right? I check the time. That's only two hours away.

Sudden footsteps at the top of the stairs, the Town Hall side, make me jump to my feet. I snatch the gun from my waistband and aim, still not even really sure how to use this thing but trying to look confident. "Who's there?" I call out.

The footsteps keep descending down the stairs, echoing off the concrete walls.

"Show yourself!" I yell, which prompts Parker and Trevor to hurry in from around the corner. They each have their guns at the ready.

Finally, the figure emerges from the shadowed stairwell, hands raised in the universal sign of surrender. It's an Elder.

"I am just here to pass along a message. A warning," he says, his voice trembling. "It's about the sergeant and the Mayor."

I look back at Parker. "Watch Eddie, and don't let *anyone* leave for any reason." He nods in confirmation and heads back around the corner. I can't risk anyone taking Nova up on her "special promotion."

Talia comes around the corner, and I look at her with questioning eyes.

"Amanada's losing a lot of blood," she whispers, and her voice shakes as she says it.

"Tell us what you know," Trevor barks at the Elder, ordering him to speak with a threatening upward flick of his own gun.

"I'm in charge of the maintenance of this building," he begins, lowering his hands and fidgeting with the sleeve of his gray Zone uniform. Dark wrinkled eyes behind thick glasses dart between us as he speaks. "I was cleaning the bathrooms when all the commotion outside started, and I've been taking cover inside since. I heard Sergeant Nova's voice in the Mayor's office, and I went over there to see if she had a plan, if she could help me get to safety, but I heard..." He trails off.

"Heard what?" I prompt, but then I kind of feel like maybe I don't actually want to know.

He chews the bottom of his lip. "I... I heard her talking to someone through the Mayor's comms radio."

He looks so shaken up I'm suddenly terrified of what he's about to say. What could he have heard that was this bad?

"Spit it out gramps," Trevor hisses impatiently. A few other Seniors have grouped behind us to listen in, but I don't tell them to leave. They have every right to hear this as I do.

"The person on the comms said, 'Bring anyone with potential. Discard the rest.'"

My lungs feel like they've dropped to my feet.

"Discard?" Talia whispers, voicing what we're all thinking.

The Elder nods, wringing his hands. "They gave her two hours."

The noise level in this stairwell escalates as all of the Zoners around me talk to each other and put the pieces together like I am.

Nova is cleaning out the Zone.

She's going to kill us all.

The FPA really gave her the go ahead to do this? How can they get away with this? How will they explain this to the parents Upstairs when they get word that the place their children were sent to for protection was actually burned to the ground, their children included?

"Everybody shut up!" I yell, pressing my hands into my temples, feeling nearly deaf with how loud it is in here, combined with my pulse throbbing in my ears. I can't even think straight.

"There's one more thing," the Elder says, and he holds up a folded scrap of paper. "Mayor Ramos dropped this when Nova was escorting him back out of the Hall. I assume it's for you. He must have seen you all running for the building."

Trevor and Talia lean in as I unfold the paper. Talia begins to read it aloud over my shoulder, but I shush her. We have to be careful how we handle this going forward, and I don't know who we can trust. The three of us read it silently instead, the rushed handwriting barely even legible.

*"Extermination order—be ready. *North* 6:00pm. Map—office."*

I hold the paper in my hand really still, like it's a fragile baby bird, my muscles relaxing ever so slightly. Ramos didn't leave us stranded. He has a plan. All we have to do is go to the North gates instead of South, and he'll get us out.

This could actually work.

"So can we count on the help of the Elders now?" I ask him,

studying his wrinkled face, the years and years he's had to live, that we might not ever have.

The man rubs the back of his neck. He answers slowly. "The Elders don't particularly like Mayor Ramos... I'll relay the message, but I don't think they'll even trust it, let alone trust *him*."

Trevor scoffs derisively. "Even when their lives are on the line, too? Ridiculous."

The Elder shakes his head. "Many of them are of the opinion that they'd rather die with what they have come to know, rather than die with the unknowns."

"Teo, the babies. We can't just leave them," Talia whispers next to me.

It was never even a possibility. "I know."

"The best I can do is get you in," the Elder says with pressed lips. "I plan to make a break for it at 5:30. I can leave the Nursery unlocked when I go in, but only for ten minutes, no more, considering everything going on." The Elder locks eyes with me, an intense expression crossing over his face. "But I have to ask a favor in return."

I share a look with the group. We're cutting it really close to Ramos's deadline for the gate already, how can we do an additional favor? "What is it?"

His head droops, and he looks overcome with emotion. "I really thought I'd get out of here one day, and I'd be able to get her myself, but"— his voice breaks— "my granddaughter... she's in C12."

He sees the look on my face and quickly adds, "Doesn't have to be right away... just at some point, whenever you are more settled somewhere. Please."

"Come with us," Talia says. "The other Elders might not trust Ramos, but who cares? You can still come. You can get her yourself."

He smiles sadly. "I've been sick for a while. Been trying to hide it. Whatever's coming will come. Please promise me you'll look for her. Milly Roberts, 10 years old."

I look around to the group, and everyone gives hesitant nods. We really have no choice, but I'm glad they agree to the trade. I'd hope someone would look for Eddie if he didn't have me.

"Promise," I confirm. "If we even survive, that is."

He nods and gathers himself to head back up the stairs. "I truly wish you all the best. I'm sorry we didn't do more for you all these years. We should have."

The door to the stairwell clicks behind him, and just like that he's gone.

Well, no time to waste.

I push past the other onlookers and grab Eddie's hand on the way to the main area of the basement. It's dim and stuffy, way past capacity with too many Zoners sitting on the ground shoulder to shoulder, scared but trusting.

So trusting.

They just believe so wholly that I know what to do, that I'll keep them safe.

If my mom could see me right now, stepping up and being the man she always trusted me to become, would she be proud? Would she believe I could actually do this?

The others have followed me out and gather behind me. The exhaustion in the room is so palpable that it's like my body absorbs it, sending a wave of fatigue over me. I'm suddenly very aware that there will be no rest, no relief, for who knows how long. I have absolutely no idea what's ahead, and my body knows that. But I shake it off. That's not what's important right now.

I clear my throat, squeezing Eddie's hand as I address the room. "I'm sure you all received that message from Nova." I gesture to my wrist to remind them, but I doubt anyone has forgotten. How could they?

"There have been some updates," I continue, fidgeting with Ramos's paper in my pocket with my other free hand. "But before I can tell you anything further, lines have to be drawn. This is everyone's last chance to pick a side. We are going to try to get out of here. But if you want to leave with Nova, this is your very last chance to go."

A Senior near the front speaks up. "What if we don't want to leave C9 at all? Who knows what's out there? It could be way worse."

I press my lips together. "You're right, I won't lie to you. I can't guarantee you'll be safe if you come with me. I have no idea if our plan will work. But what I do know is if you walk out that door, you'll die for sure." I pause to let those words sink in before delivering the final blow. "Nova has been given the order to exterminate the entire Zone. You'll be dead within the hour if you stay."

The Zoners in the room mutter to each other, taking the time to process this news just like I had to minutes ago. Talia kneels next to a group of Minors who have begun crying, pulling them in close. Eddie sits by her to help, putting his arm around a small boy that can't be that much younger than him.

"If anyone wants to leave, I won't stop you, but you have to go now."

The tension is thick as everyone looks around, the same questions on everyone's mind. Will anyone be dumb enough to go to Nova? And will anyone be even dumber and choose to stay behind in the Zone?

I raise an eyebrow at the Senior who asked the question, but he sinks back down on to the ground slowly.

I give it another minute, more for my own conscience than anything. In case something bad happens tonight, I need to be sure they chose to be here. I have to know they were informed of the risks and chose to come anyway. There's no way I can live with myself otherwise if things go south, if anyone gets hurt.

I look at Trevor next to me. Parker on the other side. Talia and Eddie helping the children in the front row. Rachel with Amanda's head in her lap. Unexpected friends that have given me the motivation to not give up, to not accept this life that was assigned to us. Their support has kept me going. It still does. They each give me nods of encouragement.

Okay. Let's do this. Let's get the hell out of here.

TYRO B-29

Ella snores peacefully on the couch next to me. The adults are talking in the other room, and I'm trying to listen. I can only pick up pieces, but what I've gathered is they don't know what to do with me. The adult whose home we're in—Penny—seemed kind when we first met, but she was the first one to suggest leaving me behind, so they could all make a clean break without me.

I make things too complicated, she had said.

It's been a few hours since we escaped, which means it's only a matter of time before I start showing symptoms of the missed sync. Last time, it was the very next day that I was completely hospitalized. How long will it take this time?

I know they're right. I know I will slow them down—I already am. Maybe if I had been able to run faster, Steele wouldn't have had to do what she did...

I don't even know the full extent of what will happen the longer I go without syncing. All they told us is that our bodies will slowly shut down, but I really don't even know what that means. But judging by the last time, whatever it is isn't good.

I look at the pile of cables and wires by my feet that I

brought with us. I think I got everything I would need... I can probably figure out how to hook us up pretty easily. I mean I've done it enough times. I can probably have a sync done within minutes.

But it just feels wrong now, knowing what I know.

Especially with her sleeping so peacefully, a little color finally returning to her face now that there isn't a parasite sucking the life out of her.

That's all I am.

A parasite.

All of the reasons for my creation I have thought of, since learning who Aunty truly is behind the smiles and the fake affection, are all bad. Why else kidnap healthy kids, if not for evil purposes? I still can't remember what I'm supposed to know about "Sam," but he must love her if he came all this way to find her.

She was happy and healthy and loved before I came into the picture.

I decide to try and sleep while I can. Soon they'll decide to either let me come along, or they'll leave me behind, but I'll be feeling the full effects of the skipped sync either way. Probably a good idea to rest before then.

Just before I drift to sleep, a scene comes to mind. A memory.

I'm on a swing set. There is a sensation in my body of falling, but not an unpleasant one. The up and down rocking motion of the swing is exhilarating and exciting. I giggle in the memory.

I feel the hand of someone behind me, strong hands, pushing me gently but firmly.

"You ready?" the voice behind me says, a voice that is familiar and warm, a sound my body seems to know more than any other sound it's ever heard.

I shriek excitedly. "Yes!"

Footsteps stomp around me in a rush, and suddenly the voice is no longer just a voice but a body too. A boy. Brown hair, brown eyes—kind eyes. He stops a short distance in front of me, nearly close enough for me to kick him when the swing rocks in his direction.

The comfort and burning in my chest I feel around this person is almost overpowering. I trust this person with my life, with everything.

This must be him.

Sam.

He holds out his arms, a wild grin spreading across his face. Infectious. I can't help but smile with him. I seem to know what he wants me to do without instruction.

He begins to count, the excitement growing even bigger as the countdown begins.

"3... 2...1...JUMP!"

I let go of the swing with a squeal, and for a moment I'm flying. Flying through the air, weightlessly. I'm not even scared. I know he'll catch me.

And he does. We laugh as he holds me in his arms.

And as I drift off to sleep in my own reality, tears stream down my cheeks knowing that memory wasn't for me.

WHEN I WAKE UP, I'm somewhere unfamiliar, and it sends a shock of fear through my body, which feels groggy and stiff. I think I'm in the back of a vehicle, and I panic, remembering Ella's memory of arriving to Aunty. Against her will.

I sit up quickly, too quickly, and I feel dizzy as the blood rushes to my head. I make sense of what is around me and feel a little better seeing Ella there, awake and speaking quietly to Lala and Red. We are tucked away in the back of some kind of van. There are boxes and boxes that appear to be arranged in a way to conceal us.

They notice I'm awake and sense my panic.

"Hey," Ella says, with a small smile. She looks better. Healthier.

And that sends a guilty slice through my insides.

"Hi," I say back, my voice small and timid, rife with the shame and guilt I feel by looking at her, by just existing.

I suddenly feel nauseous. There is a familiar tickle on the back of my neck, a warm tickle, and I know if it spreads down my back I'm going to pass out. I try to take deep breaths.

"Are you okay?" Red asks, his voice soft but carrying across the small distance of the van.

I nod, trying to swallow down the vomit that is threatening to come out.

A line of sweat breaks out on my forehead.

It's happening sooner this time. My symptoms.

Breathe in, breathe out.

The warmth travels down my back against my will, blackness creeping into my vision.

No, no. Not this soon...

I wanted to at least meet him first. *Sam.* I wanted to match the memories, the feelings ingrained in my body, to a real person. I wanted to experience it for myself.

Love.

Just as the blackness is about to consume me, the vehicle jerks to a stop and startles me so badly I snap back to consciousness. We look at each other as we hear the muffled voices outside. Red moves toward the back door, but before he even has a chance to investigate, the doors are thrown open.

The sight of her face sends an electric shock through my body that makes me start to fade to black again. Like my very heart has stopped beating altogether.

Aunty.

I'm about to fade, I'm on the very cliff of unconsciousness, but I see her sickly-sweet smile and hear her say, "You really thought you could get away from me that easily? Since you want to be so involved, let's go for a little drive, shall we? We have somewhere to be."

21

DO OR DO NOT, THERE IS NO TRY...
OR SOMETHING LIKE THAT

MATEO

Now that everyone in the room has chosen to stay, I take a deep breath, aware that we're crossing a metaphorical threshold here. The very next step we take is either the first step into our new lives, or it's one foot into our own graves.

"Okay, here's the plan."

And just like that it's like the energy shifts in the room. It was like a spark that just needed to be lit, a hope that needed to glimmer just long enough to hang on to. The Seniors who had given up are now determined. The Minors who were scared now want to help.

They've tried so hard to pit us against each other and encourage an atmosphere of apathy for each other, but they just didn't want us to realize how strong we are when we care. When we have friends to fight for. And this is how we beat them. Together.

We spend the next half hour strategizing and organizing our priorities.

Priority one - Gathering food and necessities, including medical supplies for Amanda. Parker still has the keyring he swiped from the Guard to get our cuffs off. He's going to take a group of Seniors and raid as many supply sheds as they can find.

Priority two - Defense. Whatever Guards are left are going to start coming any time now to carry out Nova's extermination order. We have an advantage that we're in a secluded spot with only two ways in or out. Trevor and anyone else who managed to collect firearms off bodies on the way here will monitor the two entrances to the basement. A Guard even gets close? They're dead in seconds.

Priority three - Transportation. The abandoned trucks the rebels came in are our best bet of escape. Talia will sneak out and find as many truck keys as she can, hopefully before any of the intruders or Nova's people do.

Priority four - Ramos's office. He said something about a map in his message. We've decided he means a map of the Underground, which is pretty vital, or else we'll just be traveling in blind circles if we even do make it out of here. I have the code to Ramos's office that he gave me last time I visited him in his cell, which I'll use to find this map.

And finally - The babies. Since the Elders aren't going to help, we have no choice but to take the babies by force. This will be our very last objective, so we can hurry them into the trucks and speed for the Northern Boundaries right after. It will also require basically every hand on deck. I'm particularly terrified of this step, considering I know close to nothing about babies, and I would never forgive myself if one of them got hurt. But luckily some of the babies' older siblings are in this room, which makes at least a little less responsibility for me.

As the details start to come together, the anxiety in my body that has been growing and spreading all day, reaches a strange level of numb. Almost like it has reached capacity and just decides to stop there. I guess my body has finally realized that worrying is not only unproductive, it's dangerous. I need to be composed. I need to be clear-headed. Nothing can hold me back, not even my own mind. Because if it does, people will die. *Eddie included.*

There is a noisy bustle around the basement as everyone makes preparations for their task with their groups, like soldiers preparing for battle. Except there isn't that heavy dread or cold fear you'd expect, considering we may be facing our deaths the moment we leave this basement. I think so many of us are just ready to finally act, to finally put a foot down after all this time, so instead of fear there's just a buzz of anxious but hope-filled adrenaline.

I kneel in front of Eddie. "You ready for this?" I ask him, putting a hand on his shoulder.

He looks at me with those brown eyes that I swear have aged ten years overnight. "I'm ready," he says with determination. "How can I help?"

"I think I want you to stay here and help with the little kids." I put emphasis on 'little' to make him feel big and important, even though many of them are his age. "Especially if Guards start coming, they might get scared."

He nods, accepting the assignment bravely.

"And help Rachel and Jess if they need any help with Amanda." I pull him in for a hug, squeezing progressively tighter until he laughs. "I love you, *Lalito.*"

"Love you too." He sets to work on his assignment right away, leaving me to go sit by a group of children. I smile as I watch him for a second. I can't wait to create a new life for him. Anywhere will be better than here. We'll make it so.

I step around the Zoners scattered across the basement floor over to where Trevor is already posted at the trapdoor. He has it propped open just a few inches, only enough to remain mostly hidden while also able to see anyone coming. I jog up a few steps.

"You good, bro?" I call up to him.

He glances down just for a second to see it was me who spoke before returning his watchful gaze back to the outside. "Yep, can't wait to get some target practice in if any Guard gets ballsy enough to approach."

I leave him be, knowing he'll protect these kids like I would. I know Eddie will be safe here.

From a cursory glance around the crowded room, it appears Talia has already headed out with her group to collect the truck keys. I look for Parker next. He's readying a group of Seniors. They've collected a myriad of mismatched sacks and boxes among the clutter of the basement to hold the supplies they'll be gathering in their raids. Parker raises his chin in greeting when he sees me coming. "Hey, man."

"You guys all good?"

Parker pats the gun tucked into his waistband with a chuckle. "Ready as I've ever been."

The group hoots in enthusiastic agreement, and I join them. "Well, I hope you don't need it, but if you do... kick some ass."

"You too, boss." Parker gives me a salute, and I return it over-dramatically.

Last stop is Rachel and Jess's group, and I'm dreading this one the most, knowing Amanda's state probably hasn't magically resolved. I kneel next to them. Amanda is fading in and out of consciousness. They have packed her wound with hodgepodge layers of fabric and clothing. Rachel is pressing it with both hands. Jess has gotten a shirt wet from the sink of one of the holding cells and has laid it over her forehead, stroking her hair. Jess's brother sits close by, and I regret not even asking his name when we spoke outside the school.

"How's she doing?" I whisper.

Jess looks at me, her eyes puffy from crying. She shakes her head, sharing a look with Rachel. "It's not looking good, Teo." Her voice breaks. "I don't know what else to do."

I take her hand, and her brother puts his hand on her shoulder comfortingly. "It's going to be okay," I tell her. "You've done everything you can do."

"She's lost so much blood. Without supplies, a tourniquet, *something*. I—" she breaks off, her eyes filling with tears.

I give her hand a squeeze. "Parker will find something in the supply sheds. Don't give up. Let's hold out for a miracle."

She nods, sniffling, turning the wet fabric on Amanda's forehead over. "Tell him to hurry. I... I don't think she has much time left."

"It will be okay," I repeat with as much of a smile as I can muster, pulling myself up to my feet. Rachel stands too, and another Senior takes over pressing the wound. Rachel's hands are covered with blood.

I walk with her across the room toward the holding cell area, tousling Eddie's hair as I pass. He and the other children are sitting in a circle, playing some kind of game with marbles they've managed to find somewhere, probably from the pile of forbidden shenanigans he and Ella hid down here. I give him one more parting look over my shoulder, and he smiles back reassuringly.

I lean up against the metal frame of Ramos's empty holding cell as Rachel steps inside to wash her hands in the dirty sink in the corner. "You okay?" I ask her.

She doesn't answer. She washes her hands, scrubbing more and more aggressively until I walk over and put a hand on her shoulder.

"Rachel." I switch off the water.

Her head drops, and a sob that she seems to have been holding back for a while breaks free. She steps into me, and I pull her in for a hug.

"We were so harsh to her when everything happened with Steven," she sobs, her voice muffled by the thick fabric of my uniform shirt. "It wasn't her fault, but we were so mean."

"I know." I just let her cry, knowing there's not really anything I can say to make it better. She's right. We really were so hard on Amanda when everything happened, but it could have been any of us that the Guards overheard.

Rachel steps back and wipes her eyes with the back of her hand. "You better get going," she sniffs.

"It's going to be okay," I repeat, thinking maybe the more times I say it, the more times I will it to be so, maybe it'll actually be true.

She gives me a tight smile and leaves.

Okay. It's time.

I turn the corner to the stairwell and I'm relieved to see that it's Jordan posted at the top of the stairs keeping watch. He has two Minors of his own down here, little twin sisters. I know he'll defend this basement with his life. Eddie is in the best possible hands.

We fist bump when I reach the top of the stairs, and we share a look of understanding. Not many people in the Zone understand what it's like to have had the overwhelming pressure of caring for a younger sibling, while also enduring Zone life themselves. Being in survival mode and responsible-for-others'-survival mode at the same time is exhausting. He gets it.

He gives me a single nod as pull the gun out of my waistband. I open the door into Town Hall. "I'll knock three times when I come back," I whisper over my shoulder.

The hallway that the stairs spit me out into is cold, dim, and empty. It feels like a morgue. It takes me a second to orient myself and figure out where I am, since I've never come into the Hall from this direction before. I keep close to the wall and make short sprints from doorway to doorway, in case any Guard comes passing by. The Mayor's office is at least on this side of the building. I think.

I recite the numbers of the code Ramos gave me to his office over and over again to keep calm as I sprint.

9-7-1-1-4-2-0-0.

I make it to the end of the hallway. *9-7-1-1-*

I flatten myself against the wall as I hear approaching footsteps.

It's a Guard.

22

OR DIE

SAM

When I awake to the artificial sunlight of morning filtering in through the window, it takes me an extra second to adjust to reality. I feel dazed as I try to wake up from the first deep sleep I've had in weeks, maybe *months,* taking longer than usual to get my wits and figure out where I am.

But then I feel her warm breath on my neck, and I allow myself to decide that she's real. This is real. We fell asleep only a few minutes after our kiss, both succumbing to the exhaustion of the day. But despite being on the thin carpet of Jones's apartment, I don't think I've ever slept better. And even though I'm pretty sure I have no feeling left in my arm from her sleeping on it, feeling the warmth of her body nestled up next to mine, I never want to wake up any other way.

But now I'm terrified to move because what if this didn't mean anything to her, and whenever she wakes up it'll be over? What if she says it was all a mistake, and I never get to feel her this close again? I don't know how I could live with that.

I close my eyes and ignore the sounds of shuffling of feet, the flush of the toilet from the bathroom, Luna's paws pacing back and forth excitedly as everyone awakens, the coffee maker whirring to life in the kitchen, and try to pretend like real life isn't carrying on around us, trying to hang on to the final seconds of this moment before everything ends.

Q's head turns on my arm, which puts her face right in front of mine. I wish I could take a picture of how she looks at this exact moment. I swear she's never looked so chest-achingly beautiful. The glow of the morning light in the room is making her skin practically shimmer like bronze that has caught the real sunlight at just the right angle. Her face is perfectly relaxed and content, not a trace of the makeup or stresses that come with Ei. Her lips are full and *so breathtakingly close*. I desperately want to kiss her again.

Her eyes flutter under her eyelids as she begins to come-to, and I brace myself for it all to be over. Her eyes blink open and look around for a moment with sleepy confusion. Her eyes flick over to me, and something in me crumbles as a look of horror crosses her face, confirming my nightmare.

She pulls the blanket up over her face and groans. Her voice is muffled through the blanket. "Ughhh I'm so embarrassed."

There it is. I knew it. She regrets it.

She's still lying on my arm, so I don't pull away, as much as I want to. Even with the incessant pain intensifying in my wrist, this hurts worse.

I clear my throat, deciding to play dumb. If she's going to rip my heart out, I'm not going to make it easy for her. She's got to spell it out, so I know clear as day to never go there again. "Embarrassed about what?"

She's still talking into the blanket. "I never cry. I feel so dumb."

"*That's* what you're embarrassed about?"

She pulls the blanket down and looks up at me, her eyes wide. "Why, was there something else too?"

I blink at her, dumbfounded. "Q, there's nothing wrong with crying, are you kidding me? You had a heightened human moment. I thought you regretted—" It catches in my throat.

She comes off my arm and up onto her elbow, sending me a bewildered look of her own. "Kissing you? Of course not—"

"You did what now?" Beardsley saunters out of the bathroom at just that moment, running a towel through his wet gray hair.

Q sits up cross-legged, pulling Luna in close and squeezing her face to hers. "Can you be any more annoying?" she groans at Beardsley. "It's only 9am. It was a kiss, and it was a good one. Get over it, old man."

"It's actually 10am," Jones corrects cheerily from the kitchen as he sips a mug of coffee. I didn't even know he was over there, but something about being the one that gets to be here next to Q while he's all the way over there makes me feel way less of the Neanderthal urge to growl and beat my chest at him like I did yesterday. What is it about a beautiful girl that makes guys completely de-evolve?

Beardsley puts his hands up in surrender, but I think I hear him mutter something Southern about kittens and biscuits as he walks into the kitchen. But I don't care enough to register it, as my thoughts have completely fixated on those three words she said.

I lower my voice to a husky whisper. "A good one, was it?"

Q nails me in the face with a pillow. "Don't push it."

Beardsley fills himself a cup of coffee. "Little Miss Sunshine out for a morning stroll?"

That's when I realize for the first time that Zara's couch is empty. She's gone.

I should have noticed immediately the lack of squeals and shrieks when the topic of kissing came about.

Q and I share a look of worry at the sight of Zara's empty couch, knowing how nervous she was to be back here. I send a silent hope to the universe she wasn't found out. I have no idea what the consequences are for what she's done, but I know it can't be anything good, especially with the talk of rebellion we were spewing *loudly* last night.

"Maybe she just needed some fresh air," I joke dryly, knowing the musk of way more humans alive and breathing down here than Earth ever intended is anything but fresh.

Jones is catching Beardsley up about what happened while he was sleeping over coffee, and I'm a little relieved I'm not the one who has to tell him about Cade's message. I stand and stretch out, offering a hand to Q. To my surprise she doesn't slap my hand away like she usually does, and she actually lets me help her up.

She doesn't drop my hand once she's up, which sends a hopeful warmth through my chest. Could this mean we've officially crossed a threshold, that we've passed into new territory with a new physical closeness? While I will never prefer the alternative, there are so many new unspoken rules to stress about, like can I hold her hand any time, or only certain times? Am I allowed to kiss her again? I still don't know if the kiss meant the same to her as it did to me, but knowing she doesn't regret it fills me with a light I haven't felt in so long. I want to stay as close to her as she'll let me.

But then I notice she is chewing on the side of her cheek again, like she was doing yesterday. I decide to test the new territory and tug her hand to pull her in closer to me. She doesn't pull away, but her brows pull together.

I whisper into her hair. "It's going to be okay," I assure her, followed with another test of the new territory: "We do today together."

She takes a deep breath into me. "Together," she repeats. *Together.*

There is so much more I want to say. She's giving me an inch, and I want to sprint a whole 5k, spill my entire heart out on the ground in front of her and say, "Take it or leave it." But I know this isn't the right time or place. We have too much work to do. I can tell her everything after the work is done.

So instead, I press a small kiss into her temple and rest my forehead on hers.

"How do you do that?" she murmurs.

"Do what?"

"Ground me so easily. Who knew the cure for my anxiety would just be someone telling me everything is going to be fine?"

I chuckle. I'm about to tell her that I'm just giving her back what she gives me, when the door to Jones's apartment opens. Luna barks once to notify us, as if we couldn't have possibly heard the door open ourselves with our mere human ears.

It's Zara, hands full of several to-go bags.

Q sighs in relief. "Oh, thank God you're okay."

Zara smirks in my direction. "Yeah, I can tell you were really worried about me."

Q glares at her, taking some of the bags to help her carry them to the kitchen. "*I was.* Where have you been?"

Zara's voice rises a noticeable octave. "I was just getting breakfast, see?" She pulls out pastries from the bags to demonstrate.

I join them in the kitchen and happily accept a croissant, tossing half to Luna.

Q does too but narrows her eyes at Zara. "You *only* went to get breakfast," she repeats pointedly, taking one for herself.

Zara doesn't answer and busies herself with taking out the various jams and butters from a bag and prepares a pastry for Jones.

"Z," Q says sternly, like a mom who knows when her kid is lying and is just trying to extract the truth she already knows.

Zara gives the pastry to Jones with a smile and makes one for herself, still ignoring Q.

"What, am I just a ghost around here or somethin'?" Beardsley says with his hands out.

"Maybe if you hadn't slept all night and left us to do all the work, you'd get special treatment too," I grumble with my mouth full. "Jones helped, and he doesn't even know what's going on."

"It's true, I've never been more confused in my life," he answers, taking a bite of his croissant. "Happy to help though. Sure beats washing dishes at VIVA."

Q hasn't given up. She's still glaring at Zara, who is now preparing one for Beardsley. "Spill."

Zara hands it to him with a sigh. "Fine." She folds a napkin into a tiny square to avoid meeting our eyes. "I *may have* gone back to my place."

Q gasps. "You could have been caught, what were you thinking?"

"I know, I know." Zara's eyes begin to water. "I just had to see if it helped..."

Q steps next to her and puts a hand on her arm comfortingly. "With remembering? Did it?"

Zara shakes her head, a tear falling down her cheek. "I still can't remember anything about my last day here."

I offer some positivity in spite of the fact that it's very unlike me. "It'll come back," I insist. "Probably when you least expect it."

"Not to be the bearer of bad news," Beardsley interrupts gruffly. "But if we're doing this, we gotta get movin'."

"Oh, *now* he wants to help," Q jokes with a roll of her eyes.

"If there's one thing I've learned in all these years of working for Cade," he answers with a tone that runs a chill down my spine, "is that what he says goes."

He's right. I mean Cade was *married* to Vegas for God's sake and now look where we are. Prompting an all-out rebellion just to one-up her. Just shows what happens when you get on his bad side. I know that's a place I never want to be.

So, we better get to work.

NERVES TICKLE on the back of my neck as we await our turn in line an hour later. We're standing in line for the magtrain, and the thought of boarding that unnatural beast of machinery is making me nervous. I'm far more comfortable on the safety of the ground and also bummed I've been in E1 for 24 hours now but haven't gotten to ride my magboard at all yet. However, Zara insists the train the quickest way to get to L'Deaux from here. Jones had to go into work, but he promises to see us tonight at the meeting.

We split up the playing cards we prepared equally, so we can each help distribute them on our way. I have a few in my pocket and the rest in my backpack. Beardsley and I have put our same outfits on from yesterday—I swear I'm going to burn these tassels as soon as I get out of here and just ask Mack for forgiveness later— while Q and Zara have traded outfits. Zara now wears the black one-piece and Q sports the glittery rhine-stoned one. There is a C-shape of jewels glued to both sides of her face that frame her eyes and cheekbones, and her lips are painted a metallic silver. Half of her hair is pulled back from her ear in three rows of tight braids while the other half is huge and bouncy with silver tinsel tied into it. Luna's leash is wrapped tightly around her hand, her fur and snout adorned with matching silver glitter paint.

Q sees me staring and gives me a wink that just about kills me. "What, never seen a girl in diamonds before?" she teases.

"Every time I think you couldn't possibly get more gorgeous, you somehow do," I answer honestly.

She blinks at me in speechless surprise, and Zara sighs dreamily.

"Oh dear Lord, give me a break," Beardsley growls. "I did not sign up for this puppy love nonsense. Get a handle on yourself, Prettyboy."

Zara pats him on the head. "Aw, has no one called *you* gorgeous today, Beardsley?"

The line moves forward as the magtrain swishes to a stop in front of us, floating eerily above the magnetic track. Luna backs up with lowered ears as it approaches, tugging on her leash with a soft whine. She seems just as leery of the beast as I am.

Beardsley scowls. "Once we get Steele, Red, and Lala back, I'm killin' them myself for leavin' me on babysitting duty with you lot."

We all laugh at his despair as we board the magtrain, especially when he has to pick up Luna and carry her inside when she refuses to step inside herself, even despite Q's persistent tugging.

The seats inside are filled with a mixture of Elites. Some sleepy and hungover, just now heading home after an all-nighter, and others like us are fresh and ready to go. I feel a pang of pity for them. Even at my lowest points in C9, having Ella at least gave me something to live for, some kind of purpose. This kind of lifestyle just seems so pointless.

The doors slide shut before we've even taken our seats, and I'm instantly queasy as the magtrain takes off above the track, wobbling up and down with the magnetic push and pull of the track. Q sits in the seat next to me but is folded in half to hug Luna from above as she sits shaking at her feet.

"It's okay, Loon, we're safe," she coos.

There is a tug in my chest, seeing Luna like this. I've never seen this side of her. She's always so fearless.

Zara gives me a reassuring smile from the seat on the other side of me. "See, isn't this fun?"

I look out the window behind me, despite wanting to puke, and see the blur of E1 pass by. We're level with some rooftops, but the tallest skyscrapers still tower above us. Even during the brightest time of the daytime overhead shell lights, the bright neon of the club signs lined up and down the road are still mesmerizing, creating a sort of flashing blur as we whiz by. The blur turns green as we pass under a line of impossibly huge trees that have grown up and around the track in a leafy tunnel.

Beardsley is standing in front of us, holding onto the upper handles, and I'm about to make fun of his face, which is looking just as green as the tunnel, to distract myself from my own nausea, when the train suddenly comes to an immediate stop. I have to root my feet to the floor to keep from flying forward like Zara does. Beardsley throws out a hand to catch her. Q nearly somersaults upside-down into Luna but holds onto my arm before she falls. I look around to find that many of the other passengers have fallen into each other and are all in various levels of distress.

Luna whines, too scared herself on this vessel to go into defense mode, and Q's lips are pressed into a hard line as she holds her, stroking her fur. A bad feeling settles in my gut as the havoc on board tells me this is not a normal occurrence. The look on Zara's face confirms it.

Do they know we're here? Did they find us?

"Y'all wait here," Beardsley instructs us as he stands to investigate.

We ignore him, obviously.

We follow Beardsley to the front of our section of the train, Q gently dragging Luna to follow behind us. The doors are all still sealed shut and don't open for the passengers trying to get out, which creates a more urgent chaos.

We're among the first of the passengers to gather our wits quick enough, so we're lucky to have a clear view out the window. Luna puts her front paws up on the seat, so she can look out the window, too. Even though she doesn't quite under-stand what's going on, she wants to. Our section is near the front of the magtrain, so the electric engine is just a few sections ahead, with the empty winding track just ahead of that. The magtrain bobs a little with the push and pull of magnetic force below from the movement aboard, and I imagine this is how it feels to be on a boat.

Beardsley points to the track. "There!"

I squint, trying to make sense of the blur he's pointing to.

The girls both gasp, but it takes me a moment longer to register that it's a *person* on the tracks.

Our gasps get the attention of the rest of the passengers, who begin to crowd around the windows, stretching their necks to see around each other. Luna growls when they get too close, her patience level thin. Beardsley pushes up the window, which only opens about a foot, probably so no one can squeeze out of it. The people at the other windows down our section do the same.

The person on the tracks is standing there very still, arms raised in surrender, dressed in all black except for a red X painted on their front.

Q covers her mouth in horror. This can't be good.

Did they hope the train wouldn't stop? Or did they know it would, so they could send whatever message they're trying to convey here? What does the X mean?

I wait breathlessly, watching as the person just stands there.

"Cavalry's here," Beardsley grunts, poking his head out the window to look at the scene below.

There is a crowd below the track. They are watching the person in awe just like we are. A group of guards in black have also gathered. They are setting up a large inflatable on the ground below. Everyone inside quiets down to a pin-dropping silence as we all strain to try to hear what the guards are saying, but it's still impossible to hear from this distance. Zara is clutching my forearm, her nails digging into my skin as we watch.

"They're telling them to jump," Q whispers through her hands.

The person doesn't jump. They stay completely frozen there, like they can't even hear what the guards are saying.

Just jump, I mentally beg them. Do these Elites even know what the FPA is capable of? What these Guards are instructed to do if we don't comply? At C9 we knew the outcome for something like this. We knew it clear as day, and we wore our fear daily like a uniform. Here the Elites are so carefree, they lack that same fear... do they even know the consequences?

We jump as the *bang, bang, bangs* pop outside, muffled but unmistakable.

People scream.

"No!" Zara cries. She's nearly broken through the skin on my arm with her nails.

The person sways for a moment, and part of me prays the guards missed. *Please.*

They sway nearly a full 180, enough to where we get a clear view of what is painted in red on the back of their jacket. Two words:

Or die.

They fall to the ground.

I act quickly, so I don't have to see if their body lands on inflatable or crunches into the concrete. I pull my stack of playing cards out of the front pocket of my backpack, and before I even know what I'm doing I've dropped the entire stack out the cracked window. They flutter to the ground like butterflies.

Q looks at me in impressed shock, and I'm just as shocked as she is. She pulls out hers quickly and does the same. The Elites all over the ground below are expecting them this time and reach for them as if they're dollar bills. The Guards are too distracted with the body to even notice. Beardsley shuffles us away from the window as the magtrain begins moving again. The girls lower onto the seats, and Zara cries into Q's shoulder. Q hands me Luna's leash, a silent instruction to try to comfort her, her body shaking again once the train started back up.

I pet her absentmindedly as the magtrain speeds along like normal, as if that person's life was nothing. Just a bug on the windshield. I can't help but feel the weight of guilt riding on my shoulders. *Or die.* I know the "live free or die" propaganda was spread by Vegas long before we decided to steal it, but I feel especially responsible since I'm the one who set things in motion. I'm the reason they will actually have to choose between the two. *Today.*

This person's message was clear - they were ready to die if they couldn't be free, but what about the rest of the Elites? Are they ready for that choice? Especially after witnessing this, will this scare them away from the cause?

The reality finally dawns on me that no one could show up to Willie's after seeing what the guards are truly capable of. It's possible no one here will actually want change enough to fight for it. And then what? Tell Cade I failed, and have to figure out a different way to get Ella? No. I can't let that happen. This has to work.

This is my last chance.

ALL OF IT CAN BE OURS
L'OCEAUX TONIGHT 7PM
LIVE FREE
OR DIE

23

CODEWORDS ARE OVERRATED – CAN WE JUST STICK TO ENGLISH OR ESPAÑOL?

MATEO

I tighten my grip around the cool metal of the gun as the Guard's footsteps in the hallway nearby get closer. I tuck myself into the closest doorway and hope he continues straight instead of turning down this hallway.

Breathtaking seconds pass, and to my relief the footsteps fade the other direction. I wait a few extra seconds before moving. I peek around the corner at the end, looking both ways before sprinting down as lightly as I can.

I make one more right-hand turn and arrive at Ramos's office nearly on the verge of passing out because I'm trying to be quiet, so I can't gulp for air like I need to. With shaking hands, I input the code into the keypad next to the metal frame of the door.

9-7-1-1-5-2-0-0

To my horror it blinks red. *Error.*

I recite it in my head. Wait, was it a 5 or a 4? Will this sound an alarm if I do it wrong again?

I press the numbers more slowly, trying a 4 instead.

9-7-1-1-4-2-0-0

I hold my breath, ready to take off for the stairwell if an

alarm sounds. To my relief, the metal door slides open with a swish, a cool blast of air smacking my face from inside the office.

I step inside and press the button on the inside to close the doors as quickly as I can, my hands still shaking.

Okay. I made it.

If I were a super secret map of the Underground, where would I be? I approach the closest bookshelf and rummage through the books and papers there aimlessly, not even really sure what I'm looking for exactly, but hoping I'll just know it when I see it.

No luck.

I move to search the other bookshelf near Ramos's desk. On this side of the office there is a window that overlooks the whole Square. I take a hesitant peek out the window, trying to stay as hidden as possible. My stomach turns as I take in the scene outside.

Bodies. *So many bodies.*

It seemed like a lot as we were running through the warzone but seeing it from this vantage point is so much worse. Fortunately, the trucks are still where the outsider rebels left them, and I don't see Talia and her group sneaking around, so they must have already collected all the keys they could find. But that's the only good thing from what I'm looking at.

It's an actual graveyard out there.

It looks like most, if not all, of the outsiders lie dead on the ground. There are many bodies of helmeted Guards mixed in, to where I wonder how many there could even be left, but the number of outsiders' bodies far outnumber the Guards. Did they really think they could just storm a federal Zone, with a couple dozen men and basic artillery, and survive? They were either misinformed about the security here or just irrationally overconfident.

It's no wonder the rest of the Guards haven't come for us

guns blazing yet. They simply don't have the manpower. Nova has to strategize now. And somehow that scares me way worse.

Reminding myself I need to get back to my search, I turn to search the closest bookshelf. That's when I notice out of the corner of my eye that Ramos's deskTab is still on, so the whole top surface of his desk is lit up with its last activity. I lean down to look at it closer. An outgoing call lasting only 1 minute and 43 seconds.

This must be the call that the Elder overheard.

There is also a pop-up on the screen that hasn't been swiped away yet, with a calendar reminder from this morning. *Supply delivery, auto gate gap - 2:47pm.*

I think of the delivery truck that came speeding toward us from the Southern Boundaries. The outsiders must have hijacked the truck right as this "gap" happened. There's no other way they could have gotten in.

My eyes scan across the surface of the deskTab and a thought crosses my mind. What if it's not a paper map I'm looking for? Did Ramos leave his deskTab unlocked for a reason?

I lower myself down into the rolling chair that has been strewn to the side and roll myself back to the desk. It should be easy enough to search through the deskTab, since its interface looks similar to my wallTab by my bed and the tableTabs in the Mess Hall. I tap the little house icon on the left side of the desk. It closes the outgoing call and calendar reminder and takes me to the home screen. The file folders on the home screen are all labelled and seem pretty ordinary. Financials. Logistics. Scheduling. Contacts.

But then I see a smaller one in the corner called X. I tap the folder icon to open it. It opens to nothing except another folder called X. I click that one, and inside it is another one. And then another one. And then another. Finally the folder opens to a line of files. They aren't named, but instead are each titled only a seemingly random series of letters and numbers. I open the first one. It's a list of names, each preceded by the title 'Mayor.' There are 20 of them, one for each Zone I'm guessing. Some of the names have an O next to them, and the others have an X.

I close it and open the next file. It's another list of names. Ella's name is at the bottom. All of the names above hers have an X next to them, but hers has an O. I think of the children Ramos told me about that this Vegas person has been experimenting on, and I feel a little nauseous seeing, what I assume to be, their names listed here with an X next to their name. Each one a real person with a name, not just an idea. And not just a person, a child. And experimented on like some sick science project.

I continue scrolling through the files, my heart pounding with each one, aware that my time is running out here. I really need to get back there—Jess had said Amanda didn't have much more time left. We don't have any wiggle room for delay. I blink in confusion as the next document opens. The entire page is just full of numbers, no breaks in between them. It's hard to tell if there is any kind of pattern or sequences, but I'm sure that's the point. It must be something important, though, if it's tucked away this deep in a random folder.

I open the next file and find a series of encrypted messages. The sender is marked as "C" and the messages are basically gibberish that seem to be in some kind of code, except for what seems to be dates and times mixed in with the code. I scroll all the way to the end of the correspondence and see a final message from "C." It's from this morning. Ramos couldn't have even seen this. All it says is: "Plan change. Today."

I tap on various places around the messages, trying to figure out how to send an outgoing message. Maybe "C" can tell me where to find the map, or at least give me an idea of where to go once we're out of here. No matter where I tap, though, I can't seem to figure out how to send an encrypted message back. It just seems like a static document. I puff out a frustrated sigh and move to the next file. There are only three left.

The next is the same thing, a separate series of messages, but with what appears to be a different person. These ones are labelled with an "H." This conversation is also mostly unintelligible. The last one was from a few days ago, and I can't tell whether they are code words, a different language, or just words I don't have stored in my vocabulary. English is my second language, after all. It says, "Coup d'état à venir."

Huh?

My brain feels so packed full of information that I don't have the ability to process or the proper context for, feeling a bit like when something is just barely out of reach and you're stretching for it, but you can't quite reach it.

I move on to the next file. It's a document that is several pages long of blueprints, I think. Blueprints of *Zones*. With just a quick scroll of the document, I'm seeing resources, labelled exits, surveillance hotspots, highlights of vulnerable spots and potential weaknesses. Ramos has been gathering intelligence on the other Zones. But why? What was he planning?

My conspiracy-theorist heart is really wishing I had more time to dig deeper into all this, but the clock is ticking, and I need to get us all out of here.

The final file. I hold my breath as it loads on the screen of the desk surface.

I pump my fist in victory. It's the map. I touch and drag the image around to familiarize myself with it. I don't think I've even looked at a map since elementary school before we all came Under, much less had to rely on one for survival. It seems like it was put together quickly rather than precisely, as the boxes and shapes around the image look a little haphazard.

Am I supposed to memorize this?

It takes me a minute to find where C9 is among all the small squares that are supposed to represent the Common Zones.

We're apparently the last Common Zone on the west-side of the Underground and seem to be the most isolated. According to the map, C9 is the furthest away from anything else. E1 is North of us, but it's hard to say exactly how far, considering there is no key or scale that I can see. Wouldn't that be a kind of important detail on a map?

I zoom out on the image now that I've found C9. Exit... exit... where is the exit? With a little more zooming and dragging on the screen, I locate E2, remembering Ramos's theory about Ella possibly being there. I hope Sam is there right now, getting revenge on whatever sick monster took her.

Wait. My hands freeze over the screen.

Ramos.

A thought dawns on me, and I lean back in his chair as the weight of it settles down on my shoulders.

He sent me to find this map. A map that is on *his* Tab, in *his* office. One he's already seen, and probably already memorized easily, since it's not very detailed.

A map he wouldn't need me to find... if he was coming with us.

Ramos doesn't think he's going to make it out.

I never would have expected, even two weeks ago, that the thought of Ramos going down with the Zone I was busting out of would almost bring me to tears.

After all he's done to help Sam, and now, Eddie, me, and the rest of the Zone... he thinks we're going to let him go down with the ship? No, I won't let him. I'll find him and make him come with us. It has to be that way. If I ever see Sam again, there's no way I could look him in the eye and tell him I didn't even try. No way.

My hands shake now as I lean back over the deskTab. I've looked over the west area and the middle section of the map, but still nothing of importance has stuck out. I drag my finger across it to move it as far east as it goes and zoom in to get a better look at one of the squares near the edge that has a smaller icon next to it. This must be it.

I zoom in and groan as it comes into view, slamming my hand on the edge of the desk in frustration. Although it's not a surprise, seeing it here in front of me makes it a glaring reality. The icon is an outline of stairs, next to a square labelled E3.

Of course.

The exit is in E3. The Zone for our very own government.

24

VIVA L'DEAUX!

SAM

The rest of the train ride to L'Deaux is solemn. Many passengers have deboarded to their various destinations around E1, but the new passengers coming on are just as sobered. If they didn't witness it firsthand, I'm sure they've all heard about it. News travels fast in places like this.

My legs are shaky as we step off the magtrain and down the ramp to solid ground. Part of me wants to puke from the nausea, and the other part of me wants to cry from the guilt, but I know neither of those are an option right now.

Q helps Zara clean up the makeup streaks down her cheeks that her tears have created as Beardsley leads the way to Willie's. I'm hoping if we get there early enough, we'll have time to warm him up to the idea of the meeting before it begins, and maybe he won't want to kill me as much. I give Luna a pat, relieved just as much as she is that we're back to solid ground.

Beardsley and Zara keep it as discreet as possible— since we don't want to draw too much unnecessary attention to ourselves, especially since the Guards will probably be on high-alert after what happened—and they pass out their cards as we walk to L'Deaux, murmuring "live free" to each person.

I take Q's hand, and she interlaces her fingers through mine. "You okay?" I ask.

She nods, but I know she's lying.

"It's going to be okay," I tell her, but I'm lying too. The closer and closer we get to Willie's the more worried I get myself. As we step through his front doors, an anxious chill runs down my back and through my legs.

It's lunch time at L'Deaux, and it's relatively empty, apart from a few groups playing pool and a few loners sitting at the bar.

Willie is behind the bar, the tattoos that are covering every inch of visible skin just as bright as ever. He is wiping down the countertop with a rag when he spots us coming his way. His eyes immediately lock with mine, and I see the flash of recognition, even though we had only met the one time... when I was out cold on his office floor one minute and then begging him for information about Vegas the next... I'm sure I left quite the impression, and now this. He doesn't seem surprised to see us, though, as if he was expecting our arrival. He must have heard about the meeting.

"Get out," he yells from behind the bar.

My heart drops. He really won't even hear us out? We look at each other in frozen surprise, except Beardsley who still marches toward the bar anyway, looking like he's about to give Willie a piece of his mind.

"We're closing early today, everybody out," he yells again, and the other patrons in the room all slink out one by one.

"Well, well, well, look what the cat dragged in," Willie says to Beardsley, in a way that makes me want to melt right out the door with the others.

"If it isn't the week-old roadkill possum himself," Beardsley retorts, his face completely expressionless.

Just when I think they might actually fight each other over the counter, Willie's face breaks out into a huge grin. He cackles an unapologetically loud laugh, shaking Beardsley's hand and pulling him in to clap him on the back. They whack each other on the back a few more times, probably way harder than necessary, before Willie's attention turns to the rest of us.

I see a flicker of fear in his eyes behind his joking exterior, the colorful tattoos all over his face and long beard that mask what he tries to hide inside. I remember seeing it last time. I remember how scared he was of Vegas then, just to tell us even minimal details, and now we've painted a red target on his back. I suddenly feel so selfish.

I step toward the bar. "I'm so sorry, Willie, about the meeting... We should call it off. I shouldn't have mixed you up in this."

He doesn't answer right away. He picks his washcloth back up and dries a few glasses as he seems to think about how to respond. Eventually he meets my eye with a sigh. "The last time you were here, something changed in me, I think."

We all take seats at the bar as he talks. He tosses an extra rag to Beardsley who grumbles but walks behind the counter and helps him dry anyway. Standing next to each other, they look like a color and grayscale copy of each other with their matching long beards and skinny frames. One face colorful and vibrant, one graying and weathered.

"You and Q came here banging on my door, asking all these questions, and I thought... if these *kids* can be that fearless, why can't I?"

"Fearless," Beardsley snorts. "Y'mean stupid?"

Willie chuckles. "Either way. It made me want to stop hiding."

"For Beck."

His eyes well up at the mention of his daughter, but he smiles. "For Beck."

Q suddenly gasps next to me, and it makes me nearly jump out of my skin. By the looks of everyone else, they feel the same. She grabs my arm, looking around the group with wide eyes like she's had an epiphany.

Zara curses breathily. "You nearly gave me a heart attack."

"The last time we were here..." Q muses with a busy look, and I know the wheels must be turning a hundred miles an hour as she thinks out whatever this is. "Willie."

He sets down a glass. "Yes...?"

"The last time we were here, you gave Prettyboy here an antidote. It worked almost immediately, and I don't think he had any side effects." She turns to me to confirm, and I shake my head affirmatively, though I bristle a bit that even after our shared moment last night the awful nickname still perseveres.

"Yeah?" Willie responds, and I share his confusion.

Zara puts her hands on her hips outraged. "Wait a minute. You're saying there is an antidote that could have saved me from a miserable hangover that I'm *still currently having* on top of *this*?" She waves her wrist at us.

I smile at her sheepishly. "Sorry."

She huffs and folds her arms across her chest.

Q doesn't respond, still so deep in thought. "What if—" She cuts herself off. "No, it wouldn't work... Would it?"

"Ya wanna let us in on the conversation, or do you and the voices in your head have it covered?" Beardsley jokes, and I snort which he appreciates.

Q ignores both of us and turns back to Willie. "Do you have more?" He blinks at her. "Of the antidote."

"Oh, um, yeah, I think I have a dose or two left for emergencies. A friend and I developed it for the times we go a little too hard at the clubs. It just happened a time or two and we wanted a solution." He laughs, reminiscently. "I tell ya, every time we—"

"Yeah, okay." Q waves to cut Willie's anecdote off. "Do you think it can be showered?"

We are all quiet as we process what she's suggesting. *Showered.*

Does she mean instead of the drugs they often put in the air here, that are absorbed quickly and often unknowingly through Elite wristTabs, that we shower an *antidote* instead? Now I'm as curious as she is if that would work.

"Why?" Willie asks, breaking the thoughtful silence.

"To give them a chance," Zara answers quietly. The outrage has melted away, and she looks at Q with a grateful smile.

"Is it possible?" Q repeats, chewing her lip.

Willie mulls it over. Beardsley sets his washcloth down, and I can see him thinking it over too.

"Maybe," Willie finally answers unconfidently. "It wouldn't be as potent if it's showered, but in theory it could still work... It might just take longer for it to take effect."

"I might be able to help," Beardsley adds slowly. "I remember a thing or two from my medic days in the military."

"Can it be done in"— Q cranes her neck to look at the clock on the wall behind the men— "seven hours?"

"Guess we'll find out."

WILLIE LEAVES us the key to L'Deaux and tells us not to get into too much trouble as he and Beardsley leave to work on the antidote. Willie's friend works at a supply warehouse nearby and supposedly will be more than happy to assist a long-awaited uprising.

We decide to take the few hours we have before the meeting to retrace the step of Zara's last day here to see if it jogs her memory and pass out the last of our playing cards as we go.

We start off by making our way down the main strip toward the bar Jones works at, VIVA, because Zara insists that seeing him first will help get her brain in the right mindset and has absolutely nothing to do with the fact that she thinks he's hot.

We're halfway down the street when Q suddenly grabs my arm and looks at me with an excited grin. "Can I give Zara a ride there?"

"Good thinking." I pull off my backpack and take out the square metal box that's just been useless dead weight since we've been here. I press the button on the top, and it whirs to life, the box opening and morphing into my magboard, an LED of blue lighting up the bottom. I drop it, and it floats just above the ground, reacting to the mag-treated pavement just like the train does. My heart twinges in my chest thinking about Mayor Ramos giving this to me and staying behind to pay all the repercussions of me leaving. I can't wait for this all to be over, so I can head back there to make sure he's okay and properly thank him for giving me my best shot.

The girls take off on the magboard, giggling and screaming with joy, and I stay earthbound with Luna. We trot along the sidewalk, which isn't as crowded as it is at night, but there are still plenty of people out and about.

I pick up my pace as the girls get farther ahead, and Luna jogs next to me happily. That's when I see them. A group of E1 guards ahead, easily recognizable by their sleek black uniforms and the menacing glares they throw at the Elites passing by. My heart pounds in my chest at the sight of them, memories from C9 flooding my head and sending a visceral reaction through my body.

They seem to be looking for someone among the passing Elites. Luna lets out a low growl, sensing my unease. I grab her collar and pull her with me into an alleyway, so we're out of the wide open strip. The alley stinks from the large dumpster, but I'll wait here for a few moments until they pass and catch up with Q and Zara at VIVA. If the guards are looking for intruders, all they have to do is take a closer look at the bandages where my wristTab is supposed to be, and they'd know right away.

If they're looking for me specifically... well, that's a lot worse.

I peek around the corner of the bricked building and see them begin to scan the Elites with more determination. One of the guards gestures to his team to spread out and search more thoroughly. My heart races as I press myself further into the shadows, praying they don't come down this alleyway.

Luna whines softly at my side, and I run a hand through her fur, trying to calm both of our nerves. The sound of boots against pavement grows closer, and I hold my breath, willing them to pass by without noticing us.

Just as the guards reach the mouth of the alley, a commotion erupts from the main street. Shouts and screams fill the air, drawing their attention away from where I'm pressing myself into the brick. My heart stops for a moment, and I hope with everything in me that whatever this is, it has nothing to do with Q and Zara. Luna growls beside me, her hind legs tensed and ready to go. I grab her leash, and we race out of the alleyway, taking advantage of the distraction.

I run with Luna toward the direction of VIVA, while trying to make out the scene around me. Guards and Elites alike are moving in toward two figures in the street. One of the figures is crumpled on the ground in front of a vehicle, and another has a vehicle screeched to a stop mere inches away from their body. They both are wearing black sweatshirts just like the one from the train track. Black sweatshirt with painted red X's on the front.

The guards don't even reason or negotiate with the people before roughly throwing them to the ground and cuffing their hands behind their back. Luckily the one hit by the car seems to be able to walk as they are pulled roughly to their feet. They are taken off into custody within seconds.

Sure enough, the back of their sweatshirts say: *Or die.*

A chill shoots down my spine, grateful at least these protesters didn't meet the same fate as the last one, though I can't imagine what the guards could have planned for them wherever they are being taken.

I finally make it to VIVA with Luna and burst through the door with a heavy breath. We weave through the partiers to the kitchen, and I breathe a sigh of relief when I see Q and Zara talking with Jones at his dishwashing station. Thank goodness they're okay.

I go right to Q, and she tenses as I hug her from behind. When she realizes it's me, she relaxes into me, and her scent instantly calms me. She's here. She's okay.

Everyone in the kitchen dotes on Luna as I catch everyone up on what happened outside. We decide to hide out in here for a few extra minutes before continuing on, and I don't mind as long as Q is right by my side. I decide in this kitchen that I won't let her out of my sight again until we're safely out of EI.

A FEW HOURS LATER, we're dejectedly making our way back to L'Deaux after stop after stop. Although we successfully passed out our remaining playing cards, including Beardsley's stack that he gave to us before going to play science lab with Willie, we unfortunately made no progress with Zara's memory. She keeps telling us it's okay and not to worry, but I know she's disappointed. I would be.

There is a quiet between our trio as we walk, apart from the clack of Luna's claws on the pavement. It takes me a moment to realize that the street itself is also relatively quiet. It's far too early in the evening for Elites to be turning in. Zara is deep in thought, probably still trying to sort through what she last remembers, but Q is also looking around questioningly. I feel a pang of anxiety in my gut the further we get down the sidewalk and the emptier the streets get. If everyone is home, or off somewhere else, will anyone show up to the meeting?

"What is going on?" Q mutters, looking around with the same confusion. "Where is everyone?"

We round the corner of the last block to Willie's and stop dead in our tracks at the scene before us.

"Woah," breaths Zara, coming out of her distracted daze.

"Guess we found everyone," I say, blowing out a breath.

In front of us, waiting in line to get into L'Deaux, seems to be nearly every single Elite in E1.

"Do we think they're here for the meeting, or is L'Deaux just suddenly really trendy today?" I ask through my teeth as we pass the line of people that winds down nearly the entire block, even though there are still several hours until the meeting. The overhead shell lights haven't even begun to dim yet, so it can't be later than 4 or 5.

There is a general tone of excited impatience in the people we pass. I realize that for a lot of this crowd it could just be a herd mentality mindset. All it takes is for the right Elites to say they were coming here, and others would follow just to be a part of the trend. I wonder if even half of them support the cause or at least know what they're getting into.

I look at their faces as we pass. So many people with the strangest distortions and modifications, so many colors and shapes, and outfits, and personalities. You couldn't have picked out a more ridiculous looking bunch, but I know there is unexpected strength in a common experience, in that communal pain that binds us all together regardless of how different we all look. A strength that the people in charge can never understand, a force they can never really replicate.

What will Cade think of his army when he sees them?

We get to the front doors of L'Deaux and have to push the people in the front out of the way. They give us angry looks and shout at us for cutting in line, but when they see me fumble with the key, they begin pushing their way closer, hoping they can be the first ones in.

People are pushing me so much I can't get the door unlocked. I hand it to Q and use my loudest voice to begin pushing people back.

"Back UP," I yell. They ignore me and continue relentlessly pushing forward, nearly forcing me into Zara and Q and squishing them into the glass of the doors.

I yell again and push them back, but it barely makes a difference. It's not until Luna puts her bossy pants on and gives them one of the most menacing growls I've heard her muster that they listen. They hold their hands up in surrender and step slowly backwards, pushing the line behind them further back.

I praise her with a nuzzle to the face, and she licks my face in return.

Q finally jostles the lock open, and we squeeze inside. We have it locked behind us before anyone else can push through. I try to catch my breath.

We take a seat at the bar, and Zara steps behind to pour us each a glass of water. She sets one on the ground for Luna. The clock behind the bar confirms that it's only 4:30 as I suspected.

Two and half hours left until the meeting is supposed to start, and there are already hundreds of people waiting?

I feel that anxiety tug in my gut again, but it's different now. Before I was worried no one would show up. Now I'm worried we bit off more than we can chew.

Am I in over my head here?

Can we even manage this big of a crowd until Cade sends reinforcements? Which he *is* still planning to do right? He has a plan for this supposed revolution, or am I expected to lead the charge myself straight through the electric gates?

Beardsley and Willie aren't anywhere around, which means they are still concocting their antidote. What if it doesn't even work, and they just wasted all that time? When we could have been making a better plan instead?

The knocking on the glass doors outside gets more persistent.

"Willie is going to kill me if they break anything," I groan. "And he's already considering killing me for this whole thing anyway."

I sip on the cold water from Zara gratefully.

Q is chewing on the side of her cheek. "That big of a crowd outside is going to raise suspicion," she says, tapping her fingertips on the side of her glass.

"Do you think we should start early?"

She shrugs. "We want them riled up for the cause but clearheaded, right? Maybe we get the party going, but keep it tame? Zara and I could work the bar, make all the drinks they order virgin instead? Then at least there isn't alcohol mixed in with whatever they've taken already, especially if the antidote doesn't work."

Zara refills Luna's water, that she slurps up happily, and sets her elbows on the counter across from us. She thinks it through aloud. "So disguise the next couple hours as a pre-party to sober them up as much as possible and then get to business at 7."

"Right. Business," I repeat with total absolute confidence, with no doubts whatsoever about my ability to follow through with this, my competence, my aptitude, my very soul for that matter.

"We have the numbers." Q nods her head in the direction of the crowd outside. She squeezes my hand reassuringly, so I know she can tell I'm totally freaking out. "I'm sure Cade has a smoother plan, but if it comes to it, I really think they'd let us out without much trouble. I guarantee if we all storm the front gates, the guards there will crap their pants at the sight of all of us and just let us through."

"And if they don't?" I put it out there hesitantly, posing the question even though I don't want to hear the answer.

"Then we reevaluate," Zara says, and I feel better at her positive tone.

I nod. Q nods. I look at Luna for good measure, and her tail wags the second she sees me looking at her. I take that as confirmation. Guess that settles it.

I put my hand in the middle. "'Beardsley's gonna kill us' on three, ready?"

They laugh and stack their hands on top of mine. I count to three, and we all cheer in unison, "Beardsley's gonna kill us!"

Luna barks supportively, hopping up and down in excitement at the shift in tone.

Well, we're doing this. We're doing this now.

We take a few moments to make any quick preparations we can think of. I locate Willie's sound system which is already pre-loaded with club playlists. I listen to a few samples and select the most rambunctious one while the girls push all the tables and chairs to the sides of the room. We really don't have much space to work with, but it's better than hundreds of them waiting suspiciously outside like sitting ducks obviously up to no good. At least if we have a good party going, any guard walking by will just think we're the trending spot of the night.

And boy are we.

I cringe as I help the girls pour all the alcohol bottles out into the sink, knowing Willie would probably keel over on the spot if he saw this. The scent of the alcohol reeks and stings my nostrils. We quickly fill as many of them as we can with water and put them back into place on the shelves and counters.

Q gives me a halfway-confident thumbs up, Zara gives a half-hearted smile, Luna's just happy to be here, and I guess that means it's time. I jog over to the door, pausing for a moment to take a breath and center myself. Inhale, exhale.

For Ella.

I'm doing this FOR Ella.

This is the last step to getting her back.

I turn the lock.

Let's do this.

25

ROSE COULD HAVE MADE ROOM
FOR JACK

MATEO

I curse under my breath the entire way back to the basement, one hand tightly on the first aid kit I swiped on my way out of Ramos's office and the other one tightly on the gun in case there's trouble.

My mind races as fast as my body does through the quiet hallways. Yes, it makes sense that you'd have to pass through the literal government to escape a prison created by said government, but I guess I just thought maybe there'd be a second option or something. Wouldn't they want a backup exit just in case?

But I scoured the map for several more minutes, looking for just that, with no luck. Ramos could be wrong, of course, but according to his map, E3 has the only exit.

This complicates things. We can't really just show up to E3 and tell them we're Zone runaways, and we'd like to exit now thanks. Especially considering the orders Nova has received to get rid of us. They clearly want us all dead, not showing up at their front door.

I knock three times on the basement door once I get back to the stairwell, winded from sprinting through the hallways all the way here. Jordan opens the door just a crack to confirm it's me before he lets me through.

"How's it going?" I ask him breathlessly.

"It's been quiet..." he says slowly. "Way too quiet."

What is Nova planning? If she was only given two hours to get rid of us, wouldn't she have come knocking by now?

I try to keep the concern off my face. "Okay." I check the time on my wristTab. It's nearly time to get the babies. "Let's give it twenty more minutes, and then we'll head out."

"You got it, boss," he answers with a trace of mockery.

"Hey," I say with a laugh, "you're welcome to take over. I never wanted to be in charge."

He laughs too but unfortunately doesn't take me up on my offer to transfer leadership. My footsteps echo as I jog down the stairs. I'm anxious to check on Amanda. I doubt anything in this first-aid kit will even be helpful, so I'm really hoping Parker and his crew found something more useful on their raid.

The second I reach the holding cells at the bottom of the stairs, my skin prickles alerting me that there is a different kind of energy down here now. *Something's wrong.*

I take off in a run around the corner to the main basement area and look around quickly. Eddie? *Please, God, don't let it be Eddie.* There is anxious commotion in the room, a growing volume among the onlookers. I push through Zoners, shouldering my way through the tight space to where the commotion is. My heart drops when I make sense of the scene. Trevor and another Senior are dragging someone down the stairs, shouting at people to move out of the way.

"Back up! Everybody back up!"

It's Talia.

She is clutching at her throat, gasping for air. Blood. *So much blood.*

"What happened?" I yell to Talia's group who are shuffling

in behind them, faces tear-streaked and panicked, as I help Trevor and the Senior lie her down.

A girl from the group answers me through sobs. "A Guard. He came out of nowhere. His bullet ricocheted off a support beam, I think. Hit her in the neck."

I press my hands over Talia's that are clamped on her own neck. She looks at me, her gray eyes so full of fear it's like she's looking straight at Death itself. Her blood is gushing everywhere, so sickeningly warm on my hands it's making my stomach turn.

"Talia," I tell her, hoping to sound reassuring, but my own throat feels like it's being choked too, I can barely squeeze the words out. It's like my voice knows it's a lie before I even do. "It's going to be okay."

"What do we do?" Trevor's hands and clothes are also blood-soaked. He kneels on the other side of her, eyes panicked and urgent. "Teo, what do we do?"

Rachel screams and runs over to us from the other side of the room where she's been helping Amanda. She collapses to her knees next to me, wailing into her hands. "Talia! No God, please, no."

A sob lingers at the base of my own throat. I keep my hands pressed into her neck as tightly as I can. Her gasps for air are growing more frantic. Maybe if we pack the wound well enough...

My hands are shaking so violently that they're sending tremors up my arms and through my whole body. *Try to stay calm,* I order my body. Eddie slides in next to me, and feeling his presence, knowing that he's here, and he's okay, helps me at least take my next breath.

"First aid kit, gauze," I bellow to Trevor, trying to choke down my own cries. I have to pull myself together. "Where's Parker? Is Parker back yet?"

"He hasn't come back yet," Trevor responds as he sprints

around us and rifles through the first aid kid I found in Ramos's office. He hands me gauze with shaking hands. I remove one hand from Talia's neck to take it, carefully replacing my other hand with the gauze. Trevor keeps handing me gauze and mismatched fabric that other Zoners are contributing off their own bodies. I press layer after layer onto Talia's neck, but it soaks through immediately.

A bubble of blood gurgles at Talia's lips. Her eyelids droop, threatening to close.

"Hey," I bark at her, and her eyes flutter back open. "You stay with us. You hear me?"

She puts her hand on my wrist and her eyes, once full of fear, now cloud over with a tired calm. She squeezes my wrist gently. Blood drips from her mouth as she opens it to speak. I can barely hear her, but I am completely shattered at the single word she manages to utter: "Steven."

I break.

The tears stream down my face as her eyes slowly close. I tap her face, begging her not to give up. "Talia. *Talia.*"

Trevor wraps his arms around Rachel as she sobs into his chest.

Talia's hand falls from my wrist, her arm dropping to the ground next to her.

No pulse.

She's gone.

Eddie hugs my arm as my blood-soaked hands drop to my lap in defeat. I cry into his hair.

Everyone suddenly freezes as we hear a groaning creak from the trapdoor at the top of the stairs. Trevor and I jump to our feet at the exact same time, guns aimed. We look at each other in silent agreement: No one is getting in this basement without our permission.

Trevor creeps forward as a figure steps into the door, their face hidden by the shadows of the basement. "Hey!" he yells. "Show yourself!"

The figure comes into view. "Woah, it's just me."

It's Parker. I lower my gun, but it's more like my arm just completely gives out, flopping to my side uselessly.

He jogs down the stairs with a box in hand, his team of Seniors lowering themselves through the door one by one behind him.

"I found something I think will help Am—" He cuts off when he sees our faces. "What happened?"

I lower my eyes, unable to answer him. I physically can't. If I even open my mouth, I really think I'll completely unravel from the inside out.

The box in his hands drops when he sees Talia. The complete silence as everyone allows him to process the scene is so unbelievably painful. Sharp, like thousands of daggers cutting through the air at once. It's like finding out myself all over again.

He curses loudly, the pain in his voice slicing through the thick silence. He punches the closest wall. "If I had just gotten here faster—"

Rachel slides up next to him, putting a comforting hand on his shoulder, tears streaking down her own face. "Parker, there was nothing you could have done."

He jerks his arm away roughly and kneels down in front of the box he brought in from outside. He tears through the items in the box and holds up a huge metal syringe, eyes sparking with pained fury. "This could have saved her life."

WE ALL KNEEL around Amanda as Parker prepares the syringe, flipping through pages of the instruction manual that came with it. We couldn't save Talia, but I'm praying there's still time for Amanda. Her eyes are closed, but her chest rises with short and labored breaths. She's still breathing.

Thank God she's still breathing.

Parker gives orders as he skims the instructions. "'Remove any prior dressings from packed wound.' Okay, take off all those layers."

Jess carefully peels off the layers around Amanda's abdomen, revealing the angry red wound underneath. I send Eddie away to help Rachel look for something to wrap Talia up in, but really, I just don't want him to see this in case it takes a turn for the worse. Watching one death is surely enough trauma for one day for a nine-year-old.

"'Clean the affected area before use,'" Parker reads. I hand Jess the bottle of saline solution that came in the first aid kid I found, and she dumps it all around the wound, patting it dry with a fresh strip of gauze.

"Okay." Parker sets down the manual and presses a button on the outside of the syringe. A winding strip of blue lights up around the gray metal, casting a blue haze around Parker's hands, which are remarkably steady. He looks at me, his eyes hopeful but not very confident. "Ready or not, I guess."

If there's any chance of this working, of saving Amanda, we have to try. I promised her that she would be the one getting her sister out of here. I have to believe this will work. We can't lose her too.

Parker presses the syringe into the wound, and I'm really glad Amanda's out because this would probably be excruciating. I wince on her behalf. Parker presses another button on the body of the syringe and a timer lights up beneath the blue lights. It ticks down from 30 seconds, and we all wait with bated breath.

"It says it injects high-tech capsules that expand once

they're in there to pack the wound, absorb shrapnel, and release antibiotics into the bloodstream," Parker explains, not taking his eyes off the syringe he's holding in place. "And it can be cleaned and reused up to five times."

The timer counts down its last five seconds with short beeps, and then the blue lights turn themselves off. Parker slowly removes the syringe, the end of it covered in blood. He hands it to Jess, and she cleans it off with a wet fabric before setting it back in the box. I hand him new gauze and bandages from the first aid kit, which he presses over the wound gently.

The blood doesn't soak through.

"It's working." I puff out a triumphant breath, relief flooding through my body.

Parker's smile fades, and he sits back on his heels, looking down at his hands.

"Hey," I say, knowing what he needs to hear, whether I believe it myself or not. "It probably wouldn't have worked on Talia anyway. The placement of the gunshot... how fast it all happened. Even if you had been here when she came in, I still think it would have been too late."

He nods, accepting my offer of comfort. I force myself to believe it too: *There was nothing I could have done for Talia, either.* I repeat that to myself mentally a few times. If I keep fixating on what could have been, I won't be able to do what needs to be done for everyone else here. The night isn't even close to done yet. Parker knows that too. He stands up with determination and offers a hand to help me up.

I give Jess a tight-lipped smile, who stays with Amanda, putting a fresh wet cloth over her forehead. I pull Parker over to the stairs where Trevor is keeping watch, so we can have a quick briefing at the top of the stairs.

"What else did you guys manage to get from the sheds?" I ask Parker. Trevor flicks his eyes our direction to acknowledge that he's listening, before turning his attention back to outside, the trapdoor just barely cracked. I read the stiffness of his back loud and clear — no one else is getting hurt on his watch.

"We just grabbed basically every box we could carry," he replies, gesturing over to stacks and stacks of boxes he and his group brought in. "I think there's enough basic essentials for a few days."

"Water?"

He grimaces. "Not as much as I hoped, but we'll have to make it work."

I check the time on my Tab, and my gut twists with piercing anxiety. It's time.

"We'll need every single hand on deck." I grasp the reality of the challenge before us as I say it, and it seems nearly impossible when I voice it out loud. "We have to get the babies and load up the kids and supplies pretty much all at the same time. The kids can't just wait in the trucks. They'd be sitting ducks. Was Talia able to..."

Trevor finishes my sentence. "They found all the keys except three. It'll be a tight fit."

My brain sprints a mile a minute with the vague pieces of a plan that don't all quite fit together yet. All I know is no one else dies.

"What are you thinking?" Parker asks, reading the busy look on my face.

"We need some kind of distraction while we get everyone in the trucks..." I think aloud. "What if we...?"

Parkers lips stretch to a devious smile as if he's reading my thoughts. "We go out with a bang." He looks absolutely thrilled by the prospect. "Say no more. I happen to know how to get on the roof of the hospital. Perfect spot for a little diversion."

Goosebumps pop up across my arms from the nervous energy. Okay. It's coming together.

Trevor looks down from the trapdoor. "How can I help?"

"We'll need to split up the rest of the Seniors. Me, you, and one half storm the Nursery—then Jordan and the other half get the kids to the trucks."

Parker claps his hands together. "Let's do this. Let's burn this shithole to the ground."

26

SOMETIMES SMALL REVENGE
THEY'LL NEVER EVEN KNOW ABOUT
IS MORE SATISFYING

SAM

Only an hour later, and I'm running around like a headless chicken, putting out fires in every direction. One minute I'm breaking up a fight near the bar, and the next minute I'm breaking up a fight near the exit. There are so many people in here that it's hard to squeeze from one place to another, but luckily with most of them not being in their right minds yet, it's easy enough to move them out of the way. With the music this loud and this upbeat, people usually forget conflicts quickly, but I have had to forcibly remove a few persistent short fuses here and there.

But it's going surprisingly okay. Could it be possible that this all just works out?

Every so often when I feel like there is a beat about to drop in the music, I yell at the top of my lungs "LIVE FREE" and the crowd shouts back "OR DIE!" and it's like straight fuel to my body, an audible confirmation that I'm taking control of Vegas's followers little by little. Me. *I am.* They are here because of me.

The clock ticks closer and closer to 7:00, and there is still a huge rowdy line outside that stretches all the way down the block. We must be far past the recommended capacity in here, but people keep squeezing through the open doors anyway.

I watch Q work the bar with Zara. They are smiling and engaging with people so effortlessly as they mix flavors and purees into water from the alcohol bottles, putting on a show of shaking them up and pouring them into glasses. Luna has her front paws up on the counter like she's taking orders herself, her tongue out happily as she soaks in all the attention from the waiting Elites.

I smile. Something about seeing all these spoiled Elites unknowingly sipping on tap water like any regular Zoner just brings a certain peace to my heart. A harmless revenge of sorts.

Q sees me watching and grins, holding up a stack of money she must have earned in tips. I send back a wink and a thumbs up. She's so cute when she dupes Elites.

A dancing group behind me nearly pushes me over, but I find my balance quickly and move to keep putting out fire after fire. Dealing with this many people in a social situation would normally put me in an immediate grave, but luckily the adrenaline on the brink of chaos in the room is contagious and energizing. I don't hate it.

It's 6:45 now, and there is still no sign of Beardsley, Willie, or this supposed backup Cade promised. The idea of storming the gates without an antidote or reinforcements isn't my favorite, but it's a possibility we may have to come to terms with. All we have to do is cause enough ruckus at the gates to make the guards back off, and hopefully Cade will swoop in to handle the rest.

I have to trust that Cade will handle the rest.

I blow out a breath. It's now or never.

Luna nearly tackles me as I let myself behind the bar. I laugh as she puts her paws up on my shoulders as if she's not nearly 80 pounds. I hug her huge furry body. She hops along cheerily next to me as I step up next to Q, who is making some kind of smoking red concoction for an eager Elite with a huge gold bullring hanging down from their nose.

Zara closes in on my other side, passing a fizzy blue drink to her waiting customer. I do a double take because I'm almost positive her customer is an actor from a movie I watched with my parents a long time ago. I can't remember the name... something with cars and a lot of explosions.

Zara gives me a smile. "Is it time?"

I turn my head to Q on the other side for confirmation. She presses her lips together in a nervous but determined way. "Let's bust these brats out of here."

"And hold out on the hope that extra help gets here soon." I press my hands down into the counter, poised to hop up onto it. "This is really dumb, isn't it?"

"So dumb," they both repeat emphatically.

Q laughs but puts a hand on my arm with a squeeze. How does she manage to infuse assurance directly into my very veins just with a single touch? I lean in, resting my forehead on hers, and despite the mayhem and the eardrum-shattering music and Zara squealing excitedly next to us, it feels for this second like it's just us.

I wish it was. My chest feels simultaneously like it's going to shrivel up inside and like it's going to explode at the same time. There is so much I want to say but only seconds to say it.

"Q." I swallow, my throat feeling tight. "Just in case I don't get the chance to do this later... I want you to know... Well, it's just that I feel—"

I'm messing this up.

She presses her lips into mine, saving me from myself like she always does. "I know," she replies simply. "Me too."

I kiss her back, savoring this moment of pure simplicity where I can just be a boy who might love a girl.

And she apparently might love him back?

We'll for sure be circling back to that later, but for now

there's work to do. I jump up onto the counter and turn back to offer my hand to help them up.

"We do this *together*," I insist, giving them a stern eyebrow when they protest.

With a fair share of grumbling and complaining, soon enough we're all standing on top of the bar. Zara turns down the music volume with a high-tech looking remote we found in Willie's office. She switches on its microphone feature and holds it out to me, but I shake my head.

"Nope. Your turn. Speak your truth."

Her eyes widen in terror. She shakes her head fervently. "Absolutely not."

"They need to hear it from you, Z," Q adds, backing me up, even though it's probably partly for selfish reasons. If Zara speaks, it's less likely she'll have to herself. "We don't know them like you do."

"She's right." I grin at Zara and push her forward ever so slightly. "Good luuuck!" I repeat it in the same sing-songy way they did to me the other night when they threw me to the wolves just like this.

She swallows. "Okay. I can do this." She nods, trying to hype herself up. "I can do this."

She brings the microphone to her lips and closes her eyes. She takes a deep breath.

When she opens her eyes, it's there. The fire we need.

Q sees it too, and she whoops, and we smack each other excitedly like children. It's about to get good.

"I've been out there!" Zara yells into the microphone, and she commands the crowd instantly. She has their *full* attention. There is a buzz of whispers, with an undertone of the bass-filled music on a lower volume.

"I got out," she repeats with emphasis. She nudges both of us with her elbows. "They helped me. And when I was out there, I realized what a LIE this is. All of it! The high society, the fancy parties, the luxury... it's all just a pretty cage," Zara continues, her voice cutting across the room like lasers. Every pair of eyes in the club is on her. People are even straining to listen outside through the open door.

"I realized that we're no better off than the Common Zones. They told us we were special, and that's why we 'got' to live here. But they just keep us distracted with sparkly fun, so we don't realize we're prisoners just like everyone else. It's not right."

She sniffs the welling tears away, hanging onto the anger, channeling the fire. "We have a choice! But we have to act quickly. We can keep living in this illusion, or we can demand more!"

The cheer from the crowd is deafening. A few people try to jump up onto the bar, but Luna growls at them across the counter like she's our personal security detail.

Zara hands me the microphone with a proud smile.

"You did amazing." I return her smile.

I hold the microphone out to Q. "You have anything to say?"

She gives me a "*why not?*" shrug and takes the mic, immediately screaming into it, "LIVE FREE."

They repeat "OR DIE" and she says it over and over again like we're in a football huddle getting hyped for the game.

I feel a sudden moisture above my head followed by a hissing sound. I look up to see a huge plume of mist spraying out of three places in the ceiling above the bar and into the audience.

I turn and see Luna hugging Beardsley up on her hind legs, tail wagging, by Willie's office door. Willie stands near the sound system, pushing some kind of lever. He sees me looking and gives me a thumbs up.

They're back.

I put my hand on Q's arm and then Zara's, nodding back in that direction to let them know. Q grins at Willie, a huge genuine smile that makes me wish I could take her somewhere she could smile like that all the time. With even more enthusiasm now, she keeps working the crowd. I meet Zara's eye and see that they've welled up with tears again. She smiles gratefully at me, and I squeeze her hand while we let Q do her thing.

Some from the audience see the mist and cheer, thinking they're going to enter some kind of psychedelic state. Little do they know, they're about to be more sober than they've probably been in a while and will get a full dose of a fun experience called reality.

Please work.

"Well? What do you say tonight we show them what we're made of? We show them *tonight* that they can't keep us locked up anymore," Q yells into the microphone. They cheer. They absolutely love her. I have a feeling they'd do just about anything she tells them to do.

Parade straight into an invisible electric gate monitored by armed guards? No problem, say when.

She's incredible.

"Tonight, we march to our freedom! LIVE FREE OR DIE!"

The crowd goes absolutely insane. People are jumping, cheering, pushing each other to hype each other up. We've crossed into a new energy. This energy isn't just listening energy or "*here for a good time*" energy.

No. This is *action* energy.

Maybe it's the sobriety finally peeking through, their consciousness begging to be let free and demanding action, but I can just feel it vibrating in the air around us.

Q opens her mouth to say something else when loud commotion erupts near the front door.

My heart drops to the counter below me.

A dozen guards have pushed their way through the door.

No.

Some of them are blocking the exit. The others are hitting

everyone within distance with batons, shouting indistinguishable commands over the music.

No, no, no.

I jump down and help the girls off the counter.

Shots fire, the *bangs* ringing out loudly even over the music. People scream.

I peek over the counter and see that their guns are raised to the ceiling. They're trying to de-escalate. That's a good sign. They aren't simply out for blood. That probably means they don't quite know what's going on here. If they heard anything that was said, they'd already be making arrests or filling body bags.

The audience is not being cooperative, though, and I fear how long this patience from the guards will last. The Elites are finally pushing back. How much pushback will be tolerated?

Beardsley has crouched behind us and is trying to usher us toward the back door behind Willie's office. "We have to get outta here."

"We can't just leave them," Q hisses. "And Cade said he'd send backup. We can't lose this momentum."

"Don't be stupid, Q," Beardsley scolds. "Staying safe is more important than any of this."

She yanks her arm out of his grip. "Not to me."

More guards march in through the exit all huddled around someone in a circle. It takes me only a second to make out who it is.

Someone whose face has haunted me every time I close my eyes.

Vegas.

Her hair is pulled back into a tight bun. Her clothes are impeccable, like she's just come from work.

Beardsley and Q are still arguing but they stop when Luna starts growling. Some canine instinct deep within me wants to too. I can barely spit out a single word to aid their confusion.

"Her."

Her.

Q looks over the counter and gasps, recognizing her immediately too. Luna bares her teeth, growling deeper. It's like she senses her very presence, not even needing to see her. *Her.* The one who nearly killed her. I put a hand on her furry sternum to keep her back, but I can't tear my eyes way. Zara must put the pieces together quickly because she takes hold of Luna's collar, picking up the leash from the ground and clicking it into place. She whispers to Luna reassuringly, pulling her away from the counter.

I watch over the bar as *she* speaks to one of the guards. They're obviously going to tell her to leave, right? Zone security is official FPA business. Why would they let some random lady get involved?

But then I see the way they nod when she speaks. The way their eyes follow where she points. The way they lean in to listen for more.

She is giving them directions.

And not just to a couple of them. All of them.

She's not just some random lady getting involved.

We thought by coming in here and riling up her followers that it would one-up her, stunt her power.

But little did we know she already owns the entire Zone.

Vegas is in control here.

27

FLAMMABLES, FIREWORKS, AND FALSE HOPE

MATEO

I'm kneeling in front of Eddie, deciding to treat him like the "big kid" he's earned the right to be, as much as I wish I could still make all his decisions for him. I lay the options before him. He can come with me to the Nursery, or he can help load the kids and supplies in the trucks.

He takes a moment to consider, so wise beyond his years. I wish life down here didn't do that to him. "I want to help with the babies. I think it's what Ella would have done."

My heart squeezes. He's right. Ella and Sam would have been right beside me tonight. Their absence is tangible. They should have been here. They deserve as much as any of us to get their vengeance on this place. If anyone deserved to light the first match, it would have been them.

I pat his shoulders. "Okay. You ready?"

He takes a long exhale, looking into my eyes. "I'm ready. We got this."

I nod in agreement. "We got this."

Parker and his gang have already headed out, and I almost don't want to know what they have planned. They seemed a little too excited on their way out, clutching handfuls of fireworks and other flammables from Eddie and Ella's collection.

Rachel and Jess have bundled up Amanda in a blanket, and covered up Talia in layers of dusty shower curtains they managed to find down here.

Rachel smiles at me sadly. "I wish we could give her better."

I take her hand, and Jess takes her hand on the other side. "Me too. Do you want to say a few words before we go?"

I regret I didn't really know Talia—or any of them, really—before Parker created this little group. I didn't even know her name. I wish I didn't let the "everyone only worry about themselves" culture they created down here get so ingrained in me. I even tried—really hard, as a matter of fact—not to be friends with Sam, but he pretty much gave me no choice.

I laugh sometimes thinking about how Eddie and I used to talk to each other only in Spanish, so everyone would leave us alone, but then Sam found a translation dictionary in the library so he could butt into our conversations like the nosy pest he is. Who knows how different the last seven years would have been for me if he didn't try so insufferably hard to be my friend? I should have gotten to know people here better before it was too late, instead of just keeping to myself so closely like they encouraged us to. But all I can do now is do differently. I can let people in.

The rest of the group gathers around to listen. Rachel sniffs. "Talia was the best person I knew. She made this hell a better place."

"And now she'll make heaven a better place too," Jess adds, her voice cracking with restrained sobs. "Tell Steven hi for us."

"To Talia, Steven, Foster, and every other Zoner lost down here—" I kiss my hand and stretch it outward, and everyone gathered around does the same. "You paved the way."

"Time to go," Trevor calls down from the top of the stairs.

He's not being cruel. I know he's dealing with the grief in his own way. He's right though. Time is up.

I clear my throat. "I need half of the Seniors here to come with me to the Nursery. We have some babies to steal. The rest of you will help get the Minors into the trucks. I'll let you choose which of the risks you'd rather take."

There is a shuffle for a few minutes as everyone picks a side. To my surprise, there are slightly more Seniors who have chosen to help in the Nursery, but still enough helping the kids that I think it will be fine. I instruct each Senior heading to the trucks to make contact in some way with as many of the kids as they can. I won't risk anyone getting left behind. Holding multiple hands, shoulder rides, piggyback rides, whatever, just don't let go under any circumstance. I've given two of the strongest Seniors—Alex and Xavier— the task of getting Amanda to a truck. She is still in and out of consciousness, but she mutters incoherently and lolls her head around as they pull her up, sliding her arms across their shoulders. Rachel has a small Minor on each of her hips, and Jess is giving one a piggy-back ride and holding the hand of another. Jordan holds his little sisters' hands, and they are each holding hands of another one too. The rest of the group gets paired up and every free hand is given a box or bag of supplies, anything they can manage.

"Wait for Parker's diversion, then sneak to the trucks. Wait for us there. We'll head to the Northern Boundaries all together exactly at 6:00." I toss Jordan, Jess, Rachel, and two other Seniors the keys to the trucks that Talia and her group rounded up. We stare at each other for a moment as we all simultane-ously realize none of us know how to drive.

I shrug. "How hard can it be? Stay quiet, stay safe. We're almost out. We can do this."

We wait at the bottom of the stairs for Trevor's signal. I hold Eddie's arm, keeping him close to me while we wait. Trevor steps out of the trapdoor, and it creaks loudly as it opens the rest of the way. I hold my breath for what feels like years. Eventually he peeks his head back in and gestures for us to follow. Alex and Xavier go first with Amanda, and Trevor helps them pull her out of the trapdoor.

Eddie and I hang back, waiting for everyone else to get out first, so we can make sure no one is left behind. One by one, the paired groups creep out of the basement and wait quietly up top for whatever Parker has planned. I send a silent prayer up to whatever Gods will listen that no one else gets hurt tonight.

I send one last parting look over my shoulder to Talia's body, including her in my silent prayer, hoping she can find some kind of rest in her afterlife with Steven and anyone else she lost down here. We've all lost so many. Too many.

Eddie and I step up from the basement. The overhead lights of the upper shell have dimmed into a moody winter twilight, not completely dark and not completely light. Light enough to see where we're going, with perfect shadows for hiding. There is nervous energy as everyone huddles tightly in the small corner this emergency exit is tucked away in. The younger children are getting tired and hungry, but they luckily stay quiet. There's not nearly enough room here for everyone, but we have to make it work anyway.

I move through the crowded space with Eddie to take a peek around the corner of Town Hall. It's eerily deserted in the Square. There isn't a single person in sight. If Nova has something planned, she's running out of time.

The Nursery is on the Mess Hall side of the Square. If we sprint the whole way there, using the support beams as checkpoints, sticking to their shadows, we should be able to get there quickly and without much trouble. It's getting darker and darker with every minute it ticks closer to nightfall.

Suddenly there is a loud popping sound coming from the hospital building near the Southern Boundaries where Nova is no doubt congregating with her remaining Guards, waiting for any traitorous Zoners to show up. The pops continue, echoing off the upper shell and the surrounding beams. This must be it.

"You stay right by me," I order Eddie. "Ready?" I ask the group, and I'm met with enthusiastic replies. Everyone is just as ready as I am for this to be over. To finally be free. This is one step closer.

"Go!" I yell, and chaos erupts. The Minors and their escorts run toward the trucks, and we take off for the Nursery. I force my legs to go as fast as they can, sprinting from beam to beam, pausing only to make sure Eddie is still by me before bolting for the next one. My breaths are short, and my wristTab warms on my wrist to warn me of the increased blood flow. I'm almost there.

I sprint the final stretch to the Nursery, using the shadows of the Mess Hall building to shield me as I approach the door. It's 5:33. Perfect timing for when the Elder will have it unlocked.

I pull the gun out of my waistband, and the other Seniors with stolen guns do the same. We wait breathlessly for everyone to reach the building before moving any closer. I look over my shoulder at them and count down from three, conveying to everyone they need to be ready for anything.

3 - 2 - 1

I reach for the door handle and tug. My heart falls to my ankles.

It doesn't open like the Elder promised it would.

It's locked.

28

RED-COLORED GLASSES

SAM

Even with the music blaring persistently, the crowd yelling and fighting to be let out of the building, the screams when a guard fires another warning shot or doles out a whack with a baton, I still hear her voice clear as day when she says my name. Her voice is like a whisper inside my very brain I can't escape from.

"Oh, Saaaamuellll," she singsongs, not even loudly, not even with much effort. But I still hear her as if she were right next to me. And it lights my anger on fire to hear her utter my name after all she's done.

How did she even find out about this meeting?

Q puts her hand on my arm as the rage I've kept simmering so deeply manifests itself and nearly propels me forward on its own.

Beardsley curses behind me. "What is she doing here? And where the hell is Cade? We need to leave *now dammit.*"

But I'm barely listening. All I see is red.

Q pulls me down with a firm grip on my arm. "Be smart," she yells in my ear, but her voice feels far away.

I don't want to be smart. I just want her to pay for the pain she's caused.

She speaks again. *Her.* "Come out, come out, wherever you are."

Like we're playing hide-and-seek. It's always a game to her. She knows where I am.

Willie is letting Elites hop over the counter. He stays low, crouched and out of view, but guides them to the back door.

"I knew our Sam would need a little extra motivation. The rest of the dream team too." Vegas waves a command at the guards by the exit, and a small group shuffles through the guarded doors.

Beardsley growls a curse at the sight of them, knocking over a stack of plates that shatter on the ground.

The group that comes through the door is huddled together, handcuffed. Their mouths duct-taped shut. My eyes flick to each of their faces.

Ella.

Red.

Lala.

There is a fourth person by Ella but it's not Steele... A small child.

Wait...

Illusion surely, but I don't even wait until it makes sense in my brain before leaping over the counter and pushing my way through the crowd to her.

It's really Ella.

She tries to move toward me, but the guard keeps her back. Tears are streaming down her pale face. She looks sickly and frail, like she is starting to recover from some kind of flu. No sparkle in her eyes, barely any life within them at all. She's scared.

But not scared of me.

What has she been through since the last time I saw her? I

hate being right. I hate that Vegas must have turned out exactly as I thought she would.

I'm going to kill her.

I need to get closer. I need to reach her. I'm so close.

But then I do a double take again. The small girl huddling into her closely *looks exactly like her.* I push through the crowd, shoving Elites out of the way to get to her. I don't know what's going on, but I don't care. It'll all make sense if I can just *hold her.*

"There's our pretty little hero!" Vegas sings. A burly guard has my hands behind my back before I can even blink. Guards have found the back door entrance behind the counter and are closing in on the others. I can hear Luna's throaty warnings from here.

I shove my elbow into the guard and scream into the crowd of Elites, "LIVE FREE OR DIE! NOW! TO THE GATES, NOW!"

The Elites answer the call with an atomic level force, and it's like they've been waiting for permission to finally detonate. They explode into action. Bodies blur around me. Shots fire. Glass breaks. I take the opportunity to punch the surprised guard behind me in the face. I glance back and see Luna taking bites out of the guards advancing on them behind the counter. They howl in pain. Such a good girl.

Q scales the counter and runs toward Red and Lala, relief and desperation on her face, pushing people out of her way just like I am, and it's like we're parting the sea from two separate directions.

Luna has tasted blood, and she's hungry for more. She soars over the counter, her loose leash flapping behind her like a cape, and pounces on the closest guard, his gun clacking to the floor.

Beardsley helps Zara over the counter and throws a glass bottle at the head of another guard as he does. Zara grabs a couple bottles off the counter too and doles them out with equal force.

Vegas is shouting commands at the guards as we get closer. She knows just what to do to get me to stop in my tracks.

The guard behind Ella points his gun directly at her. She sobs, and it absolutely breaks me. I freeze instantly, holding my hands up in surrender.

This girl that somehow looks exactly like her begins to cry too. They lean into each other like they're keeping each other upright.

Who the hell is she?

Vegas sees my busy expression, and her lips curl into a nasty grin.

She knows she has me.

The guards have their guns on Lala and Red now too, mouths hidden under duct tape, but their eyes flash with fear. I feel a pang of guilt, knowing they're only in this position *again* because of me. But thank God and every universe they're alive. *They're alive.* I send up a silent plea that Steele is just late to the party.

I feel Q's presence arrive next to me, Beardsley's and Zara's too, but I can't take my eyes off Ella and the girl next to her. I'm looking back and forth between the two of them now, and the longer I look at them, the more I'm doubting myself on which one is real. Who is this girl? How is it possible she looks exactly like Ella?

"Are you okay?" is all I can manage to croak out. Noise is compounding all around us, screams, shots firing, breaking glass.

Both girls nod.

The one on the left—that's her, isn't it? I'm sure that's her.

But the other one... no that's not her. Right?

Vegas laughs. "Oh, it's even better than I pictured. Your reaction."

I don't even look at her. I'm not playing into her games anymore. I'll get answers later. Everything will make sense *later*. All I need now is to get her out of here. I don't even care about revenge. I don't care about this revolution. Seeing Ella here like this, no longer the hopeful happy girl I had to leave behind in E2... it changes everything.

Her tears change everything.

This is no longer my fight. Screw my IOU to Cade. I need to get out of here.

"What do we do Beardsley?" Q asks through her teeth without moving her mouth.

Beardsley doesn't reply, but his eyes are busy. He is tense like a coil that is getting tighter and tighter and tighter, waiting for its chance to spring. The fury at seeing his friends like this is emanating off of him like a noxious gas. His grip tightens around the broken bottle he wields like a patient weapon.

"Where is Steele?" Q whispers, bending slowly to pick up Luna's leash—Luna's teeth bared at Vegas, just waiting for her opportunity to pounce—and thankfully she winds it tight. We don't want history to repeat itself here.

The room begins to thin as Elites and guards take their fight outside. A quick glance out of the broken window shows a different world out there than we left it earlier. Elites are storming the streets in every direction—working together to take down guards, damaging buildings, destroying everything in sight—as they advance further down the road toward the gates. They're doing it.

For better or worse, E1 will never be the same.

Vegas takes advantage of the empty space, like she's stepping onto a stage. Her hair is different, her bangs now parted in the middle and framing her overly made-up face. Her skin is just as glowing and dark gold as I remember it, not a single bit creased or even disturbed by the atrocities committed by it daily. Her snarling teeth are just as white.

You'd never know by looking at her what this woman is capable of. I assume she likes it that way.

She has made it center stage now. "Did you really think I wouldn't find out what you were doing here?" She cackles a laugh like it's the most ridiculous thing she's ever heard. "Honestly guys, does no one even bother to do their research anymore?"

She pulls out a few cards from the tiny pocket on the front of her gray skirt and throws them at us. They flutter to the ground like ash. The playing cards we've been distributing.

"If only you had paid attention to the details, then you would have known I use the other suits for direct messages only. My E1 cards are all on the red queen of hearts. *Obviously.*" She holds out her arms like she's being introduced for an award. "Seriously, a child could have done better than this."

She turns to gesture to Ella and the... other girl. "And speaking of child, oh, I really should introduce you." She holds her arm out to the one I originally thought was Ella. I hate how her eyes widen with fear just to be looked at by this woman. *What did she do to her?* "Sam, Ella, Ella, Sam, you remember each other, I'm sure."

She smiles wickedly as she moves her arm to the other girl. "It is my pleasure to introduce you to my own creation, Ella-B. You've actually met before, don't you remember? Back in E2, the last time you visited? Isn't she magnificent? Oh, if only the boys in charge knew what kind of scientific breakthroughs I'm making down here by the second. They'd kill themselves for even a shred of my technology."

What is she talking about, *creation*? Ella-*B?*

Though I try to keep my face neutral, she must see the flicker of confusion.

She groans in exasperation. "Ugh such is my lot in life. Always having to slow down for people who simply can't keep up. She is Ella's *clone*, Samuel, catch up dear."

My throat suddenly feels like I'm being choked.

I must have misheard her.

Q brings her hands to her mouth in silent shock. She looks at me with wide eyes, confirming I must have heard it correctly after all.

Clone?

What is this, *Star Wars?* Willie must be showering hallucinogenics after all, because there is no way this is reality.

Vegas steps next to the girl and pets the top of her head fondly. The girl flinches at her touch. She speaks to her in a high, buttery way like she's a baby. "We have a few kinks to work out obviously, because *this one* got a little more cognizant than she was supposed to and got us into quite the pickle back home. But a few tweaks should get us back in business, right my darling?"

This one? Does that mean there are *more?*

Vegas pulls the girls chin up to look at her, and she beams down at her like a proud parent. The girl's eyes well up with tears. Ella inches her body even closer to the girl's. *Protectively.*

Everything starts to feel like it's spinning around me. I'm two seconds away from blacking out when Q's touch on my arm brings me back to earth. I try to zero in on the placement of her hand, trying to stay focused on what I understand. I take a few deep breaths to keep from passing out. Inhale, exhale. *Plan, make a plan.*

Vegas notices Q's closeness and gasps with delight. "Oh, to be young and in love!"

Beardsley utters a low growl as if he's morphed into Luna, but it's not at what Vegas said. My eyes follow his to the slow movement from the broken window behind the guards who have Red and Lala.

My insides twist as I realize it's Willie.

Beardsley hisses under his breath, "Idiot."

Willie is creeping up slowly behind them, wielding a bat in

his hands like it's a sword. He's raising it to strike, so slowly and silently that I hold my breath. But Ella's guard sees the motion from the corner of his eye, and before I can even blink he has moved his gun from the back of Ella's head and straight at Willie.

Bang. Bang.

Q screams. "Willie!"

Luna howls, her leash going taut as she tries to leap to his aid. Zara stumbles as she tries to help Q keep her held back.

Willie's tattooed face is forever frozen in beautiful colorful surprise. He falls face-first through the window, his body crunching into the broken glass of his own shop.

Beardsley lets out a battle cry and charges forward with his broken bottle, not even caring that the guard is pointing the gun at him now, but Red and Lala shake their heads at him so fiercely with wide fearful eyes, their panicked pleas muffled by the duct tape, that he comes to a stop. He throws the broken bottle on the ground in fury, screaming expletives at the guards, but he doesn't move an inch forward. He won't defy his friends' wishes, no matter how much he wants to.

Ella and the girl burst into scared tears. They lean into each other.

Vegas tsks Beardsley, her mouth curled in mocking pity. "Look what you've done, you've scared the children."

I put my arm around Q, and she cries into my shoulder, stretching out her own hand to hold Zara's even when she's needing comfort herself.

I look at Willie's lifeless body. *We did this to him.* This was the fate he was so afraid of, by the very hands he feared most. And we served him up to her on a silver platter.

"Just let us go," Q yells through her tears. "You won, okay? What more do you want from us?"

Vegas smiles, her eyes crinkling at the sides. "I'm so glad you asked, Miss Mia Davis, ward of the sunny state of Texas.

Well, what's left of it, that is. Daughter to..." She cuts herself off with a wicked laugh. "Oh wait, I can't reveal all my secrets, can I?"

Q's entire body freezes, like she's been turned into granite.

Is she talking about *Q*? Does Vegas know her somehow?

"What do you know about my parents?" Q whispers breathlessly, stumbling forward like her knees have been kicked from behind. Luna pulls at the leash even harder now that they have gotten closer, barking at Vegas like she's begging for vengeance of her own. Vegas ignores her, like she's nothing more than a pest.

Vegas steps toward Q with her arms out, like she's inviting her in for a hug. "I saw a spark in you that reminded me of myself. You hide it well, but like calls to like, my dear."

Q flinches.

"Make history with me," Vegas croons, her voice low and gentle. "Do something important. We can move *actual* scientific mountains together. It'll certainly mean more to the world than"—she waves her hand like she's shooing away a fly— "being some ragtag delivery girl. So much potential wasted for so long. God knows we need more girls in charge around here. Come with me, sweetheart, and I'll tell you anything you want to know about your parents."

Q is still as a statue. I can't see her face, only the back of her hair, but her stiffness is telling. Her silence is telling.

Is she actually... considering this?

Zara and I share a look, a concern flickering in her eyes that I'm sure matches mine. She's worried too.

A sudden motion startles me out of my skin. A group of men charge through every open window and door, using the guards' moment of surprise to knock the guns out of their hands. They have the line of guards disarmed and in headlocks within a matter of seconds.

Punches fly, batons are thrown, shots fire. They fight each

other, men and guards alike each trying to get the upper hand, now too distracted with each other to worry about us.

I yank Q and Luna back, pushing them and Zara behind me. We stumble back into the bar counter as Red and Lala act quickly amid the commotion. Despite their hands being cuffed behind their backs, they use their elbows to push Ella and the girl off to the side, away from possible crossfire of guards and these newcomers. *Who are they? Elites?*

Red and Lala step in front of the children, shielding them from harm with their own bodies.

I'm already halfway across the room to them when Vegas steps right in front of me, blocking the way. She pulls her own gun from the back waistband of her skirt with a sigh, like it's an inconvenience to have to use it.

"Nice try," she says darkly, her carefree look slipping by the second. Her eyes hold a trace of hysterics because she knows she's losing control the longer her manpower stays distracted.

I'm having major déjà vu here. How do I keep ending up in this exact situation with this woman, her gun pressed to my head?

"Sam!"

It's Ella's voice.

Her *real* voice. I'm actually hearing her real voice. It's not just a dream or a hallucination.

Red and Lala have helped each other remove their handcuffs and have carefully taken the duct tape off Ella and the girl's mouth. Red keeps her from running to me, stopping her from putting herself in harm's way. He gives me a nod, a silent promise, and I know without a doubt that no matter what happens to me, she is safe with him. That brings me an unexplainable comfort, even with the cool metal of Vegas's gun in my forehead.

I smile reassuringly at Ella. "I'm okay."

On the other side of the room, while Vegas and the guards

have been distracted, I'm relieved to see that Beardsley has shoved Q, Luna, and Zara toward the broken window that Willie's body lies beneath. I can hardly hear Q yelling out for me with how ferociously Luna barking her head off at the sight of me like this again.

I point at Luna, growling and poised to pounce. "STAY, Luna. Don't you DARE. Keep her leash tight Q, don't let her leave your side no matter what happens."

I will not let Luna take the fall for me again. If this is the end I'm meant to have, so be it. I feel a certain amount of pressure off, a peace knowing Ella is safe with Red and Lala regardless of what happens to me. She's away from Vegas now, and that's all the matters. That's a peace I haven't felt in a long time.

Vegas opens her mouth, I'm sure to rub my nose in my fate, but a rumbling voice from the front door interrupts her. "Let the kid go."

My heart soars as Cade himself saunters in, his hands in his pockets like he's simply showing up to another day at the office. Axel prowls in at his side.

The backup he promised. These must be *his men* fighting with the guards.

I'm so relieved I could cry.

My head whips to Zara who lets out a loud gasp, standing frozen just off to Beardsley's right side, her face completely white, eyes wide like she's seen a ghost.

Is someone hurt? I hate being so helpless.

Vegas lets out a scream of frustration as Cade walks across the floor, gliding like a glorious red-haired Hercules, and I think I might have to break the news to Q that I am in love with someone else. He stops right in front of Vegas and me. He folds his arms across his chest, his face looking like he's already on the brink of losing his temper like he did back at the Catacombs. I'd hate to be the one on the opposite side of that look.

"Hello, Ronnie," he says, his voice clipped. "Long time, no see."

RECIPE: FOR MAKING YOUR OWN CLONE (QUICK AND EASY!)

PREP TIME: 3–4 WEEKS
SERVES: UNLIMITED

INGREDIENTS:

-A HAPPY/HEALTHY CHILD, PREFERABLY BETWEEN THE AGES OF 6 AND 9. (AVOID ONES WITH OLDER BROTHERS FOR BEST RESULTS)

-A TEAM OF DEDICATED DOCTORS AND SCIENTISTS WITH NO SOULS OR MORALS

DIRECTIONS:

-USING WHATEVER METHODS YOU DEEM NECESSARY, OBTAIN CHILD

-MAKE THEIR TRACKING TECHNOLOGY USELESS

-HAVE CHILD UNDERGO WEEKS OF BIOLOGICAL AND NEUROLOGICAL TORTURE

LIKE A LAB RAT

-BE SURE TO MONITOR VITALS, IT CAN BE ANNOYING TO START ALL OVER

WHEN THEY DIE.

-TAKE AS MANY BIOLOGICAL SAMPLES AS NECESSARY, BUT DON'T DRAIN

THEIR BLOOD COMPLETELY. WE NEED THEIR BRAIN FOR DOWNLOADS.

-AND FINALLY LET SCIENCE RUN ITS COURSE!

AND THAT'S IT! ENJOY!

29

YIPPIE-KI-YAY

MATEO

I jiggle the handle to the Nursery, hoping maybe I just did it wrong the first time, or maybe it was a figment of my imagination. But it still stays firmly closed.

I slowly turn to face the group, panic beginning to prickle at the back of my neck. This wasn't supposed to happen. He said it would be open. I pose the question to the group silently. *"What do we do?"*

A Senior, Malik, who has a one-year-old brother inside the Nursery steps forward to input his passcode into the keypad below the handle. A red X flashes on the screen. Another Senior, Myah, tries her code. Another red X. The last few with baby siblings inside try theirs too with no luck. I see the panic growing on their faces by the minute.

They kick the door furiously, taking turns, getting more and more distraught the longer it doesn't budge, Trevor among them. He kicks again and again.

I shush them, trying to stay calm, but I can feel my pulse in my ears. "We are drawing too much attention. We have to figure something else out."

"Is there another way in?" Eddie asks the Seniors with baby

siblings, but they say there isn't. This is the only entrance and exit.

A couple people volunteer to sneak around either side of the building to look for windows, and they creep off into the shadows. If they can find a window we can break into, then maybe someone can open the door from the inside.

I decide to try something drastic while they do that, remembering scenes from movies I watched as a kid.

"Back up," I tell Trevor, as I raise my gun shakily. He understands immediately and pushes Eddie and the rest of the group further back. I pull the slide down on the top to cock the gun, surprised that it's harder to do than I imagined.

I channel all the anger I feel toward the Elders into this hunk of metal in my hands as I point it at the door handle. How dare they just sit and hide in there, keeping innocent babies hostage while they cower away like the spineless old wrinkled pieces of trash they are? I pull the trigger, and the gun recoils a lot more than I expect, so the bullet lodges into the roof above the doorframe. My ears ring. I try to account for the recoil this time and fire off a second shot. It hits the keypad, bursting the screen into shattered pieces. I fire another, and it hits the frame.

I look at Trevor, and he takes a turn. He runs at the door at full speed, kicking it as hard as he can. It still doesn't budge. He falls backwards onto his butt.

The Seniors come back around the corner with apologies in their eyes.

"I'm not leaving him." Malik rips the gun out of my hand and fires off shot after shot desperately at the door, until it clicks. Empty. He tosses the gun to the side and barrels toward the door like a linebacker, throwing all his weight into his shoulder as he rams into the door. It may have bent inward an inch or two, or that could have been my imagination, but it still remains firmly locked.

Suddenly there is a series of pops from all directions,

louder than the fireworks at the hospital building. I cover my head instinctually and pull Eddie down, the group doing the same. I peek around hesitantly as the pops continue, their echoes filling my already-ringing ears and see smoke rising all around the Square.

Explosions.

They're blowing up all the Living Quarters one by one, getting closer to the Square with each one.

I curse. They're pushing us toward the Southern Boundaries, where Nova waits. The exact opposite direction of where Ramos told us to wait.

The explosions continue.

"We have to head for the trucks!" I yell, and it kills me to have to say it. If we have any chance of getting out, we have to leave now.

Malik looks at me, and I know he knows this. I see the decision painted out clear as day in his eyes. "I'm not leaving him."

He holds out his hand to shake mine. My brain is spinning, trying to see another angle, another option. Malik lowers himself onto the ground in front of the door, and I shove away the tear that streaks down my cheek furiously. This can't be the only way. The other Seniors with siblings join him on the floor. One of them, Myah, begins to cry. She buries her head in her knees.

The explosions continue, closer now. One pops right behind the Mess Hall next to us. Trevor hands Malik his gun. We have to leave.

The explosions are so loud that I didn't even hear the trucks approaching behind us, the delivery truck basically limping as its blown tire does its best to keep up.

Jordan yells at us from the open window of the pickup in front. "Come on!"

Malik gives me a nod, giving me the go-ahead to do what I need to do for my family, while he does what he needs to do for his. I hate this. He puts his arm around Myah and comforts her as she cries. I take a grudging step toward the truck, tugging a begrudging Eddie with me as everyone else loads solemnly into truck beds and roofs and wherever there is empty room. I help him into the cab of the front truck, and he slides in next to Jordan's sisters. Just as I'm about to hop into the passenger seat, I hear a noise from the Nursery.

The unmistakable swish of the door sliding open.

Malik and the other Seniors scramble to their feet.

"No way," Jordan breathes behind me at the steering wheel.

Hot tears burn in my eyes at the sight.

One by one, Elders step out of the Nursery door, arms full of bundled babies and diaper bags packed tightly for travel.

Seniors immediately jump to action, hopping out of truck beds to help load babies into trucks, setting them carefully into the arms of their siblings or other responsible Zoners. Malik takes his sleepy baby brother gently from the arms of an Elder with a dazed awe on his face.

I know what Malik was prepared to do. My whole body sighs with relief that he didn't have to. He didn't have to go down with the Zone with his brother locked helplessly inside.

In the middle of the group of Elders, taking the lead and barking out orders, is the Elder from the basement. My heart swells. He must have convinced them after all. I jog over to him.

"You really had me there for a minute," I say to him breathlessly. "I thought you changed your mind. Come on, let's get you guys loaded up. You can squeeze into the back of the delivery truck, or wherever there's room."

The Elder directs a few other Elders who still have bundled babies in their arms to load themselves into the trucks, and they obey, squeezing into cabs and beds wherever they fit. Many, however, like the Elder from the basement, linger.

"Come on," I tell them. "We have to hurry, let's go."

The Elder from the basement gives me a sad smile. "We're tired, Mateo. My decision remains the same."

"So you're just giving up?" I throw out my hands in fury.

He shakes his head. "We're doing what we should have done a long time ago. We want to give you your best chance."

I meet the stares of the wrinkled faces and grayed hair that surround me, some men, some women, their eyes unanimously set on this decision. Who am I to turn away their help, after years of wishing they'd do exactly this? That they'd finally wake up and decide we were worth making a splash for? And now they stand here in front of me, ready, waiting for me to tell them where they can make the biggest splash.

I nod, accepting their offer, but not sure how to best put it to use. "Okay. Parker's really the diversions guy, I wish he—"

As if on cue, Parker and his group nearly slam into the trucks as they run in. They are breathless and noticeably more somber in contrast to the hooting enthusiasm they left the basement with. I notice there are two less of them now. That's not a good sign.

Paker runs up to me, panting, holding out something in his hand. "I found this on the run over."

He tosses it to me. It's another truck key. I cheer, clapping him on the shoulder. "We can redistribute everybody once we get the hell out of here."

Eddie moves to get out of the truck.

"Ah," I stop him with a single syllable. "Stay with Jordan. I'll meet you out there."

He opens his mouth to protest, but I shush him again and repeat with emphasis, "I'll see you out there."

He nods with a grimace, knowing from my tone there is no room for argument.

I slam the truck door shut and lean in through the window to give parting instructions to Jordan. "Wait until exactly 6:00 for the gates to go down. Test it first, don't be dumb. Watch out for landmines along the way." I slap the side of the truck. "Be careful."

He gives me a salute and then thrusts the shifter into drive. He makes a hooting sound like a cowboy collecting his herd and makes a gesture out his window to the drivers behind him. The tires fling up gravel as he peels out, turning around and flying toward the Northern Boundaries, where pops of explosions are still blasting along the trail they will have to drive down.

As the trucks drive away and the dust settles, I make out the faces of the figures who have remained.

It's Parker and Trevor. Idiots. Instead of loading into trucks like everyone else, like a sane person would, they are instead standing next to the group of Elders, waiting for further directions. I give them a look.

"You thought we were just going leave you here?" Parker mirrors the look back at me.

"You'd probably try to do something stupid and heroic if we didn't come with you," Trevor adds, and I have to laugh. He's probably right.

"Parker was just at the Southern Boundaries where Nova and the Guards are," I announce to the group. And then to Parker, "How can they help?"

Parker rubs the back of his neck, exhaling loudly through his teeth. "We almost didn't make it back, man. I didn't see Nova, but I'm sure she's lurking in the shadows around here somewhere. There are probably a dozen Guards left. They're all just waiting there by the gates. Armed."

The Elder from the basement nods. "Sounds like the place we need to be."

The other Elders agree and begin gathering themselves to leave.

"Wait." I stop them. "What are you going to do? Just show up? They'll kill you on the spot."

A graying Elder from the group speaks up, rolling up her uniform sleeves to her elbows. "You boys get loaded into the last truck, and we'll get you a head start out of here."

I make eye contact with as many of them as I can, trying to confirm without a doubt they're actually agreeing to this. Is this really how they're choosing to go out? This is really what they want?

I'm met with conviction, eyes that are hardened and ready.

I give them a tight-lipped smile. "I wish it didn't have to be like this. But thank you. All of you." How do you put into words the gratitude for a sacrifice like this? Ending their lives so brutally... for us? I don't know what else to say, but I know it's time to get going. 5:49. Only 11 minutes to get to the Northern Boundaries.

We can do this.

I exhale, readying myself, and Parker and Trevor are at my sides in an instant.

"One last run through the Square for good measure?" I clap their shoulders, and they crouch, preparing to sprint. I take off for the Podium where the last few trucks sit deserted.

Parker and Trevor run at my side, and the Elders run behind us like warriors charging into battle. I'm surprised at their speed and agility. They've found their backbones and chosen a cause worth fighting for, and it has given them new life, breathed youth back into brittle bones. Youth that is about to meet its end... No, I can't dwell on it. It's the choice they've made. I just can't let it go to waste.

I race toward the closest truck as fast as I can, hopping over bodies of Guards and rebels like they're hurdles in a track meet. The Elders separate from us and race toward the Southern Boundaries, many of them letting out actual battle cries as they dive headfirst into the battlefield.

I race around to the drivers' side of the closest truck and

throw open the door, leaning in to shove the key into the ignition. *Please be the right one, please be the right one.*

The key doesn't turn.

Only 9 more minutes.

I sprint to the next one. Still nothing.

Okay, last one. This has to be it. I move to open the final truck door, but I feel a hand on my arm stopping me.

"Teo," Parker whispers.

"Wha—?" The words are snatched right from my throat as I see the pair that has crept out from the shadows of the Podium.

No.

It's Nova, one arm tightly around Mayor Ramos's neck, and her other arm in its gun form, aimed right at his head.

Nova drags Ramos closer to us. He looks terrible. His face, which was already nearly black and blue when I saw him earlier today, is now lined with fresh wounds. His nose is bleeding, and a cut near his eye has reopened. His eyes are wild with desperation now that he has seen us. He's been trying to keep us out of Nova's range of fire this whole time, but now it's too late.

We've walked right into the trap.

"Mateo—" Ramos croaks, but Nova presses her gun into his head to cut him off.

"We can do this the easy way or the hard way," Nova hisses at us, her lips stretched into an infernal sneer. "Drop the keys or watch your Mayor die."

I drop the keys in front of me right away and put my hands up in surrender. Parker and Trevor do the same.

My throat tightens as I hear the pops of unmistakeable gunshots near the Southern Boundaries. I try not to picture the Elders on the other side of those gunshots. I try not imagine them dropping like flies, completely outnumbered and weaponless.

It was their choice, it was their choice.

"Come with me," Nova orders, gesturing with her gun-arm to follow, still gripping Ramos tightly in a chokehold. "All of you."

I grimace at Parker and Trevor, sending them a silent apology. They didn't have to be here. I wish they weren't. I wish they had loaded into the trucks when they had the chance.

We were so close.

I send a silent grateful prayer upwards that Eddie is on his way out. I'm so glad I had the good sense to send him with Jordan instead of letting him come with me. It's like somehow all the forces at play knew before I did that I wouldn't be getting out.

It was too good to be true.

We follow Nova to a tiny building near the Guards' Quarters that I've never really paid much notice to before. It's not exactly hidden, but it doesn't really stand out either. It's just a small unimposing shed, the same gray of the steel condos the Guards live in. 5:58. This must be the place that controls the gates. I can't think of any other reason Nova would have us all here, so close to her own deadline.

How will she tell her higher-ups that she failed? That the explosions she set up to kill us or push us all South failed? That when Ramos opens the Northern gates right now instead of the Southern ones as ordered, all of the Zone children she was supposed to have exterminated will run free instead? She relied too much on us turning on each other, that we'd simply jump at the very prospect of her bogus "special assignment." She was wrong. We beat her together.

It kind of warms my heart at the thought, even though I'm probably facing my own certain death whenever she's done with us. At least they'll get out. It won't be for nothing.

They'll get to the exit, and Eddie will be free.

It dawns on me, the horror of the realization freezing my entire body. *No, they won't.* Because I'm the only one who saw the map in Ramos's office. No one else knows where to go, or that the exit is even in E3.

I suddenly feel lightheaded. When they do get out, they'll be lost Underground, still prisoners just to a larger jail cell. With only a few days' worth of supplies, if that.

Nova throws Ramos at the door, and he stumbles forward, nearly hitting his head on the smooth metal. "You're lucky my FPA bosses have gone quiet, otherwise I would've killed you days ago. Unfortunately you're my only way out."

Ramos catches himself and looks at us over his shoulder, his eyes busy, trying to figure out how to get us to the Boundaries, how to make it all work still. I give him a tight smile. "*It's okay,*" I try to tell him with my eyes, begging him to stick to the plan.

Even lost Underground is still better than here.

They'll figure out what to do.

Jordan, and Rachel, and Jess. The other Seniors. The few Elders who came to help escort babies. They can all figure something out together.

Just get everyone else out. Get Eddie out.

I don't know if he understood me or not, but Ramos turns to the keypad on the doorframe, inputting an excessively long code into the screen. Then a small platform spits out underneath the keypad, and he presses his thumb into it.

The keypad blinks green in confirmation, and the door slides open with a clank.

Nova flicks her gun-arm into the small building. "All of you, in. Now," she barks.

Parker, Trevor, and I pass them and shuffle into the small space, trying not to trip over each other, squeezing closely together as an auto-light flickers on above our heads.

Nova pushes Ramos into the room. "Do it now."

"What do we do?" Parker whispers, eyeing me sideways.

All I can do is lift my shoulders in a shrug. "Got any ideas?"

The far wall of the shed lights up at Ramos's touch, a Tab taking up the entirety of the wall. It's not the same as the deskTab in his office. Instead, it's dark and blank, and a cursor blinks for code to be inputted. This must control the entire security of the Zone. I wonder what else can be controlled from here. Surveillance cameras? The wallTabs in our own Quarters?

Ramos starts typing quickly into the source panel, a series of unintelligible commands line after line. He looks over his shoulder, pretending to wait for her command. It's 6:00.

"What are you waiting for?" Nova pushes him into the keyboard impatiently. "Open the gate."

He presses a final single key on the keyboard, and at the same time there is a deafening boom that shakes the building and the ground under our feet.

Nova smiles wickedly. "Oh, did I forget to mention that if you opened the Northern gates instead, it would set off my final explosion? Thanks for getting rid of the rest of those little brats for me before I head out."

My soul leaves my body. "*No!*" I scream, lunging at her. I claw at her face, pushing, shoving, ripping anything I can reach.

It can't be true. It can't be.

Eddie.

I sent them driving right into their graves.

I push Nova to the ground, punching her across the face. Ramos stands at the keyboard dumbly, in frozen shock. Parker and Trevor try to get me off Nova, trying to quiet my screams.

Nova just laughs, even as blood runs out of her nose, her black eyes completely void of any emotion. Soulless blackholes.

They pull me off her, holding me by the arms, knowing her retaliation will be swift. But I don't even care.

I deserve the punishment.

I killed them all.

Ramos looks at me with wide tear-filled eyes as Nova pulls herself up. "Mateo, I had no idea. I'm so sorry."

I fall to my knees, the sobs clawing themselves out of my chest.

We heard the explosion, *felt it.* Anything even remotely close would be absolutely obliterated.

Eddie's really gone.

The other children.

The babies.

I sob into my knees, wishing I could just melt into this ground and disappear forever. Parker and Trevor stand stiffly behind me, not even bothering to comfort me. I know they feel it too.

This is our fault.

Nova aims her arm-gun at Ramos again, shifting her weight as she regains her balance. "Now, let's try this again. Do it right this time, and I'll let the Three Musketeers here come with me. I know a certain someone who can put them to use. She usually likes her recruits... *younger*, but I'm sure she can make do."

I barely hear the clicking of keys as Ramos puts in the new commands. Everything around me feels like it's already gone, like the whole Zone has already burned to black ashes, and I'm in the middle of the smoke, not allowed the fiery bliss of burning with it. Cursed to just stand in the middle of the smoke forever, completely untouched.

Ramos clicks a final key, and Nova yanks me up to my feet, pushing me toward the door. I stumble out of the shed and see the indisputable cloud of black billowing out from the Northern Boundaries. It was true. They're really dead.

I don't even feel my legs as Nova escorts us to the Southern Boundaries. We pass Town Hall, pass the emergency exit nook where we all gathered just minutes ago. The last place we were all together. It's like their ghosts linger in this spot, sending a chill through my body as we pass. *You did this to us.*

We pass the hospital building, and I'm too numb to even react to the wrinkled bodies we have to step over to get to the gate where the Guards wait.

"Kill me," I beg Nova, but she just ignores me. "Please just kill me."

She storms past me and puts her gun right on Ramos's nose, her face twisted in fury. "You," she snarls.

He didn't open the gate. The air still buzzes with the unseen electricity of the invisible gates. A trap for a desperate onlooker. The path to freedom is right there. You can see it there just beyond the threshold, and maybe even convince yourself you can't actually feel the deadly energy pulsating around the space, until it sucks you into its embrace.

The only embrace I deserve.

The second this Guard lets loose even an inch, I will be running for the gate. Any end is better than being forced to live in a world without Eddie.

Nova screams at Ramos, the cool control she's had the whole time she's been here quickly dissolving into hysterical rage. "I'm getting really fed up with your games!"

To my horror she fires a shot at Ramos, the blast cannoning out of her prosthetic. He flies back into the brick of the hospital, crumpling to the ground on impact.

"Mayor Ramos!" Parker yells, trying to yank free, but his Guard shoves him to the ground onto his belly, shoving a gun into his back.

I can't move, I can't even speak, my brain unable to send the proper commands to the proper limbs. I'm still just stuck in the middle of that same helpless smoke, forced to watch without action and without end of my own. Ramos's head lolls limply, dark blood pooling beside him.

Another person I failed.

Nova rips a knife out of her belt and turns toward Ramos.

My stomach turns as I put the pieces together. She still needs his thumbprint.

She barks an order to the Guards, and they begin marching toward the Square. Parker's Guard yanks him back up to his feet. They pull us away from the buzzing gates, in the direction of the Square. Trevor yells and thrashes, trying to fight off his Guard, but it's no use. I don't even have the energy to try. I let mine drag me wherever he wants me to go. There's no point in resisting. No point to anything.

Nova remains behind, the knife outstretched, approaching Ramos's unmoving body.

Suddenly the formation of Guards in front of us separates, Guards diving to opposite directions as something comes barreling through them.

A black truck. Rachel behind the wheel.

She's alive?

Could that mean...?

She speeds in our direction, and I have to dive out of the way as she swerves past, accelerating faster straight into her target.

Nova.

The truck rams into her at such a speed that her body flies through the air, seeming to defy gravity, flying right into the electric gates of the boundaries.

Rachel screeches the truck to a stop and screams out the window with the rage of a lion, "That's for Talia and Steven, you cyborg bitch!"

The gate flashes to life like lightning.

I duck instinctually, covering my head as sparks and cracks explode in front of us. Blasts of electricity zap, energy pulsating out of the gate in waves that whip my hair back. A sickening burning scent fills the air, and it's so overpowering I gag.

There is a lull for a moment, the space quiet as my eardrums ring from the cracks of the gate. Trevor doesn't hesitate. He leaps to action before the Guards even realize what has happened. He rips the gun out of his Guard's hand and pulls the trigger immediately, sending his Guard flying back. He lets bullets fly, bodies dropping all around him.

My body jolts back to life, the hope that Eddie may still be alive sending life back into my veins. I punch the nearest Guard in the face, ripping his gun from his hands and hitting him over the head with it.

Parker does the same.

We duck as we run toward the truck, gunshots peppering all around us. Rachel whips around and drives straight into the group of Guards. They jump out of her way.

"Get in!" she screams, the sounds of the gunshots ricocheting off all the surrounding steel.

"Help me get Ramos!" I shout to Parker and Trevor, and they run to me right away, shooting off rounds behind them, barely aiming, just hoping they'll hit a Guard one way or another. The gun in my hand skids across the ground as I drop to my knees in front of Ramos. To my relief I see his chest shudder with shallow breaths.

He's alive.

I count down from three as each of us grabs a side of him. We look at each other and brace ourselves, knowing it's up to chance if we will even be able to lift his weight into the truck.

3-2-1

We heave him up, and my muscles strain. I groan through my teeth, forcing my body to keep moving. We shuffle him to the truck bed, the tailgate mercifully already down. I count down from three again so we can hopefully use combined momentum to get him up into the bed.

All of us grunt and strain, pushing as hard as we can to lift him high enough.

By a sheer miracle we get him up, and he drops into the

bed, his head bouncing off the metal of the bed. Oops. But better a bruised head than left for dead, I guess.

Guards advance, their gunshots getting closer, pinging off the truck. Rachel yells at us to hurry. We push him in just far enough to close the tailgate. Rachel doesn't even wait for us before the wheels turn, trying to gain traction in the gravel. The truck lurches forward, and we all hop over the tailgate and into the truck bed, crouching as low as possible as Rachel speeds out of the alley and into the Square. Guards shoot at us as we fly by, but luckily the bullets lodge into the sides of the truck or above our heads into surrounding beams.

Within seconds, we're speeding across the Square and toward the Northern Boundaries.

Alive.

Eddie might be alive.

I yell at Rachel through the broken rear windshield as we fly North, swerving around bodies and rubble, bouncing over sidewalks and other landmarks. "What happened at the gate? We heard the explosion."

"Everyone's okay," she shouts, and it feels like the noose around my neck snaps free. "We were far enough back."

"Is the gate—?" I don't even have to finish my sentence.

"It's open," she confirms. "Everyone got out."

My cheer is like a garbled overjoyed sob. Parker and Trevor punch each other and hoot. Pure relief washes over my body, immediately cleansing me from the guilt and pain.

He's okay.

Not only okay.

He's out.

We are about to pass the Podium when an idea strikes. "Stop the truck!" I yell.

Rachel screeches to stop, and Trevor nearly flies out of the truck bed.

"What the hell, bro?" He tries to regain balance in frustration, but when he sees where we are the realization crosses his face.

The other truck.

In a swift movement, I jump out of the bed, and run to the spot where I dropped the key. Darkness has fallen and the overhead lights have dimmed to their nighttime glow, so I pat the ground sightlessly for a moment, hoping to feel the cool metal beneath my hand.

I find the key and leap to my feet victoriously. I throw open the door to the truck, and it thankfully cranks to life when I turn the key in the ignition.

Rachel has already started back across the Square, and it takes me a minute to figure out what to do. I fumble with the pedals and the gear shift dumbly for a moment, trying to think of movies I've seen, anything I can pull knowledge from to do this.

I press down one of the pedals hesitantly.

D - Drive, I'm guessing?

To my relief, the truck staggers forward clumsily. I press the other pedal with my foot, my head nearly slamming into the steering wheel as the truck slams to a stop.

A moment later, and I'm moving, albeit gawkily, in the right direction, following Rachel down the sidewalks I've walked down for the last seven years.

Tears sting at my eyes, momentarily blurring my vision, the reversal of everything I thought happened still processing through my body. My hands shake at the steering wheel as I separate the nightmare from the reality.

He's alive.

We did it.

We got out.

30

CAUGHT IN THE CROSSFIRE, AND
IT'S HOT

SAM

Cade mutters a command to Axel, whose eyes flash with the registered instructions. He leaps into action, and I watch in horror as he rips a piece of flesh off the nearest guard's forearm. The guard howls in pain, but only for a second because Axel goes for his throat next. He cuts off the guard's screams, ripping it out clean with razor-sharp teeth, blood splattering all over his metal frame. He doesn't even bother activating the gun on his back. He doesn't need to. His teeth are enough. He doesn't hesitate before he leaps to his next victim, fighting alongside Cade's men with steel and unbridled brutality. The guards don't stand a chance against him. He picks them off one by one. Their screams ring in my ears.

Vegas's face has reddened into such a combustible fury that I'm worried she might explode, and I'll be collateral damage by just being next to her.

"Get out of my Zone, or I will blow his head off, Cade. I mean it." Her voice is low and deadly and even though I'm the one she is pointing the gun at, I'm way more worried for Cade.

"*Your* Zone?" Cade replies with a cocked eyebrow, subtle mockery laced throughout his tone.

I watch back and forth between them, my eyes feeling like tennis balls. I take in the two of them together, trying to make it make sense in my head now that I see them both in front of me, but I still don't get it. How could these two ever have had enough in common to get *married*? They are like oil and water. Fire and ice. How much more different can you get?

Vegas barks out a harsh laugh. "When will you learn that everything in this godforsaken Underground is *mine*. I will give you one last chance to see yourself out, and consider yourself lucky I'm even giving you that, Arcadius. Or did you forget what happened the last time you tried to take something that was mine?"

Cade's face darkens, a furious vein pulsing in his neck.

Vegas's bubbly tone returns now that she has the upper hand in the conversation, even as Axel makes her men drop like flies around her. "Did you need me to jog your memory? C9? No survivors? Just the other day? I mean I'm sure you remember, considering you lost... what was it? All of your men?" She laughs. "I will say I was a bit bummed to lose my best general, but woes of battle, I suppose."

No, no, no.

My insides coil. Did I just hear her right? My eyes flick to Lala, but luckily she didn't seem to hear her from all the way over there. Her and Red are mercifully distracted trying to find a way out.

Mateo... Eddie... Mayor Ramos?

I feel sick.

I stumble forward dizzily, the cool metal of her gun digging further into my forehead. "What happened at C9?" This can't be true, it can't be. "What is she talking about, Cade?"

Cade ignores me. His voice is basically a growl. "Let the kid and his sister go, Ronnie, and we can settle this ourselves."

Vegas sighs like her hands are tied by some external force. "Unfortunately, no can do. I only brought her over here to be a little reminder for Sammy here to stop meddling in grown-up business." She *boops* my nose with her gun. "But I need the girl for my next batch. Also, her poor double over there wouldn't survive without her, and you wouldn't want that on your conscience now, would you? They're one now." She smiles dreamily over her shoulder and blows a kiss at Ella and the girl.

I shake my head, my mind reeling at all the consecutive bombs dropped right now.

What?

I feel like I'm three miles behind here and still moving further backwards. Did she just say that she can't...survive? Without Ella? How is that possible? Who is she?

Cade examines the two of them, and I can see similar questions all over his face as he looks back and forth between them. Vegas is thrilled as he puzzles it out, nearly vibrating with smug pride.

"Aren't they just amazing? I absolutely cannot wait for batch two, I have so many upgrades planned."

His whisper is so low I can barely hear it, even though I'm right next to him. He shakes his head, seeming genuinely aghast. "What have you done, Veronica? This is sick, even for you."

She beams. "Not that I needed your approval, but thank—"

"Ronnie, these kids won't bring him back. You know that, right?"

Vegas looks like the air has been completely knocked out of her. She is so stunned that the arm she was pointing the gun at me with falls to her side. She looks like he has just slapped her across the face.

I don't waste any time. With the gun finally away from my head, I sprint over to the other side of the room, forcing my body to move faster than I ever have before and scoop Ella up in my arms.

The air explodes around us, my movement like the first

domino in a line falling down, sparking action after action. Vegas and Cade screaming at each other. Shots firing. More glass breaking. Guards and Catacombs men alike fighting for dominance by the exits. Luna restrained and howling wildly, not knowing how to help.

I crouch low as more gunshots are fired. I don't even look to see whether it was Vegas or Cade, I just run faster and faster with Ella in my arms, past Beardsley, over Willie, away from the gore of Axel's victims, and out the window behind Q, Zara, and Luna. I follow them out of L'Deaux and don't look back.

Ella screams at me to stop, hitting my arms and shoulders, trying to squirm out of my hold, reaching behind us with an outstretched hand. "We can't just leave her there, go back, go back!"

But I just ignore her. I don't care. If what Vegas said is true, I don't want that parasite anywhere near my sister.

I leave the adults to fend for themselves, knowing they can hold their own, and jog after the girls across the street, away from any possible crossfire of the power struggle happening in L'Deaux. Luna hops and barks the whole way there, pulling at the leash Q grips onto for dear life, begging to be put to use. The lights overhead have darkened to evening. There are small fires in many of the windows down the strip. There are still so many people in the streets that it's hard to tell if anyone even managed to get out. The ones left are fighting, vandalizing buildings, looting stores. This isn't exactly what I hoped to inspire, but I can't worry about any of that now.

I just have to make sure she's ok.

I set Ella down on the sidewalk breathlessly and drop to my knees in front of her. I touch her shoulders, her hair, her chin, confirming sure she's real, she's here, she's okay. Her anger at me melts away as I bring her face in my hands to look at her.

"It's you."

Her eyes fill up with tears. "It's me."

I pull her in for a hug and have to choke back a sob as she clings to me. The feeling of her warmth in my arms again feels like a dream, one that I've dreamed so many times in her absence that it's hard to believe it's really true.

"It's really really you," I repeat, my throat tight.

Q and Zara watch our reunion with their own tears, holding onto each other, happy to be safely away from L'Deaux.

Ella cries into my chest, and I can tell she has tried to be strong for so long, that this has just been building and building. I let her cry, stroking her hair and breathing her in. *This is real.*

Beardsley and Red run out of the broken window next and work together to move Willie's body gently to a quiet alley next to L'Deaux. I watch them lay Willie to pitiful rest with a stabbing guilt.

I hold my hand out to Q's as I kneel here with Ella, and she takes it, though she doesn't quite meet my eye. I know that look... What is she thinking about?

Lala jogs up to us, holding the hand of that girl—that *thing.* She's crying. Probably scared. I'm repulsed by the sight of her, seeing her wear Ella's hair—our mother's hair—her smile that looks like mine, like dad's. Everything about her is stolen.

Q immediately breaks into tears at the sight of Lala and runs to her.

"La," she cries.

"*Mija,* come here, baby." Lala holds her, and they cry together, tears streaming down both of their cheeks. I feel another stabbing guilt, knowing I'm responsible for their separation too.

"Steele?" Q croaks. All Lala can manage to do is shake her head.

I'm gutted. *Not Steele too.*

They cry into each other. I hold Ella tighter, feeling even more grateful for her safety, wondering if it was because of Steele that she's even here and safe.

Zara allows us our reunion, taking a turn keeping the girl under her wing, trying to talk with her and get her to stop crying. She speaks to her in a gentle singsongy way. But I can't watch. I can't even look at her.

And then as if I couldn't possibly feel more guilty, as if there couldn't possibly be more death on my hands, I remember what Vegas said. About C9. I fall from my knees to my backside with Ella in my lap, like I've completely deflated from the inside out. I tuck Ella's head into my chest, wanting to cry myself.

Mayor Ramos. Mateo. Eddie.

Lala.

She doesn't know.

Could Vegas be lying? I've never hoped so much for that. I think back to any small details from before we left the other day, desperate for anything that can prove this wrong.

"Q," I gurgle, saying her name almost involuntarily like an exhale. Q and Lala's heads snap to me, their tear-streaked cheeks still pressed together in their embrace.

Ella peels herself off my chest to look up at me in concern as I barely manage to breathe correctly. She puts a hand on my face. "Are you okay?"

I take her hand and kiss it, knowing she'll be hurt by this too if it's true. She's already been through so much, and Eddie is her best friend. But I have to know... Lala has to know...

I look back at Q, my throat tight. "When we left the Catacombs, you said Cade couldn't help because he was preparing the trucks for a delivery. Right?" Please say I'm wrong. "Where were they going?"

She thinks about it for a moment. "C-Zone drop-off, I think. Why?"

I was hoping I misremembered. I look down at Ella's hand in mine, unable to look Lala in the eyes.

"Lala, I'm so sorry—"

Red and Beardsley have joined us. Q pulls away from Lala

and gets a running head start to jump into Red's arms. They embrace tightly, crying into each other.

"What is it?" Lala asks, stepping toward me, and just hearing the concern in her voice wrecks me.

"I—" My voice breaks. I can't even say it.

I swallow. I look around at the group, unsure if I want to trample all over this happy of a reunion. What's the right way to completely shatter someone's entire world?

Lala repeats herself, crouching in front of Ella and me. She is nearly in tears already with only the anticipation of bad news. "Sam?"

Q holds onto Red's arm, her brows pulled together at the look on my face. She can tell it's bad. She feels so far away.

"I don't know if it's true," I start slowly, squeezing Ella's hand in mine. "I'm so sorry, Lala. I heard Vegas say C9 was destroyed. She said Cade had a part in it." I gulp. "She said there were no survivors."

Q covers her mouth with her hands, eyes widening. "What?"

"No," Ella squeaks. I pull her in tighter as she cries, wishing I could comfort her somewhere other than the sidewalk of a smoking wasteland.

Luckily Beardsley is at Lala's side in the blink of an eye because if he hadn't been so fast, she would have fallen straight to the floor. She falls into him, letting out such a deep guttural wail that only a mother can. A cry filled with years of pent-up pain and restrained rage finally set free. It's the most heartbreaking sound I've ever heard.

Q drops to her knees next to me, her eyes busy and confused. "Are you sure she said *Cade* was involved? That's impossible. He wouldn't do that."

Zara clears her throat uncomfortably, shifting her weight on her feet and suddenly paying very close attention to the girl's hair. *Ella's hair.*

"What do you know?" Q asks her, loudly enough that everyone is listening in now.

Zara looks away as her eyes fill with tears. Q leaps to her feet and is by her side in seconds. "What is it?"

"I remembered everything," Zara blurts, and then covers her mouth with her hands as if she's just thrown up.

"About your last day? What did you remember?"

"As soon as I saw him, it all came back..." She shakes her head and has to take a breath before she's able to say more. I can see her hands shaking from here as she recounts this memory. "He forced me into his car. I remember him pushing me through the door by my face and pulling my hair when I tried to get away. I... I think he drugged me." Her voice quivers. "The last thing I remember was him saying I was a message, that he needed to teach my dad a lesson... He didn't save me. He abducted me."

"*Who?*" Q asks incredulously.

Zara's reply is bone-chilling. "Cade. I think Vegas is telling the truth. He's not a good man."

My chest feels tight. "And we just gave him an army."

"We've gone over this before," says a low voice from the shadows that makes me jump to my feet and push Ella behind me.

Luna growls in a protective crouch as the two shadowed figures approach. It's Cade, Axel walking mechanically next to him.

"Speak of the devil and he shall appear."

31

BATTLE ROYALE

SAM

Red and Beardsley hold Lala back as Cade approaches. She paws at him like a tiger in a cage, but they keep her restrained tightly as Axel growls threateningly, daring her with teeth crusted in blood to come closer.

"How could you do this?!" she screams. "My boys! MY BOYS!"

Cade is completely unruffled by her reaction. He's too collected, like he was prepared for this. And somehow that's the only confirmation I need.

They say if something seems too good to be true it usually is, and I guess that's true. He's always just been too calm, too calculating, TOO DASTARDLY HANDSOME AND COOL.

Apparently he and Vegas are one of a kind after all. She wears her crazy loudly and proudly. His crazy lurks in secret, under the guise of seemingly good deeds and fake refuge for vulnerable people.

More figures begin to appear out of the shadows, closing in slowly on every side like a dark fog. Our group tightens together as they fold in around us.

I keep Ella's hand in mine tightly. I will not lose her again. I don't care what I have to do. We're leaving here together.

"Easy girl," Q whispers to Luna, gripping her leash tighter as her growls rise in volume. The fur on her spine is sticking straight up as the threats around us get closer, as Axel gets closer.

The adults throw threats back and forth, Lala's especially graphic, and understandably so. I brush my shoulder on Q's next to mine, needing the reassurance as things get progressively tenser that she's close. She turns her head to smile, but it doesn't reach her eyes. Why do her eyes look like goodbye?

"Q?"

Red, ever the peacemaker, is trying to negotiate with Cade's men, who are now completely surrounding us. Ella and the girl are whispering to each other, and my stomach coils at their closeness, but I don't intervene. Q's eyes have dropped to the ground, her brows pulled together.

"Q," I repeat, more firmly, but still keeping my voice low. "Talk to me."

Her eyes flick back to mine and hold my gaze. She doesn't answer, but she doesn't have to. Every thought and emotion fighting for dominance inside her is painted across every inch of her face. Fear, pain, regret, but also hope. Love. Determination.

I feel a crushing sadness as I layer all her emotions together into the only possible conclusion. I feel dizzy, like I'm spinning on an eternal merry-go-round.

"You want to stay with her," I whisper hoarsely, the words feeling so heavy that they might knock me to my knees. I can't even bring myself to say that woman's name. "Is there anything I can say that would change your mind?"

It's useless to even ask. I know she's already made the decision. She just didn't know how to tell me.

She twists her mouth to one side, trying not to cry. She

takes my other free hand and keeps her voice low so no one else can hear. "I have to, Sam. I don't care about the power, 'moving mountains,' whatever she was saying. I don't care about that."

"I know you don't," I force myself to say, through a throat that feels like it is made of clay.

"If she knows anything about—"

I shake my head and cut her off. "I wish there were another way. I hate this. I hate her." I swallow down the hurt. I know this isn't about me— I'm trying *really hard* not to make this about me. "If you're sure, tell me what you need me to do."

A tear has let itself out of her eye despite her best efforts and streaks down her face in a single line. I drop her hand, so I can wipe it away, trying to force myself to breathe. I stroke her face with my thumb, pressing a kiss into her forehead.

I want to scream. I want to break something.

But more than anything, I want her to be happy.

I want her to get the answers and the peace she deserves.

"Thank you," she whispers, her breath cool on my lips. "I'm going to find them."

"You're going to find them," I repeat.

I know she will. She can do anything she sets her mind to. That's what I love about her.

She puts her hand on my cheek. "If you promise me one thing, I'll make you a promise back."

"Anything."

"Promise you'll help me get away. They'd never let me leave." She nods to Beardsley, Red, and Lala, who are still yelling at Cade and the other men—the people they've been working alongside with for years. She's right. They'd never let her do this.

I don't want to let her do this.

Inside I'm screaming. I hate this.

I want to say, "Please don't leave me."

But I know it wouldn't do any good. *This isn't about me.*

So I close the distance between us with a relenting kiss.

A short-lived closeness. A momentary happiness cut short by what feels like an inevitable goodbye.

It's always an inevitable goodbye.

Too good to be true. Too good to last. Like everything else.

She returns my kiss, and on her lips, I feel every single one of those conflicting emotions her face gave away. But most of all I feel the hope, the determination. I know this is what she feels she needs to do, no matter how much it kills me to let her go.

"LubYouQ," I blurt in a jumble, my mind knowing this is my last chance but my mouth sabotaging the attempt. I sigh, trying again. Might as well own it. "*I love you.*"

"I love you too." And somehow it hurts even worse to hear her say it. "My promise to you is once I get the information I need, I'm going to take her down from the inside out. I swear I will."

I try to smile. I hate that she wants to go, but I take comfort in knowing she'll burn the place down while she's there. If there is anyone who can give Vegas the true run for her money she deserves, I know it's Q. She is a damn force to be reckoned with, as long as I don't get in her way.

"I'm going to take Lala back to C9," I whisper. "I just have to see it for myself that it's really gone. And she deserves some closure."

"And then?"

"I'm going to find the way out of this hellhole and give Ella the life in the sun she deserves." I nod down to Ella next to me, who still whispers with the girl, clutching onto her with her free hand.

Q's voice falters. "And then?"

"And then I'm going to do the same for you."

She smiles, squeezing my hand a final time. "Three months should do the trick."

"Three months it is," I repeat. I like that way better than 'goodbye,' even if it is doused in delusion.

A series of gunshots fire close by, and it's like we are both yanked back to reality. All of us crouch down instinctually, making a sort of sphere around each other. I hunch over Ella, not sure which direction it came from.

I peer over Lala's shoulder and see Vegas shooting rounds off from the entrance of L'Deaux, walking drunkenly, her hair loose from its bun and her nose bloodied. It's hard to tell if she's aiming at Cade or at us.

I evaluate the scene, and I know every member of this circle is doing the same. Cade's men have us surrounded on all sides, just waiting for orders and ready to strike.

Cade stands in front of Beardsley, Axel at his side, waiting to do the same.

Vegas nears, bringing a storm of haphazard bullets with her.

"Calix, go take care of my wife please. It's time to go," Cade says, with a sighing tone that is almost bored. "Unfortunately, you've all become a liability to my goals."

And sure enough, his trusty right-hand steps out of the circle, wearing all black like he did that night we played paintball.

"After all we've done for you over these years, you're just going to throw us way like the trash?" Red's voice is such a low growl, I wonder for a moment if Luna has learned how to speak.

Q is whispering to Zara on the other side of her, and by the gasp Zara lets out I know she's told her what she plans to do. Maybe Zara will have the good sense to stop her or talk her out of it. Maybe she can say all the things I wasn't able to say.

"It's nothing personal," Cade says to Red dismissively. And with a turn on his heel, he walks away, taking half of the men in the circle with him. He sends one last command over his shoulder. "Axel, *fass.*"

It's like that single word transports me back years. Visiting the K9 unit with my dad at the police station. I remember that word because it was the one I was most fascinated with as a little boy watching the dogs train, with their trainers in huge marshmallow-like suits.

Fass.

It means *attack.*

Axel's LED lights in his eyes click brighter as the command activates in his computer system. He stalks forward slowly like a lion, straight to who he perceives as the largest physical threat. Red.

We all back up as a unit, prepared to run, but the semicircle barricade of Catacombs men behind us prevent it, and Vegas advances furiously in the other direction. There is nowhere to go.

Axel bares his knife-like teeth and pounces, his back legs springing him into the air right at Red.

Red braces himself for impact and tightens his fists, ready for the fight.

Time moves to double speed as several things happen all at once, feeling like the very earth itself is spinning faster.

Luna rips free from her leash in Q's hand and leaps to action, shooting through the air and intercepting Axel midair. Before I can even take a second breath, she has Axel's metal throat in her teeth, and they fall to the ground in a *crash,* rolling around in a flurry of fangs and snarls.

Beardsley whips out a thumb-size accessory from his back pocket and with a push of a button it enlarges into a baton, similar to the ones the Guards used to give me Penalties with in C9. He pulls two more from other pockets and tosses one to Red and Lala, keeping the third for himself. The adults waste no time with the batons, immediately throwing hits at the nearest men. The semicircle explodes as an all-out fight breaks out. Fists, batons, the Catacombs men's hodgepodge array of weapons fly through the air in every direction.

I pull Ella behind me, and she reaches out for the girl, trying to tell me they are a package deal. Zara picks her up and holds her closely, giving Ella a reassuring smile.

"I've got her," she assures her, and crouches to dodge a hit from an incoming man, the girl tightly in her arms. Red is there in a second, yelling in fury as he lands a blow to the man's knee, then his shoulder, and then his head. He crumples to the ground. Red moves on to the next.

Q and I lock eyes through the commotion. With every effort I can summon, I nod. Now is her chance. She has to go *now*. She blows me and Zara a sad kiss and takes off in a sprint straight toward Vegas, whistling at Luna as she passes.

Luna and Axel are still rolling in a growling, snarling mess of foamy saliva and grease. With a feral howl, Luna rips off one of Axel's mechanical limbs, like she's a wild hyena devouring a gazelle. She goes in for the kill, ripping out the wiry mainframe from his chest and spitting it to the side. The severed cables spark and sizzle on the ground. The LEDs in Axel's eyes go dark, and what's left of him falls to the ground in a heap. Luna barks at him one last time for good measure, a final warning that this is what happens when you mess with her humans.

That's something Cade didn't account for in Axel's design. He can follow the most brutal of commands without question, can defeat hordes of men at the drop of a hat. But he's nothing without heart. Heart creates the fiercest warriors because they have more at stake. The need to protect who we love is more brutal than any programming ever will be.

Luna charges after Q, and as much as it hurts seeing them go, I take comfort knowing Luna will protect her with her life.

I know that from experience.

As the fighting consumes the space all around us, I focus on making an exit plan to get Ella out of here. If we can just get to the exit, we can join the throng of Elites that are hopefully there wreaking havoc on the gates and blend in with them as they push their way out.

Zara is still close by holding the girl. She ducks to avoid a hammer that has been thrown. She looks at me with worried eyes. *"What do we do?"* her eyes ask me.

A figure advances on me from the other side, and I throw out a punch in the direction of his nose. It's Calix.

He blocks my punch and twists my arm, forcing me to let go of Ella's hand as he throws me to the ground. I land on my shoulder hard as I fall to the ground. It sends a lightning bolt of pain down the same arm my wristTab was on. Now pain radiates from both directions.

Ella and the girl scream in unison. "Sam!"

Lala flies in and hits Calix in the stomach with her baton. He doubles over in pain with a groan. When another man comes up behind Lala, Zara takes over and begins kicking Calix everywhere she can reach. Ella and the girl help too. Lala whips around to throw a punch at her assailant's throat with a follow-through of a knee to the balls. He falls to his knees, and she kicks him down to the floor before leaping to the next opponent.

I pull myself up and stalk toward Calix with fists clenched in front of me to help Zara finish him off.

"Wait," he croaks, massaging his stomach as he stretches back to full height. "Take this."

He holds out a circular item, which I eye suspiciously. Zara and I share a wary look. Beardsley nearby grunts as a punch lands in his shoulder which he then returns with double force to the man's nose.

"It's just a smoke bomb," Calix assures me with a low voice, stepping forward to set it in my hand. I pull Ella into me as he gets closer. "Use it as a distraction when you're ready to make a break for it. Run straight to the club Neon Ave, and don't stop. Jones will be waiting in the back for you, and he'll take you through tonight's service exit."

I can feel Zara's eyes on me as we process this. She has even more reason than me to not trust him.

"Why?" I ask carefully, studying him. What could he have to gain from this?

He takes a second before responding, seeming to choose his words carefully before he says them. He seems to consider whether he should tell me the truth or not. Finally, he sighs.

"I was a low-level Guard years ago for Mayor Ramos," he says, and the shock wave that sends through my body is visceral. Ella's attention perks up at the sound of Ramos's name. "I sent him a warning before Cade's trucks moved in, but I never heard back. I'm sorry. He was a good man."

I feel that confirmation heavily on my shoulders. "He was."

Zara shifts the girl onto her other hip and whispers something to her that I can't hear.

"And—" Calix stops, nodding at Lala who runs by with a warrior battle cry toward her next victim, channeling all of her rage and pain into a single punch. A flash of guilt shadows Calix's face. "And I— I didn't know her sons were there. I'm so sorry."

I nod, my throat tight. "Thank you."

Finally, he looks at Zara, who straightens at his eye. "I didn't know what he had planned for you, or I would have tried to intervene," he says sincerely. "I'm sorry for what he put you through."

Zara shifts under the weight of the girl, but she squares her shoulders. "Thank you."

And with that, Calix turns to leave, looking over his shoulder to say, "I have some motives of my own, and I need to bide my time with Cade until then. I'd appreciate it if you didn't let him know about this." He slaps me on the shoulder amiably before making his way back into the group. He throws a few pretend punches to look busy and involved.

I look down at Ella with a sad smile and kiss her head, knowing how hard this all must be for her to hear.

"Ready?" I ask Ella.

"We are *both* ready," she emphasizes stubbornly, noticing I've barely even acknowledged the girl this whole night. I seethe internally, but that's a fight for another time.

I reach out to put a hand on Zara's shoulder. She's been through a lot tonight. Being back here with those memories so fresh must be hard. I admire how she's keeping it all together. "You okay?" I ask her.

She lifts her chin. "Let's get out of here."

I take a quick look over my shoulder. Vegas is gone, and so are Q and Luna. I hope she stays safe. *I need her to stay safe.* My chest squeezes, and I wonder if my heart will ever have both halves, or am I just destined to only have one at a time?

"Now or never." I shrug.

I pull the plug on the smoke bomb and toss it into the middle of the fight. It explodes and casts a heavy smoke over the entire street. I pull Ella down low and take off through the smoke. Zara follows right behind.

"WEST!" I yell as loudly as I can into the void, hoping the rest of the group will hear and recognize my voice. Zara yells it into the darkness too. I hope it's enough.

I don't wait for confirmation if they heard us or not. All I care about is getting Ella out of this godforsaken place as soon as possible.

As soon as we're out of the thickest smoke, I break out into a run. Ella takes a moment to warm up but soon she's keeping up with me. Zara takes the lead since she knows where to go, and I have to say I'm impressed at her sudden surge in superhuman strength as she carries the girl in her arms the entire way to the club Calix named. Neon Ave.

I look over my shoulder and with a sigh of relief see Lala and Beardsley running toward us. Red tumbles out of the smoke cloud with a burly man of a similar size. They roll out onto the sidewalk, Red rolling an extra time until he's on top. He punches the man in the face until he's unconscious, dusts himself off, and breaks out after us.

The further I get from L'Deaux, the more I consider throwing Q's wishes out the window and making her leave with me whether she likes it or not. But I force my feet to keep moving because Ella needs me to be strong. She doesn't need a heartbroken brother. She needs a brother who can do what needs to be done.

So I don't stop, and I make sure Ella doesn't stop either, because that's just what you do when you have someone depending on you. You keep going even when your heart begs you to stop.

I follow Zara through the near-empty club and to the back, ignoring the adults behind me who are asking where Q and Luna are.

Zara sets the girl down and bursts into tears when she sees Jones waiting for us. He pulls her in for a hug and lets her cry, and I feel so guilty that this weekend has been so hard for her. She's been holding back so much, staying so strong so she could be what we needed her to be. It was already hard enough for her to come back here before she remembered what happened, but she did it. She helped us anyway.

And for what?

All we accomplished was to take a huge number of vulnerable and moldable people from the hands of one power-hungry person and hand them to another.

All we did was give Cade the numbers he needs to take over the entire Underground.

And it was my damn idea to do this.

I made him unstoppable.

Jones keeps his arm around Zara as she cries but points to the counter where he has water bottles for us. I make Ella drink her entire bottle, and she mutters under her breath the whole time. It makes me smile because it's a glimpse of the old Ella. The grumbling Ella I know and love.

I sigh when Beardsley announces that something must be wrong, so he is going to go back for Q. I know I have to come clean.

If I thought Beardsley hated me before, he's sure going to now.

32

FREEDOM TASTES LIKE DIRT, BUT IN A GOOD WAY

MATEO

I'm glad Rachel is driving ahead of me, fearlessly paving the way through the Northern Boundaries, or I may be tempted to slam on my brakes as we approach the gate, especially after what we just witnessed with Nova. We're supposed to forget that all happened and just drive right through? Trusting that we won't be burned to a crisp just like Nova?

I can't help but cringe, watching from behind as Rachel speeds straight through the gate, half expecting the flashes of lightning I saw just moments ago, but once I get close enough, I can see the dark outline of the other trucks waiting on the other side, and the shadow of Eddie standing close by, nearly bouncing in anticipation.

It's enough to give me the boost to drive through the gate myself, seeing his smiling face just on the other side of this threshold. *He's really alive.*

As soon as I'm passed the boundary, the truck is barely parked before I'm throwing open the door and running to him at full speed like a quarterback.

I scoop him up in my arms, crushing him into me. He groans happily at the tightness.

"You're going to break me in half," he laughs.

I set him down, squeezing his face in my hands to make sure he's really here. "You're okay," I choke out.

He hugs me, bringing me back to reality in that way he always does. A reality where he's here, he's safe.

And we're out.

Rachel, Trevor, Parker, Jess, Jordan and several others have hopped out of their trucks and congregate around us. The joy is physical. The laughs, the cheers, the pure elation, as we all experience this inch of freedom for the first time. I smile as I see Amanda, conscious, sitting in the back of the open trailer of the delivery truck, holding her baby sister in her arms. I look around at them, my body feeling packed so full of happiness and relief that I have to release it, or I might burst.

"We did it!" I yell at the top of my lungs.

The cheers that follow are uninhibited and unbridled. Loud and chaotic and *free*. It feels so freeing to just yell as loud as I want to yell, to have something worth cheering so loudly for. Our celebration reaches the top of the upper shell, and echoes back down at us, amplifying the excitement we all feel. Rachel and Jess hug each other and jump up and down in place. I find myself in some kind of bouncing football huddle with Parker, Trevor, and Eddie. Jordan tosses his sisters up in the air one at a time, and they squeal with joy. Even the Elders laugh and cheer, despite missing most of their comrades that should have been here too. Everyone, for this one singular moment, is just happy. When was the last time we were allowed to feel this way?

I know we can't bask in this for long. The remaining Guards are probably on their way over here, considering this is the only way out. Ramos needs medical attention. We need to head to the exit. But I let everyone enjoy it a second longer. We deserve it.

AFTER ALLOWING ourselves a brief moment for celebration, we get back to business and find the box with Parker's syringe. I'm relieved to see the physical proof of its efficacy—Amanda awake and happy, knowing we can hopefully expect a similar miracle for Ramos. I just knew I couldn't leave him there after all he's done for us. For Sam and Ella.

We clean, pack, and fill his gunshot wound the same way we did Amanda's, trying to get him comfortable where he lies in the back of the truck bed, propping his head up with rolled up uniform shirts. It's not perfect, but he's still breathing, and that's what matters.

Rachel and Jess rush to layer the bandages over his torso while we all get loaded back into the trucks, everybody redistributing now that we have one more truck to load people into. It's still way too tight and pretty unsafe, considering it's basically standing room only in the trailer of the delivery truck, and with how many are squeezed on the exposed truck beds, infants and children without car seats. But at least we're out.

I take a moment to visualize the map from Ramos's office, knowing my job isn't over yet. It's still on me to get everyone to E3. I have no idea what we're going to do when we get there, how we'll explain to the government that we left their Zone in ashes, but we would still very much like their help please. But we'll figure it out.

I feel a growing flicker of hope inside me that I've never felt before. We've made it this far against all odds, so I start to believe we can make it the rest of the way too.

We start up the trucks. Eddie is sharing the front seat with another boy around his age, and a little pigtailed toddler sits at their feet. Parker and Trevor sit in the cramped backseat with four other Minors who chatter excitedly, and loudly, about "going outside." But no pressure or anything.

I look behind me to make sure all the trucks behind me are good, and I give one last parting look to C9. On the outside it looks exactly how it feels inside. Like a giant prison. Smoke billows toward the upper shell, curling through the dimness of the artificial evening.

Trevor sees me looking and spits on the ground out his window. "Good riddance," he says.

We all spit out our own windows too. "Good riddance," we all say in agreement, like we're doing a toast.

And with that we take off into the night and drive down the Eastward road until the lights of morning come on overhead.

IT'S ALMOST 9:00 AM now, and Ramos assures us we're nearly there. He's looking much better and is in annoyingly improved spirits. Improved enough to make critiques about my driving and offer backseat advice. He slept through most of the night and woke a few hours ago when we stopped to let all the drivers switch out. He was well enough to sit himself up and with help was able to move from the truck bed to the cab of the truck. I sat with him and the kids in the back, let Parker take the wheel, and dozed lightly in the backseat for a few hours with Eddie on my lap.

Now I'm back at the wheel, and Ramos is in the front. He says we'll know it when we see it. The plan is to park everyone a ways out, then Ramos and I will go inside to find his contact. We'll come back and get everybody once we know it's safe. Ramos is confident that his contact will be able to get us to a safe place.

I told him about the promise I made to the Elder... about

his granddaughter in C12. We agree that we will cross that bridge when we get to it, but we first need to get everyone to safety. He nearly buzzes with excitement as we get closer, and I can't help but match his energy. I never realized Ramos was a prisoner too, like us. He was a prisoner of a much cushier prison... but trapped still, nonetheless.

It's definitely much easier to drive now that the overhead lights are back on. Much easier to avoid potholes and bumps when I can actually see them, even though Ramos claims I hit them on purpose.

I do sometimes.

The kids laugh when we go over them. It makes me smile.

"Look!" Eddie yells through the middle console between the front seats, leaning forward and pointing out the windshield.

I push his face backward, shushing him. "Get back in your seat," I tell him, but I see it too.

Buildings bigger than anything I've ever seen before come into view ahead of us. They stretch so tall, nearly all the way up to the top of the upper shell. Impossibly huge trees create a border around the Zone, with the buildings of different size and design scattered among them inside.

E3.

Our very own government. I could cry with relief.

I did it.

I really got us here.

Now the rest is up to Ramos. I can finally breathe again.

Parker, Trevor, and the kids in the back get even louder as their excitement grows. But I don't blame them. After living in the gray of C9 all this time, seeing the grandeur before us, the sheer magnitude of it all... it's breathtaking.

I bring the truck to a slow stop, and the trucks behind me do the same. I step out of the truck and stretch, my muscles sore from sitting. I don't think I've ever sat that long at once.

The children from the different trucks all find each other

and immediately run around and jump and play, finally able to let out their pent-up energy, for some, energy that has been building for years. And they do so. *Loudly.*

"Well, shall we?" I say to Ramos, crossing an arm in front of my chest and stretching it tightly.

"You don't want a break?" Ramos says with a breathless laugh. "We're just hopping right in?"

I forgot he was on the brink of death only hours ago. I apologize to him. "If you want to take it easy—"

"Nope, let's go. I've waited long enough. And I'm excited for you to meet my contact."

He says it with a smile so bright, I can't help but wonder who it could be.

I hug Eddie goodbye, waving to the others. I hope they agree we might as well not waste any time. We make our way through the sandy dirt, and I keep a hand on Ramos's elbow as we walk, even though he insists he doesn't need help. His breaths get louder and louder as we get closer.

"Do you need to sit down?" I ask, worried about him exerting himself too much. Maybe we should have waited after all.

"This is the closest I've been to sunshine in years, son, I'm not quitting now." He gives me a determined look.

We step over a mound, and I trip a little on a small hole at the base of it, twisting my ankle just a little bit, but I press on. If he can make the trek with a bullet hole in his side, I can walk on a sore ankle. "How did you find out that the exit is in E3 anyway?" I ask.

"I have been researching the ins and outs of the Underground pretty much ever since I took the position. I've feared for awhile that things may start to get a little too out of control as different power groups went head-to-head. It's inevitable in a place like this. A new frontier is just too tempting for people wanting power."

"And your contact?"

"We reconnected only a few days ago," is all he says, and I blink in surprise, wondering if he's referring to "C" or "H." All the coded messages from both files I saw on his deskTab seemed to go back much further, but I guess they just had a lot to talk about in a short timeframe.

We finally arrive at the main entrance, which kind of resembles what I imagine the entryway of a castle would look like, fortunately minus a drawbridge or moat filled with alligators. We approach a stone archway that has tall watchtowers on each side, bright ivy growing all the way up the sides. I don't feel a buzz or hum from any kind of electric gate. The entrance appears to just be wide open. *Huh.*

Ramos stretches his neck to look up at the watchtower. He waves over his head, trying to get the attention of whoever may be up there. "Hello," he calls up the stone. "I am Mayor Victoriano Ramos of Zone C9 seeking refuge. I can provide any credentials you require."

There is a quiet moment as we wait for some kind of response. Seconds go by. Nothing. We look at each other in anticipation, and he looks just as confused as I am. Is there even anybody up there? Some watchtower.

"Okay," Ramos says slowly, after we've waited several minutes without a response. "I guess they are used to people driving in, maybe they just don't see us."

We hesitantly step under the archway, and even though I know there's not an electric gate, I still cringe as we pass under it, half expecting something to come out and bite me.

We walk slowly into the Zone. I feel grateful and lighter now that someone else has taken up the torch, and I am finally allowed to go back to what I do best: follow.

The entrance spits us directly into some kind of industrial plaza. There is a courtyard with a marble fountain and some ornately crafted benches, overly green fake grass in neat squares, the whole thing surrounded by massive corporate buildings. It's impressive, but there's something off. I feel it as we get closer, a weird layer of unease that coats the whole place. The fountain doesn't have any water in it, and it looks like it's been dry for a while. There is thick dust on the benches. No cars, even though there are streets that stretch out on all sides of this plaza.

I look at Ramos, and I can tell this isn't what he was expecting either. Confusion is etched across his face.

We approach the closest building, and he opens the door to peek inside. The hinges creak loudly. It's dark in there, cold. Not a single person inside as far as I can see. I move to step inside, but Ramos stops me with a hand.

"Hello?" he calls from the doorway.

No answer. The uneasy feeling tickles at the back of my neck, growing. This isn't right. Where is everybody?

Never in all my days would I have ever expected that the Zone, which was supposed to belong to the government, the government responsible for keeping us all down here, to run the entire Underground, to uphold order... would be completely and utterly *abandoned*.

A voice from behind startles me, and I nearly leap out of my skin.

"Vic?"

We turn, and to my surprise Ramos laughs heartily, the sudden loudness slicing through the eery silence and making my heart rate spike. He closes the distance quickly despite his injuries to give a tall man across the courtyard an enthusiastic hug.

Ramos's contact. Is this "C" or "H?"

I try to make out his face, but it's mostly covered by shadows from a black baseball cap and a thick salt and pepper beard.

They hug and laugh, slapping each other on their backs so hard you'd think it would hurt.

"I can't believe it's really you. I thought you were dead, you bastard." Ramos claps the man on the shoulder.

Ramos gestures me over, and my eyes widen as the man removes his hat, revealing familiar brown eyes. It's like my heart completely stops all together.

"Mateo," Ramos says, holding the man's arm and presenting him to me, but I already know. He's the older, grayed-out version, of course, but I'd know that face anywhere. "I'd like you to meet Henry Carmichael."

Henry Carmichael. H.

Sam and Ella's father.

MEMORY LANE WITH TEO
EPISODE 2

When Roger and Reggie used to live in our Quarters before they aged out, we all used to play this game right before bed where we'd each say the ONE thing we were going to do when we "got out." We allowed ourselves to pretend, to live in delusion for just a few moments, that whenever the war was over, we could go back Upstairs, and everything would be magically back to normal. We could just mold right back into our old lives, and our time Underground would be nothing more than a small blip.

It was always both cute and depressing whenever it was Eddie and Ella's turn because they didn't know what Upstairs was like anyways, but they sure tried. Like Eddie would always say something about playing in real rain every single day and splashing in puddles with real mud, but I never had the heart to tell him we lived in the desert.

I always had an answer I said out loud for the rest to hear, and one I kept inside only for me. My fake answer usually had something to do with food or movies, and yeah, of course I want to eat so much guacamole it makes me puke if I ever get

the chance, and yeah, of course I want to have a movie marathon with Eddie to show him all my favorites.

But most of all, what I really want more than anything... and something I've never allowed myself to hope for, much less admit out loud... One day I hope I can hug my mom again.

If she's still out there, still alive, I want her to know I never stopped wishing. And even when I had to push her out of my mind, I never truly forgot her. I never will.

33

HALF A HEART IS BETTER THAN NONE, JUST ASK AXEL. OH WAIT.

SAM

It's a strange experience driving away from E1 in the same truck we came in, considering every single other thing is different.

Arriving in this very truck two days ago, in denial about my feelings for Q, and not sure if I'd ever see Ella again.

Leaving in the same truck, overjoyed that Ella is safe and snoozing on my shoulder, but not sure if I'll ever see Q again.

One thing I know for sure is I'm really tired of sitting in this truck and driving away from people I love.

It took a lot of convincing to get the adults to walk out of Neon Ave without Q.

Every minute I had to spend convincing them to leave her behind felt like I was shaving off pieces of myself little by little and offering it to them on a platter. Trying to make words I didn't even believe myself sound convincing enough for them to leave, while secretly hoping they *wouldn't* be convinced and go back for her.

But I made her a promise, and even though it was one of the hardest promises I've had to fulfill, I did it. I knew there was only one way they'd leave—Ponyboy. I made them realize we have to hurry to go get him before Cade gets back. We don't have time to spare.

And I think deep down they all knew it was Q's choice to make anyway.

But now they're furious at me for not doing better at changing her mind. I don't blame them. I hate myself too.

Beardsley is in the passenger seat and hasn't even moved at all since we left. Won't speak, won't even look at me. Lala has been looking out the window the whole time, pretending she's not crying, and the two girls are snoozing on each other in between us. Red's knuckles on the steering wheel are so tight I'm worried he might break it off completely.

At least Zara and Jones don't hate me.

It didn't take much to convince Jones to leave E1 behind and come with us, and Zara did most of the work with a flutter of eyelashes and a pretty please or two. Now they're sitting under the camper shell in the truck bed, talking and laughing and making up for lost time, and I'm trying really hard to be happy for them.

As we left E1 and raced across the emptiness between the service exit and the dumpster where the truck was mercifully still waiting for us, Jones told us that the guards at the gates abandoned ship when they didn't receive further orders from Vegas or the FPA—both suddenly went radio silent apparently —and after some problem-solving and teamwork, the Elites were able to get the electric gates disarmed.

They got out. And not just the Elites. Jones told us service-workers and disabled "employees" there fled in masses too, taking the opportunity to get out while they had it.

As we took off in the truck, we saw all of them gathered outside the gates, celebrating and waiting there for someone new to imprison them.

Seeing them all there, knowing it's my fault they will be fed to Cade like lambs to slaughter, it ignited something in me. I feel this nagging, burning responsibility to hold up my promises to them. I promised them freedom, I promised them safety.

And all I did was lead them straight into a new cage.

Not to mention all the other Zones that could face the same fate as C9 now that Cade's manpower has tripled. And the other children getting the life sucked out of them just like Ella because of Vegas's desperate need to beat Cade. How will I sleep at night knowing every other child down here is in danger because I created not just one, but two unstoppable monsters?

Once I get Ella to safety. Once I figure out what to do about this parasite wearing Ella's face. Once I know that the rest of my friends are safe. Once Q gets the information she needs about her family...

Maybe then we can figure out how to save the Underground from Cade and Vegas before every single child down here becomes collateral damage in their conflict.

Obviously the FPA isn't doing anything about it, if what they said about C9 is true, so if we don't, who will?

In the meantime, we're hopefully going to make it back to the Catacombs first while Cade is tied up with his new army, get Ponyboy, and steal whatever supplies we're able to squish into our vehicle before we make our way to C9.

I dread what we're going to find there. I hope they were wrong.

I know Ella will need me, when we see the physical evidence right in front of us of what happened to her best friend. I know Lala will need a shoulder to cry on seeing the destruction her boys fell to. I know I will need to keep it together, no matter how much I will want to fall apart too—losing Q, Mateo, Eddie, and Mayor Ramos all in the same day. But I have to stay strong.

I have work to do.

And I only have three months to do it.

TYRO B-29

I wish Ella would let me die. I wish she would let me stop syncing. I hate the way it makes a little bit more of the color fade from her eyes every time. I hate what my existence is doing to her.

I'm a freak of nature.

And I can't even escape when I close my eyes because when I do I still see his face.

I can't get his face out of my head. It's like it is burned into the very cells of my brain, imprinted there forever.

The look of disgust. Hatred.

Sam is disgusted by me.

I feel so silly that I allowed myself to believe he would have room in his heart for me too. That I could match the memories — the unconditional love, the safety, the comfort— to a person. To him.

So silly.

How could anyone love something like me?

I wish she would just let me die.

DEAR READER...

K please don't hate me!! But c'mon, you had to know those cliffhangers were coming— it's ME we're talking about. I swear I won't make you wait as long for answers this time, though. Pinky promise! Don't give up on me! In fact, I have a special surprise just for you. Drum roll please.......

Presenting the third and final book in The Underground Series.
COMING SOON!!

I truly could not have written this book without YOU. I am eternally grateful for everyone who would always ask when Royale would be done. You are the reason it's finally here. I can't wait for you to read book three <3

XO, Kennedy

ABOUT THE AUTHOR

Kennedy is a former middle school teacher-turned-author who currently resides in Arizona with her high school sweetheart, Aaron. She stays busy with their five beautiful children (a blend of biological and soon-to-be-adoptees) and their two fur-daughters, Granger and Bellatrix (Trixie).

She welcomes you to follow her on Instagram @kenn_plumb and TikTok @kenn_plumb and @bookishkenn

DM's are open if you feel the need to lovingly yell at her for her cliffhangers <3

instagram.com/kenn_plumb